LONDON IN CHAINS

An English Civil War novel from a highly-acclaimed author

London, 1647. Lucy Wentor, a young lady who was attacked by soldiers during the Civil War, and then rejected by her sweetheart, hopes to start her life afresh in the capital with her uncle and aunt. London, however, is in chaos and her once well-to-do uncle is now almost bankrupt. Unwilling to go home, Lucy finds a job in publishing and excitement, love and independence soon follow…

LONDON IN CHAINS

Gillian Bradshaw

Severn House Large Print
London & New York

This first large print edition published 2012
in Great Britain and the USA by
SEVERN HOUSE PUBLISHERS LTD of
9-15 High Street, Sutton, Surrey, SM1 1DF.
First world regular print edition published 2009 by
Severn House Publishers Ltd., London and New York.

British Library Cataloguing in Publication Data

Bradshaw, Gillian, 1956-
  London in chains.
  1. Publishers and publishing--Political aspects--
  England--London--History--17th century--Fiction.
  2. Great Britain--History--Civil War, 1642-1649--
  Fiction. 3. Historical fiction. 4. Large type books.
  I. Title
  813.6-dc23

ISBN-13: 978-0-7278-9876-0

Severn House Publishers support The Forest Stewardship Council
[FSC], the leading international forest certification organisation. All
our titles that are printed on Greenpeace-approved FSC-certified paper
carry the FSC logo.

MIX
Paper from
responsible sources
FSC® C018575

Printed and bound in Great Britain by the
MPG Books Group, Bodmin, Cornwall.

...the people's expectations that were much greatened, and their hopes of relief in their miseries and oppressions, which were so much heightened, are like to be frustrate, and while you look for peace and freedom the flood-gates of slavery, oppression and misery are opened to the nation.

The Case of the Armie Truly Stated

Acknowledgements

In researching this book I have taken shameless advantage of other people's expertise. I am particularly grateful to printer Martyn Musgrove and the staff of Blists Hill Victorian Town, and to Brian Russell, who volunteers in the print-shop. They not only allowed me to work on the Victorian hand printing press and enthusiastically shared their extensive knowledge of printing, but also went out of their way to get me on a British Printing Society junket to visit a replica Tudor/Stuart press reconstructed by Alan May. All of this was invaluable, and a lot of fun, too. Any printing-related errors are mine, not theirs.

One

It was as though they were riding into Hell.

A dirty smudge had been visible against the blue sky ahead when they started on the road that morning. It broadened as the day went on, and now it was all around them, stealing the brightness of the afternoon sun. A haze of smoke filled the air; buildings were blackened with layers of grime; even the leaves of plants were filmed grey. The expected scent of coal-smoke, though, was almost swamped by the reek of butcher's offal and rendered tallow, the tannery stink of rotting hides and the acrid bite of fullers' shops, the stench of the urine and dung of animals and men. Lucy breathed through her mouth, blinking hot eyes.

There was noise, too, everywhere: the clatter of iron-shod wheels and hooves on rough cobbles, the rumble of carts and cursing of drivers. Passing a coppersmith's, she was deafened by the ringing of hammer on metal; even before the din began to fade, it was overwhelmed by the thudding of the neighbouring cooper's mallet. Everywhere there were voices: talking, shouting; raised up in long swooping howls as vendors tried to make themselves heard.

'EE-ee-EE-ee-EELs alive O!'

9

'Any KNIVES to GRIND?'

'MIIILK-below, MIILK-O!'

Lucy looked round at the milkmaid's cry, thinking of the dairy at home, but, instead of the strong young countrywoman she expected, saw a dirty, white-faced girl in a tattered skirt. The April weather was chilly, if bright, but the milkmaid's arms were bare; the heavy milk-can on the girl's head seemed to press her down into the mud, and the mugs and ladle hooked to it rattled at each step like a cough. A ragged beggar-woman, her face covered in sores, held up a hand pleading for a sip for the child huddled against her. The milkmaid brushed past her without a glance.

On the next corner, two men begged side by side, one blind, the other missing both legs; the blind man still wore the buff-leather coat of a cavalryman. The legless one had an evil face and was muttering to himself. The jostling passers-by didn't appear to notice him but still managed to give him a wide berth, despite the press of the crowd.

Lucy had never imagined so many people. When she first saw the crowds in the street before them, she'd asked Cousin Geoffrey whether they shouldn't wait until the march or riot, or whatever it was, was over. He'd laughed at her.

'This is *London,* girl! It's thus all the day – and half the night!' He guided his nervous mare through the thick of it. His servant William followed on his sturdy gelding, and Lucy, sitting pillion behind William, tightened her grip on the servant's belt. Behind them, the pack-mule tossed her head resentfully.

London. They'd been travelling for eight days, with one halt to keep the Sabbath, and now, at last, they'd reached their destination: the new Jerusalem, the new Babylon, the seat of government and the fountain of rebellion. Lucy wasn't sure what she'd expected London to look like, but it hadn't been this.

'London Bridge!' announced Cousin Geoffrey, drawing rein and sweeping a hand at the street ahead of them. 'Our uncle lives in Southwark, yonder on the other side.'

He had been to London twice before, as he liked to tell people. He was an eldest son, the heir to the family farm, and he thought highly of himself; Lucy's opinion of him was not nearly as elevated, but she kept it to herself. She peered round William. For a moment her eyes couldn't make sense of the scene: there was a river, broad and brown and crowded with boats, but the street seemed simply to continue across it, the tall buildings overhanging the road. Then she realized that there were houses built on the bridge, their back walls hanging out over the river. Shops, too – the signs for them dangled just above the heads of the men mounted on horseback. Londoners busily sold soap and spoons, pewter and plaster, suspended above the current of the river.

The traffic slowed as they made their way forward, then came to a halt. Lucy peered round William again: there was a jam where two carts had clipped one another in the narrow passage between the shops. Through a gap between two

11

of the buildings on their left she could see the brown water foaming and tumbling around the piers; it seemed to drop several feet. Below the bridge, though, the stream was tranquil, and the boats moved up, down and across it, as many of them as there were carts on the road.

William, who'd accompanied his master on the two trips to London, grinned at her over his shoulder and jerked a thumb towards the boats. 'Plenty of folk take to water to speed them over the river,' he explained. 'A bridge crossing can be slow.'

Lucy nodded, but did not reply. William had become overly-familiar during the journey, encouraged, perhaps, by the fact that she had to sit so close behind him on the horse every day. If she gave him the slightest encouragement, he'd start to take liberties – and Cousin Geoffrey would blame *her* for it.

'When we came before, we mostly stayed the Southwark side of the bridge,' William informed her. 'Southwark's a *grand* place. There used to be theatres, four or five of 'em. I saw fine shows then! *The Revenger's Tragedy* – that was a good one, with more murders and poisonings than a man could count on all his fingers. The maid I took to see it, she screamed and hid her face in my jerkin.' He grinned smugly at the memory.

Geoffrey glanced back reprovingly. 'You'll have to do without such licentious fare, Cousin Lucy. Our godly Parliament has closed or torn down all the theatres, and I say, well done!'

I didn't want to see murders anyway, thought Lucy, *not even make-believe ones,* but she knew

12

there was no point in saying so. Geoffrey would only be annoyed that she'd talked back.

'Mayhap there's still bear-baiting, though,' said William hopefully. 'You ever seen a bear-baiting?'

'Nay; nor do I wish to!'

'It's good sport!'

'Parliament has banned it!' snapped Geoffrey, giving his servant a stern glare. 'It gave occasion for license and depravity!'

William subsided, muttering something that might have been 'Roundhead killjoys!' He shot Lucy a conspiratorial look, which she ignored. She found his assumption that she'd *agree* with him exasperating. He surely knew that her family was just as Puritan as Geoffrey's! Did he think she was soiled, or was she just supposed to have been won over by his loutish charm?

They edged forward, halted, edged forward again. The pack-mule suddenly snorted and kicked, and then Cousin Geoffrey's mare danced nervously: a pair of ragged boys had squeezed past on foot, one of them actually darting under the mare's belly. Cousin Geoffrey cried, 'God *damn* you!' – an oath he would have rebuked if anyone else had uttered it. He dismounted to soothe his horse, and Lucy took that as permission to slide down from the gelding, relieved at the opportunity to ease her aching rear – and get away from William. The servant, however, also dismounted. 'A good notion,' he said, grinning at Lucy. 'Spare the poor beast's back and our arses!' His eyes lingered on her backside as he ostentatiously rubbed his own.

She said nothing, only went back to check on the mule. The animal bared yellow teeth threateningly. 'There's a good girl,' Lucy whispered approvingly. 'Look after yourself!' The mule snorted and canted her ears forward, and Lucy patted her shaggy neck.

They made the rest of their slow progress on foot, leading the animals. At the far end of the bridge there was a tower: the road passed under the arch of its gateway. The parapet above it was decorated with black lumps on posts.

'See the heads?' William asked gleefully, pointing to them. 'All that's left of traitors! I reckon there'll be a mort more of 'em before long!'

Was it true, or was William simply trying to scare her? (*'She screamed and hid her face in my jerkin!'*) She stared at the objects, and her eyes snagged on the unmistakable curve of a skull, showing white where the blackened skin had pulled away. She shuddered and looked down at the street, wondering whose head it was and what he'd died for. Who were the *traitors* in this new upside-down world where the king was imprisoned by his own Parliament?

They reached the southern end of the bridge and led the horses and the mule under the arch with its grim decorations. Geoffrey mounted up again, and William vaulted on to the gelding's back and offered a hand to Lucy.

'I would be pleased to walk a while, if I may,' she said, looking down demurely. 'To stretch my legs.'

'Your arse, more like,' muttered William,

14

disappointed, but Cousin Geoffrey merely shrugged. 'Please yourself. It's no distance now.'

He turned the mare left, into one of the wider streets. Lucy followed, already regretting her decision to walk: the street was filthy. There were narrow channels cut on either side for drainage, but these were half-choked with dung and sweepings from the shops and houses. At one point a channel was completely blocked, and half the street was flooded. A pig was wallowing in the dirty water, chewing with evident pleasure on something it had found in the drain. Lucy held her skirts up and tried to pick her way around the side of the puddle without stepping in anything foul. The horsemen had been drawing further and further ahead, and when she looked up after negotiating the obstacle, she found that they'd vanished.

She stood still for a moment, alone on a strange street. She was cut off from everyone and everything familiar, adrift in a world where she knew no one and no one knew her.

It was exhilarating.

She drew a deep breath, shocked by her own response. It was because she knew she was in no real danger, she told herself. Geoffrey and his servant had simply turned up the next cross-street, and even if she had lost them, she could ask directions, now that it was 'no distance' to her uncle's house. She was not, she told herself, so desperate for escape that she really *wanted* to be alone on the streets of London. She drew another deep breath, then let it out again and picked her way onward.

The men were indeed just around the next corner, standing outside a shop; they had taken off their hats respectfully. The shopkeeper was speaking to Cousin Geoffrey, but he looked round when Lucy came up, then smiled broadly. She halted, shocked. Yes, it was Uncle Thomas, but he was *old*. It had been only six years since she saw him last, but from his looks it might have been twice as long: his face was lined and his hair was mostly grey. She remembered her manners abruptly and curtsied.

'Lucy!' he said and came forward to kiss her in greeting. 'Little Lucy! Oh, Lord, how you look like your dear mother! Welcome!'

Being embraced by a man who was to all intents a stranger jerked a scream into her throat. She swallowed it, forced her fists to unclench, tried to smile. Uncle Thomas didn't notice: he'd already turned back to Cousin Geoffrey and was telling him where he could stable the horses.

'And you, child, come in!' he exclaimed, taking Lucy's arm and leading her to the door. 'Agnes! They've arrived!'

There was no one in the shop, and nobody responded to Uncle Thomas's call. Lucy, catching her breath, glanced round. Thomas was a mercer – a wholesale dealer in cloth – and the family had always referred to him as 'rich Uncle Thomas, the London mercer'. His shop, however, didn't look rich. It was dingy and dark. The sample racks around the walls were half-empty, and what cloth they did hold seemed all the same drab colour.

'Agnes!' Thomas called again.

A flabby old woman in an apron appeared, scowling, mending in hand; Lucy took her for the maid, until she demanded, 'What is it?' in a tone no maid would use to the master of the house. Lucy stared. She'd met her uncle's wife only once and her memory was of a fine young matron, vain about her plump good looks.

'They've arrived,' repeated Uncle Thomas. 'You remember Lucy, my poor sister's girl?'

Agnes regarded Lucy with unfriendly eyes. Lucy curtsied, and her aunt sniffed. 'Well, you still *look* like an honest woman! That's well.'

Lucy felt her face heat, and her hands fisted again. 'Why should I not look like an honest woman, Aunt?' she demanded sharply.

Agnes blinked, taken aback by the tone and offended by it. Lucy glared at her, choked by the impulse to start shouting. She struggled to crush it. Why, she wondered despairingly, did she keep getting angry? It was a kindness in her aunt and uncle to take her in: she could not begin by shouting at them. She forced her eyes down and made herself flatten her hands again. 'I beg your pardon.'

Her voice came out wooden and insincere, and Agnes scowled.

'It's a weary journey,' said Uncle Thomas with false heartiness. 'Agnes, Geoffrey's off stabling his beasts at Fleur-de-Lis; I'll go and help him. Take Lucy upstairs and make her welcome.'

Agnes sniffed again but turned and beckoned for Lucy to follow her.

The next room was a parlour, and the stairs led

up from it, wooden and nearly as steep as a
ladder. Agnes climbed them slowly and stopped
at the top, wheezing a little and pressing a hand
to her side. Lucy perforce stopped behind her,
halfway up. She found that she was taking shal-
low breaths: the scent of the house was strange
and unpleasant. It was because there were no
animals, she decided. She was accustomed to the
farmyard smells that constantly tracked into her
father's house, so that the scents of dung and
dairy were mingled with the human ones. Here
the mingling was with the London reek.

'You'll bed down with our Susan,' Agnes said
abruptly, glancing back over her shoulder.

For a moment Lucy's mind spun, trying to
remember who Susan was. Her cousins – her
aunt and uncle's children, the two who'd survived infancy – were named Mark and Hannah.
Mark, though, was dead, killed in the war, and
Hannah had married and left home just a few
months before. Lucy had never heard of any
Susan in the family.

'Geoffrey will lie in Mark's room,' said Agnes,
and there was something defensive in her tone,
'and we mean to find a lodger for Hannah's.
Susan sleeps in the loft.' She started moving
again.

Lucy suddenly understood that Susan was the
maid. She froze where she was, halfway up the
stairs. Agnes looked back at her impatiently.
'Come along!'

'I might lie in Hannah's room,' Lucy said
tightly, 'until you do find a lodger.'

Her aunt turned back and stood at the top of

the stairs, scowling down at her ferociously. 'Nay. Tom, fool that he is, agreed to take you on, though we've scarce enough to keep ourselves. Well, I must obey my husband – but you're not lying in my child's bed! Understand this, miss: you're no heiress. Your place is with Susan.'

Lucy clutched the step above her. It was hard to breathe: all the air seemed full of needles, and her throat was clenched shut on them. Her aunt's face above her was unnaturally clear: the loose skin folded where the chin was tucked in, the spots of colour in the cheeks, the resentment in the eyes. Lucy imagined that prim mouth shrieking, spewing teeth and blood. She shut her eyes hurriedly: God forgive her this sinful anger!

'Keep your surly look to yourself!' commanded Agnes. 'What, did you think you could step into our daughter's place? There's no undoing what's done, girl: you must make the best of things, not puff yourself up with sinful pride, as though you were still a wealthy maiden! If we're to keep you, we need to get some profit from it. *Charity*'s fine for them that have money.'

So she was to become her uncle's *maid-servant*? She clenched her teeth and stared down at her feet, motionless on the stairs. Her old shoes poked out from under her petticoat; the hem of the petticoat was splashed with mud from the street. She made herself concentrate on that stain: imagined scrubbing it off and throwing out the wash-water. Her soul was stained, too, with rage: she begged God to cleanse her. A woman should be humble, modest and obedient, and if she wasn't, she should at least pretend to

19

be. If she offended Thomas and Agnes, she had nowhere to go but home again, and no one there would be happy to see her.

Agnes waited a while, but Lucy said nothing and did not look up. At last there was a creak of floorboards, and Lucy, glancing up quickly, saw that her aunt had moved off. Lucy followed, moving stiffly, afraid that the fury inside her would burst out and break anything she touched.

To get to the loft they had to climb a ladder fixed to the stairwell above. Half of the loft held bales of fabric for Thomas's customers; the rest was bare under the roof-beams. A window above the stairwell provided reasonable light. The chimney, brick and solid, ran up the right wall, and the maid's bed stood next to it. A shift and some petticoats hung from a nail in the wall beside the bed, and there was a small chest at the bedfoot with a washbasin and pitcher. Lucy told herself that it was no worse than her bed at home, and she was used to sharing that, with her cousin, with the occasional visiting relative or friend.

But not with the *maid*!

'There you are!' said Agnes. 'Space aplenty!'

Lucy clenched her hands together to keep them still and kept the angry words tight-locked behind her teeth.

'Susan is at the market,' said Agnes. 'She knows to expect you. Your things are on the mule? Then you can bear them up later. I'll leave you to refresh yourself from your journey.'

Lucy stood where she was and listened as her aunt descended the ladder. When the footsteps and the huff of breath had gone, she went over to the window. It was unglazed, the panes covered with waxed paper in place of glass, but it was hinged. Lucy flung it wide and leaned out. The scream of rage was still caught in her throat, and she took deep breaths of the smoky air, trying to dislodge it.

From the window she looked out on to a jumble of tiled roofs, with, further away – across the river? – the stone bulk of a church. As far as her eyes could see, there were houses. So many people!

London. She had wanted to come here to start a new life – not to take Cousin Hannah's place but to regain her own. Before the war, she'd been (*a wealthy maiden, yes!*) a prosperous freeholder's only daughter, able to look forward to a house and husband and children. She'd lost all that through no fault of her own and she'd hoped that in London she might be able to make a fresh start. It seemed, though, that she'd been naive. *There's no undoing what's done.*

The hurt and rage grew as the full measure of the blow made itself felt. She'd expected to help Uncle Thomas and Aunt Agnes, in the house and in the shop. She'd hoped to make herself useful, even valuable. She'd never in her life been idle and she was perfectly willing to work hard – but this, this was a *humiliation!* She was Thomas's *niece*. She'd expected to be treated as *family*. Instead, it seemed that she was expected to work as a servant, unpaid, and to be grateful that she had a place at all!

When she last saw Uncle Thomas, at home in

21

Leicestershire, he had teased her, saying that a girl as pretty as her would certainly marry a fine gentleman, and then she would have to be kind to her poor old uncle. Six years ago; before the war, before...

Your place is with Susan. Would Agnes have said that two years ago, before...

She'd known that the rage would bring the memories down. She held on to the window frame, seeing the soldiers' faces, feeling their hands on her, hearing...

She swallowed the scream, though it churned in her stomach. She swallowed several times more to try to settle it. Then she went over to the washbasin, poured in some water from the pitcher and washed the cold sweat off her face. By the time she dried her hands she'd almost stopped shaking. She sat down on the bed and inspected the mud on her petticoat, then glanced about for something to brush off the worst of it.

There was nothing suitable in the loft. She would have to go back downstairs, but she wasn't ready for that yet. If Agnes said anything more to her, she would *hit* the woman, and she knew that if she did, she'd have to go straight back home. London might not be what she'd hoped, but going home would be worse.

Understand this, miss: you're no heiress. Your place is with Susan.

It suddenly struck her that perhaps this was nothing to do with what had happened two years before. Agnes had lost her son; her daughter had married and moved out. Now her husband had proposed putting a stranger into the place that had been occupied by their children. Agnes might very well dread that, without any sense that Lucy was defiled and dirty, unworthy of Hannah's maiden bed.

Lucy drew another deep breath, this time in relief. She didn't have to hate her aunt, and she might yet find a way to make a new life for herself. She made a fierce vow that she would *not* settle for a servile dependency: she would find a way – somehow! – to be mistress of her own life. She checked that her hair wasn't coming loose and repinned the white coif that kept it decently covered, then went downstairs.

Uncle Thomas and Cousin Geoffrey and his man had returned from the stable and were sitting in the parlour with mugs of beer. Thomas waved a hand at Lucy as she descended. 'There you are, my girl! All well?'

He sounded nervous and embarrassed. Lucy hadn't been sure whether he'd approved the decision to send her to sleep with the maid: now she was. She curtsied. 'Aunt Agnes says that your maid Susan is at the market, sir, but has been told to expect me.'

Thomas nodded, relieved. 'I'm sorry you can't have Hannah's room, sweet, but your aunt wants to let it.'

'Oh?' asked Geoffrey, surprised.

'We could use the rent,' admitted Thomas. 'Trade in this town has gone to ruin, Geoff, to ruin! If I make enough in a week to pay my costs, I bless God for my good fortune!'

'Lodgings are dear,' said Geoffrey thoughtfully. 'I was told by one I met on the road that he'd paid ten shillings and sixpence a week for two rooms, and he had to supply his own coal and candles.'

Thomas nodded eagerly. 'Aye! I've been told I could get as much. Since the war ended, all England's coming to London to solicit Parliament.'

Geoffrey smiled. His own errand was to solicit Parliament – or, at any rate, a parliamentary clerk – for the right to buy a strip of land. It had belonged to a supporter of the king and was now at the disposal of Parliament. He raised his mug to his host. 'I'm grateful, Uncle, that my lodgings are free.'

Agnes had appeared in the doorway just before he said this, and Lucy noticed her sour expression: she, obviously, would have preferred a guest who paid. Perhaps it wasn't maternal feeling that made her want to keep Lucy out of Hannah's room. Perhaps it was simple greed.

'There you are, girl!' said Agnes. 'Your things are in the kitchen. You can take them up.'

'Thank you, Aunt,' said Lucy meekly. 'Aunt, my petticoat's muddy: please, where should I clean it?'

Agnes gave her a distrustful look but showed her into the kitchen and pointed out the scrubbing brush.

Lucy cleaned her petticoat, then carried her small case of possessions up the stairs, the damp hem flapping against her shin. She set her case down at the foot of the bed and looked at the maid's clothes hanging on the wall. She would have to find some more nails so she could hang up her own.

When she went back downstairs, she found that the maid had returned from the market and was busy preparing supper. Susan was about Lucy's age, a pock-faced young woman with work-reddened hands. She was chopping onions when Lucy came into the kitchen, but she stopped and the two of them looked hard at one another.

'This is Lucy, of whom I told you,' said Agnes, who was also in the kitchen.

Susan bobbed a curtsey, then stared at Lucy some more. She was clearly wondering whether Lucy would go to work beside her, like a fellow-servant, or sit down in the parlour, like a guest.

Lucy might have offered to help prepare the meal if she'd been given Hannah's room and there'd been no doubt as to her status. Because there was doubt, she stood and smiled, as though it hadn't even occurred to her that she might do a servant's work. If Agnes wanted her to serve, she would have to order it.

Agnes, however, was craftier than that. 'Lucy has been long on the road today,' she told Susan. 'Tonight she will rest.'

Meaning, of course, that she'd start as a servant *tomorrow*. Lucy felt her smile stiffen. Susan ducked her head and went back to chopping onions.

The evening meal was barley soup; with it they had maslin bread, of wheat mixed with rye, cheaper than wheat bread. It was full of grit from the millstones and Lucy nibbled it cautiously. The men talked: Cousin Geoffrey was eager for

25

hints as to how to get his business done quickly. Uncle Thomas was discouraging.

'If I'd known how the world would run over last month, I'd have advised you not to come,' he said, shaking his head unhappily. 'I pray the peace holds!'

Geoffrey was startled. 'What? The war's *well* ended! Hasn't Parliament reached a settlement with the king yet?'

Thomas shook his head again. 'No. Parliament sends him proposals, and he says only that he will take them under advisement. I fear he is fishing in troubled waters. The Army – have you really heard nothing of this, up in Leicester-shire?'

'The Army is to be disbanded, surely?'

Thomas let out his breath unhappily. 'That's what Parliament wants, certainly. The trouble...' He stopped, then, leaning forward, said, 'There was a petition from the Army last month. The soldiers asked, first and foremost, that before the Army was disbanded they should receive their pay – they have had none, not for months, and many of the men have not enough money to carry them home, let alone pay debts for their food and board. They also asked for indemnity for any acts done in furtherance of the war—'

Geoffrey gave a snort of contempt. 'What, so they need not repent their thieving?'

'There are some who have been hanged as horse-thieves because they collected horses *requisitioned* for their troop!' Thomas protested.

Geoffrey snorted again, unconvinced. He'd be delighted to see soldiers hanged for horse-stealing: his family had lost most of their own stock. He only had his mare and the gelding because he'd been using them when soldiers arrived to 'requisition' the rest.

'They had some other demands,' Thomas went on nervously. 'Just and reasonable demands.'

It was Agnes who snorted now, and Thomas glared at her. '*Reasonable* demands, I say! Fair and reasonable demands! Pensions for men crippled in the war, so that they need not beg in the street, and provision for the widows and children of those who died for the cause of Parliament! But Parliament denies them. Worse! Parliament has passed a Declaration of its high dislike of their petition and decreed that anyone who furthers it shall be proceeded against as an enemy of the State.'

There was a silence. Then Geoffrey asked, 'And?'

Thomas subsided into his chair. 'And there, at present, it stands. But I cannot think it wise for Parliament thus to set itself against the Army, and I do fear that there will be trouble from this.'

'It's the business of the officers to control the men!'

'The Army,' declared Agnes, 'is full of heretics, and many of them *are* officers!'

Thomas looked alarmed. 'Peace, wife!'

Agnes snorted and rolled her eyes, but fell silent. Geoffrey gave Thomas a quizzical look.

'The Army,' said Thomas reluctantly, 'does have many men who are Independents in religion – though to call them *heretics,* wife, because

27

they don't agree in all things with Jock Presbyter...'

Agnes sniffed. Thomas glared at her. 'A man
may be a good Christian and still disagree with
another man about church government! I have
had many profitable discussions with Independents, and I've found them godly people.'

This was surprising and interesting. Thomas,
like all his family and Lucy's, had always been a
strict Presbyterian, deeply suspicious of all other
forms of Christianity. Lucy had developed
doubts of her own over the past two years, but
she'd been afraid to acknowledge them even to
herself, in case doing so led to damnation. She
hadn't expected her pious uncle to preach
toleration.

Agnes sniffed again, conveying a world of
indignant disgust without a word.

'Even where a man is *mistaken*,' Thomas
insisted, 'what benefit is there in demanding he
should *lie* about his beliefs – on pain of imprisonment or branding with irons, as the proposed Blasphemy law would have it? It would
be worse than the tyranny of the bishops, and it
would make hypocrites, not believers!'

'And what of the Covenant?' Agnes asked
acidly.

Even Lucy knew that Parliament had engaged
to establish a Presbyterian state church throughout England – had made a Covenant to that
effect with the Scots, in return for their help in
the war. She hadn't realized, however, that there
were so many Independents in the Army; it
wasn't the sort of thing that was discussed in

rural Leicestershire. The Independents would obviously oppose a Presbyterian settlement. If they had a lot of support in the Army...

This was frightening. The one good thing about the bitter and bloody war was that it was over with, or so Lucy had thought.

'Lord General Fairfax is an honest man,' said Geoffrey confidently. 'I cannot believe he will countenance mutiny!'

'But Cromwell's an Independent,' said Agnes shortly.

There was a silence. Everyone knew of Lieutenant General Cromwell, second in command of the New Model Army, victor of Marston Moor and Naseby. Lucy put a hand to her mouth. Parliament chose to antagonize the Army, when they knew a man like Cromwell was already opposed to them?

Into the stillness came a knock on the door. Susan went to open it and presently came back with a burly man who carried a shabby hat in a dirty hand. Thomas jumped to his feet and came to take his hand. 'Will!' he exclaimed warmly. 'Come, sit down and sup with us!' Lucy noticed that Agnes's face had grown stony.

'You've company, Tom, I won't,' replied the visitor, glancing at Geoffrey and Lucy. 'I brought the petition round since you missed the meeting last night.' He took a sheaf of paper out from under his jerkin and set it down on the table. 'I brought a dozen copies: will that suffice you?' Lucy, craning her neck, saw that they were printed sheets, not a letter.

'It should,' replied Thomas. He scanned the

paper, smiling, then asked, 'Do you have pen and ink, Will?'

Grinning, the visitor removed a quill pen from the band of his hat and a capped inkwell from a pocket. Thomas took them and, with a bold flourish, signed the top paper. He noticed Geoffrey and Lucy staring and waved the pen at them vaguely. 'It's a petition,' he explained, 'for the release of Mr Nicholas Tew, a brave man who's been unjustly imprisoned for defending the liberties of freeborn Englishmen. Geoff, this is my friend, William Browne. He's brought me copies of the petition so I can take up signatures here in Southwark. Will, this is my nephew Geoffrey, my brother John's eldest, from Hinckley in Leicestershire.'

William Browne cheerfully offered his hand to Geoffrey, who took it gingerly. Lucy realized that the black on Browne's hand wasn't ordinary dirt but ink. 'Well met!' Browne exclaimed. 'You're a Mr Stevens? Like your uncle? Have you just arrived in London?'

'Aye,' agreed Geoffrey, still perplexed. He glanced sideways at his uncle. 'What's this petition?'

'Mr Tew was arrested last month,' explained Browne. 'He was defending the right of subjects to petition Parliament, and the Committee he spoke to took offence at his vehemence and had him cast into prison without so much as stating a charge against him. This petition asks Parliament to release him – or, at the very least, to allow him due process of law – and to defend the right of subjects to petition.'

30

'I see,' said Geoffrey, and Lucy could tell that he was wondering what connection Nicholas Tew had with Uncle Thomas for their uncle to take up signatures on his behalf. She wondered the same.

'Would you care to sign?' asked Browne hopefully.

Geoffrey hastily shook his head. 'I know nothing of this matter, sir; I only arrived in London today!'

Browne took this with a good-humoured smile. 'I'll let your uncle tell you more of it, then!' He retrieved his pen from Thomas and put it back in his hat, then recapped the inkwell and returned it to his pocket.

'How go things?' Thomas asked him.

Browne sighed and rolled his eyes. 'Difficult times, Tom, difficult times! We've finished printing the latest, but the sheets hang all about the works since we've no one to stitch them together.'

A possibility suddenly occurred to Lucy, so irresistible that she blurted out, 'Sir, are you looking to hire a needlewoman?'

Everyone turned and stared at her in surprise: a young woman shouldn't have spoken out uninvited. She pressed her hands together in her lap and tried to look innocently hopeful.

'This is my niece,' said Thomas, while Agnes frowned at Lucy for her forwardness. 'Lucy Wentnor, my poor sister's daughter.'

Mr Browne glanced from Lucy to Geoffrey. 'She's not your wife, sir?'

'Indeed not!' exclaimed Geoffrey with a horror

that was far from flattering.

No one else seemed inclined to explain the situation, so Lucy did. 'Cousin Geoffrey brought me to London. My aunt and uncle have offered to take me in for a time. I am very sensible of their goodness to me, and I thought, sir, that if you were looking to hire someone to stitch these sheets of yours, I could use the money to ... to ease the burden on my family.' *To avoid becoming a servant in the house of my own blood-kin!* she thought fiercely. 'I'm a quick needle-woman.'

There was another silence, startled and uncertain. Mr Browne looked at Uncle Thomas and said, 'It's true we could use a trustworthy young woman to stitch the pamphlet, and we could afford to pay her a small wage, if—'

'It's out of the question!' exclaimed Aunt Agnes furiously. 'Tom, tell him so!'

'Peace!' ordered Thomas.

'No, I will *not* hold my peace!' cried Agnes. 'How can you even *think* of allowing it? Send a simple country girl to stitch those foul seditious pamphlets for your trouble-making friends? Bad enough that *you* have anything to do with – with *these people!*' – she spat the words at Browne – 'I won't have you involving the rest of the house!'

Thomas slapped the table. 'Peace, I say!'

He was flustered and alarmed: the head of the household was supposed to command respect, and Agnes was embarrassing him in front of guests – not for the first time. She had, in her family's view, married beneath her, and she had always been more forceful than her husband. Lucy remembered her father laughing at his brother-in-law: 'Small wonder if a capon's hen-pecked!'

For her own part, she was surprised. She hadn't appreciated that the 'sheets' to be stitched were pamphlets, let alone 'seditious' ones: she'd thought she was volunteering to work as a seam-stress. She found, though, that the prospect made her more eager, not less. She looked at her uncle with fresh appreciation: so the capon had trou-ble-making friends who printed seditious pam-phlets, did he? He'd never mentioned it in his letters.

'You stupid girl!' exclaimed Agnes, turning her fire on Lucy. 'The man you want to go to work for has *twice* been arrested for selling seditious libels!'

Browne laughed, looking pleased with him-self. 'Aye, and gave the constable the slip both times! But you're right, child, to think that there's no wickedness in what I print. Indeed, it's the wicked who want the pamphlets suppres-sed! Can you read and write, as well as sew?'

'Aye,' Lucy said eagerly. 'I read and write very well.'

Browne looked at Uncle Thomas. 'I could pay the girl tuppence a day.'

Thomas hesitated, looking troubled; Lucy thought he was about to refuse, but Agnes chose that moment to cry angrily, 'You agreed that she would help me in the house!' and he decided he had to assert his authority.

'Very well!' he decreed. 'Lucy may try her

hand at stitching pamphlets, since she wishes it.'

Lucy bowed her head respectfully, heart beating hard in triumph. She didn't have to become her aunt's maidservant: she had *paid work*! True, tuppence a day wasn't much – only half of what her father would give the poorest day-labourers on his farm – but she'd never been paid before in her life. She supposed she would have to give most of the money to Uncle Thomas, to pay for her keep, but perhaps he'd allow her to keep a little of it? Even a penny a week would be more money than she'd ever had at her disposal before.

Mr Browne went off, and the supper ended. Lucy tried to slip up to bed immediately, but Agnes was too quick for her. When Lucy started up the stairs from the parlour, Agnes struggled huffing and wheezing after her and stopped her at the foot of the loft-ladder with a peremptory 'Girl!'

'You shameless little minx!' she said, advancing on Lucy like a dog on an intruder. 'Too proud to serve, are you? There are worse places in the city than this house, girl, and if you go to work for Browne, you'll find them. You'll end up in Bridewell, mark my words!'

Lucy set her teeth against another surge of rage and bowed her head humbly, keeping her angry eyes down. 'I'm sorry if I displeased you, Aunt. I only hoped to be able to give you and my uncle something for my keep. You told me earlier that you've scarce enough.'

'Oh, a clever tongue! You should remember what the scriptures say: that the tongue is a fire and a world of iniquity. A woman should be humble and obedient and do as she's told without argument!'

'As you did just now at supper?' asked Lucy, looking up.

There was a silence: Agnes seemed to swell with rage. 'Well, you've got your way,' she said at last. 'I pray you don't curse the day you won it!' She turned and stamped back down the stairs.

Lucy went on up to the loft, unnerved despite herself. It was growing dark and her eyes tried to tell her that there was a man hiding behind one of the bales of cloth, another waiting beside the chimneypiece. She stood still a moment, heart pounding, then made herself walk slowly from one end of the space to the other, proving that there was nobody there. She went again to the window and looked out: the sky still held the last of the daylight, but the streets were already black. For some reason the sight soothed her. Fear and anger both fell away and she was left with only the weariness of a long journey. She undressed to her shift and got into bed. She could *smell* Susan in the none-too-clean linen – a scent of onions, soap and old sweat; she could feel the shape the other woman's body had worn in the flock mattress. She was too tired, though, to care much, and she snuggled under the thick blanket.

She was just falling asleep when Susan came in, holding a candle. Lucy looked up sleepily at the maid, then moved over to the other side of the bed to make space for her.

Susan set the candle down and undressed to her shift, hanging her skirt, petticoat and gown up on the nails. She blew out the candle and climbed into bed. Lucy felt the mattress shift, adjusting to the weight; the other girl's shoulder brushed hers, colder than her own sleep-warmed skin. It was impossible to lie in Susan's bed and ignore the fact that the maid, too, was being forced to share and that she must have her own view of the matter. Lucy wondered if she resented the intrusion, or if she'd looked forward to having another pair of hands to help her work.

'I'm happy to lend a hand, if it's needed,' Lucy said abruptly. 'On a wash-day, like. And I can pick things up in the market and run errands. I don't mind work. But I didn't want to be maid-servant to my mother's brother and his wife, and if they were like to offer me tuppence a day for my labour, I never heard them say so.'

'I've not seen my own wages this twelve-month,' Susan said unexpectedly. 'Not that I'd complain: with things as they are, there's plenty who'd be glad of enough bread to fill their bellies and a roof to keep off the rain. I'll speak plainly: if you'd taken the maid's place, I would've feared being turned out of it.'

Lucy remembered the hard look they'd ex-changed in the kitchen and suddenly understood that she was not the only one worried about being sent back to a home where she'd be a burden. She began to relax. 'Of that, I'm not so sure. My aunt is very angry with me.'

'She don't like anyone,' replied Susan. She paused, then said, more gently, 'She used to. It broke her heart when her boy Mark died.'

Lucy was quiet a moment, thinking of all the dead. 'It was a cruel, unnatural war. I pray God it truly is settled! I'd not heard any of this that my uncle was saying, about Parliament and the Army.'

'The master is eager in suchlike,' said Susan. 'Always buying newsbooks and drinking in taverns with men of the same humour as himself. And he knew John Lilburne, back when Freeborn John was an apprentice mercer.'

'Who's John Lilburne?' asked Lucy.

Susan raised herself on an elbow. 'You never heard of John Lilburne?'

'No.'

'Eh! Well. He used to write pamphlets against the king, but now they're against Parliament because, he says, Parliament's become more tyrannical than the king was. He's been locked up in the Tower this past year.'

'Oh!'

'The pamphlets Mr Browne sells are his, some of 'em. I can't believe you never heard of him!'

'Leicestershire's a long way from London.' Lucy could feel all those miles in the ache of her muscles and the heaviness of her eyelids. She had never seen any pamphlet at all, let alone one so dangerous that it got its author locked up in the Tower. She was too tired to wonder what it was like.

She was just about to fall asleep when Susan said, 'They said you came here because you were ravished by soldiers during the war, and your sweetheart wouldn't have spoiled goods afterwards, and your mother died of grief. They said you were pining away.'

Lucy was abruptly fully awake again. 'My mother had been ill a long time. Grief ended her illness but didn't cause it. And I wasn't pining: I was angry.'

'Aye?' said Susan with sympathetic interest. 'I'd be angry, too. If a woman jilted a man because he lost a leg in the war, everyone would call her a false jade, but if a man jilts a woman because she's lost her maidenhead, the other men just nod. Half of them think the woman must've played the harlot to have suffered so in the first place, and the other half say they wouldn't want spoiled goods either.'

'I think Ned fancied he could marry a bigger dowry,' Lucy said bitterly. 'With so many men dead, those that are left fetch more at market, and my father couldn't supply even what he'd promised before. The men who took my maidenhead also took all our cattle. You say you were told about this, about me?'

'Oh, never fear!' Susan said, immediately understanding the concern. 'Nobody in the neighbourhood knows. Your uncle told *me*, but to the neighbours he gave out that you've come to stay in London because times are hard for your family. He says that's true as well, anyway.'

'Aye,' agreed Lucy. 'All our wealth was in those cattle.'

She had milked those cows every morning and evening; she had given them the old country names – Daisy, Clover, Sweetbriar – and they'd come trustingly to her call. Sometimes she still dreamed of them. The thought that they'd almost certainly been slaughtered for meat still caused a surge of pain and anger, even two years later. It was worse, somehow, than the anger she felt on her own behalf: you weren't *supposed* to mourn cows.

Her father had been slow to replace the cows. He'd promised Ned Bartram a dowry and he'd tried to keep his promise – until Ned declared that he wouldn't take spoiled goods. Then the dowry-money was spent on cattle. Lucy had said nothing but she'd noted the assumption: no one would wed her now.

Still, now she was in London, where nobody knew of her disgrace. She allowed herself a small sigh of relief. One of the things she'd most longed to escape was the way everybody *knew* what had happened to her. She could feel them looking at her when she walked past: 'There goes Lucy Wentnor, who was ravished by three soldiers when she went to milk the cows. Her father found her lying on the barn floor, naked and covered in blood.' She didn't know which was worse, the pity or the revulsion.

Now she was in London, she thought again, already half asleep. It might be a hellish place but at least it was a new one.

Two

Lucy woke before dawn, at first disturbed just because she was in an unfamiliar bed. Then the thought struck her: *I start my work today!* and it became impossible to go back to sleep.

She wanted to jump up at once, but there was nothing to be gained by it, and it would wake Susan. The maid deserved better than to have her sleep disturbed to no purpose. Lucy lay staring up into the darkness for what seemed like hours, thinking about Parliament and seditious pamphlets, until at last the window over the stairwell turned grey and Susan stirred, yawned and sat up.

The previous night it had been arranged that Thomas would walk Lucy over to Mr Browne's shop. Cousin Geoffrey made a half-hearted offer to do it, but Thomas said it wasn't on his way and, anyway, the place was difficult to find. Agnes, who was required to mind the shop while he was out, scowled at them resentfully as they set off.

It was just after dawn, but already the streets were full of people: apprentices hurrying to work, children to school, and women to market; vendors on their rounds and tradesmen opening up their shops; craftsmen fetching this or that needed for the day's work; ragged beggars pleading for alms. Lucy felt as overwhelmed by the noise and bustle and stink as she had been the afternoon before. She did notice this time, though, that the citizen-women all wore gowns – new or shabby; kilted up or loose and half-covered by aprons. She suspected that her skirt and waistcoat marked her out as a country bumpkin, and bit her lip. She had no money to buy a gown.

Thomas walked very quickly, and Lucy struggled to keep up with him, particularly since she had put on footwear suited to the muddy streets, high wooden pattens that kept her petticoat-hem out of the mire but were clumsy to walk in. She was relieved when her uncle paused near the foot of London Bridge to talk to a vendor. The woman smiled and offered him what seemed to be a chapbook from the satchel-like apron she wore around her waist. *'Weekly Account,* Master Stevens?'

Thomas shook his head. 'I'll wait till Monday. I miss *Britanicus,* Kate, indeed I do.'

'We all miss him,' replied the woman, returning the booklet to her apron with a sigh. 'If he takes up his pen again, I'll keep a copy for you, shall I?'

'Do that!' Thomas ordered and walked on. He glanced at Lucy, hurrying after him, and explained, 'I used to buy a copy of *Mercurius Britanicus* every Thursday when it came out, but, now, alas, I have to make do with *A Perfect Diurnall* on Monday.'

Lucy was confused, and Thomas noticed.

'Newsbooks, child! Ah, but you wouldn't have seen a newsbook, would you? They're not printed out in the country, and I never troubled to send any to your father. He would've reckoned it a terrible waste of money!'

Susan had mentioned that Thomas was a great reader of newsbooks. 'What is a newsbook, sir?'

'A sort of chapbook, or short pamphlet, that recounts the news of the week. Some call them mercuries, because many of them take the title *Mercurius* after the heathen god who carried messages. It's an apt title for them, for, like the gods of the ancients, they are full of lies. To read them, one would think that all Parliament-men are wise and fair, and that only the malignants differ with them on any matter whatsoever!'

Lucy wondered why Thomas bought them if they were full of lies, but they were now struggling to cross London Bridge and too busy trying to dodge the traffic to continue the conversation. She thought about it, though, staggered by the idea of buying a book *every week* to tell you what had happened. Her father owned two books: the Bible and Foxe's *Book of Martyrs* – heavy and valuable volumes, which were treated with reverence. The only other printed materials Lucy had handled were the blackletter ballads she'd swapped with her friends – song sheets which cost a penny new but were passed from hand to hand for years. She wondered what you did with a book that was worthless the week after you bought it.

Getting across the bridge was quicker on foot than on horseback: it was possible to squeeze

42

past obstacles by nipping in and out of doorways. When they reached the northern bank of the Thames, they paused a moment to catch their breath. Thomas smiled at Lucy and said, 'You've not been to London before, is that so?'

Lucy nodded.

'A fearful city,' said Thomas. 'I remember when I first came here, thirty years ago, it seemed to me a hell on earth.'

'Aye,' agreed Lucy, a little too quickly, and Thomas smiled again.

'One grows used to it. Here, let me show you the shape of it, in case you get lost.' He led her to a point on the riverbank where there was a view. *'That,'* he pointed across the bridge, 'is the borough of Southwark, which is reckoned almost a separate city. That tower there, that's St Mary Overie – see it, the great church? *This,'* he waved at the shore about them, 'is the City of London. Now *that,'* he pointed west and a little north to a tower which rose above the crowding roofs, 'there, that is London's cathedral, St Paul's. If ever you are lost, look for the towers of Paul's or St Mary's, and then you can find Southwark. Downriver yonder – see the ships? That's the Pool of London, the port where all our merchandise comes and goes. That great fortress above it, that's the Tower.'

'Where prisoners are kept, sir?' asked Lucy, remembering what Susan had said, that the author of Mr Browne's pamphlets, a friend of Thomas's, was imprisoned there.

'Aye, where men whom the state fears are kept prisoner, but also where all the coin of the realm

43

is minted. There's a menagerie there, too, with lions and other strange beasts, well worth three farthings to view. But today we are bound north, to Moorgate.'

At first Thomas continued to point out the sights: Lombard Street, where the rich bankers had their offices; the fine shops on Cheapside; the merchants' Exchange on Cornhill. After that, however, he trudged in silence. Lucy was wondering what the matter was, when suddenly he burst out, 'Lucy, my girl, I confess I am having doubts whether you should take up this place. In fact, I–I should never have agreed to it!'

Her heart gave a jolt: the prospect of returning to the house *now*, and resigning herself to becoming Aunt Agnes's maidservant, was utterly abhorrent. 'I like the notion of it very well, Uncle,' she said quickly. 'Shouldn't we at least make trial of it?'

He frowned. 'There's a matter. I should have spoken of it last night, but ... well, Will was eager, and your aunt was pressing me.'

This, Lucy suspected, was going to be about the *seditiousness* of the pamphlets and ending up in Bridewell. 'Yes, Uncle?'

'The printing press is unlicensed,' said Uncle Thomas. He peered at her anxiously. 'Do you know what that means, child?'

'No,' she admitted, taken aback. 'Do most printing presses have licences?'

'Now, that I'm unsure of,' Thomas said with a nervous smile. 'There's no doubt, though, that they're *supposed* to. The Stationers' Company is responsible for licensing them, and every printer

44

in England is required to get his name on the Stationers' register, and afterwards submit all he wishes to publish to the licensors before he prints it. But since the war began, regulation has been all at sixes and sevens, and there are many unlicensed presses in London. The Stationers' men strain every sinew to find them out, but London is a very great city, and they've no more hope of finding every unlicensed press than of catching every pickpocket at Bartholomew Fair. However, when they do find an illegal press it ... it's better if they don't catch the people who were working it. Particularly if those people were printing something the Parliament-men dislike. In January our other press was found, and those who were printing on it were used very ill. Poor Mary Overton, who was stitching the pamphlets, was barbarously dragged through the mire and over the stones to Bridewell, even with her infant crying in her arms. She's still there, poor brave woman! Now, they might not treat a stranger so inhumanly – but, still, the more I think of it, the less I like the risk of exposing you to such danger. What would I say to your father? No, in good conscience I must disappoint my friend William!'

Lucy took several steps on along the road, imagining a woman with a baby in her arms being dragged along the street to prison – for stitching a pamphlet! So, it seemed that Aunt Agnes hadn't just been trying to scare her.

She felt, though, that if she went back now she would be trapped for ever. She would become her aunt's unpaid serving-maid, and everyone around her would gradually forget that she might ever have been anything else. *I don't care if it's dangerous*, she thought fiercely: *I want to do it. At least I'd eventually be released from Bridewell!*

'Is it against the law for me to stitch your friend's pamphlets?' she asked cautiously.

He sighed. 'Of that, I'm not sure. It's against the law to print them or sell them, but is it against the law to *stitch* them? A lawyer could argue not. But, ah, the present government is most grievously offended by our pamphlets. They very much wish to silence us.' He hesitated, then went on, 'I doubt that Will would have been so eager to take you on if he'd properly understood how little you know of all this. He's been managing this press for us since poor Mr Tew was imprisoned and he finds it hard, or he would have asked more about you.'

'Managing it?' repeated Lucy, confused again.

'It's Nicholas Tew's press,' said Thomas. He peered at her. 'The petition Will brought me last night – remember? Will's run back and forth between the press and his own bookshop ever since Tew was cast in prison, and that's dangerous, since Will's known to the authorities and might be followed. That was one reason why he was so eager to have you there instead. You're unknown in the city, and yet, as my niece, you're trustworthy.'

Lucy wondered if he would have assumed a *nephew* was trustworthy, just because an uncle was: men never seemed to get lumped in with their relatives the way women did. 'Sir,' she said, 'Who is "us"?'

'Eh?'

'*Our* pamphlets, you said; the government wishes to silence *us,*' she pointed out. 'Who's "us"?'

'Oh! I see. Well.' Thomas drew a deep breath, then showed her over to the side of the road and stopped in a doorway, out of the traffic.

'When this war began,' he said, speaking suddenly with clarity and fervour, 'we were told that we must support Parliament to secure our liberties from an oppressive tyranny. We believed it – at least, *I* believed it! – and we spent our treasure, and shed our blood, and lost – God *knows* how I loved my sweet boy; I would rather have lost my own life! And now that we've given Parliament the victory, what do we find? A persecuting prelacy is to be replaced with a persecuting presbytery, and we are to have no more rights than we did before! Still it goes on: imprisonment without charge, monopolies and corruption, punishment for those who complain, privilege for the rich and misery for everyone else. Aye, and this present everlasting Parliament, that was elected nigh on eight years ago and has waded through so much blood – when will it *stand down* and call fresh elections?

'There should be reform. We should get what we fought for! There should be an election and a new settlement of the government! As our victory is stolen, more and more of us have come to believe that we must fight again – not with swords, this time, but with petitions and the law. We've banded together to demand a settlement

47

that secures our liberties as freeborn Englishmen.' Thomas frowned at Lucy and added,
'Agnes calls it "sedition" because this present
corrupt Parliament does – but the king called it
"sedition" when Parliament set itself against his
will, and who believes that now? There *are*
honest men in Parliament; we *do* have support
in the Commons, for all the arrogance of the
majority, and in the Army there are many who
agree with us. I hope and pray that our oppon-
ents have the good sense to realize that they
must make concessions. Then this so-called
sedition will become the new foundation of our
commonwealth, and England's liberty will be
the glory of the world!' He paused, cleared his
throat, and added unhappily, 'In the meantime,
though, I fear that working on our pamphlets is
dangerous.'

Lucy tried to digest all this. She had never
really cared about the claims of Parliament or
King: the 'liberties of freeborn Englishmen' had
very little to do with English*women*. For her the
war had meant ruin and suffering, without sense
or reason, and the thought that anybody might be
stupid and wicked enough to start it up again
appalled her.

On the other hand, she still wanted the job.

'I'm not afraid, Uncle,' she said. Inspiration
struck. 'I would be ashamed if you disappointed
your friend on my behalf, particularly as he
might think you did so only from fear of my
aunt.'

She'd won: she saw that at once.

'We should make trial of it,' she coaxed.

'Then, if I think it too dangerous, I can tell Mr Browne as much, and the blame will rest on me.'

Mr Browne's bookshop was on Coleman Street, near to Moorgate. When they arrived he was perched on a joint-stool outside the shop, but he jumped up, beaming, as soon as he saw them.

'There you are!' he said, shaking hands with Uncle Thomas. 'And your pretty niece from the country! What was her name again, Tom?'

'Lucy Wentnor,' Thomas informed him. 'My sister Elizabeth's child. I've told her of the dangers she faces, Will, but she swears she's not afraid.'

'Excellent! Brave girl! Liza!' Browne called the last back into the shop.

A girl of twelve or thirteen came into the doorway, regarded Lucy a moment with curiosity, then smiled. 'Good health!' she said. 'My da told me you were going to stitch Freeborn John's pamphlet. You're from the country, aren't you?'

'Aye,' said Lucy, smiling back. She felt safer with Browne, knowing he had a young daughter.

'I could tell!' said Liza. 'From the waistcoat. I don't know why nobody in London wears one; it's pretty. Will you come back here for your dinner?'

'Aye, I expect so,' said Browne before Lucy could answer. 'Mind the shop, chick, while I show Mistress Wentnor the press.' He turned to Uncle Thomas. 'I'm much obliged to you, Tom. We need it done as soon as possible.'

'Aye,' agreed Thomas, looking serious. 'I'll let you get to work. Lucy, sweet, I'll see you this evening!' And with that he set off back to South-wark. Lucy watched him go, frightened, despite herself, at being left with strangers in this huge city.

'Well, then!' said Mr Browne. He started off down the street, gesturing for Lucy to follow him. She took a deep breath, steeled herself, and trotted after him, with only one apologetic wave at the girl Liza. She would have liked to talk to Browne's daughter and perhaps ask the sort of questions she didn't dare ask Browne. She wished, too, that she could have had a look at the bookshop. She'd never set foot in a bookshop.

They went up one lane, down another and into the yard of a tavern. Two great curved white beams framed its door; Lucy took them to be wood until she saw the inn-sign naming the place as The Whalebone. She stared at the white beams, impressed, trying to imagine a whale and wondering what part of the animal the bones came from. They looked a bit like a wishbone.

Browne, however, ignored the relic and turned right to unlock one of the stable buildings. Lucy thought it might be a carriage house, but there were no carriages inside. Instead it was festoon-ed with sheets of paper, hung up like laundry on lines that criss-crossed the room in fluttering ranks. In the centre of the laundry lines stood a wooden construction which looked like the bas-tard offspring of a poster bed and a cider press. Lucy stared at it curiously. So that was a printing press! She'd never seen one before: there was no such machine in the whole of Leicestershire.

'Here we are,' said Mr Browne with satisfaction. 'Now, the first thing is safety.' He walked over to the far wall, where there was a table set under a dusty window. 'If ever you hear any disturbance out in the yard, you climb up on this and go directly out of the window. If the alarm turns out to be for nothing, well, there's no harm done; if it's the Stationers' men, then at least you're safe. Do you understand?'

'Aye, sir.' With a nervous glance at Browne, she climbed up on to the table. She opened the window and looked out. It stood over a coal-cellar, and she saw that it was an easy step from the window to the roof of the cellar, and another easy step down into the yard. She closed the window and climbed back down from the table, reassured that if she did have to go out of the window, she wouldn't break her ankle.

'Once you're out of the window, you should be well,' said Browne. 'Just walk off. Don't run. If anyone questions you, say that you had business with the keeper of The Whalebone. He's one of us and will back you up. I'll tell him you're here, and he'll likely come by this morning and make himself known to you. His name's Trebet, Ned Trebet.'

The name *Ned* was an unpleasant reminder of the man who'd rejected her – but it was a common enough name. She settled her nerves by picturing an old, fat innkeeper in an apron, bustling about, giving orders to his wife and children: a man who'd be no threat. 'Aye, sir.'

'You must take care, though, not to let any stranger know what you're doing here, even if they seem well-meaning: London's as full of

51

informers as a dung-heap is of worms! When you're on your way here, if ever you think someone is following after you, don't go in. Walk on by and come back when you're content that no one is watching to see where you go.'

Lucy swallowed. She'd never imagined that *bookish* people engaged in such behaviour. This was like poaching, or levelling a hedge to let your cattle graze on land a lord had enclosed for his own private use. Her father and her brothers had done both, and she knew how carefully they went about it: the checks to see that no one was watching, the excuse made ready beforehand in case someone was. She supposed, though, that what Mr Browne was doing was similar to levelling a hedge: he was breaking down the fence the Stationers and Parliament had put around the printed word. She ducked her head and uttered another subdued 'Aye, sir'.

'Don't look so frighted, girl! I hope you'll have no trouble, but it never does harm to take care. Now, as to what you're to do...' He went to one of the laundry lines and took a paper from it. 'Have you helped to make books before?'

'No, sir,' admitted Lucy, looking at it with some alarm. She'd imagined that books were printed page by page and that it would be straightforward to stitch them together. This sheet, however, was larger than the Bible in a parish church and it was covered on both sides in dense blocks of print. Obviously, you had to manipulate it somehow before you had pages.

'Ah. Well, this is the first sheet. It's printed in *octavo,* which means that it must be folded to make *eight* pages, thus.' He took the sheet to the table, took a kind of bone spatula from his belt and proceeded to fold the paper, flipping it one way, then another with the edge of the blade and smoothing the creases with the flat. 'When you've done it properly, the pages will run in sequence.' He handed her the folded sheet, and pointed out the page numbers in the corners. 'This pamphlet is fitted to a single sheet, so there's no need of more stitching than that.'

She studied it delightedly: what he'd just done seemed like a magic trick. 'I stitch it here?' she asked, running a careful finger down the left-hand side.

Mr Browne smiled back. 'No.' He took the booklet and opened it out again, then picked up a box from under the table and removed a needle on a stick. He punched a series of holes along the crease of the paper, using his bone spatula as a guide. 'You stitch it there, along the crease.'

He had her fold some sheets herself, to make sure she had the way of it, meanwhile telling her more about how to make a book. He used a lot of strange words: *folio* and *quarto*; *recto* and *verso*; *quire* and *signature*. As far as she could see, however, her instructions boiled down to folding the sheet, then punching and stitching the crease. He showed her the needles and the fine linen thread, and he watched as she stitched the first sheet – the first *signature,* it was called, once it was folded; when it was stitched it was a *quire*.

'No need to be so careful!' he told her cheer-fully. 'This isn't a gentleman's shirt. Nobody will care if your stitches are uneven. Speed's the thing! We wanted these by the beginning of the week; if we can get them out by the end of it, you'll have done very well.'

When he was content that she could do the work, he handed her his spatula – *bonefolder* was the proper name for it – and left her to get on with it, closing the door of the carriage house behind him.

She made some mistakes folding the first few sheets and had to do them over. She also punched some of the holes in the wrong places and had to try again. The shed was unheated, too, so that after half an hour or so she had to pause every now and then to warm her fingers under her arms. Still, it was warmer work than weeding or cheese-making, and easier as well.

The pamphlet itself was more worrying. She didn't read it from beginning to end – she'd taken Browne's call for speed to heart – but she kept picking up bits of it as she stitched. It was called *A New-found Stratagem*, and the anonymous author seemed to be arguing that the Army should not be disbanded; that, in fact, the proposal to disband it was a trick, intended merely to leave the people defenceless against the tyranny of Parliament. She found herself whispering the difficult words under her breath, chewing the ideas like gristle: 'just demands ... denied contrary to duty, oath, and covenant'; 'a shelter and defence to secure them from oppression and violence'. She could see why Parliament would dislike the pamphlet, but she wondered what Mr Browne and his friends thought they could achieve by printing it. Presumably Mr Browne thought he could sell it, but what were the buyers supposed to do about the disbanding of armies?

After a while she got up and walked around the shed while she sewed, partly to keep warm, partly because she was curious. The printing press drew her irresistibly: she would fold and punch a sheet, walk over to the press as she stitched, gaze a moment, then walk back to the table as she tied off the thread. She thought she could see how the machine worked: the flat part, the bed-like bit, would slide under the cider-press-like screw. The bed was covered by a sheet of canvas in a wooden frame, like a blank painting, and after a while she worked up the courage to lift it and peer beneath. There was another piece of cloth, folded; under that was a kind of frame full of words, lying on a flat stone. She tried to read the words and couldn't.

She went back to the table, vexed, and folded and punched another sheet. Everyone had always told her she read well; during her mother's long decline she'd spent hours sitting at the bedside, reading from the Bible – yet she couldn't read the words in the frame at all! She returned to the press, busily stitching, and tried again.

The letters in the frame were written *backwards*, she realized: that was why she couldn't read them! She stared at them, her tongue between her teeth: *To the rigg ... To the right honourable the Commons of England af ... affemd ... assembled in Parliament...*

It was the petition Mr Browne had brought Uncle Thomas the night before: it had been printed here, on this press. There was something wonderful about that: those printed words, as black and formal as the Bible itself, had been put on paper *here*. It was like discovering the secret of a juggler's trick.

The door banged open.

She dropped the paper she was stitching and bolted for the window; she was up on the table when a voice yelled, 'Hey! It's only me!'

She turned back, heart pounding, and saw a young man in an apron standing by the press and grinning at her.

'Will told me you were here,' he said. 'The niece of Mr Stevens the mercer, he said. I'm Ned Trebet.'

Ned Trebet was not fat and old. He was about her own age, tall and sturdy, with sandy hair and long legs like a stork. His eyes were a bright blue, and they regarded her with a mixture of amusement and ... something she didn't like. She gritted her teeth: she was going to have to lift her skirts to jump down from the table again, and Ned Trebet, damn him, would *enjoy* it.

'Will said you were a pretty thing,' said Trebet, still grinning. 'He didn't do you justice!'

Since it had to be done, she picked up her skirts and jumped down quickly, then gave him a cold look. The wretch merely grinned some more. Then his eyes fell on the stack of papers she'd already stitched and the expression changed. 'You've done all that already?' he asked in amazement.

'Aye,' she replied cautiously.

'Why, you'll have it ready in no time!' He looked her up and down once more, then leered cheerfully. 'I wouldn't have thought a beautiful girl *needed* to be a hard worker!'

'Nay,' she said sharply, 'any woman must work hard if she wishes to make an honest living, and if she's pretty, she must work twice as hard or she'll suffer ill-use by dishonest men.'

Trebet merely grinned. *'Use,* certainly, but *I* certainly wouldn't term it *ill!*'

'If there's aught you wish to know, you should ask of Mr Browne,' she said pointedly. 'For myself, I came to London only yesterday and I'm still learning the work.'

'Aye, I can see you are a country rose,' Trebet said gallantly. 'I only came to make myself known to you and to say that I can give you dinner.'

'I think Mr Browne meant me to go to his house,' she replied at once. The cost of dinner in an ordinary inn would swallow up the whole of her day's wage: if Trebet was expecting her to pay, she couldn't afford it; if he was offering to feed her for free, she didn't want the debt.

Trebet, however, frowned. 'It would be better if you didn't parade up and down the street, so that any informer watching has the chance to notice something's up. I'll speak to Will about it. No sense wasting the time, either! We need these in Saffron Walden by the week's end.'

'Saffron Walden?' she repeated, frowning.

'Aye. Didn't you know? They're for the soldiers. Parliament's commissioners are already on their way to the Army's headquarters at Saffron Walden and they mean to persuade the men to disband or go to Ireland. If we lose the Army, we lose all hope of a just settlement.'

The pamphlet's point suddenly appeared very clear indeed: persuade the Army to mutiny. It was confirmation, if she'd needed it, that her uncle and his friends weren't just playing: they really were engaged in sedition – and so, it seemed, was she. 'I didn't know,' she said, feeling slightly sick.

'*This* will make it clear to the soldiers what's at stake!' said Ned Trebet enthusiastically. 'With you finishing it off so speedily, perhaps we should print more. I can work the press, once Will's set the type.'

Will, however, when he came to collect Lucy at noon, reckoned that there was not enough time to print more copies. Lucy wasn't sure whether to be disappointed or relieved. Disappointed, she decided: if she was arrested, another hundred copies would be neither here nor there, and at least she would have seen the press working.

Mr Browne did, however, accept Ned Trebet's offer to supply Lucy with dinner – without consulting her. 'Generous!' he exclaimed warmly. 'And, in truth, I think the less traffic there is between my shop and your tavern, the safer it will be for both of us. I'm obliged to you, Ned.'

'It's a small matter,' replied Trebet modestly.

Lucy was afraid that he meant to stay and flirt while she ate, but it seemed he was busy in his tavern at dinner-time. He brought her bread, small beer and a dish of stewed beef, then excused himself and hurried back across the yard, apron flapping. She was relieved: she wanted nothing to do with lusty young men, particularly ones named Ned. The food was good, but she still regretted Browne's shop. It would have been pleasant to have some *safe* company, and she still wanted to look at the bookshop.

She stitched until the sun was low, then stopped and put away the needles and thread: she did not want to walk back to her uncle's in the dark. She was arranging the quires in stacks when Mr Browne came in to tell her she should get home before dark.

'All of those?' he cried delightedly. 'You're a fine needlewoman indeed!'

'Thank you, sir,' she said, feeling herself blush at the unaccustomed praise. She knew very well that she was not a fine needlewoman: she tended to hurry, and her stitches were uneven and too large. She was just lucky that that was exactly what was required to rush out a pamphlet.

'Tomorrow you must trim these and finish them off,' said Browne. 'Do that before you stitch any more and we can send the first batch out. Can you come early tomorrow?'

'As soon as there's light, sir.' She wondered if he'd pay her now.

'Good girl!'

'Sir, *how* do I trim them and finish them off?'

'You ... no, I'll show you tomorrow. But I'll give you another pamphlet tonight: have a care to study it, and use it as a guide tomorrow.'

'Thank you, sir!'

59

They left the printworks separately, like poachers, and met again outside his bookshop; this time he showed her in. The shop was small and dark; it smelled of leather and dust. Liza wasn't there. The books stood in locked cases all around the walls, their dark spines barely visible through an iron grille. Lucy stared at them in fascination. She had never seen so many in one place.

'No use looking there!' Browne told her with a smile. 'I don't keep the pamphlets on the shelves, where any informing knave could see them! Here!' He went to a case, opened it and then knelt and swung a whole shelf out of the way. He reached down into the concealed space behind it. 'Now, what have we?' He began pulling out stacks of pamphlets, printed on the soft, greyish, poor-quality paper Lucy had been stitching all day. *Regal Tyranny Discovered* – that would do, but, mmm, this copy is most sluttishly put together. *London's Liberty in Chains*, together with *The Charters of London* – too thick. Ah! *An Arrow Against All Tyrants* and *The Oppressed Man's Oppressions Declared* – either of these would do; they're both much the same length as the *Stratagem*. Which will you have?'

'Uh, whichever you wish, sir!' said Lucy, taken aback.

Browne weighed a pamphlet in either hand, then put one aside. He stacked the rest back in their hiding place, replaced the shelf of books and closed and locked the case. 'Here, then!' he said, handing her the pamphlet he'd selected.

It was *An Arrow Against All Tyrants*. Lucy

took it gingerly and thanked Browne again.

'Have a care not to study it on the street!' Browne warned her. 'Informers, remember! Keep it out of sight until you're safely home.' He got to his feet, then smiled at her. 'Ah, but I almost forgot your wages!' He dug two large pennies out of his purse and set them in her hand, one, two: the heavy cold rounds filled her palm. She wondered if the surge of pleasure she felt was sinful. Money was the root of all evil, said scripture, but she'd worked hard all day, and didn't scripture also say that the labourer was worthy of his hire?

'Thank you, sir!' she said, smiling.

She'd worried that she'd get lost going back to Southwark, but she discovered that the landmarks her uncle had pointed out that morning had stayed with her and she had no difficulty. It was just beginning to grow dark, and the streets were crowded again, this time with people hurrying home; jostling among them on the same errand, Lucy believed for the first time that perhaps she *could* get used to London, after all.

Crossing London Bridge was slow, and by the time she arrived at her uncle's house it was dark. She knocked on the door, out of breath from having hurried the last part of the way.

The others were already at supper, eating by the light of a single tallow candle, but her uncle smiled and told Susan to fetch another bowl of soup. Lucy slid into place at the table. Mr Browne's pamphlet, which she'd slipped into her apron pocket, caught against her leg, and she straightened it carefully.

'You should have been home before dark!' Agnes said disapprovingly. 'No decent young woman should be on the street this time of night.'

'I had to wait to cross the bridge,' explained Lucy.

'Don't you talk back to me, girl!'

'I beg your pardon, Aunt.'

Susan brought the soup, and Lucy began to eat it, uncomfortable under her aunt's glare.

'Did he pay you?' Agnes asked suddenly.

'Aye, Aunt Agnes.' Lucy dug the two pennies out from under the pamphlet and set them down on the table. 'Here are my wages.'

Agnes snatched both coins, examined them a moment, then slipped them in her own pocket with a sniff of contempt.

Thomas frowned at her, cast an uneasy glance at Cousin Geoffrey, who was pretending not to notice, then frowned at Agnes again. 'I did not give you leave to take those,' he pointed out at last.

'It's money for the girl's keep!' snapped Aunt Agnes, turning the glare on him.

'We didn't ask her *father* to provide for her keep when we offered to take her!'

'Indeed!' replied Agnes vehemently. '*You* wouldn't ask, lest he learn you were not the great man he took you for! But you promised *me* that the girl would help me in the house, and now you've sent her to work for your trouble-making friends! You owe—'

'Her keep doesn't even *cost* tuppence!' interrupted Thomas, his voice rising. 'Will's providing her dinner, and, as for bed and linen, we'd have to supply Susan whether Lucy were here or not! You lazy slut, give that money back!'

'It's my money!' exclaimed Agnes, going red in the face and clutching her pocket.

'Scolding shrew!' cried Thomas, jumping to his feet. 'Give it here!'

Lucy cringed and called, 'Please, Uncle!'

Thomas paused, casting a puzzled look at her. He was defending her, and she protested?

She wasn't sure what to say to him. He was within his rights to beat his wife for such open defiance; indeed, it was what was expected of him. She didn't want to see or hear it, that was all. She remembered cowering at the table while her father beat her mother; remembered her mother's sobs and her own helpless desperation. Her parents' quarrels had been rare and all the more disturbing for it.

She found she knew exactly how it would end: Agnes, red-faced and crying, yielding up the coins; Thomas, flushed with anger and guilt, taking them and perhaps handing them to Lucy. It would set a pattern: Thomas defending his niece, Agnes hating her. The quarrel would fill the house like a noxious vapour, poisoning all of them.

'Don't let me be the cause of a quarrel, please!' she said desperately. 'I'm sure I'd rather my aunt kept the money than we quarrelled about it!'

Agnes glared at Lucy as though she'd struck her. Lucy swallowed and met her furious eyes directly. It was not that she didn't want the

63

money: she did. If freedom cost tuppence a day, though, she couldn't complain, and if it purchased peace as well, it was a bargain.

'You crawling lick-spittle hypocrite!' Agnes exclaimed furiously. She dug the coins out of her pocket and threw them at Lucy, then stamped out, bursting into tears as she went.

Lucy picked the two pennies off the floor, her hands shaking, then set them down on the table in front of her uncle. 'Give them to my aunt, please! Give them to her with soft words, so she won't be angry with me!'

'You're a good, sweet girl,' said Thomas, picking them up and offering them back to her. 'You keep them.'

She shook her head: no amount of money was worth filling the house with poison. 'Perhaps ... perhaps you could give my aunt *some* of the money, sir?' she asked. She remembered her excuse for putting herself forward and added, 'I only took the work, sir, because I wanted not to be a burden on you and my aunt, and I fear my being here *is* a burden to her. It's only fair that you should give her something extra for the housekeeping.'

Thomas thought about it, then nodded. 'Very well. I'll give her these, but I'll tell her that tomorrow you'll keep half of what you earn.'

'Thank you, Uncle,' she said in relief.

She hoped it would be enough. She could imagine Thomas being magnanimous and superior as he gave Agnes the money, and that would only fuel Agnes's resentment. She hoped, though, that it would still be enough to keep the peace.

After supper Thomas and Geoffrey sat down in the parlour to smoke a pipe and talk about Cousin Geoffrey's day at Westminster. Lucy hesitated, wondering if she could take a candle upstairs to study the pamphlet Mr Browne had given her, or whether that would be regarded as a waste of a candle. She decided to give Agnes no cause to complain and crept into the parlour to look at the pamphlet there.

'What's that?' asked Thomas.

'A pamphlet, Uncle, that Mr Browne gave me to study, so that I could see how to put pamphlets together.'

Thomas nodded and turned back to Cousin Geoffrey's account of the laziness and greed of parliamentary clerks. Lucy turned the pamphlet in her hands, taking careful note of how the pages had been trimmed and the spine glued. The title letters stood out black in the flickering candlelight: *An Arrow against all Tyrants and Tyranny*, and then, in smaller letters, *shot from the prison of Newgate into the Prerogative Bowels of the arbitrary House of Lords and all other usurpers and tyrants whatsoever.*

She mouthed the words silently, as she had when confronted with particularly challenging words in the Bible – *Melchizedek*, for example, or *recompense*. What, she wondered, did 'prerogative' mean? She glanced up at Uncle Thomas, found him still listening to Geoffrey, and decided not to ask. She was not altogether sure, but she felt that Geoffrey wouldn't like the pamphlet and that drawing attention to it would cause awkwardness between him and Uncle Thomas. She read over the title again and this time grasped that the author was calling the House of Lords 'usurpers and tyrants'.

She was shocked. The government of England had always consisted of King, Lords and Commons, and no one had gone into the war to *change* that. It was true that the Commons and many of the Lords had risen up against the king, but now that the war was over everyone expected King Charles to be restored to his throne, this time with defined limits to his power. Both sides of the conflict had claimed to be defending ancient and traditional rights.

Maybe, she thought, the author – this man John Lilburne? – was referring to the Lords who'd supported the king during the war. *Then* it would make sense to call them tyrants. She looked at the bottom of the page for a date, and found it.

1646.

Only last year! The year the king surrendered and the Royalist Lords fled to the Continent, or else submitted to Parliament. Lucy came reluctantly to the conclusion that the author really did mean the present House of Lords. Troubled, she read the title again, this time continuing on:

... usurpers and tyrants whatsoever. Wherein the original, rise, extent, and end of magisterial power, the natural and national rights, freedoms and properties of mankind are discovered and undeniably maintained...

By Richard Overton

She felt a moment of relief: so the author *wasn't* Uncle Thomas's friend. The name *Overton* was familiar, though, and after a moment she remembered why: it was a Mary Overton who'd been dragged through the street to Bridewell with her baby screaming in her arms.

For stitching *this* pamphlet? Her husband or father's pamphlet? Lucy felt a surge of indignation: why did women and children always suffer for the misdeeds of their menfolk? She was not entirely sure that the pamphlet *was* a misdeed, but she could certainly understand why the House of Lords thought it was.

Natural and national rights. There was a concept she'd never encountered before. What on earth was a *natural* right?

She thought again about levelling hedges: her father and her brothers had broken down the lord's new enclosure because it fenced off common land where village cows had been accustomed to graze for time out of mind. The lord said it was his, that he had a *legal right* to enclose it, and apparently the law courts agreed with him. If he had a *legal* right, then maybe what the villagers had was a *natural* one.

Lucy's heart gave a sudden fierce leap of agreement. She put the pamphlet away, disturbed by her own reaction. She did not want to agree with Richard Overton: she could see that his ideas were trouble. All she wanted, she repeated to herself, was honest work and an honest independence. She curtsied to her uncle and went upstairs to bed.

Three

All the printed sheets of *A New-found Stratagem* had been turned into pamphlets by Friday afternoon. When the last copy was finished, Lucy went to inform Mr Browne with a flutter in her stomach. She'd believed that her place would be more than temporary, but it struck her now that this had never been discussed, let alone promised. Her two and a half days of work might be all she could hope for, and, while Aunt Agnes had grudgingly agreed that two-thirds of Lucy's earnings would pay for her keep, the truce between them was at best an uneasy one.

Lucy set her teeth and told herself that as long as she had other work *sometimes* she would manage to keep her independence. Agnes couldn't rely on Lucy as a serving-maid if she was going to be off earning money even occasionally, and surely she'd done well enough that Browne would hire her again the next time he needed a pamphlet stitched?

She needn't have worried. 'Well done!' Browne told her warmly. 'Now we can start typesetting the next one!'

'The *next* one, sir?' asked Lucy, scarcely daring to believe it.

Browne glanced about, then picked up his cash-box and showed her a stack of paper beneath it. The pages were covered with large, scrawled, uneven letters.

'Freeborn John's latest,' Browne told her, with a proud smile. *The Resolved Man's Resolution.* His wife gave it to me only yesterday.' He looked at her speculatively and went on, 'You've nimble fingers, girl, and quick wits. I've no doubt you can learn typesetting as easily as you learned to stitch a pamphlet.'

Lucy goggled wordlessly. *Typesetting?* It was a skill so exotic to Leicestershire that he might as well have said, 'You can as easily learn to fly'.

'It's nothing but setting out the letters you see on a page,' Browne told her cheerfully. 'I'll do most of it, but any help would speed the matter, and the more you learn, the more you'll be of help.' He considered a moment, then went to the door of his shop and looked judiciously at the sun. 'Too late to start now,' he concluded. 'Tomorrow morning, then.'

Lucy walked slowly back to Southwark. It was a grey, damp day, and cold for April, but she had glorious sunshine in her heart. She had been worried that she would lose her job, and instead ... *typesetting!* However casually it had been offered, she was sure this was an opportunity she must seize eagerly. Typesetting wasn't like sewing or cooking, a woman's skill, domestic and cheap. Men learned it: it was real work.

It would be dangerous. She'd known that, though, and she was already convinced that the risk was worth it. What was fascinating and disturbing was the *nature* of this sedition. She was beginning to grasp it now, and it was either no sedition at all or the worst ever.

Treachery and sedition had always been as common as poverty and injustice, but until the war they'd meant conspiracies of nobles trying to overthrow the king and replace him with somebody else. Now, though, the king had already been overthrown, Parliament wanted to restore him on its own terms, and here was a group of men – *ordinary* men, not nobles! – who wanted to change not the king but the *terms*. They wanted to replace not one man or even one Parliament but the whole system of government. She'd never heard of anything like it. This man Lilburne seemed to be their leader, but Lucy had the distinct sense that it was the *ideas* these people had that really identified them and set them apart.

She thought of the arguments in *An Arrow Against All Tyrants*, which she'd now read through – twice.

For by natural birth all men are equally alike born to like propriety, liberty and freedom; and as we are delivered of God by the hand of nature into this world, every one with a natural, innate freedom and propriety ... even so are we to live, everyone equally and alike ... The safety of the people is the sovereign law, to which all must become subject, and for the which all powers human are ordained.

It was a far cry from the preaching she'd grown up with: that God ordained the ranks of

men in their several degrees, from lord to beggar, and that to rebel against that order was rebel
against Him. It took her breath away.

Well, she was involved in it now, by her own
free choice; and she *still* preferred it to sinking
tamely into the role of poor relation. Besides...

She thought again about the lord of Hinckley's
hedge. He'd not only stolen common land; he'd
turned five poor tenant families off their farms,
leaving them to beg bread of the parish. If a lord
said he had a right to a piece of land, what
chance did a poor tenant have of proving the
contrary? It wasn't *right*, though – not *naturally*
right, however the law stood.

Typesetting was *not* as easy as stitching a
pamphlet.

Lucy had barely noticed the cases of type
before: the big boxes had been closed, and she'd
thought they were something to do with the
carriage-shed. Now Mr Browne opened them,
and she found they held drawers and drawers of
little letters on stems. They were called *sorts,*
and there were all sizes and styles of them. The
reason Browne had mentioned her 'nimble
fingers' became clear at once: the sorts were
tiny, and it was very easy to fumble them.

Finding and arranging the letters was hard
enough; what made things worse was that
margins had to be straight and even – *justified,*
like sinners – which meant varying spacings and
moving words from one line to another to try to
get everything to fit in neatly. It took her a whole
morning to set her first paragraph; Mr Browne

set the rest of the first and fourth page in less than an hour, and then went off to his bookshop.

He reappeared at dinner-time with Ned Trebet. She'd stopped worrying about the tavern-keeper: he still tried to flirt with her but he kept his hands to himself. She showed them her miserable few lines.

'Never mind,' Browne told her kindly. 'It will come, with time. Let's print it off and see what it looks like.'

At last she got to see the press working. It was much as she'd imagined – the bed slid under the screw – but there was a lot of fuss first, much like checking over a cart and team before setting off to market with a full load. The machinery was clearly very heavy: Trebet pushed the bed in like a man ploughing a field full of stones. Lucy had had visions of working the press herself, and began to suspect she couldn't.

The bed was hauled back, the paper was removed from the press and the first impression was carefully examined. Ned Trebet began laughing. 'Resolb!' he exclaimed; 'freebom!'

Lucy stared at him, puzzled. With a smile Browne showed her the page. The paragraph she had typeset was a mess: every letter *d* had been replaced with *b,* and vice versa, and the same thing had happened with the *p*'s and *q*'s.

'The letters on the sorts are *reversed*,' Mr Browne gently reminded her.

'Free bomb!' repeated Ned Trebet and mimed an explosion.

Lucy, red with shame, bit her lip and said nothing.

'Never mind!' Browne comforted her. 'An easy mistake to make, and almost as easy to correct. Ned, I think we need more pressure *here* and *here*.'

Lucy, still red in the face, replaced the errant letters. Browne arranged some scraps of loose paper under the formes in the spots where the impression was faint. The press was worked again, and this time the result was judged satisfactory.

'Five hundred copies, I think,' said Browne, with satisfaction. 'I'll work the press for the next hour, Ned. Then you can take over. Lucy – you do the inking.'

Inking was done with two *dabs,* leather balls on sticks which you rolled in ink, then blotted over the forme two-handed, as quickly as you could. Printer's ink was thick, like set honey, and it smelled of linseed and soot. It took a full day to dry, so between dabbing ink Lucy ran around hanging up the printed sheets. She went home that evening exhausted, but at the same time satisfied. They had made something that day; turned scribbled words into a sheet that would soon be in men's hands and minds.

She arrived back at the house at supper-time, but when she sat down at the table, Aunt Agnes stared, then squawked angrily, 'You're filthy!'

Lucy glanced down and saw that her hands were black with ink; what was worse, there were tiny splatters all over her sleeves as well. She jumped up in horror, bobbed her head at her aunt, and ran into the kitchen to wash it off before it dried.

Too late. The ink wouldn't come off with water; laundry soap only smeared it. She was dismayed. Ink-stained hands were one thing, but she *had* only two shifts.

'You'll have to stitch yourself some over-sleeves,' said Susan, who had been eating her own supper in the kitchen with Geoffrey's William. 'I'm sure Mr Stevens has some old scraps of linsey you could use for it.'

'Aye,' Lucy agreed unhappily: oversleeves might protect her shift in future, but they wouldn't get the ink out.

William gave a bray of laughter and leaned back against the wall. 'Got your hands dirty, Mistress High-and-Mighty?'

She gave him a cool look and didn't reply. Susan slapped his arm. 'Leave her be!' she ordered. 'Where's the shame in dirtying your hands with honest work?'

'She wouldn't dirty them on *your* work, though, would she?'

'As though you cared for that!' Susan replied tartly. 'Your grievance is that she wouldn't dirty them on *you* – and for that I don't blame her!'

Faced with this female solidarity, William's only reply was a grunt. Lucy smiled at Susan, who grinned back.

She wondered if she could clean the splatter-marks by rubbing soda and ash into them and leaving them to soak overnight. That would mean she had to wear her best shift instead, but the next day was a Sunday, so she'd be wearing it anyway. She went upstairs to change.

* * *

74

Lucy wanted to rinse her shift next morning, but Uncle Thomas forbade even that much work on the Sabbath. She'd forgotten that he was so strict: on a farm, where cows needed milking regardless of the day of the week, Sabbath-keeping tended to be more lax. The household – including Cousin Geoffrey and his man – went to the parish church of St Olave instead, and listened to a long sermon on a text from Jeremiah. Lucy usually enjoyed sermons – the high-flown rhetoric, the dramatic story-telling, the ingenious reasoning and heartfelt emotion. St Olave's preacher, however, was a long-winded mumbler, and she spent a tedious two hours worrying about her shift.

In the afternoon they walked across the bridge to visit Cousin Hannah and her husband in Stepney. Lucy had met Hannah only once, twelve years before when Thomas had taken his whole family north to meet his relations. She remembered a soft, fat, timid girl who hadn't liked the countryside and who'd cried to be taken home to London. Meeting Hannah again, after so many years, she found her perfectly recognizable: still soft and timid and anxious. Her husband, Nathaniel Cotman, was a loud, large man at least a decade older than his wife, a mercer like his father-in-law. He engaged in a long lament about the ruin of trade; Thomas occasionally added an 'Aye! Very true!', while everyone else sat mute. Lucy found herself wishing for the morning: printing was a lot more interesting than the Stevens family Sabbath.

She finally managed to rinse her shift that

evening. By candlelight it looked as though most of the stains had come out. In the morning, however, daylight showed the marks had merely faded from black to grey. The shift was damp, too: it had not had enough time to dry. She put it on anyway – she didn't want to ruin *both* shifts – wrapped herself up in a thick shawl, and set off for The Whalebone Tavern, shivering and scowling.

Ned Trebet was in the yard of The Whalebone, helping to unload a dray. He glanced at Lucy, glanced again, then set down his barrel of beer and came over. 'What's amiss?' he asked with concern.

'Naught,' she said sharply.

'Your face is as pinched as a mildewed apple! Come, what's the matter?'

'It's only that I got ink on my shift,' she said, showing him the sleeve, 'and I cannot get it out again.'

'Is that all!' he said in relief. 'You cannot *shift* it, you mean! Ha, ha, ha!' He laughed with great gusto, then, at her look, stopped abruptly. He touched her sleeve. 'Here, that's damp! Why did you put on a damp shift? You must have others; your uncle's no pauper!'

'What, and spoil another one? I'll not be using less ink today than I did Saturday!'

'You'll catch cold!'

'I have this.' She waved the end of the shawl. 'I'll be warm enough.'

'Nay, it's a chilly day! I'll speak to our girls here, see if one of them can lend you—'

'Nay!'

76

He stopped, surprised by her vehemence. She looked him in the eye: she had no intention of changing her shift anywhere he might spy on her. 'I thank you, but there's no need.'

He frowned, surprised and hurt. 'What ails you? You treat me as though I were a rogue out to cozen you, when I've never treated you with aught but kindness!'

Her face flushed: it was true. 'I'm sorry.'

He continued to frown at her.

'It's only that I'm ... that London is such a fearful place and so full of strangers.'

His expression softened. 'You've not been here a month, have you? I had forgotten. You're from ... from somewhere up north.' He waved a hand vaguely towards Moorgate.

'Hinckley, in Leicestershire.'

'Aye, and your father has a dairy farm, freehold. Will told me. Aye, I suppose London is a fearful place, to one not used to it, and perhaps you think your uncle's seditious friends must be desperate men, hey?'

She risked meeting his eyes and managed a small smile. 'Are you not?'

'No more than your uncle. These are uncommon times, mistress, and many ordinary men are desperate.'

She considered that a moment, then responded honestly, 'Aye. It was a cruel war.'

'God knows it!' replied Trebet, with feeling. 'My brother and I fought at Newbury. I brought him home after, but he died of his wound anyway.'

She looked at him with sudden understanding.

So, like Thomas, he fought now to make the sacrifice worthwhile. The phrase *throwing good money after bad* came to her mind, but she put it aside. How could anyone who'd lost a son or a brother *not* want their death to count for something?

'You were in the London militia?' she asked instead, then bit her lip: of course he had been in the militia. The service was required of freeholders.

'The trained bands, aye. I'm a sergeant.' He said it proudly. 'My regiment trains at Moorfields once a month, but since the Army was new-modelled we've not been called upon.' He paused, looking at her, then said, 'Are you sure you'll not borrow a dry shift? I've three servingwomen here who might lend one.'

'Nay,' she said, but more gently this time. 'I might smut it with more ink, which would ill return their kindness. My shift is almost dry now, and the work will keep me warm.'

By the end of the week she'd stopped worrying about ink spots. Her new oversleeves caught most of them and there was no point worrying about the rest. Ploughmen had muddy boots; printers had ink-stained sleeves, and there was nothing to be done about it. Like her hedge-leveller caution going to and from work, it became something she no longer even thought about.

It was a good week: they printed half of *The Resolved Man's Resolution*, and Lucy's typesetting gained speed and accuracy. Sometimes

Mr Browne worked the press, sometimes Ned Trebet, sometimes one of the ostlers from The Whalebone, who, like his master, was enthusiastic for the cause. Twice Lucy found herself printing on her own and was pleased to find that she could, after all, manage the heavy machinery, though it was an effort and she didn't think she could keep it up for a full day.

Mr Browne's daughter Liza turned up at The Whalebone at dinner-time on Tuesday. 'I come here,' Liza said ingenuously, 'cause it's raining, and da's gone to Westminster.'

Ned Trebet, who was working the press at the time, rolled his eyes and exclaimed with comic exaggeration. 'More mouths to feed!'

'Nay!' protested Liza. 'I have my dinner, here.' She held up a covered dish. 'It's only I mislike being at home when da's at Westminster.'

There was no Mrs Browne at home: Lucy had gathered that she'd died in childbirth some years before. 'What's your father doing at Westminster?' she asked.

'Shouting at the Parliament-men,' replied Liza woefully.

Ned Trebet caught Lucy's frown and explained: 'We're pressing Parliament for an answer to our petition. Well-affected people stand outside the hall every day and ask the Parliament-men about it when they go in.'

'Isn't it too early for an answer?' asked Lucy in surprise. The petition had been printed only a week before, and if it had been handed in, neither Uncle Thomas nor Browne had mentioned it.

Trebet shook his head. 'Not the *new* petition. The last one, the large one. The one that asked for the reforms we want. Mr Tew was arrested over it.'

'Oh!' Lucy had believed that Tew's arrest was something to do with unlicensed printing, though now that she thought of it she remembered that Thomas *had* mentioned a petition. So now Mr Browne was at Westminster, doing what Tew had done? She glanced at Liza, guessing that this was the reason the girl misliked being home without her father: she feared that she'd find herself left that way. 'Well, I'm glad you're here,' she said impulsively. 'I mislike eating alone, too.'

She and Liza became firm friends after that.

The policy of the 'well-affected', however, caused trouble in a completely unexpected quarter. She came home on Friday to a row between Thomas and Cousin Geoffrey.

'...seditious and scandalous!' Geoffrey was shouting as she came in. She froze, one hand still on the door.

'That is a lie!' Uncle Thomas replied hotly.

'Why would he lie?' demanded Geoffrey. 'What was I to say? Your friends have been standing around Westminster calling like fishwives! All week I've been courting this man's favour, and it's all for nothing! He told me to my face he much misliked my company in London, that you and your friends—'

'These *ambitious*, encroaching Presbyterians would have no opinions spoken but their own! Do you know what they plan? Have you heard of their foul and tyrannical Ordinance against what they call blasphemy?'

'I do not *care*! I wish only to buy some land and go home! And now I find that—'

'Is it *my* fault, then, that they would deny you your purchase merely because you lie in my house?'

Lucy closed the door and came into the parlour. Geoffrey, who had been short of an answer, seized upon her arrival. 'If you wish to court trouble, Uncle, it's your affair, but why should the rest of your family pay for it? It's not just *my* business you're ruining: here's my cousin Lucy – a simple country girl whose father trusted you to protect her – and you have her printing these scandalous pamphlets for your trouble-making friends! Will you go to Daniel Wentnor and tell him his daughter's in prison?'

Thomas flinched.

'Don't fear for me!' Lucy put in hurriedly: any more of this and Thomas would forbid her work. 'I *offered* to take this work, Cousin Geoffrey, and I like it very well!'

Geoffrey glared at her. 'As though a silly girl could understand anything of what she's tangled in!'

Lucy glanced down at her ink-stained hands, then up at her cousin's face. He was, and always had been, a selfish, self-important ass; she'd kept that view to herself all her life and now she couldn't think *why*. 'I understand this much,' she said evenly. 'You save ten shillings a week by staying here as our uncle's guest, and you are berating him, *your father's brother,* at his own table, about his choice of friends.'

Geoffrey flushed. Thomas gave Lucy a look of astonished gratitude.

'If you are so eager to please this clerk at Parliament,' Lucy went on, 'why don't you tell him you've resolved not to lie under your uncle's roof a night longer? – though in fact I'd wager your business would be better served by giving the ten shillings to the clerk!'

'You – you brazen hoyden!' exclaimed Geoffrey incredulously.

'Better brazen than a silly child!' replied Lucy. 'Better either than a selfish dolt!'

Geoffrey drew in his breath sharply and raised a hand.

'Enough, enough!' said Thomas hastily. 'Lucy, you shouldn't speak thus to your cousin. Ahem.' Despite the reproof, he was smiling. 'Geoffrey, you are always welcome under my roof; I would never turn away my brother's son. If you *wish* to leave, though, because it impedes your business here, I will not hinder you.'

Geoffrey floundered: he did not wish to leave. The whole trip to London was proving much more expensive than he'd expected and he couldn't afford to pay for his lodgings. He scowled and grumbled an apology.

His words had, however, hit their target. Thomas climbed the ladder to the loft when Lucy was preparing for bed.

She and Susan were both in their shifts with their hair loose: they'd been combing out one another's tresses and checking for lice. They both gasped when Thomas's head appeared in the stairwell.

'Be easy!' said Thomas. 'I only want a word with Lucy.' He climbed the rest of the way into the loft, regarded the two young women for a moment, then smiled. Lucy had had a moment of terror that his appearance preceded some lustful advance, but the smile was one of extraordinary sweetness. 'Lord, how pretty you are! So much like your dear mother.'

Lucy had a sudden vision of her mother as a girl, sitting before the fire of the big farmhouse now owned by Uncle John, combing out her hair while little Thomas sat beside her reading aloud: two children, long ago.

Then she remembered her mother as that last skeletal shape, lying on dirty sheets, dull eyes staring at the wall. 'Oh Lord God, have mercy, no more!' had been her last words. 'I'm not made of iron.'

Lucy twisted a hand in her long dark hair and pulled it behind her head, then pulled her coif over it, as though she could stifle the memory. 'What is it, Uncle?'

He sat down on the boards of the loft, acknowledged Susan's presence with a nod and a weak smile, then returned his attention to Lucy. 'Child, I'm troubled by what your cousin said. I was entrusted with keeping you from harm, and this employment of yours is like to put you in danger.'

'I like it very well,' Lucy said. Her heart speeded up again.

'My dear, that's nothing to the purpose.'

She searched for his eyes, held them. 'Uncle,

you know what manner of thing we print. It's work you would see done, or so I thought. Why would you hinder it?'

He winced. 'I would not *hinder* it – but I'm sure Will Browne could find another girl to help him, if he set his mind to it.'

'And that would be *better*?' Lucy asked sharply. 'What's dangerous for me is just as dangerous for another, and the one to replace me might not have as much will to the work as I do.'

'I would not be answerable to your father for somebody else,' replied Thomas. 'I fear that your cousin will carry him a report, and he will be angry with the both of us.'

'My father never wants to see me again!'

He stared, shocked.

'He's ashamed.' She'd never said this aloud before and she was surprised that she could speak of it now without tears. When she'd first realized that her father was shunning her, she'd been so sick with rage and grief that she'd been unable to eat. 'I was ravished in his own barn, and there's nothing he can do to revenge it or mend it, so whenever he looks at me he feels less of a man. He hates the sight of me! I've no doubt that you're right – that Cousin Geoffrey will tell him tales – but if you think he'll reproach you, you're much mistaken.'

Thomas looked at her for a long time in silence. Then he sighed. 'Oh, Lord God, man that is in honour and understands not, he is like the beasts that perish! When a man is cast down, he should turn the more urgently to God – not punish his family with his own idolatrous pride!'

Thomas always had been a godly man. Lucy bowed her head humbly, though privately she wondered why her own suffering should be so purely incidental to her father's casting down. 'Amen,' she said vaguely; then resumed, 'Do you see, though, Uncle? You don't have to answer to my father for me, let alone to Geoffrey. As to the work, I like it well, and I ... I think it tends to the good of the Commonwealth. I know that you and your friends think the same. Since we are agreed on that, don't, I beg you, put me from it.'

Thomas sighed, then raised his hands in surrender. 'How can I argue against my own heart? So be it! Oh, Lucy, you're a brave girl! I wish your dear mother could see you: she would be so proud!'

She felt her throat catch: it had been two years since anyone had been proud of her. She went over to Thomas and kissed his cheek. He gave her another of those sweet smiles and said goodnight.

Susan was looking at her curiously. 'Do you really think that?' she asked, when Thomas had descended from the loft. 'That printing these pamphlets is for the good of the Commonwealth?'

Lucy considered that a moment. 'Aye,' she said at last, 'if the Commonwealth heeds them.'

She reminded herself of that the following week when William Browne was arrested.

It happened at Westminster. Browne had let his boldness carry him away: he'd been overheard saying, 'We have waited many days for an answer; we should wait no more, but take another course.' When he was asked his name, he'd replied, 'The time may come when I will take *your* name!'

This, however, Lucy learned later; the first she heard of the matter was when she arrived at The Whalebone and found Liza sitting huddled against the press.

It was the first day of May, but still cold and rainy. They had finished printing *The Resolved Man's Resolution* two days before; Mr Browne had carried off the first batch of freshly assembled copies, but the carriage house was still aflutter with printed sheets and Lucy had expected to spend the day stitching. Instead she was confronted with Liza, wrapped in a blanket. The girl looked up miserably when Lucy came in, and announced, 'My da's in prison.'

'Oh, Liza!' cried Lucy, shocked. 'Don't you ... isn't there somewhere you can go?' If Liza didn't have an aunt or cousin or neighbour to take her in, Lucy knew she was going to have to beg Uncle Thomas to give her house room. An illegal printworks in a disused carriage house was no refuge at all.

Liza shrugged. 'I'll go to Auntie Moll this morning, but I came here last night with the books.'

'The books?'

'Aye. Da said if there was trouble, bring the books here, the ones he don't want the wrong people to see,' elaborated Liza.

Lucy noticed the neat stack of pamphlets on top of the cases of type; on the floor beside the cases was the bundle of *The Resolved Man's Resolution* which Browne had proudly carried off the day before. She stared at it, her stomach cold. She'd *known* that this might happen, so why was she so shocked?

There'd be no wages for Lucy now and no sales for the Brownes. What would Liza do? What would Mr Browne do, locked up in prison? Jailers were notoriously greedy, charging their captives extortionate rates for food and bedding: how long could the Brownes afford to pay? 'Have you told Mr Trebet?' she asked, flailing for some solid ground.

'Aye, of course!' said Liza impatiently. 'He helped move the books, and he gave me my supper, and this.' She plucked at the blanket and eyed Lucy unhappily. 'I didn't want to go home last night, in case the men came to search.'

The door to the carriage house opened and Ned Trebet came in. He looked pale and anxious, and he stared at Lucy in surprise. 'Oh, I'd forgotten you! You should have stayed home!'

'Why?' she asked – and suddenly the chill in her stomach turned to iron. 'Would Mr Browne have asked me not to come?'

'He's in prison! Didn't Liza tell you?'

'Aye. But by what I can see, the pamphlets still need stitching. If we need to hide them, they're easier to hide folded and stitched than loose.'

'Well, that's true,' admitted Trebet, frowning. 'But I can't pay your wages for doing it.' He paused, then went on cautiously, 'If you're willing to work unwaged, of course...'

'I can't,' Lucy said, without thinking. She was

a little surprised by her own certainty, and slightly disgusted. If she believed in what she was doing, why was she so determined to get her tuppence a day?

It paid her way, that was why. Aunt Agnes had now settled on an arrangement of taking tuppence one day and a penny the next: she'd grudgingly agreed that it covered Lucy's keep. Without that money Lucy would be nothing but a drain on the household, and while Thomas might agree to support the cause that far, Agnes certainly would not.

Lucy turned to Liza. 'Do you know who your father's customers are?'

'Some of 'em,' said Liza cautiously.

'*I* know 'em,' said Trebet, blinking. 'The leaders meet here every week.' He stared at Lucy for a minute, his eyes beginning to brighten. 'You're right! We don't need Will to sell Freeborn John's *Resolution*. I'll just offer it here – aye, and take up a collection for Mr Browne while I do!'

Liza clapped her hands. 'Thank you, Ned!'

He grinned at her, then at Lucy. She grinned back. 'So,' she concluded, 'we have the pamphlets and we know we can sell them. I'll take my wages when we have a profit. Why should I go home?'

When Lucy finally got back to the house that evening, tired from a full day's work, Agnes rushed into the shop to meet her before she'd even closed the door. 'Where've you been all the day?' she demanded.

'At work, Aunt. I—'

Agnes slapped her. 'Liar!'

Lucy stood in the open door, the mark of her aunt's hand burning on her face, so indignant that she couldn't speak. She could feel her fingers curling into claws; Agnes's face once again became unnaturally distinct – the wattled neck and hot eyes, the spots of colour on the cheeks, visible in the last daylight. 'You greedy, preaching harridan!' Lucy said at last. She turned about on her heel and walked out into the street.

She walked down to the corner, to St Olave's Street, which led to London Bridge. There she stopped. The light was fading and there were few people on the street; the air was heavy with coal-smoke from a thousand kitchen fires. She told herself that that was why her face was wet with tears – hot on one side, cool on the other, where Agnes had slapped her. She tucked her trembling hands into her sleeves and swallowed repeatedly.

She remembered her mother dying – *'Oh God, no more!'* – and then her mind fell into the well-rutted track of the soldiers in the barn; always, always when she was angry she remembered that. She supposed it was because she'd fought them so hard. They'd laughed at her at first; then, after she'd bashed her head into one man's face and made his nose bleed, they'd beaten her and told her she was making it worse for herself. She probably had – but she'd felt such immense, overpowering *outrage* that it had been impossible not to fight.

She wiped her face with an ink-stained oversleeve and tried to set the memory aside so that

89

she could *think*. For a moment she remembered *hitting* Agnes; then realized that she'd only *wanted* to; that, in fact, all she'd done was call her aunt names. She could probably go back and apologize, and things would limp on ... but she wasn't going to apologize. Agnes had struck her. Lucy hadn't even realized that that was a line she'd drawn; she recognized it now that it had been crossed. She would do the chores Agnes assigned while she was in the house; she would give her aunt most of her money – but she would not accept being beaten.

So what now?

She could walk back across the bridge, go to The Whalebone Tavern and ask Ned Trebet if she could stay in the carriage house. He'd agree, she had no doubt of it. He was a *friend*, or so she was beginning to believe. Tuppence a day wouldn't pay rent, but perhaps she could help at the tavern as well as—

'Lucy!' came Thomas's voice from behind her. She turned and saw her uncle running down the street, hatless and coatless. 'Lucy! Where are you going?' He stopped beside her, panting a little.

Lucy touched her cheek. 'Your wife struck me!'

'But where are you going?' Thomas asked anxiously.

'I will not stay to be beaten!'

'Child, child! We heard Will Browne was arrested and we had no idea what had become of you!'

'And therefore I should be beaten?'

90

'She feared for you,' said Thomas. 'We both did. If she struck you, it was because her spirits were overwrought. She says you came in as though nothing were amiss and said that you'd been working!'

'But it was true!' She eyed her uncle warily. 'We mean to finish the pamphlets and sell them – Mr Browne will surely need the money! I was going to take my wages from the profit.'

'Oh!' said Thomas, as though this had never occurred to him. 'You should have explained.'

'Agnes called me a liar and struck me before ever I had the chance!'

Her uncle shook his head. 'It was a misunderstanding; clear, it was. Come back to the house, child; beg your aunt's pardon—'

'Why should I beg *her* pardon? She struck me and called me a liar!'

Even as she said it, she felt her indignation ebb. Agnes was her *aunt*, and Lucy had called her a greedy harridan. It might be true but it was still a sin to say so.

'Oh, come, you used a proud tongue, or so she told me! I will tell her that she was mistaken, but you *must* kneel and beg her pardon.'

Running off to The Whalebone was all very well, Lucy realized, but all her things were in Thomas's loft. She sighed and nodded.

She followed Uncle Thomas back to the house in silence. Agnes was in the parlour. Supper was on the table but Agnes sat glowering at an untouched bowl of pottage. Cousin Geoffrey was out, which was a mercy.

Agnes came to a stand, glaring, as Thomas

entered with Lucy trailing behind him. 'She had but gone down to the corner,' said Thomas. 'And she says she was at work all the day, finishing the pamphlets so they can be sold to supply money for the Brownes. She will get her wages from the profit.'

Agnes opened her mouth, then closed it again.

Lucy knelt and bowed her head; the bare *possibility* of running off somehow made it easier. 'I beg your pardon, Aunt, for my proud words. I spoke out of sinful anger and I do much repent it.'

'So you should,' said Agnes shrewishly.

Lucy took that as forgiveness and got to her feet. She looked down at her aunt's bowl of cold pottage and felt suddenly sorry for the woman. Agnes had once been young and pretty, with a prosperous husband and a string of children; now the husband was old and struggling and all the children but one were dead. She was an ageing woman in poor health, trapped in a house and a marriage that were nothing but the ashes of her hopes.

Lucy was lucky: she could still escape. She had a choice and she felt a sudden hot conviction that once she'd really mastered typesetting, she would have more choices. The threat of Bridewell Prison was a small thing compared to that freedom.

Four

The Resolved Man's Resolution sold all of its five hundred copies within three days. When Lucy went with Ned and Liza to Newgate Prison to visit William Browne and give him the money, he suggested that they print another five hundred.

'We can't, sir,' Lucy told him, blushing a little. 'Our friends want us to print flysheets, urgently. I'll bring you money from those, though. Can you tell me where to buy more paper and ink?'

The conflict between Parliament and the Army had intensified and become a wellspring of flysheets. The commissioners sent by Parliament to Saffron Walden to convince the Army to disband had returned to London in failure: the Army wanted its pay and a settlement of its grievances before it gave up the sword, suspecting that once disbanded it would receive neither. It was vocal in its defence, issuing declarations and petitions as fervently as its well-affected friends in London.

Ned Trebet came into the printworks the day after Lucy was given the first of the Army flysheets. 'Have you heard *this*?' he asked, joyfully waving a sheet of paper.

She finished the line of type she'd been

setting, then looked up at him and raised her eyebrows. 'Heard what?'

He grinned. 'The Parliament-men's report from Saffron Walden.' He held up the paper and read out, '"The Army is become one Lilburne throughout, and more likely to give than to receive laws"! And this: "Lilburne's books are quoted by them as statute law." That's what *our pamphlets* have done!'

Lucy thought of all the copies of *A New-found Stratagem* that had gone north to the Army – not the first of Lilburne's pamphlets that had moved in that direction, she was quite sure. She looked down at the paper on the table, with the half-set forme she'd assembled beside it. The *Petition and Vindication of the Officers* had arrived at the printworks the previous afternoon, but it was not handwritten. It had been printed: the Army now had a press of its own. Print was flowing in both directions now: mutiny to the Army and sedition to London. She felt a moment of vertigo and clutched the edge of the table. What if Parliament *didn't* compromise? What if this was the start of another war?

She did not have the confidence in the Army that Ned or Thomas did. They had fought as soldiers; she had been raped.

'What's amiss?' asked Ned, taken aback.

'What's that paper?' she replied, gesturing at the sheet in his hand.

'Oh, this! It's nothing to fear – only a letter from one of our friends in Parliament. He must miss the meeting this evening, so he bids me show it to the others.' The grin began to creep back. 'Have you heard that the soldiers have *elected* spokesmen? The common soldiers, not the officers! They've chosen two out of each regiment, all the men voting for those they best trust, and these spokesmen – they call them *Agitators* – meet with the officers to determine what the Army should do!'

What do the officers think of that? Lucy thought, then looked down at the sheet she was working on, which answered the question. The officers, like the men, were angry and indignant. They had fought for Parliament's cause: now Parliament denied them their pay, scorned their sufferings and called them traitors for petitioning about it! The officers might be willing to let the men take the lead in this dangerous game but they weren't going to stop it.

'What does Parliament think of that?' Lucy asked instead. 'Does your friend say?'

Ned made a face. 'The Presbyterians aren't pleased. But think of it, Lucy! An Army behaving as "one Lilburne throughout", electing its own choice of men to speak for it!'

Lucy thought of it. Parliament was elected, of course, but only by the handful of men who were entitled to vote. In some boroughs that included all the freeholders, but in others a dozen aldermen sufficed. Only gentlemen came to Parliament, and the gentlemen of the House of Commons were undoubtedly alarmed by this uprising of an armed rabble.

'What will Parliament do?' she asked worriedly.

That just provoked another of Ned's grins.

'What *can* they do? They have no *second* army to counter this one!'

'There's the Scots!' Lucy pointed out unhappily. The Scots would obviously be extremely angry if England broke its Covenant to establish a Presbyterian church.

'Let them wail!' Ned said airily. 'Parliament will come to terms; they have no choice else!' He tapped his letter against the table, then eyed her speculatively. 'Why not come along this evening? Hear the talk for yourself!'

'What, to your tavern?'

'Nay, to Whitehall Palace! Of *course* to my tavern!'

'Do honest women come?'

Ned was surprised, then offended. 'Do you think I keep a *bawdy house*?'

Lucy felt her face go hot. 'Nay, indeed not, but – but in Leicestershire, godly women don't frequent taverns.'

For a moment she thought Ned would say something sharp, but he frowned. 'Aye, your uncle's a very godly man, so I've heard. He'd take it amiss, would he?' He folded his letter and tucked it in his jerkin. 'I'll speak to your uncle if he comes this evening, tell him it's naught to fear. It would be well if you came to the meetings, now that you do so much of the printing.'

Lucy almost told him that whatever Uncle Thomas thought of this suggestion, Aunt Agnes would be outraged, but she held back. She didn't want to embarrass Thomas and she wasn't entirely sure what she wanted herself. She hadn't previously considered this as something she *might* do; now she was both intrigued and alarmed. It would be interesting to hear the talk, but it would mean crossing another line. She'd come to the cause as hired help, an onlooker; she'd become a sympathizer; if she started attending meetings, she would have enlisted.

Thomas did go to the meeting at The Whalebone that evening. He returned after Lucy had gone to bed, but when she came downstairs in the morning she saw that Ned had spoken to him because he gave her a very anxious look. 'I've business in the City today,' he announced. 'Lucy, I'll set you on your way this morning.'

Agnes muttered angrily, *'Whose* business in the City? Not *yours,* I'll warrant!' When Thomas looked at her, however, she fell sullenly silent.

Thomas started on the subject as soon as they were out of the door. 'Lucy, child, last night it was suggested that I should bring you to our council meetings at The Whalebone, at least while Nick Tew and poor Will are in prison.'

'Council meetings?' she repeated, surprised. It seemed a very grand name for drinks in a tavern.

'Aye, our common council meets in The Whalebone on Thursdays,' said Thomas impatiently. 'The others thought it a fair notion that you should attend, but they defer the decision to me. I ... well, you know, child, that I mislike the risk to your safety, and I fear what your father would say.'

He said nothing about any *scandal* in her attendance. 'Do women come to these meetings, Uncle?'

'Oh, yes,' he said, surprising her. 'Mrs Lilburne comes, and the wives of some of the other men. Mary Overton came, until she was imprisoned. Katherine Chidley – a most outspoken soul – never misses a meeting; her son, Samuel, is our treasurer—'

'*Treasurer?*' repeated Lucy, surprised again.

'Aye,' said Thomas, blinking at her. 'He keeps the common fund that pays half your wage.'

'It does?' Browne hadn't mentioned that. Where, she wondered, did the money in the common fund come from? But that was an easy question: it came from collections among the 'well-affected'. Another reason, she suspected, that Agnes disapproved of her husband's friends. For her own part, she was intrigued. Villagers might band together to oppose an enclosure, but this sort of *organisation* – a council with regular meetings, a common fund managed by a treasurer – was something more.

'Aye, Will asked for help,' Thomas continued, 'and we agreed that he was entitled to it. But this strays from the point! What I meant to say was that this notion of your attendance troubles me. Already I fear that your father will be wroth with me on your account. If he learns that I've brought you to ... well, you and I know it's honest business, undertaken in goodwill to the Commonwealth, but *some* would call it a nest of heresy and sedition.'

'What need has he to know?' asked Lucy. 'Cousin Geoffrey will leave London before long, and once he's gone, who'll tell my father? *I* won't, you may be sure of it!' She realized even as she spoke that, yes, she *did* want to attend the meetings. If she was going to risk arrest, it should be for what *she* was doing and not just because she was William Browne's hired help and Thomas Stevens' niece.

Thomas stared at her for a long moment, taken aback. 'It would scarce be *honest* of me to—'

'My father won't care anyway,' Lucy interrupted. 'I've told you: his wish is to forget that he ever had a daughter. It's Cousin Geoffrey who'd stir up trouble, and Cousin Geoffrey has no rights in the matter! I doubt he cares a fig what happens to me, but he's offended with *you* because his parliamentary clerk fobbed him off. Waiting until Geoffrey's gone would not be dishonesty but – but simple avoidance of a quarrel!'

She could see that the argument carried some weight, but still Thomas frowned. 'Sweet, I would not risk my own daughter thus: how can I risk my poor sister's?'

'Uncle...' Lucy began, then had to smile. Thomas stared in surprise. 'Uncle, can you imagine *Hannah* ever doing such a thing as this? She – well, she's a sweet, gentle soul, but...'

Thomas suddenly returned the smile. 'She would be affrighted and she would beg me to take her home.'

Lucy nodded. 'I'm not Hannah! I like the work very well, and ... and I like this *cause* very well, if it can succeed without bloodshed! You are not risking me: I am risking *myself.*'

Thomas considered that for a long, uneasy minute. Then he drew a deep breath and nodded. 'Well, then, I'll tell the others you'll attend after your cousin has left London.'

Cousin Geoffrey left the following week. A daily attendance at Westminster and a heavy expenditure in bribes had failed to get him the strip of land and at last he gave up and went home. Ned, who listened with interest to Lucy's account of the matter, said probably a Parliament-man had his eye on the land. Geoffrey, however, blamed Thomas.

'This is what comes of rebellion!' he muttered angrily, as he mounted his mare on a wet Monday morning. He glowered at Thomas from the saddle and added, 'I will tell them at home how you fare, Uncle!' He made the polite words a threat.

Thomas was distressed: he loved his brother, Geoffrey's father, and was afraid of a breach; he was also frightened of Daniel Wentnor, despite Lucy's assurances.

Lucy, however, was simply relieved to see the back of Geoffrey. Even if she'd been inclined to worry about what he'd say, she had little time for it. The flow of print had continued unabated, and in the middle of it they'd had to move the press.

The carriage house of The Whalebone had never been intended as more than a stopgap printworks: the authorities were well aware of the tavern's clientele. The only reason the press had been located there at all was that The Whalebone had been searched immediately beforehand and it would be a month or two before anyone searched again. The 'common council' meeting which discussed Lucy's attendance had also settled on a new location for the press. This was a disused barn outside the city wall by Bishopsgate, over towards the parkland of Moorfields. It was immediately beyond Bedlam – Bethlehem Hospital for lunatics – which meant any casual traffic was disguised by people coming to gape at the madmen.

The barn was only a ten-minute walk from The Whalebone, but moving the press was still a huge task. It was too big and heavy to travel in one piece: it had to be taken apart, loaded on a cart, driven to its new home and then put back together again. The actual move was done using a dray borrowed from a brewery. Lucy packed up the cases of type, paper and ink, took down the drying lines and helped to disassemble the press. It was heavy work and left her with a sore back and a torn fingernail. She was glad of the nagging aches, though: it distracted her from the prospect of working *alone* in a *barn*. She'd been unable to do that since she went to milk the cows early one morning, two years before.

Ned was in the thick of the move: he borrowed the dray and drove it out to Bishopsgate in the evening, its incriminating load concealed under a stack of empty beer barrels. The next morning he turned up early at the barn and helped to reassemble the press before rushing off to put in a day's work at his tavern. He paused only to speak to Lucy. He handed her the key for the padlock that was to secure the barn door and said, 'Come back to the tavern at dinner-time. You'll be in need of a hot dinner, working here!'

She was relieved: the prospect of The Whalebone at dinner-time would distract her from being *alone* in a *barn* – and, what was more, next door to Bedlam. The thought of finding an escaped lunatic terrified her.

When Ned had gone, she made herself walk right round the barn, checking that it was indeed empty. The place was draughty, damp and, worst of all, dark. The only way to get decent light was to leave the door open, but the spring continued cold and wet, and opening the door meant letting in the wind and rain. The press had been set in the middle of the room, and she strung the drying lines behind and to the side of it, where they wouldn't be rained on. She put the table and the cases of type against the wall near the door, though, protecting them with spoiled sheets of paper: she would need light for typesetting. She could already tell that that was going to be a miserable job here.

Setting up took her until noon, by which time it was raining hard. She padlocked the barn, then ran to The Whalebone with her shawl over her head. She entered in a rush, then paused to let her eyes adjust to the dimness. The tavern was dark and low-ceilinged. There was no fire burning on the hearth – it was, after all, May – but the room was crowded enough to feel warm after the cold outside. It smelled of unwashed bodies, dirty wet woollens, beer and stale tobacco. It was about half full; most of the customers were men but, to her relief, there were also a few women. A vaguely familiar older woman in an apron came over to her and asked, 'What do you lack?'

'I...' began Lucy, then stopped, unsure how to

102

answer. 'Is Ned here?'

The woman looked at her more closely. 'Oh, it's *you*!' The business-like attention dissolved into a warm smile. 'Well met at last! I'm Nancy Shorby; I've been here since old Mr Trebet's day. Ned's fetching beer from the cellar but he'll be up again in a moment. You come into the kitchen and sit down by the fire!'

'What's that?' called one of the customers. 'Ned's sweetheart?'

'Never you mind if it is!' replied Nancy and bustled Lucy through another doorway and into the warmth and comparative brightness of a large kitchen. 'Rafe! Sarah! See who's here!' The cook and another serving-maid, their faces familiar but their names previously unknown, turned from their work and came over smiling. The warm welcome made Lucy very uneasy, but she rubbed her ink-stained hands on her apron and smiled and exchanged greetings.

'We've all been agog to meet you,' the younger serving-maid confessed.

'But Ned, the scoundrel, kept you all to himself,' said the cook.

Lucy smiled weakly and was spared the need to reply by Ned himself, who came up the stairs from the cellar, carrying a barrel. He beamed when he saw Lucy. 'Here you are!' he exclaimed. 'The sight of you is as good as a rest. Nan, get her some dinner. I'll be back anon!' He hurried through into the tavern's common room with the beer.

He returned while Nancy was ladling out Lucy's stew. 'All's well? Nancy, Rafe and Sarah

103

have made themselves known to you? Fine people, all of them; Nancy's worked here since I was but a boy.' He turned to Nancy. 'Nan, the party in the panelled room want more bread.'

'I'll see to it,' said Nancy and hurried off.

Ned settled Lucy in a corner of the kitchen, asked about the press, then rushed off to draw more beer. His staff hurried in and out: it seemed that The Whalebone was popular. Rafe, the only one fixed in the kitchen, told her the tavern had eight private rooms and two common ones, and that at least half were full every afternoon. The tavern was thriving, he told her, with a meaningful smile, but would do better still if it had a mistress. They'd been waiting for Mr Trebet to find one ever since the war ended.

She felt sick. She bolted the rest of her dinner and got up. Ned, on his way back through the kitchen to fetch more beer, gave her a startled look and cried, 'You're not going so soon?'

She ducked her head. 'I must. We're two days behind and still not ready to print.'

Walking back to the cold barn through the rain, she found herself furiously angry. It was clear enough that *Ned's sweetheart* was exactly what Ned's staff thought she was. What right had he to give them such a notion? She ought to demonstrate that she wasn't: she ought to stay away from The Whalebone in future.

It would mean packing herself a cold dinner and eating it *alone* in the cold *barn* – if she had enough appetite to eat at all, with her stomach in knots.

It was absurd! If she'd been a *man*, there

would have been no trouble: she could have gone to sit in the warm kitchen, talking and laughing, and nobody would suppose she owed them anything, but because she was a girl – and, worse, a pretty girl – she was expected to pay her way with kisses!

She imagined being kissed by Ned. Part of her was curious, even eager, but part of her recoiled, remembering the soldiers and her own frantic struggles, the violence and the *pain*...

She stopped in the street, telling herself that it was the rain running down her face that made her eyes sting so. *Spoiled goods.*

Oh, why should she blame Ned Trebet? His intentions were undoubtedly honourable, as far as they'd yet taken shape. He was a young man with a bit of property who needed a wife. He'd met a young woman – pretty, hard-working, a fellow-believer in a cause dear to his heart. Obviously he was thinking about her! *Your father has a dairy farm, freehold. Will told me.* She should have taken good note of that: he had spoken to Will about whether her family had enough money to make her a suitable match.

If he knew, though, that she was no maiden and that her dowry had gone to buy cows, would he want her then?

From nearby came a shriek and then a long desperate wail, and she glanced up in surprise and saw that she was next to Bedlam hospital. She shuddered and hurried on back to the barn and the work waiting for her.

The next two days were miserable. She did not go to The Whalebone for dinner but ate bread and butter alone beside the press. The various people who'd come to help her with the machinery – or, like Liza, to talk – didn't make the additional walk over to the barn, and she was left on her own. Operating the press by herself was as exhausting as she'd feared, and she had to keep stopping for a rest. She became expert in checking the bolts and greasing the slides.

The following evening, however, was a Thursday, the day of the 'council meeting'. She didn't go back to Southwark but met Uncle Thomas in the City instead. He said it would save her walking across the bridge and back again, though they both knew that the real advantage was that it postponed the argument with Aunt Agnes.

It was after supper when they arrived, and growing dark, but the common room of the tavern was better lit than it had been the rainy afternoon when she first visited, and busier. Tallow candles on sconces about the walls cast a warm yellow light over a dense crowd of men and women. Lucy noticed a thin, tired-looking woman, heavily pregnant, sitting in a chair in the middle of the room; she later learned that this was Elizabeth Lilburne, Freeborn John's wife. (She was permitted to visit her husband and even to stay the night; when the baby was born, it was christened 'Tower'.) Next to her sat a round-shouldered older man, and behind them stood a crop-haired soldier in a cavalryman's buff-leather coat, with a sword and a pistol in his belt. Nearby, an elderly lady in a lace-trimmed collar was talking to a young man with a notebook; over at the side was another young soldier, this one elegantly dressed, with long dark locks and an officer's sash. He was talking to a slim gentleman in a fine blue coat and lace ruff.

Ned hurried over to them, looking anxious. 'Lucy!' he said; then, quickly, 'Mr Stevens, you are welcome. Lucy, I ... never mind; we'll speak after. Will you have a draught?'

They accepted mugs of beer and squeezed into places on a tavern bench just as the crop-haired soldier rapped on the table and the room fell quiet.

'We've a deal of business tonight,' said the soldier briskly, 'so let's not delay!'

The older man got to his feet; he was tall and heavily built, but his wide face was exceptionally gentle. 'Thank you, Mr Sexby,' he said, with a polite nod to the soldier. 'My friends, let us take a moment to beseech God's guidance on our counsels!'

Everyone bowed his or her head. 'Oh God, let us "walk circumspectly",' said the big man, '"not as fools, but as wise, redeeming the time, because the days are evil".'

Some of the 'Amens' which greeted this were fervent, some perfunctory. Lucy, glancing round the faces, wondered what they believed in, beyond the need to reform the government. Many would be sectaries – Anabaptists and Brownists, who had the most to lose if religious toleration was denied. She wasn't sure what Anabaptists believed but she knew her Calvinist father abominated them. The thought of how angry he would be if he knew she was here was oddly cheering.

'My friends,' the big man began, 'I fear the news is bad. As most of you have heard, Parliament commanded our last petition to be burned by the public hangman. We must petition again, but I fear that there is little hope of a better outcome unless we have means to win Parliament's attention.'

'You have that, in *us*,' said the crop-haired soldier, Sexby.

'Oh, you and your friends in Saffron Walden have indeed won Parliament's full attention,' said the blue-coated gentleman in a dry voice. 'But I fear that my colleagues are of two minds. While I and the more sensible part favour making concessions – as you saw at the start of the month – Mr Holles and his friends are outraged at your defiance. They believe that if they cannot bring you to heel, no gentleman in all England will ever again be master of his own servants, and they are determined to put you down. They have proposed an ordinance to win them control of the London militia.' There was a stir through the room, and he raised his hand and went on, 'The new Militia Ordinance – which I have no doubt will pass – takes control of the Militia Committee away from Parliament, and grants it instead to the Common Council of the City of London – a body which, as I am sure you're all well aware, is entirely in the hands of good Presbyterian friends of Mr Holles, and, unlike the Commons, untroubled by inconvenient Independents such as myself.'

'Common Council was unjustly stolen from the people!' said Sexby angrily. 'Taken over by the rich, in defiance of the ancient charters of London!'

'Aye, as our friend John Lilburne has shown!' agreed the gentleman. 'But we need a *solution* to the difficulty, not a history!'

A familiar voice spoke out: Lucy recognized it, with pleasure, as Ned Trebet's. 'Common Council may appoint as they please: the militias won't *obey!* Why should we fight our brother-soldiers to keep Holles and his friends in the saddle?'

'I hope you may be right,' said the gentleman seriously.

'I am sure of it!' said Ned. 'My men don't trust Common Council!'

'Aye, but they're *your* men, Ned,' said the dark-haired officer. 'What of all the other militia men in London?'

'The sheets we print are taken up all over the city!' protested Ned. 'The men of London can read the truth for themselves. They will not be belied into war!'

There was a ripple of pleasure, then of applause.

'Well said, Mr Trebet!' said the big man. 'But let us not be complacent. You speak of what we *print* when we have but one press left in the city, and the Stationers' men are hunting for that. We must keep it safe. You moved it this week, did you not?'

'Aye.' Ned hesitated, looking around the room, then gestured towards Lucy. 'And here is Mr Stevens' niece, Mistress Lucy Wentnor, who has been working it for us, despite all dangers!'

At that everyone looked at Lucy. She got up

109

and made a little curtsey, her face burning.

'Welcome!' said the big man, smiling at her. He had little white peg-teeth with large gaps between them, but the smile was kind. 'We are grateful to you, Mistress Wentnor. I am William Walwyn; I hope the rest of us will make ourselves known to you as they have occasion to speak. How is the press? Is there anything you lack?'

Lucy felt breathless: she'd never had to speak in front of so many strangers. 'The press is safe, sir,' she said − then realized that there *were* things she lacked. 'But I need help with it, sir. When it was here at The Whalebone, Ned came often to help with it, and Tim, and Mr Browne, but now no one comes, and it's very heavy. Also, when I must both ink and work the press, it makes for slow work, so I hope you can find some help.'

'Fairly spoken,' said Walwyn. 'What help do you need?'

She'd expected to have to plead; having her words accepted so quickly threw her, but only for a moment. 'Just someone strong, sir. It need not be anyone who knows printing. I can set the type and make up the pamphlets; it's only that the press is so heavy. It needn't be the same person helping all the day or all the week. It might be many different men, each coming for an hour or two.'

'Hold a moment!' It was the elegant officer again. 'How long would the press be safe, with a new printer coming to it every hour, as though they were going to see a monster at a fair? Won't the neighbours remark it?'

'It's over near Bedlam!' protested the man with the notebook. Several people cried, 'Hush!' and 'Don't speak of it!' He looked chagrined.

'Captain Wildman is right,' said a stocky man decidedly. 'We must do nothing to attract notice to the press, and too many visitors might do that, wherever it is.'

'We should find one steady man who can arrive and depart quietly,' said Wildman. He glanced about. 'We will have to pay a wage.'

'I am sure we might find volunteers...' began the man with the notebook.

'Aye, we would find *many* among us willing to help on the press for nothing,' agreed Wildman, 'providing they can do so for an hour here and there and still continue their livelihood. But we need but one, and we cannot expect that one to live upon air. This is no time to shave pennies! The press is our bastion against the Militia Ordinance that Mr Marten warns of. I move that we set up a fund for it.'

'Seconded!' cried the stocky man.

'Captain Wildman moves that we establish a fund for the press,' said Walwyn; 'Mr Petty seconds. All in favour?'

All around the room, people raised their hands; after a moment's hesitation, the man with the notebook raised his, too.

'Carried,' said Walwyn.

'What sum shall I set down?' asked the note-book-man.

'What does it cost to run a press?' Wildman asked.

The notebook-man was flummoxed; the old lady in the lace collar touched his arm. 'Sam, my dear, you must remember how much paper costs, after all the to-do we had about *A New Year's Gift*! And I think apprentice printers commonly earn sixpence a day.'

'Thank you, Mother,' said the notebook-man and scribbled rapidly. 'If we rate Mistress Wentnor and her assistant as apprentices both, we might manage on fourteen shillings a week.' He looked up. 'Are we planning to defray the cost by selling the sheets or are we to distribute them free?'

'Sell them,' said another man firmly. 'At least at first. The money from sales one week can be added to the press fund the following week, and the amount disbursed from common funds reduced accordingly. If, later on, we choose to distribute a sheet without charge, we merely pay nothing back the following week.'

Sam the notebook-man nodded and made another note. 'Thank you, Tom. Mistress Wentnor, can you keep accounts?'

'Aye, a little,' she said, floundering. 'I managed our dairy in Leicestershire. But – but, sir, I'm paid *tuppence* a day!'

'Well, that will save money!' exclaimed Wildman with satisfaction.

The old lady tut-tutted. 'That is most unjust!' She looked around the room. 'Would any of *you* do such work for tuppence a day?'

'A woman has not the same need of wages as a man,' said Wildman.

Sam laughed; his mother rose to her feet and

stalked over to the young officer. She barely came up to his chin but she glared up at him, hands on hips. 'Has a woman no need to *eat*, young man? The girl can no more live on air than can this *man* you wish to hire!'

'I meant only that it is her father's duty to provide for her,' replied Wildman, taken aback. 'Or her uncle's.'

'So is it a master's duty to provide for his servant! If your servant goes to work for some other man, will you continue his upkeep, or will you tell him to get his wages where he serves? If Mistress Wentnor were not engaged on our press, I have no doubt that she would be helping Mr Stevens. You men! You rate a woman's work as worthless, until you try to hire a man to do it!'

'Peace, Kate, peace!' said Walwyn with a wide smile. 'You have poor Captain Wildman on the mat, fair; let him up now!' He glanced round. 'I, for my part, do not doubt that in permitting Mistress Wentnor to work for tuppence Mr Stevens was making a sacrifice: he has ever been a generous friend. The young woman certainly deserves sixpence a day, particularly if she must now keep accounts in addition to all she did before.'

'Seconded,' said someone.

'All in favour?' asked Walwyn. There was another show of hands. 'Very well: Mistress Wentnor to continue in charge of the press, at sixpence a day; another worker to be found to help her. Captain Wildman?'

'I have a man in mind,' said Wildman hopefully. 'James Hudson, formerly a soldier in my troop, well-affected and eager for the good of the Commonwealth. He was maimed at Naseby-fight and has relied since on what work his friends have been able to find for him. I will vouch for his honesty and discretion.'

'Very good,' said Walwyn. 'All in favour? Captain Wildman to approach James Hudson to assist with the press for sixpence a day; Mr Chidley to set aside fourteen shillings a week, less returns, and the press to be our bastion against the Militia Ordinance!'

The meeting went on for some time after that, but Lucy found herself continually distracted by the thought that she would get *sixpence a day; three shilllings* a week! Her mind filled with agreeable dilemmas: should she wait until she had enough to buy a new gown, get one second-hand, or buy some cloth from Uncle Thomas and make it up herself? Would it be better to buy a lace-trimmed collar or some silk ribbons?

She was ashamed of her greedy enthusiasm. The rest of the talk was heady stuff, about the doings of friends and enemies in Parliament, about a letter Elizabeth Lilburne had taken to Cromwell from her husband; about the Army and the king. Nonetheless, the thought of that sixpence a day never entirely left her mind.

At last the meeting ended, with another prayer. Most of the men and women remained in their seats talking, but Thomas, anxious to get back to Southwark, touched Lucy's arm and gestured towards the door.

They were on the doorstep when Ned Trebet reached them, his hands full of empty tankards.

'Lucy!' he panted. 'Mr Stevens. A word with you, please!'

Thomas looked at him in surprise. Ned set his tankards down on the nearest table and said, 'I'll not delay you – here, I'll set you on your way!' He opened the door and led them out into the night.

It was overcast and drizzling. The Whalebone had a lantern above the door, but beyond it the street was dark, with only a distant glimmer at the corner showing that a householder on the lighting rota had set out a lamp. Ned reached up to unhook the lantern.

'Nay!' protested Thomas anxiously. 'What will the others do?'

'Fetch their own lights,' replied Ned. He started along the street, holding up the lantern so they could pick their way around the puddles and the foul patches, and began speaking before they'd gone three steps. 'You didn't come at dinner-time today or yesterday, Lucy.'

'There was too much to do,' she replied.

'Ah.' Ned glanced warily at Thomas. 'I thought perchance Rafe said something he shouldn't have.'

Lucy was silent a little too long, trying to think how to respond, and Ned nodded. 'I thought so.' He drew a deep breath. 'You need not take fright because of Rafe.'

'What's this?' asked Thomas in confusion.

'My cook, sir,' replied Ned, 'making free with my intentions towards your niece. Not that I ... that is, it's been only a short while since I met her, and I ... I would have spoken to you before if...'

'Don't!' cried Lucy, mortified, and Ned stopped and stared at her in surprise.

'Lucy, what is this?' asked Thomas.

'Mr Trebet's cook hinted that his master wanted a wife, and I didn't know what to do.'

'Oh!' Thomas stared in amazement from Lucy to Ned.

Ned grimaced. 'My cook said more than he should, sir; yet I confess that—'

'Stop!' Lucy drew a deep breath. 'Ned, I'm all but dowerless. You can do much better for yourself. You should know that, before you say anything more.' She hoped she wouldn't have to admit that a dowry wasn't all she'd lost.

Ned stared at her blankly a moment, then shot a questioning look at Thomas. 'I'd heard her father had a dairy farm!'

'He does,' admitted Thomas, 'but all his cattle were driven off and he spent his daughter's dowry replacing them. As for me, I – I cannot afford to supply my brother's lack. It was struggle enough to satisfy my own son-in-law last year.'

There was another silence. They reached the corner and stopped there. 'I am very sorry for it,' said Ned at last. His tone was heavy.

For some reason Lucy was more moved by that than by his flustered half-proposal. She touched his shoulder. 'So am I.' She took Thomas's arm. 'Uncle, we must get home!'

She and Thomas walked in silence almost as far as London Bridge, picking their way carefully along the dark, foul street. The bridge, however, was well lit, rain-blurred lanterns outside the door of every fourth house and candles in many of the windows. The light shimmered on the dark water of the river below.

'You might have kept your peace about the dowry,' Thomas said suddenly. 'If he'd learned of it after he'd asked for you, he might have taken you without one.'

'That would ill return his kindness,' replied Lucy. 'He's a man that might marry fifty pounds. I'd not have him marry for shame and repent the day after.'

'I suppose so,' said Thomas, dissatisfied. After a moment he added, 'I am still sorry to see you lose such an opportunity. He's a fine young man, and ... well, I wonder sometimes what will become of you.'

'Aunt Agnes will be mightily pleased to get two shillings a week,' Lucy said quickly.

Her uncle blinked. 'How ... oh! You mean to give her *two shillings*?'

Lucy hesitated. If she gave Agnes *one* shilling, it would still be an increase: surely Agnes would be satisfied?

Not if she knew Lucy was getting sixpence a day. Besides... 'If we tell her that when we come in tonight, Uncle, she won't be wroth with us and she won't nag us about it.'

Thomas looked suddenly much happier. 'That would be a mercy!'

Five

The elegant Captain Wildman turned up at the barn the following morning, bringing the new assistant. Lucy had been working the press, but when the two men arrived she stopped, rubbing her hands on her apron and staring speechlessly. James Hudson was a monster: a tall man, powerfully built but cadaverous – and horribly scarred. His right eye was missing, and the puckered socket was set into a florid mess of shiny pink and dull white skin. His right hand was similarly scarred, the first two fingers missing and the thumb reduced to a stub. His hair hung in matted ropes around his mutilated face, and he stank of brandy, sour beer and old piss. A cavalry sabre hung at his side.

Wildman merely nodded to Lucy; when he spoke, it was to his protégé. 'There you are, Jamie! That's the press.'

'Who's the wench?' asked Hudson. His voice was a hoarse growl.

'The niece of a Southwark mercer, one of our company,' replied Wildman. 'She was helping Will Browne the bookseller, but he's in Newgate, and she found the work too heavy, as I told you.'

Irritation gave Lucy her voice back. 'I am *in*

charge of the press, Captain Wildman!'

Wildman merely smiled. Hudson came over and touched the bed of the press with his good hand. 'How does it work?'

Wildman regarded the press a moment. 'I think you slide that bit in and out, and pull that handle to lower the screw.'

'Out of the way, puss,' Hudson ordered Lucy.

'Nay,' she said, suddenly hot with rage. She had asked for *help*, not a master! 'If you've not worked a press before, you're to listen to instruction before I give you leave to touch it!'

He turned his gargoyle face towards her, fixed her with a single bloodshot eye and gave her a horrible twisted leer. 'Oho! You'll give me leave to touch, will you, puss?'

'Nay, then!' she said, glaring back at him. 'If you will not heed instruction, you can take yourself off – and if you won't go, I will! For I'll not be called *wench* and *puss* at my own press – and much joy may you have, trying to set type and stitch with that *claw*!'

The leer vanished and the gargoyle head lowered, like that of a bull about to charge. 'Peace, peace!' cried Wildman, alarmed now. 'There's no call for that!'

'Yes, there is!' cried Lucy, rounding on him. 'If your swill-bowl friend heaves too hard on that handle, he'll crack the block, and then we'll have no press; and if my uncle – a godly man! – heard him speak so lewdly, he'd forbid my coming here ever again, and we'd have no one to set type! There's *every* call for me to protest: you could end printing here this month and more, all

119

for want of more courtesy than would fit a *sty*!'

Wildman was flustered. 'He meant no harm.'

'And you, what did *you* mean?' she demanded furiously. 'You did not see fit even to tell him my *name*, let alone make it plain that *I* was given charge! You are more to blame than he is!'

'I had forgot your name,' admitted Wildman, 'and I thought Will Browne had charge. I beg your pardon, Mistress...?'

'Lucy Wentnor,' she said coldly. 'Captain Wildman, I *was* given charge of the press, whether you recollect it or not, and your friend should heed me because it is *not* so simple a matter as the pulling of a handle!'

'You say if I pull too hard, I will crack ... what?' asked Hudson. The scarred face was turned towards her again, but the expression on the good half now seemed to be earnest and intent.

Lucy touched the block that contained the great wooden screw. 'Too much pressure and this could crack – or even if it holds, you might damage the type, which is set *here,* see? *I* was told to take care, and how likely am I to strain it, compared to a great ox like you? This press has its quirks, too, of placing and working, which one must have regard to, or else damage it or what it prints.'

He stared uneasily at the press, and she saw that she'd won. Her anger faded and, as it did, her hands started to tremble. Anger always brought back the memories – and here she was, in a barn, with two soldiers. She refused to look at them, refused to think about the past. Instead, she caught hold of the press-bed and hauled it out from under the screw. She lifted the canvas-and-blanket covering and peeled the latest sheet off the forme.

'It's our *Declaration*!' cried Wildman as he saw it.

It was indeed a *Declaration of the Army* – one of several that had emanated from Saffron Walden of late and more moderate than most of them. Wildman plucked it from Lucy's hands and looked it over with a smile; Lucy took it back before he could smear the ink. 'We mean to sell it throughout London, so that the citizens will not be deceived as to the justice of the Army's desires.' She was pleased to find that her voice was briskly confident, with no hint of a tremor. She hung the paper up to dry, then came back to the press and gazed across it at Hudson. 'So what will it be, Mr Hudson? Will you take instruction from me, or will you go? For I'll not hand the mastery to one that knows less of printing than I do!'

Both men looked at her, and she could see them thinking, *Insolent wench!* She crossed her arms and stared back at them implacably.

Hudson stirred, grimaced and conceded: 'I'll take instruction.' Wildman gave him a look of sympathy, slapped him on the shoulder and departed.

In fact, there was not a lot of instructing to be done. The latest *Declaration* was short, and all of the typesetting had already been done: printing was a matter of inking the forme and working the press. Still, there were all the usual adjustments to forme and paper, the normal tightening of bolts and greasing of slides, so Lucy was satisfied that Hudson knew her supervision was needed. The soldier was easily strong enough to manage the press, though Lucy noticed that he was careful with his maimed hand, pushing and pulling with the palm, not the fingers.

She'd secretly hoped that Ned would turn up to tell her she was welcome to come to The Whalebone for dinner, but there was no sign of him. At about two o'clock she gave up and took out the bread and butter she'd packed at home – she was wary of taking meat or cheese without Agnes's goodwill. 'Do you have aught to eat, Mr Hudson?' she asked, looking up at the big man.

He shook his head.

She hesitated. 'You're free to go and buy yourself some food. There's a baker's at the corner of Coleman Street and London Wall.'

'I've no money,' Hudson said hoarsely.

She sighed, grimaced and offered him half her bread and butter. He didn't take it, only stood gazing down at her, scarred face unreadable.

'Take it!' she ordered. 'I can't eat with you grokkling me like a hungry dog!'

He took it and sat down on the dirty floor of the barn. She sat down opposite at a safe distance and nibbled at the bread.

'You're not from London,' he said suddenly.

'Nay,' she agreed. 'I'm from Hinckley in Leicestershire.'

He nodded, took a bite of the bread and butter and chewed it thoughtfully. The scarred side of his face moved stiffly, but at least he didn't dribble. 'I hail from Lincolnshire myself.'

'Aye?'

'Not been back, though, since...' He waved his maimed hand at his scarred face.

Lucy hesitated again: she didn't really want to know more about this brute, but she felt she ought to, since they were working together. 'What happened? Captain Wildman said you were wounded at Naseby, but...'

'Pistol misfired.' He held his bad hand out in front of him and went on, 'This was the worst hurt. I was 'prenticed to be a blacksmith, but that's work that needs two hands. Now I'm glad to heave a press for sixpence a day.'

'I used to work in my da's dairy,' Lucy told him. 'Then soldiers stole all our cows, and there was nothing for me to do. I'm glad to find work that pays sixpence, too, Mr Hudson, but then I never earned tuppence at home.'

He fixed her with that single eye. After a moment he snorted. 'Bold child, aren't you?'

'No more *child* than you, I thank you!'

'Nor yet a *wench* or a *puss,*' he replied with a lop-sided smile. 'You are *in charge* here, after all.'

She was silent a moment, angry again. It was *funny,* was it, for her to say that? 'Aye,' she said, 'and like to stay that way, since I'll not spend all *my* earnings on drink!' She got to her feet and went back to the press.

He got up, too, glowering again. 'What do you mean by that?'

'Oh? You got that stink on you by sleeping in

a distillery and a privy by turns, did you?'

'A man that's hurt needs something to dull the pain!'

'While a *woman* that's hurt is expected to mend and mind the children, too!' She put the rest of her bread and butter in her mouth, dusted off her hands and began inking again.

They worked in silence for the rest of the afternoon. At last Lucy signalled that it was time to stop. She cleaned up, then gathered up the small stack of sheets she'd managed to print the previous day, which were now dry. 'We'll take these to The Whalebone Tavern,' she told Hudson. Since Browne's arrest, Ned had been selling the products of the press among his customers.

'Will they pay us there?' was the soldier's response.

She hesitated: she'd been taking her tuppence from Ned but she wasn't sure how things would work now. 'Probably not,' she admitted. 'We'll need to see Mr Chidley.'

When they arrived at The Whalebone, the serving-woman Nancy greeted Lucy with some embarrassment, then called for Ned. He came up from the cellar with a morose expression that became a pleased smile when he saw Lucy.

'Lucy!' he exclaimed. 'I began to fear I'd not see you today. Why did you fail us at dinner-time?'

'I ... I wasn't sure I had your leave to come,' said Lucy. She could feel her face growing warm.

'Of course you have!' Ned said. 'The press may have moved, but I hope we are still friends!

Will you come tomorrow?'

'Aye!' she said, smiling stupidly. 'I'd be glad of it.'

Hudson was watching Ned closely. 'Is this invitation only to Mistress Wentnor, or is it to all who work the press?'

Ned gave him a curious stare.

'This is Mr James Hudson,' Lucy explained, 'whom Captain Wildman found to help with the press. Mr Hudson, this is Mr Trebet, the keeper of The Whalebone.'

Ned held out his hand to Hudson with a smile. 'I'll gladly offer refreshment to those who work our press, and any friend of Captain Wildman is welcome at The Whalebone. What was it, a pistol misfiring?'

'Aye,' said Hudson, taken aback. He did not take the offered hand, but he held up his own damaged one in a sort of apologetic wave.

'I saw the like at Newbury.'

'You were with the London trained bands?' asked Hudson, his tone suddenly much less surly. 'That was a brave stand!'

Ned smiled. 'Captain Wildman said you fought at Naseby. In what regiment, pray?'

The two men began to talk about the war. Lucy listened to them in surprise at first but, as the talk moved to flanking attacks and musketry, quickly grew bored. When Ned offered Hudson a drink, she said that she must see Mr Chidley. Ned was barely willing to divert his attention long enough to tell her the address.

The Chidleys lived nearby, in Soaper Lane, so she was not gone long. When she returned, however, Ned was back at his work and Hudson was in the tavern's common room, talking war with half a dozen others. Lucy had to rap on the table to get his attention. The whole drinking party looked up at her with appreciative leers.

'Your wages,' she said curtly. She set down sixpence. 'I expect to see you tomorrow, Mr Hudson, *sober* and presentable!' She stalked out.

Chidley had, in fact, entrusted her with the whole fourteen shillings, along with an account book. 'If you've run a dairy, this should be no trouble to you,' he told her, 'but if you need advice, I am at your disposal.' She could have paid Hudson a week's wages, but she suspected that if she did, she wouldn't see him the following day. As it was, she was uneasy about leaving him in a tavern with money in his purse.

When she arrived at the barn the following morning, she was fully expecting him not to show up before noon. She made her now-routine tour, assuring herself that all the dark corners were empty. When she came into the hayloft, however, there was a rustle, and then a man's head and shoulders emerged suddenly from a pile of stale straw. Memory seized her by the throat: she screamed, bolted for the ladder and leapt from it only halfway down. She staggered, then fled out of the door.

She glanced back before she reached the street. The barn stood peacefully in its muddy field under a cloudy sky, its door wide open so that she could see the white flutter of paper within. No one was coming after her. She stopped, breathing hard, pressing her trembling hands together. She did not know what to do. She should not leave the barn unlocked and open, panting out its secret – but she couldn't possibly go back.

A figure appeared in the doorway, and she belatedly recognized James Hudson. She had run away from her own assistant! Shame and self-disgust turned her stomach: how could she ever hold her own against him now? Still she couldn't bring herself to go back, though, and the two of them stared at one another for a long time, Hudson in the doorway, Lucy sixty paces away in the track that led to the street. At last Hudson shambled forward. She knew he was going to laugh at her, and then ... she wasn't sure, but she didn't think she could work with him. It had been hard enough working *alone* in the *barn*: to work with this monster leering and jeering at her would be impossible.

'I beg your pardon,' he said quietly. 'I fear I startled you cruelly.'

It was so different from what she expected that she could only stare blankly.

'I lay in the barn to save rent-money,' he informed her. 'I thought it might serve, too, to keep out thieves.'

'Oh,' she said stupidly. After a moment she added, 'How did you get in? The door was lock-ed!'

'Loose board,' he said simply. 'You thought me an escaped lunatic, did you?'

'Aye,' she said, glad of the excuse. She took a deep breath and forced herself to take a step back towards the barn, then another and another.

Hudson stood aside for her, then followed her in. His coat and hair were decorated with straw, but he managed an air of respect despite it. She was grateful for it.

Inside, everything was as it should be: the press sitting quietly, the printed sheets drying on their lines, the scents of paper and ink vying with the smell of damp and old straw. She pushed a stray lock of hair up under her coif and wiped her hands on her apron. Hudson went to the press and looked at her expectantly.

'Nay,' she told him. Her voice was unsteady, but only slightly. 'We've done enough *Declarations*; now we're to print more petitions. Mr Chidley gave me the text yesterday. I'll set the type. You can go find yourself some breakfast if you've a mind to it. We'll start printing when you get back.'

'I've a sour stomach this morning,' he told her, 'but, if there's time, I'll find myself a drink of plain water.'

She nodded, glad of a little time to settle her nerves again.

When he came back he was carrying his coat over one arm and his shirt and hair were wet. She looked at him in surprise.

'Since I need not lie in either a distillery or a privy tonight,' he said solemnly, 'I thought I might safely wash my shirt.'

'My nose thanks you,' she said with equal solemnity.

They smiled at one another.

She hesitated, then said determinedly, 'It would be well if you drank less and had a stomach for breakfast.'

His single remaining eyebrow rose.

'It's heavy work!' she pointed out. 'You need more in your belly than last night's ale – *if* you kept that down!'

He cast his eye towards Heaven. 'God save me from nagging women!'

'I am in charge of this press, Mr Hudson, and I've a *right* to worry that you'll faint at your work!'

Unexpectedly, he smiled. 'I promise not to faint.'

Walking home that evening, she found herself smiling again. For the first time, it seemed that she really might succeed in setting what had happened behind her.

When she looked back on the weeks that followed, they seemed to her to be ordinary. There were events, yes, but they formed a pattern she regarded as *normal*: they gave shape to her ordinary life. That sense of ordinariness exasperated her, however: in truth, nothing about that spring and summer was ordinary. Power and authority were shaken to the foundations, and her unlicensed press was in the centre of things. She printed John Lilburne's *Rash Oaths Unwarrantable*; she printed the Army's *Humble Representation of the Dissatisfactions of the Army* and their *Solemn Engagement*. Print streamed around the city, to the Army and back again, a torrent of protest and demand that battered against the floodgates of Parliament.

The Army mutinied. The common soldiers rose in defence of their rights, and their officers bowed to their will or were swept aside. Parliament's orders were disobeyed and its frantic pronouncements were treated with contempt. The king, whose consent Parliament had hoped to win for its Presbyterian settlement, was suddenly snatched from his luxurious captivity in Northamptonshire – escorted off by a very junior officer, a mere cavalry cornet. Next heard of, he was with the Army. Cromwell fled London, leaving behind parliamentary outrage for his broken promise that the Army would disband; soon he, too, was with the Army and negotiating with the king for quite a different settlement. The Army assembled near Newmarket and began a slow march towards London.

All of this was exhilirating and thrilling, but – at first – none of it had much real effect on Lucy's life. The arrival, at long last, of a lodger at Uncle Thomas's house was a much bigger change.

Mrs Penington was a *gentlewoman*, the well-bred wife of a Royalist whose estate had been sequestered because of his support for the king. The gentleman himself was in France, but he had sent his wife to 'compound' for his 'delinquency' – in other words, to pay a hefty fine and get his lands back. Mrs Penington had taken both the empty rooms – Mark's for herself and Hannah's for her maidservant – and, though she paid eight shillings a week rent and not the hoped-for ten, Agnes was in awe of her and determined not to lose her. In consequence, Lucy

130

was exiled from the house during the hours of daylight: Agnes was terrified that if the gentlewoman discovered that the niece of the house was a seditious printer, she'd lodge elsewhere. Agnes didn't like Thomas's opinions, either, of course, but she couldn't give orders to him; Lucy was another matter.

'I don't want you speak to the lady!' Agnes ordered her. 'If you must, confine yourself to *decent* topics. If she asks you what you do, you are to tell her you print *wholesome* and *lawful* things!' Agnes took to serving supper early in the evening, before Lucy got home, so that there would be no chance for her and Mrs Penington to converse. The scoldings for returning after dark were replaced by encouragement to stay away; Agnes even gave up one of Lucy's two shillings, so that Lucy could buy herself a frugal supper in the City. The result, of course, was that Lucy worked late more and more, often going directly from the printing press to The Whalebone, where she could hear the latest news. The house became only the place she slept: her life was centred elsewhere.

She got to know many of Ned's other customers, particularly the Chidleys and William Walwyn; she grew comfortable enough with Ned to joke with him and his staff. Jamie Hudson no longer seemed the least bit alarming: a quiet, steady presence that made the barn feel safer. He still drank, but – perhaps because she nagged him about it – less and less. He began to gain some weight and lost his surliness.

She bought some cloth from Uncle Thomas –

131

a pretty chestnut-coloured worsted, with hints of red to it – and she and Susan spent several pleasant Sabbath afternoons discussing gowns before she cut the fabric, and then more pleasant afternoons tacking it together and adjusting it. The actual sewing, however, went very slowly as she seldom had time while there was daylight enough to stitch.

As May gave way to June, however, the public events had private effects: Lucy finally had her long-threatened encounter with the law.

She was at The Whalebone at dinner-time when there was shouting outside. A moment later a party of soldiers burst into the room with their swords in their hands.

Nancy Shorby, who'd been at the bar, screamed; everyone jumped up, instinctively recoiling from the edged metal. A tin plate fell to the floor, spilling its contents in an ugly smear. Lucy was jostled back into a corner, and the low-ceilinged room filled with noise.

'We've come by order of Parliament to search this tavern!' yelled one of the soldiers. 'Where's the keeper?'

Ned thrust his way through the packed mass of his customers. 'Here! If you have a warrant, show it!'

One of the soldiers waved a sword before his face. 'Here's my warrant, you son of a whore!'

Ned angrily thrust the sword aside; at this the soldier struck at his face with the hilt. Ned yelped and staggered, and there was a gasp of outrage. Somebody kicked the soldier, who turned angrily in the direction of the kicker. Ned at once grabbed the sword-hilt and tried to wrestle the weapon away. The soldiers' leader drew his pistol and fired it at the ceiling.

In the confined space the noise was deafening, and in its wake the room fell silent. 'Stand quiet!' ordered the officer. 'We'll do no violence to those who offer none!'

'Whoreson Reformadoes!' called James Hudson from somewhere nearby. 'Is Parliament paying you thirty pieces of silver?'

Lucy finally understood who the men were. There were many discharged soldiers in London; there had been disturbances when they demanded their pay, which, like that of the soldiers still under arms, had long been denied. Parliament had just the day before decided to make use of them, offering them the money they were due if they re-enlisted in new, 're-formed' regiments.

The officer sneered. 'Thirty pieces of silver? Nay, the New Model can sue for pennies: *we're* getting full arrears of pay! Five pounds each!'

That provoked a growl of anger. Ned, dishevelled and wild-eyed, his chin flecked with blood, cried, 'I asked to see your warrant! You've no right to conduct a search without you have a warrant!'

'You're one of Lilburne's get all right!' sneered the officer. 'I'll tell you your *rights*, tavern-keeper: you've a *right* to life and limb if you give us no trouble. Hinder us, and I swear you'll suffer for it. This house is notorious, and no one will question what we do.' He gestured for his men to begin searching.

By great good fortune, there was no stash of pamphlets at the tavern that day: the previous day's output had already been distributed, and the new sheets were still drying on the lines in the barn. Lucy was silently thanking God for that, and wondering what to say if anyone noticed her ink-stained hands, when she recognized the face of one of the searching soldiers.

For a long minute she stood frozen with shock. The man felt her eyes: he looked at her, frowned, looked back, then grinned toothily. She realized that he did not even recognize her.

The scream was in her throat again, and for once there seemed no point at all in swallowing it. *'You THIEF!'* She shrieked it, and suddenly every eye in the room was on her. She elbowed a customer aside and advanced to confront the soldier face to face. *'Thief!'* she cried again. She was shaking with rage and loathing. 'Foul cruel rogue! I never thought to see you again! What's your *name*?'

The soldier cast a look of bewilderment at his officer. 'What ails you, wench? I've not met you before in my life!'

Lucy spat in his face. His look of confusion became one of indignation, and he raised his hand to hit her; she caught the hand and fended off the blow. He tried to shake his hand loose, and she caught it with her other hand as well. He swore, jerking her from side to side. Angry exclamations sounded on all sides, and then there was a ring of steel. James Hudson stepped beside her, his sword drawn. 'Let her go!' he ordered the Reformado.

The Reformado couldn't: Lucy was the one holding *him*. He tried to draw his own sword, but couldn't get his hand free. One of his friends, however, swore and drew; Hudson turned towards him, there was a ringing clash, and then the Reformado's sword was on the floor.

'Peace, peace!' shouted the officer. He was alarmed, despite his claim that no one would question what he did. Presumably it would reflect badly on him if he couldn't even search a tavern without bloodshed.

'Keep peace yourself!' Hudson snarled, turning on him; the officer recoiled a little at the sight of his face. 'Do you think to come here and misuse the keeper of the place and this young gentlewoman, and have no one check you for it?'

'This man is a *thief*!' Lucy repeated. She realized she still had hold of his hand and flung it off with revulsion. 'What is his *name*, sir?'

'Symonds,' said the officer, blinking.

'Symonds!' hissed Lucy, turning back to the man. Her father might want to forget he'd ever had a daughter but he would still be glad to know that name. 'May God curse you for ever! May you burn in Hell!'

'You say he is a thief, Lucy?' Ned asked from across the room.

'Aye!' she agreed, turning to him. 'One of the three who came to my father's freehold, two years ago last month, and drove off all our cattle and...' she almost told the whole truth, but retained enough sense to change it to, 'and *beat* me when I tried to hinder them!'

135

'I don't...' began Symonds – and recognized her. The whole room saw his shock as he did. Any suspicion that Lucy was mistaken collapsed.

'He was of the King's party then!' Lucy said, glaring at him. 'Sir, have you brought a *Cavalier* here, to tyrannize us?'

'He's no Cavalier,' said the officer. 'He fought in Colonel Massey's regiment.'

'Then the more shame to him!' said Lucy. 'To come to a farm and steal cattle from Parliament's own supporters!' She drew a deep, outraged breath. 'My brothers were with the militia when he came! *They* were fighting for Parliament, and he took advantage of their absence to steal our cattle!'

'This – this is nothing to the point!' protested the officer, embarrassed and angry. 'There is to be an indemnity for acts done for furtherance of the war, so whether he stole your beeves or not—'

'*Milch* cows!' Lucy cried. 'Not beeves! Good milch cows, and it grieves me to the heart to think of this stinking knave slaughtering them for meat! We'd supplied cheese to the militia, many times, but after that, how could we? How did that *further the war*? *Symonds*! What's the rest of your name? What were the names of your friends?'

'Silence, you slut!' ordered Symonds, sweating and afraid.

'You dare not even give your name, do you? A brave soldier indeed! *Thief*! *Robber*! Somebody seize him! If there's any justice in England, he'll *hang* for what he did!'

'*We* are the law here!' bellowed the officer and slapped a table. 'We were sent to search this place for evidence of sedition!'

'Is my tavern to be searched by a *known robber*?' Ned shouted back. 'No, sir! And I have not seen your warrant!'

'Enough! Arrest him!' The officer struck the table again. 'And arrest the wench, too! And that one-eyed monster! You can join your friend Lilburne in prison!'

Six

A PERFECT DIURNALL, 10–16 June 1647

News is come of a strange chance at *The Whalebone Tavern*, where some *Reformadoes* employed by the Committee of Safety, coming to search for seditious printing, had the Hue and Cry raised against themselves. A Mistress *Wentnor* at the tavern recognized among the Soldiers one *Richard Symonds* who, she says, two years before drove off cattle of her Father's, to the great hurt of his house, and to her great grief, for her dowry was spent upon replacing them. Her Father kept a dairy in *Leicestershire* and often supplied cheese to *Parliament's* Army, but after his loss could do so no more. It is to be hoped that the Committee of Safety will question the Soldier, to know if he indeed be a Robber, for it would be shame to see Robbers enforce Laws against honest Citizens.

Lucy gazed at the item in the newsbook with sharp disappointment. 'It doesn't even say that they arrested *us!*'

'It does say they're robbers!' replied Ned, grinning.

The arrest had not, in fact, lasted very long. The soldiers had dragged Lucy and the two men out into the yard of the tavern, bound their hands and kept them standing there while they searched The Whalebone. It had been raining again, and the three prisoners were soon soaked and shivering. The search, however, had been in vain: the only pamphlets found were in the possession of one or other of the customers. The soldiers confiscated these, and took them and the prisoners back to the Committee of Safety which had sent them. This was a new committee, set up only the previous day to counter the threat of the Army, and it was composed entirely of the most war-like and intolerant Presbyterians in the House of Commons. It had set up its headquarters in the Guildhall, which was at least nearby.

At the Guildhall the prisoners stood dripping in an antechamber while the Reformado officer went in to report to a member of the committee; presently, however, he came out again and sullenly commanded his men to release them: 'Colonel Massey says, bring him evidence!' he said bitterly. 'As though it were our fault there was none!'

Cold and wet, the three of them were glad enough to go. Once they were back at The Whalebone, however, drinking hot spiced ale, relief gave way to outrage.

A written protest, delivered to the Committee of Safety the following day, was torn up before their eyes by a sneering clerk. Hudson then suggested that the three of them print and publish their story as a pamphlet, but this plan fell down because none of them felt confident of the skill to pen a pamphlet, particularly since printing their own story would mean *not* printing the latest remonstrance from the Army. Lucy suggested that they turn instead to a newsbook, which had the additional advantage of a wider audience than the 'well-affected' who bought most of what they printed. *A Perfect Diurnall,* Uncle Thomas's usual purchase, was the obvious choice: it was the most widely read title and, though deeply cautious and unwilling to offend anyone in power, was more honest than most.

It was easy to find the writer of *A Perfect Diurnall*: all the vendors knew him. He turned out to be a tall, thin, bald man named Samuel Pecke. He was very willing to talk to a pretty girl, though disappointed when she insisted on confining the discussion to what she wanted him to publish. He promised, however, to write something and put it in his next issue. 'For I think it shame that such a sweet child should lose her dowry and no man be punished for it.'

'He's done well by us,' Ned told Lucy. 'This would never have seen print at all, were it not for

139

your bright eyes.'

Lucy made a face. 'But it's naught but cattle-stealing and my dowry! I *told* him how they arrested us for nothing, and how that scoundrel declared his sword was warrant enough, and—'

'He's said the main thing,' interrupted Ned, grinning. *"It would be shame to see Robbers enforce laws against honest Citizens".* It *is* shame, and all who read this will know it.'

Lucy let out her breath unhappily. 'And? By what we heard at the Guildhall, that same Colonel Massey who commanded Richard Symonds during the war commands him still! Will he see justice done? He probably gave the order to steal cattle – aye, and ate of the meat! He can easily slip the whole matter off by saying that he looked into it and found I was mistaken, or lying.'

'That would be a blow,' said Ned, undeterred, 'if we had ever hoped to get justice from the Committee of Safety – but that would be like hoping to get strawberries from gorse.'

'This tale will help make the Committee odious to the citizens,' added Hudson seriously. 'That was all we could hope to do at present.'

Ned nodded. 'When the Committee's disbanded and we have a new Parliament, *then* we can get justice!'

Lucy snorted. 'You mean, when the Army's triumphed! It still seems to me a most strange thing, to expect lawlessness from the government and justice from the Army!'

'It's a strange world,' said Jamie Hudson mildly.

Lucy eyed him sourly. 'Did your fine New Model Army never take goods by force?'

'Not to my knowledge,' he replied seriously. 'We were told that we fought for the people and that it was shame to rob them. Oh, we took goods without payment often enough – when a man's not been paid himself, he has no choice about that – but we always wrote out a receipt, so that those who supplied us might have some hope of reclaiming the value of their goods. Colonel Massey's Horse was never a part of the New Model and was notorious for lawlessness. It was disbanded early for that very reason.'

'The Army will force Parliament to give us justice,' Ned said eagerly. 'There will be no second army to oppose it.'

He was almost certainly right to think so. The very day after their arrest, Parliament summoned the London trained bands to muster – and the trained bands didn't come. A ward that was supposed to supply a hundred men managed to assemble eight, or a dozen, or, in one case, a watchman and his dog. True, the new Committee of Safety was still hiring, but their few thousand Reformadoes were no match at all for the massed regiments of the New Model Army, and everybody knew it. The Army had halted, only a daymarch away at St Albans, and messengers rode back and forth between it and Westminster, while the people prayed fervently for an agreement.

'When we have a new Parliament,' Ned told Lucy, 'you can take your cattle-thief to court.'

Lucy was not at all sure that she could. She

had written to her father, telling him about Richard Symonds, but she was not confident that he'd pursue the matter. Even if he did, and even if a Leicestershire court issued a summons, nobody was going to enforce it in London, new Parliament or old.

She was thinking about her father on her way to work next morning, thinking so hard that she forgot most of her hedge-leveller caution. Daniel Wentnor was a proud man, hard-working, strong-willed and ferociously honest: the shame of what had happened cut him deep, but so did the desire for justice. She did not know what he would do and she pondered it distractedly, at one moment afraid he'd do nothing, at the next that he'd pursue justice relentlessly and call her to testify, so that everyone in London discovered how she'd been raped.

The sick feeling that thought inspired eased when she reached the barn and unlocked the door to see the sheets of their latest publication filling the dimness inside. It was yet another *Declaration of the Army* – to her mind, the best yet. She began checking the sheets to see how many were dry, her eyes snagged again and again by the noble phrases: 'We were not a mere mercenary army, hired to serve any arbitrary power of a State, but called forth and conjured by the several declarations of Parliament to the defence of our own and the people's just rights and liberties. And so we took up arms in Judgement and in Conscience.'

Somebody laughed. She looked up and saw Richard Symonds advancing on her. Behind him was another man whose face she remembered – it figured in her nightmares, though she'd never learned his name.

She screamed and recoiled. They were between her and the door, so she darted back behind the press. Symonds laughed again.

'Here I was wondering how I could get you alone,' he said, 'and here you are with an illegal press! I won't have to explain myself; I'll be *rewarded*!' He advanced towards her slowly, moving a little to the left. His friend mirrored him, moving a little to the right.

'Go away!' cried Lucy desperately.

He laughed again. 'Go *away*? From a juicy little slut like you? Why would I do that?'

Lucy bolted towards the back of the barn, ducking under the drying lines. At once both men ran after her, batting the paper aside. Lucy reached the barn wall and ran along it, looking for Jamie Hudson's loose plank. Symonds' friend crashed through the wall of paper. She screamed again, lashing out at him, and he seized her flailing hand. 'Got her!' he yelled triumphantly.

Richard Symonds arrived and caught her shoulders; his friend twisted her arms behind her back. She struggled wildly, shrieking and kicking, convulsed with horror and disbelief – not *again*! The man behind her jerked her arms up, wrenching her shoulders so violently that the pain stilled her. 'You like it rough, don't you?' he breathed into her ear. 'I remember that. Nick had the marks of your teeth in his lip till the day he died. Well, rough is how you'll get it, sweeting.'

Symonds, in front of her, grabbed her buttocks and pulled her against him, laughing; the laugh stopped when she head-butted him in the face. He swore, clapped a hand to his nose, then raised his other hand to slap her.

The blow never fell. Symonds' mouth opened and his eyes widened in astonishment and pain. Lucy, looking up over his shoulder, saw Jamie Hudson, scarred face like a devil-mask, standing behind him.

Symonds' friend yelled and thrust Lucy away. She staggered into Symonds, who grabbed at her blindly. She kicked his shin and he fell. Jamie leapt past him, sword in hand; the blade was red for half its length. Symonds seized Lucy's ankle, and she looked down and saw him writhing at her feet. She kicked at him frantically; he cried out, and she kicked again. He looked up at her, eyes wide: his mouth was gushing blood that splattered her skirt. It was only then that she understood that Jamie had run him through. 'Oh, God!' he cried, his voice bubbling through the blood. 'Oh, God, no! Oh, nooo!'

She tore her foot out of his weakening grasp. He had a knife in his belt; she stooped and snatched it, then stood holding the blade in both hands and looking wildly around. The drying lines were shaking; one fell suddenly in a ripple of paper, and she saw Jamie and the other man. Both had swords in hand now; the other man was trying to circle left, to get on Jamie's blind side. She ran towards them. Even as she did, there was another of those slithering clashes of metal, and then, just as in The Whalebone, the other man's sword was flying to the ground. He yelped and started to raise his hands. Jamie leapt forward, sword sweeping up and down again: there was a shocking spurt of red, and the man fell. He dropped on to the cut line, legs kicking, and the red spurted out across the printed pages, again, again, again – then ebbed into a weak trickle.

Lucy and Jamie stood looking at one another over the body. He made a move forward as though to embrace her. She took a step back: the thought of being touched just now, by *anyone,* was intolerable. He stood still again, his face mask-like. 'Is the other one dead?' he asked at last.

Lucy opened her mouth but couldn't speak. She shook her head and went back to see.

Richard Symonds lay twisted about on his side, one heel digging into the ground, opposite arm flung out as though he were trying to rise. He wasn't moving. Jamie nudged him with a booted foot, then rolled him over on to his back. Symonds' chin was covered with blood and his eyes stared up sightlessly. The front of his breeches were wet, and he stank: he had emptied his bowels and bladder.

Lucy knelt slowly but couldn't bring herself to touch him to see if his heart was still beating. The sight of the body filled her with horror. Richard Symonds had been a wicked man, but probably there had been those who loved him – his mother, at least; perhaps even, God forbid, a wife and children. She dropped the dagger and

145

twisted her hands together in her apron. 'May God have mercy on their souls,' she whispered.

Jamie Hudson shook his head. 'They're gone to their master the Devil.' He bent over and wiped the blade of his sword on Symonds' sleeve.

Lucy flinched. She was glad that Symonds was dead, but the thought of Hell was terrifying, and it seemed suddenly that she could almost smell the brimstone. Two men dead and damned, she thought wretchedly, and Jamie Hudson had killed them. Two deaths on his head and for *her* sake. 'I'm sorry!' she cried miserably.

He looked at her quizzically, raising his one eyebrow. 'What have *you* to be sorry for?'

'They must have followed me, and I never saw them! They must have been waiting for me, near The Whalebone, but I wasn't paying attention!'

He thrust his sword point-down in the ground, bent to find a handkerchief in Symonds' pocket and used it to finish cleaning the weapon, holding it steady with his bad hand. 'Would you have seen them, however much attention you gave it? Men who set out to commit murder usually take great care about it.'

'Murder?' whispered Lucy.

'Aye.' Jamie picked up his sword, wiped the point and dropped the cloth on Symonds' stained breast. 'They feared what you knew of them and they meant to silence you. I take it the other fellow I killed was also of the party that stole your cattle.'

'Aye,' she said and swallowed. She was suddenly feeling very sick.

'You said there were three of them, did you not?'

'Aye, but – but I think one's dead. He – the other one you killed – he said that N–Nick h–had ... had the marks of my teeth in his lip until the d–day he d–died, and ... you must know, Jamie, that they did worse than steal cattle!'

'Aye,' said Jamie very quietly. 'I guessed as much that day you ran out of the barn. I've seen ravished maids before – seen that same look on their faces when a man startles them. But I'll not speak of it without your leave.'

'Oh.' Her teeth were starting to chatter. She wrapped her arms around herself, then got to her feet. She wanted to vomit, or burst into tears – do *something* to relieve the cold heavy enormity of feeling. Instead, she walked unsteadily over to the press and leaned against it, then sat down, leaning her cheek against the rough oak. The smell of ink and paper was indescribably comforting.

Jamie came over, his sword now sheathed again, and squatted beside her. 'Are you hurt?' he asked with concern.

'Nay. Nay, just...' It struck her that he was trying to comfort her, when he must be at least as shaken as she was. He had killed twice within minutes of waking.

He had saved her life. 'Jamie,' she said, 'Jamie – *thank you.*'

He met her eyes, and the look on the good half of his face melted some of the cold sickness inside her. 'It's a rare thing to do justice,' he said. 'I am glad I was able.'

Justice? She remembered how the second man had raised his hands: he'd been trying to surrender. Could it ever be *justice* to kill a man who was trying to surrender – kill him without due process of law, with no chance to repent his sins?

Still, how could Jamie have spared him? If he'd lived, he would have gone to the Committee of Safety and told them about the press. After that she and Jamie would have been two evident malefactors caught with the evidence: the Committee would have been happy to believe any lying accusation Symonds and his friend chose to make.

The Committee of Safety, she remembered, was still in power.

'We – we must bury them!' Lucy exclaimed in alarm, getting to her feet again. 'The Committee would hang us if it knew what we've done!'

Jamie lowered his head, then raised it. 'So it would.'

They went over to the body of the second man. It lay on its back on top of a cut line of *Declarations,* head twisted; Jamie's sword-cut had opened the throat from jaw to collarbone. The wound gaped horribly, and all the pages around were stained with red. Jamie gave her an ironic look and murmured '"*And so we took up arms in Judgement and in Conscience*".'

Lucy shuddered. She picked up a bloodstained page and set it over the staring eyes, then another over the wound.'We must hide them,' she said; her voice was still unsteady but she no longer felt she wanted to be sick. 'Get them out of sight. We'll need to borrow shovels before we can bury them.'

They turned to The Whalebone for shovels. Ned for once was not busy – it was only the middle of the morning – and was willing to speak to them privately.

'What's amiss?' he asked concernedly, after shutting the door to one of his small parlours behind them.

'That knave Symonds...' began Jamie.

'The son of a whore!' exclaimed Ned hotly. 'What, has he threatened our Lucy?'

Jamie lifted his sword an inch from the scabbard, then slid it back again, *shhk.* He held out his hand, turning it so that Ned could see the stain on his sleeve. They had both tried to clean up, but there was limited washing water at the barn.

Ned stared at the bloodstain, his face going white, then looked anxiously at Lucy.

'I'm unharmed,' she told him. 'They followed me to the barn, and I was a fool and never saw them until they came in, but they didn't know Jamie was there. When they attacked me he killed them both.'

'*Both*?'

'Symonds had his friend with him. One of the others who stole our cattle. From something he said, I think the third man is dead – I mean, was already dead. Ned...'

'Oh, *Lucy!*' Ned caught her in his arms.

It was unexpected, and she flinched and nearly

cried out. She stood rigidly, and Ned let her go and regarded her in puzzlement. Jamie laid a hand on his arm.

'Give her room,' he advised. 'Did you want to be clutched, on Newbury field after the battle?'

'Aye,' said Ned, understanding dawning. 'My brother and I clung to one another like babes. But I saw many of the other sort. Oh, my poor Lucy!'

'We need shovels to bury them,' she told him determinedly. 'The Committee of Safety would hang us for killing them, whatever we said – but if they simply disappear, everyone will think they've run off for fear of being hanged as cattle-thieves.'

They decided that it would be a bad idea to be seen carrying shovels out of the city gate: if anyone did connect the disappearance of the two Reformadoes to Lucy's accusation, it would be deeply incriminating. Ned, however, regularly sent cartloads of stable sweepings out to Moorfields, and shovels were a normal part of the load. The cart went out in the evening, and the men agreed that they would slip out of the city with the cart and bury the bodies under cover of darkness.

They both told Lucy that she should go home to recover, but this she was unwilling to do. Symonds and his friend had died because of her: she could not just go home and leave others to dispose of them. Ned tried to insist on sending her home, but Jamie unexpectedly changed his mind and came to her support. 'If she has the stomach for it, she should not go home until the usual time,' he said. 'Let her be seen eating her dinner here, and her supper, too. Then if anyone asks questions, her friends can honestly swear that she followed her usual daily round and they noticed nothing amiss.'

So Lucy and Jamie washed off the rest of the blood and prepared to behave as though it were an ordinary day. They all three agreed to keep the killings a secret, but Ned suggested that someone on the 'council' should know what had happened, as a safeguard. At this Jamie decided that the best person to inform was his friend, Captain Wildman. Lucy was reluctant. 'Must it be him?' she asked.

'This is because he forgot her name,' Jamie told Ned with his twisted smile.

'Nay, it's because he thought she should work for tuppence!' replied Ned, grinning back.

'Nay!' protested Lucy. They both turned their smiles on her, and she went on reluctantly, 'He thinks I am but a silly girl, of no account.'

'I'm sure he has changed that low opinion,' said Ned gallantly.

'Lucy, he is a gentleman of great ability and honest goodwill,' Jamie said seriously. 'He studied the law at Cambridge, and he has travelled widely and has many friends. I trust him with my life and I would have his help in this, his more than that of any man I know.'

She made a face. 'Very well.'

He went off to find Captain Wildman; when he returned, later in the day, it was to say that the captain had volunteered to help them bury the bodies.

The rest of that day passed like a long night-mare. Lucy ate her dinner at The Whalebone, making sure she spoke to the staff and to several of the regulars; she went back to the barn and printed some more copies of the *Declaration of the Army* to replace those spoiled by blood, all the while horribly aware of the bodies hidden under mouldy straw in a corner. She returned to The Whalebone for supper.

Wildman turned up while she was choking down her soup, as neat and self-possessed as ever. That self-possession wavered a little, how-ever, when he was confronted with the dung-cart. Ned, smiling, took the captain's fine coat and loaned him an apron instead, and they all went back to the barn with the dung-cart. To-gether they rolled the bodies in some old sack-ing, loaded them on to the cart and covered them with dung.

'Now, Mistress Wentnor,' Captain Wildman said sternly, 'you must go home.'

'They died because of me,' she replied stub-bornly. 'I'll help to bury them.'

Wildman shook his head. 'Mistress, we must wait until full dark for this work, and in this season, night comes late. If you returned home at midnight, it would be remarked upon – or, worse still, you might be questioned by the Watch as to your business, and your name taken. *You* are the one who accused these two rogues, so you will be the one in question over their disappearance. You've done bravely and wisely to follow your daily course all this long day: you should not change now. If you are taken, you put us all in danger.'

Lucy bit her lip: it was true. 'Very well, Captain.'

She left the three men sitting in the barn with the cart and made the long walk back to Southwark. It was just beginning to grow dark when she at last reached Uncle Thomas's house, and she was sick and stupid with exhaustion. When she opened the door to the parlour and saw her brother Paul standing there, it took a moment for her even to register who he was.

Paul must have heard her come in from the street because he was already on his feet, alert and anxious. 'Lucy!' he cried and strode over to seize her by the forearms. 'Where've you been?'

'Paul!' she replied stupidly. 'How come you are here?'

He shook her. 'Cousin Geoffrey told us that our uncle had set you to printing scandalous things for his friends in the City. Father would not heed him, so I came. Lucy, it's night! Where've you been?'

'I–I worked on the press and then I supped with friends,' she said, stammering and off-balance. 'Paul, there was no need for you to...'

Agnes emerged from the stairwell, her face pinched. *'Hush!'* She glared savagely at Paul. 'You gave me your word that you would be quiet if I let you stay!'

'I must speak with my sister!' protested Paul.

'Then speak elsewhere!' Agnes ordered in a vehement hiss. 'I'll not have you disturb my gentlewoman-lodger!'

Paul scowled, took Lucy's arm and pulled her

out through the shop and back into the street. It was another chill, damp evening, and the road-way was foul with mud. 'Lucy,' Paul said, as soon as they were far enough from the house not to be overheard, 'I've come to bring you home!'

'Oh, have you?' she replied sharply. 'Well, I don't want to come!'

There was a silence. Paul stared at her, his face a pale blank. 'Geoffrey said...'

'Geoffrey is an ass!'

Another silence, this one shocked and hurt. Her numbed brain finally caught up with the fact that he had defied their father and come all the way from Leicestershire to *rescue* her. She'd never expected anyone at home to think her worth it. 'Oh, Paul!' she cried in guilt and exasperation. 'I'm *sorry!* You're a dear, kind, loving brother, and *brave* to come all this way alone, but why didn't you write me a letter first, to know from *me* how I did?'

'I don't understand,' Paul said stiffly.

She hugged him, and when her arms went round him the last of the swollen chill inside her seemed to melt, and suddenly she was clinging to him and crying.

His stiffness went: he held her close and patted her on the back. 'It's all right, Luce! I'll take you home!'

'But I don't *want* to go home!' she cried, struggling against the sobs. 'Oh, Paul! Please, I've had a hard, hard day, and I'm – I'm glad to see you, glad that you came, but ... I *like* it here! Please, I'm weary to death, but I can explain everything in the morning!'

Seven

When she woke in the morning, Lucy realized that she'd lied to her brother: she couldn't explain *anything*. She was printing seditious pamphlets on an unlicensed, illegal press, and meeting regularly – in a tavern! – with a group of sectaries who wanted to overthrow the government; she'd been arrested, and she'd helped conceal murder. Not only could she not explain it to Paul, she could scarcely believe it herself. Her life felt ordinary and natural from the inside: how could seeing it through someone else's eyes make it seem so scandalous?

Paul could not take her home by force, but that was little comfort. He might have defied their father by coming to London, but she had no doubt that if he went home with a full report of her doings, Daniel Wentnor would demand that she return immediately. She would live at home in double disgrace then, and would be utterly wretched.

Paul had come to help her, not to ruin her. Surely she could persuade him to let her be?

Paul was in the parlour when Lucy came downstairs; it seemed he'd slept there. Thomas was at the table eating breakfast, but he was silent, miserable and very nervous; it emerged that when Paul had arrived the previous afternoon, Thomas had been so unnerved that he'd remembered urgent business at the Mercers' Hall and disappeared for the rest of the day. When Lucy tried to ask her brother about his journey, Agnes hissed that they were not to discuss 'aught of this scandalous business' in the house. Lucy was forced to invite him to accompany her to the City. She did not want him to see the press – she had no confidence that he'd agree to keep its location secret – but she didn't know how else she was to talk to him.

Paul began almost as soon as they were out of the door: he'd travelled to London with a neighbour who had business in the capital; the neighbour was returning to Hinckley in three days' time. Paul meant to go with him – and take Lucy.

'But I don't *want* to go back to Hinckley!' Lucy protested again. 'I am *happy* here, I have friends, and work I like. I earn three shillings a week!'

Paul cast a horrified eye at the chaos of London Bridge. 'How can you like this hellish city? And *three shillings*, for a *woman*? Cousin Geoffrey must be right, and this work is no honest employment: else why should they pay so much?'

'It is entirely honest!' she said hotly. 'And soon, God willing, it will be lawful, as well!'

'So Geoffrey told the truth, and it's *not* lawful!'

She tried to explain about Parliament and the Army, about levelling hedges and natural law, and about Cousin Geoffrey's disappointment and the parliamentary clerk. In passing she mentioned what Ned had said about a Parliament-man having an eye on the land.

'Ned's here?' Paul asked in astonishment.

She stared at him blankly. She couldn't think how he knew Ned.

'When did he come?' Paul demanded eagerly. 'Did he seek you out?'

She realized that he thought she meant her former sweetheart; realized at the same time that she'd forgotten there'd ever been such a man. To think she might have *married* Ned Bartram! That she might have become Mrs Bartram, the obedient wife of a smug, mean-minded dullard!

'Not *that* Ned, Paul! Ned *Trebet,* the keeper of The Whalebone Tavern, where I dine most days.' It occured to her, with relief, that this might be a way to divert Paul from the print-works. 'Here, we'll stop there, and I'll introduce you. Then you'll see that my friends are honest people!'

The yard of The Whalebone was bustling: two ostlers were saddling horses, Nancy was arguing with a tradesman, and a tired-looking Ned was paying a carter for a load of bread. He broke off with a smile when Lucy came up, then directed a look of surprise at Paul.

'Ned,' she said, very glad to see his face, 'God bless you! Paul, here is Ned Trebet, keeper of The Whalebone Tavern; Ned, this is my brother Paul, fresh-come from Hinckley. He heard tales which alarmed him, and he wishes me to come home with him.'

Ned stared at Paul in dismay, then looked anxiously at Lucy. He opened his mouth and closed it again. Lucy abruptly realized that he thought the 'tales' were about murder, and hastily added, 'My cousin Geoffrey, of whom I told you, has been filling their ears at home with stories of Uncle Thomas's sedition. I've been trying to tell Paul that he's been misled, and that our friends are honest well-affected people, but I doubt I've convinced him.'

'Ah!' exclaimed Ned, relieved – but only briefly. His brows drew down into a heavy frown. 'He wishes you to *leave London*?'

'To come home, aye!' agreed Paul, frowning back. 'And I pray you excuse me, Mr Trebet, but for aught I can see Cousin Geoffrey was right, and our uncle has allowed my sister to trespass in a very dangerous business.'

'Don't blame Uncle Thomas, Paul!' Lucy said sharply. 'He misliked my work from the start and nearly forbade it several times, but I persuaded him to it.'

'He was ever a weak man,' Paul replied, with contempt, 'and unable to govern a woman.'

It was exactly the sort of thing their father would have said, but Lucy had expected better from Paul. She stared in cold anger. 'Then I must be the more to blame, for abusing his weakness!'

'Nay!' exclaimed Paul, sensing that something had gone wrong. 'It was his place to judge what was safe and to protect you from—'

'Oh, say what you mean!' snapped Lucy. 'You think Uncle Thomas must be either wicked or

158

foolish, and I am too silly to understand that or anything else! What cause did I ever give you to think so poorly of my wits?'

'Mistress Wentnor, good day!' said another voice. They all looked round and saw Captain Wildman, booted and spurred for riding and carrying a despatch bag. Apparently one of those freshly saddled horses was his.

'This is Lucy's *brother,*' Ned broke in angrily. 'He wishes to take her from London!'

Wildman regarded Paul with surprise. 'What's *this*?'

'Sir,' said Paul stiffly, 'who you are I know not...'

'Captain John Wildman, at your service!'

'...but *indeed* I wish to take my sister home, for it seems to me that here she is in danger!'

'So are we all,' Wildman replied. 'In danger of losing all we have fought for these long years; and if we preserve our freedoms, it will be in part through your sister's steadfast diligence. Sir, I am very sorry to hear what you say, that you mean to take her from London while our need of the press is so great. Will you give me leave to argue our case with you?'

Paul stared suspiciously.

'Sir. Let me first ask you this: do you believe our cause is just?'

'Sir,' replied Paul in surprise, 'I scarcely know what your cause *is*!'

'And yet would hinder it? That's as to say, I know not what my sister does, yet I will put a stop to it! Should you not first inform yourself what it *is* you wish to stop?'

'I know it puts her in danger!'

'If *danger* were reason enough to stop a thing, nothing would ever be done! Childbearing puts a woman in more danger than ever your sister suffers here in London. Would you therefore forbid her to marry?'

Paul gaped, then scowled. 'I see you are skilled at argument.'

Wildman gave a little bow. 'I read law, sir, at Cambridge.'

That had an effect. Cousin Geoffrey's account of Thomas's seditious friends had not led Paul to expect a Cambridge-educated lawyer among them.

'Paul,' said Lucy, striking while he was off-balance, 'you should speak with Captain Wildman. Why should you believe Geoffrey's report before you even hear the other side of the story? For my part, though I'm very glad to see you, and though I never want to quarrel with you, I would rather beg in the street than go back to Hinckley! You know very well that I would be wretched there. Our father has no wish to have me under his roof again.'

Paul winced. He glanced at Wildman and at Ned, then nodded. 'Very well. I'll listen.'

Lucy kissed him and went off to work, feeling much happier.

Jamie was already at work when she arrived. He stopped, leaning on the press with a smile. 'You're late. I was beginning to fear that events yesterday made you ill.'

'Oh, no, indeed, but I have a *new* trouble! My brother has arrived from Hinckley. He wants to

160

take me home, but—'

Jamie, however, had stopped smiling. 'Take you home?'

'Aye. Not because ... that is, he knows nothing of what happened yesterday. He's come because a cousin has been telling tales of my uncle's seditious friends. By God's grace, though, we met your Captain Wildman at The Whalebone.' She smiled. 'He's the quickest disputer I ever heard! If he can't win Paul over, no one can.'

Jamie was frowning. He started to speak, then stopped himself. He tried again. 'Most wenches would be happy to go home after an attack such as you suffered yesterday.'

She frowned. 'I am unlike most wenches, then.'

'Aye,' he agreed readily.

She stared in hurt affront, and he quickly raised his bad hand, as though to ward off a blow. 'You've wit enough for two, and spirit enough for three.'

She was flattered and touched. 'I told Paul I'd rather beg in the street than go home. It was bad enough just to be known ... known to be spoiled goods. If I were spoiled goods brought back from London in disgrace, my life would be pitiable indeed.' She paused, studying his scarred face. *'You* should understand that: you won't go back to Lincolnshire!'

He gave a small snort of recognition and look-ed away. 'I'd no wish to see my sisters cry when they set eyes on me. Aye, and the pretty girls I used to court would all scream and stare. I'd be spoiled goods come home, and very soon stink-

161

ing rotten with drink.'

They were both silent a moment, contem-plating the impossibility of ever going home. 'Do you write to them?' she asked.

He made a face and shook his head. 'John wrote to tell them I was wounded. He's sent them news once or twice since. I ... have tried, but it's as though I had to make myself known in some other language, and I know not how to begin.'

'Aye,' she agreed, swallowing.

They looked at one another again. He smiled warmly. 'I'm glad you won't be leaving us.'

'Ah, but whether or not I do depends more on your Captain Wildman's quick tongue than on my will!'

'You do your will an injustice, for it's a good strong one, and I'd wager on it against your brother. But John Wildman's wits are always worth enlisting. I've told you: I trust him with my life.'

Jamie's trust was justified: when they returned to The Whalebone for dinner, they found Paul thoughtfully reading a copy of John Lilburne's *Regal Tyranny Discovered.* Wildman, he said, had left for St Albans, but it was clear that he'd made a deep impression. Paul asked about Lilburne and the cause, then joined Lucy, Jamie and Ned for dinner and asked some more.

However, over the course of the meal a distraction far more potent than Lilburne emerged: Richard Symonds. Lucy told Paul all about the incident at The Whalebone, adding that she'd already written to their father – though, for Ned's sake, she described Symonds as a 'cattle-thief'.

Paul was thrilled: he had come to London to rescue his sister, but a chance to get *justice* for her was even better. He downed the rest of his ale in a gulp and set off for the Guildhall to demand that the Committee of Safety arrest Symonds and send him for trial at Leicester assizes. Lucy made no effort to dissuade him, though she felt uncomfortable about it. She told herself that to draw Paul aside to explain that Symonds had been murdered would seem suspicious to anyone watching, but she knew that really she was relieved to have found such a good distraction. Not only did chasing Symonds keep Paul's attention off his sister, it reinforced for the authorities the impression that Symonds and his friend had fled. She and Jamie went back to work.

When she saw her brother again that evening, he was white with outrage: the Committee had been as short with him as with Lucy.

'The whoreson rogues!' he complained. 'They said that they *had no legal complaint* against these men, that *no charge had been made*! I'll charge them, the stinking curs!'

Lucy thought of telling him the truth, but how could she broach the subject of *murder* in the house when Agnes had given her instructions to lie about seditious printing?

She remained uneasily silent as Paul spent the next two days marching between the London courts and the Guildhall with applications and affidavits. In all this time there was no enquiry into the disappearance of the two Reformadoes: the Committee of Safety was evidently relieved to be rid of an embarrassment. Eventually their clerk admitted to Paul that Richard Symonds had disappeared.

Paul was bound to set off back to Leicestershire with the Hinckley neighbour the following morning: he didn't have the money to stay longer.

'I'll get Da to sue for a warrant,' he told Lucy that evening. 'He'll stir himself for *this*!'

Her vision of her father descending on London returned, and she winced. A quest for *justice* now might end in Jamie being hanged for murder: she had to put a stop to it. 'Paul,' she said, 'will you ... will you come down to church to pray with me about this?' St Olave's would almost certainly be empty at this time on a weekday evening.

It turned out to be locked. Paul tried the door, then turned to go to look for a verger with the key; Lucy caught his arm. The church porch was sheltered, dark and quiet, good enough for her purposes. 'In truth I need only to talk to you,' she said nervously. 'Paul, I'm sorry, I should not have let you waste your effort, but I feared to speak where anyone might overhear! Richard Symonds is dead, he and his friend both. They came to my printworks to murder me, and Jamie Hudson killed them both, the day you arrived in London.'

Paul reeled. He demanded the details and then wasn't sure how to respond to them: glee that

164

justice had been done; bewilderment that they dared not say so; anger at the way he'd made a fool of himself with his affidavits.

'But, Paul, that helped to save me!' Lucy protested. 'It must have convinced the Committee that they'd run off and I knew nothing of it! If they'd investigated, Jamie might have been hanged, and perhaps me as well!'

It was an exaggeration, but it mollified Paul. 'Jamie Hudson is the one with half a face?' he said. 'I should thank him.'

'Nay, nay, nay! You should forget you ever heard me name him. Paul, the Committee *rules* here and it would hang him! But tell Da.'

'Aye,' said Paul wondering. 'God has revenged the innocent! All praise to Him!'

Lucy thought that God would have done better to *protect* the innocent but shunted the blasphemous thought aside.

Paul duly left next morning. He was still not really happy about what his sister was doing, but he was sympathetic to her reasons for it and he promised to tell their father that Geoffrey had greatly exaggerated. Richard Symonds and his fate were a much greater concern: Paul was still marvelling at the workings of divine justice, and Lucy decided that she must to write to him, to remind him that publicizing the mighty works of God would lead to human injustice. She kissed her brother goodbye and went back to the press with a sigh of relief.

The next few weeks were among the happiest of her life. There was now a real bond between herself, Jamie and Ned: she found that she trusted the other two more than she'd ever expected to trust men again. She woke every morning looking forward to the day, and every evening parted from her friends with smiles and laughter.

The city was bubbling with debate, with pamphlet countering pamphlet in a swirling battle. Presbyterian tracts furiously denounced the blasphemers in the Army; Royalist ballads mourned the sufferings of the king and called for his restoration; hopes of a settlement were raised, dashed and raised again. There were speeches and remonstrances, petitions and declarations and engagements. In the pulpits of City churches, preachers denounced toleration; in the conventicles of the sectaries, preachers denounced the intolerant. The City's apprentices held a violent demonstration, calling for peace, the disbanding of the Army and the restoration of the king. In the middle of it, Lucy's press laboured, banging out sheet after sheet – and the sheets *sold*. Distributed across the city through the regular meetings of the well-affected, they were taken up eagerly as soon as they appeared. The fourteen-shillings-a-week subsidy voted by the council was never needed; instead, a surplus was delivered to the fund for prisoners.

The negotiations between Parliament and Army went nowhere, but still the conflict remained poised short of bloodshed. The Army marched from St Albans to Uxbridge, but stayed out of London. It issued demands. Pay was no longer its first concern: it wanted the Committee of Safety disbanded and the Reformadoes dismissed; it wanted the old Parliament dissolved and a new one elected; it wanted religious toleration, reform to the system of justice, an end to monopolies and corruption. It presented charges of impeachment against eleven members of Parliament and called for their conduct to be investigated. It also demanded the release from prison of John Lilburne, Nicholas Tew, Richard and Mary Overton, and William Browne.

The House of Commons inclined one day towards resistance, the next towards compromise. It refused to investigate the eleven members, but it disbanded the Committee of Safety and dismissed the Reformadoes. Perhaps this was only because they'd proved so inadequate, but the news filled Lucy with huge relief: that vile oppressive force, gone! Swept away by the Commons as quickly as it had been set up! It was as though the kingdom had been released from shackles and taken two steps back from war.

Parliament, however, still refused to release Lilburne from the Tower or Richard Overton from Newgate. In another measured step back, though, it freed Mary Overton, Tew and Browne.

It was a result the well-affected had petitioned for again and again in anger and despair, and the news swept across the city. Ned announced it jubilantly to Lucy and Jamie when they turned up at The Whalebone for dinner late in July. 'They were set free without warning, early this morning! They're *home*!'

Lucy's first reaction was happiness: now Liza

could go home to her father, and soon there would be a real peace! Her second, however, was anxiety: she'd come to think of the illegal press as *hers,* but she hadn't forgotten that it was, in fact, the property of Nicholas Tew. What would happen to her when he reclaimed his own?

Her third reaction was shame. Nicholas Tew had been unjustly imprisoned: she should be glad that he was free. Instead, here she was, coveting his livelihood! She should repent and ask God to cleanse her sinful heart.

Ned hosted a celebration dinner for the freed prisoners, arranging it for a couple of days after their release, so that they could first have some time at home with their children. Lucy was invited.

William Browne was thinner and paler than he had been before his arrest. He was in better health than his fellows, however; he had only been in Newgate for three months. Tew had spent nearly five months in the dark, verminous prison; Mary Overton had been six months in Bridewell. All three were in high good spirits, though, laughing and joking, toasting the health of the Army and the release of Richard Overton and John Lilburne, which everyone was sure *must* come soon. Liza, smiling shyly, stayed at her father's side all evening; Mary Overton, little, thin and pock-faced, constantly had her arm about one or another of her three children. The baby that had been taken to prison with her had died there, and the children had been scatter-

168

ed among her friends and neighbours.

Lucy shyly went over to Mrs Overton and introduced herself: she was a little in awe of this fellow-printer who had suffered so much.

'So you're the girl who's been in charge of the press since Will Browne was sent to Newgate!' said Mary. When she smiled, as she did now, her face became almost pretty. She was still only in her early thirties, though she looked older.

'Aye,' agreed Lucy. 'I ... I'd heard you had a press, too, but it was seized.' Mary had, in fact, petitioned Parliament to get it back, on the grounds that it represented 'her present livelihood for her imprisoned husband, herself and three small children' – a piece of insolence to which Parliament hadn't deigned to reply.

'Aye,' agreed Mary with a sigh. 'And I wish I had it back, for I'll have a hard time supporting these babes without it!' She hugged her youngest child, a solemn-faced girl. 'Still, by God's mercy, we're together again!'

'What will you do?' asked Lucy. A small reprehensible corner of her mind wailed that even the place of Tew's *assistant* would be taken.

'I'll look for work bookbinding,' Mary said promptly. 'It pays badly, God knows, but friends and neighbours will help, and the great advantage of it is I can do piecework in my own home. My poor children have suffered enough: I'll be their mother a while and have no more to do with unlicensed printing!' She gave Lucy another smile and added, 'But if ever you need advice on it, that I'll give you freely!'

169

Relieved, Lucy thanked her.

There was to be music after the meal – two of the guests had brought lutes, and Samuel Chidley had a flute. While the consort was tuning its instruments, Browne came over to Lucy, leading Nicholas Tew. He introduced them, then said, as Lucy had feared, 'I've told Nick that you've been minding his press for him.'

'Aye,' Lucy agreed nervously. 'It's safe, sir, and waiting for your return.' She had not entirely succeeded in suppressing her covetous desire to keep the press, but she was determined not to let it show.

'Good to know,' said Tew, then paused to cough. He wiped his face and blinked at her. He was a small man and looked unwell: his dark hair was thin and dull, and there were sores around his mouth. 'I have not the strength to work it, Mistress Wentnor. I mean to leave London for a month or two and stay with my brother in the country to recover my health. I hope you will see fit to continue in place for a little while longer.'

Lucy could scarcely credit her good fortune. 'Aye, sir, I would be glad of it!'

The consort suddenly struck up 'A Light Heart's a Jewel', and they all turned towards the players. Tew smiled, Browne beamed, and at the second verse Lucy joined in, singing with great gusto.

Though Fortune has not lent me wealth,
As she has done to many,
Yet while I've liberty and health,

I'll be as blithe as any!
I'll bear an honest upright heart,
There's none shall prove contrary,
Yet now and then abroad I'll start
And have mine own vagary.

'He's afraid,' Jamie Hudson told her next morning, when she rushed into the barn to tell him the good news. 'He found Newgate not at all to his liking, and he won't resume his work until the Army has triumphed and there's no danger of being sent back there.'

'Jamie, he was *ill*!' she protested, taken aback. 'He really was; he *looked* ill!'

Jamie shrugged. 'Aye, Newgate's no healthy place. But he might have offered to *hire* us, rather than leave London without so much as a glance at his press. He wants to keep his distance from illegal printing.'

About to protest again, Lucy reconsidered. Jamie was right.

'I don't blame him, mind,' Jamie went on. 'Once bitten, twice shy: for my part, I've not set hand to a pistol since Naseby. Only I think we should take it to heart, you and I, that he fears to do what we are engaged upon. We've grown careless of our danger, and if we don't mend that, we'll suffer as he did.'

She made a face, but nodded soberly.

In spite of that, she had hopes that the danger would pass. The crisis seemed to be dying down: the eleven members of Parliament impeached by the Army voluntarily withdrew from the House. The Army set up its headquarters in Reading and

171

continued negotiations, not just with Parliament but with the king as well. The Council of the Army – a body that included the 'Agitators' elected by the men – arrived at proposals for a settlement of government in line with the Army's recent demands: religious toleration, biennial elections for Parliament, a monarchy bounded by law. The document they drew up – *The Heads of the Proposals* – was formally presented to King Charles as the basis on which the Army would restore him to the throne. The Presbyterians in Parliament and the City were terrified that he would accept it.

It was undoubtedly this terror that drove what happened next. It was late in July. Lucy and Jamie were working the press, printing John Lilburne's latest missive, when Ned suddenly appeared in the doorway, flustered and worried. 'Jamie,' he panted, 'have you seen John Wildman?'

Jamie stopped, his bad hand resting on the handle of the press. 'Not this week. I think he's still with the Army.' Wildman was always shuttling back and forth between the Army and Westminster: he was a messenger trusted by both the Council of the Army and by the Independents in Parliament.

Ned shook his head. 'He arrived in London yesterday and stabled his horse with us. I fear he's at Westminster.'

'What's amiss at Westminster?' asked Jamie in alarm.

It seemed that there was a mob there. Ned wasn't certain who it was composed of, but

Reformadoes had been mentioned. The Committee of Safety's forces had been dismissed when the committee itself was disbanded, but the dismissed soldiers had not left London. They could be seen everywhere around the city, angry, resentful and not infrequently drunk. 'What I heard,' Ned said grimly, 'is that they mean to force Parliament to re-form the Committee of Safety. I pray to God that the captain isn't there – or that if he is, he can keep his business quiet!'

Jamie let go of the press and swore. 'I'll go and look for him.' He marched over to the basin of dirty water they kept to rinse off the worst of the ink.

'Nay!' cried Lucy in alarm.

He paused, smiling at her. 'What, you're afraid for me? I'll be in no danger.' He swept his bad hand up and down, indicating his thin, scarred frame. 'I'm villainous enough they'll think me one of their own.'

'But how will you even find him?' asked Lucy. In her mind's eye a mob of Richard Symondses besieged Westminster.

'There are two or three places I might look for him,' replied Jamie. 'It might help him to have someone to back up his account of himself, or guard his back.'

'I'll go with you,' offered Ned.

'Nay, you go back to your tavern,' replied Jamie.

'I'm a sergeant in the trained bands!' Ned objected. His voice had an edge that surprised Lucy.

It surprised Jamie, too, and he gave Ned a

quizzical look. 'I meant no slight to your courage, friend! You know very well that all of us rely on The Whalebone as a place to meet. If you are long gone from it, messages may go astray and plans miscarry.'

Ned grimaced, then nodded. Jamie rinsed his hands, buckled on his sword and set off.

Ned watched him go, then looked at Lucy. 'Come back to The Whalebone with me,' he suggested. 'Whatever the news, we'll get it quickly there – and you know you won't get much printing done alone.'

'I must clean the type and lock up first,' she told him, 'but I'll come join you then, and thank you.'

As she cleaned up, Lucy felt strangely empty. She kept thinking of Jamie, tracing his route in her mind: now he would be on London Wall; now he had come to Smithfield; now he was on Fleet Street; now the Strand. She wished she had offered to go with him – which was *stupid*. What did she expect to do in a mob of Reformadoes? She would have been not a help but a hindrance: a vulnerable, frightened girl whom Jamie would be obliged to protect. If she had offered to go with him, he would certainly have been sensible enough to refuse to take her.

She wished, nonetheless, that she was with him.

With Jamie Hudson? she asked herself incredulously. *That scarred, hulking swill-pot?* To be fair, he wasn't drinking heavily any more – but still, he was a man without a trade or prospects, and hideous to boot.

She locked up and started off to The Whalebone, vexed with Jamie and with herself. The streets were quiet, but the tavern, when she arrived at it, was packed: the clientele had filled both the common rooms and spilled out into the yard. She waved at several people she knew, then pressed on inside to greet Ned.

He was in a huddle with William Walwyn and the soldier Edward Sexby, who was one of the Army Agitators. They all glanced up when Lucy appeared, and Sexby smiled. 'Mistress Wentnor, well met! Thomas Stevens of Southwark is your uncle, is he not?'

'Aye,' she said, taken aback.

Sexby shot a significant look at the other men.

'It's too soon!' protested Walwyn unhappily. 'We know not yet how Parliament will answer!'

Sexby spat. 'It will answer, "Aye, gladly!" like a whore offered gold. But I do not say that we must *act* now, William – only that we must be ready to act if needs be. Mistress Wentnor, will you take me to your uncle's house? I need to speak to him, and I don't know my way about Southwark.'

Lucy looked at Walwyn, who seemed worried; Ned, in contrast, was excited. With some misgiving, she agreed to take Sexby to Southwark. As they started off along Coleman Street, she asked, 'Sir, what's your business with my uncle?'

Sexby gave her a bright smile and a wink. He was a dashing, vigorous man of about thirty, and, like Ned, much inclined to flirt. 'Why, only to ask him how things stand in Southwark, sweet!'

She took several steps. 'You think Parliament will agree to reinstate the Committee of Safety and re-enlist the Reformadoes. The Army won't endure it and will march on London. From Reading it will naturally come first to Southwark.'

He grinned wolfishly. 'Army headquarters are in *Bedford* now, sweet, not Reading! Lord General Fairfax thought our struggle was done and won, and so we all stood down. Old Noll Cromwell, too: he said that anything we got by force, he looked upon it as nothing, and therefore we ought not march on London – which, I have no shame in telling you, some of us were ready to do days ago, and if we had, we would have saved ourselves time and trouble! Your uncle fought in the Southwark militia, did he not?'

'Aye,' said Lucy wretchedly. So: the Army would march, and the Committee of Safety would assemble the Reformadoes and as much of the militias as it could coax or threaten to its aid, and there would be bloodshed. How could men be so rash and wicked as to let it go so far *again*?

'Never fear!' Sexby told her confidently. 'The trained bands won't shed blood to keep their masters in the saddle, and the fat aldermen of the City have no stomach to fight on their own. It will pass over peacefully, you'll see.'

'That's what you've been saying since the mutiny started,' Lucy pointed out.

'Aye, and it was true then, too, only some in

176

Parliament don't credit it.'

'The Reformadoes don't seem to credit it, either.'

Sexby gave a snort of contempt. 'I wonder why that is?'

'What do you mean?'

'Sweet, the Committee of Safety consisted of Denzil Holles and Philip Massey and the like – men who love power, and men who, moreover, have been impeached for misconduct and have good cause to fear what will become of them once they step down. If they've not been whispering promises into some ugly ears to whip this trouble up, then my right hand never held a sword. Never fear: the Reformadoes will soon discover that it takes more than eleven members to sustain a war.' He slapped the hilt of his sword.

She winced, remembering a phrase from a sermon she'd once heard: 'The sword has two edges, but never an eye.' Sexby might be talking sense, but good sense vanished as soon as swords were drawn. She wondered if he was right that the eleven impeached members had whipped up the trouble simply to keep themselves in power.

Sexby smiled at her, as cheerful as Cousin Geoffrey's servant offering bloody murder in a play. 'Soon you'll be printing copies of our new settlement, telling all the people of their liberty!'

'God send it!' she said fervently. 'And God send that it passes over peacefully, as you say. Sir, do you *know* what's happening in Westminster? Were you there this morning?'

He shook his head. 'I meant to go this morning by water, on business of the Army, but when I got to Billingsgate Stairs there were no boats, and a fishwife told me that all the watermen had gone to Westminster to tell Parliament to bring the king to London.'

'The king?' asked Lucy. It was the first she'd heard of that.

'Aye. The poor fools think that once Charles Stuart is back upon the throne, all will miraculously be well again – as though our troubles began with somebody else! As for our enemies, they think that if they have him in their hands, they can make their own settlement and cut us out – and they're as great fools as the watermen, for King Charles has never failed to ruin those who trust him.'

She blinked, again surprised. 'But he's on the point of settling with *us!*'

Sexby spat. 'The grand officers of the Army think so, but I say they're deluded! He treats all our people with contempt, and he's fishing for a better bargain with the Scots. Had you not heard that? The Scots commissioner has called upon him, time and again, and our Grandees are so eager to please him they permit the meetings to go unsupervised. For my part, I'd be rid of him: let him bargain with the Devil in Hell! But others have determined otherwise.' He spat again, then looked back at her with a smirk. 'Enough of him! Tell me true: how did Thomas Stevens get himself such a pretty niece?'

'Through having a sister,' Lucy replied shortly and moved a step away. 'So you don't know

178

what's happening in Westminster?'

'Only what I heard at The Whalebone.'

'Which is? You took me away, sir, before I had any chance to hear the news there.'

Sexby swept a bow. 'My apologies, sweet mistress! There is a mob gathered at Westminster—'

'The Reformadoes?'

'Aye. Them, the watermen and those City apprentices who caused so much havoc earlier this month. The Reformadoes want their pay, but, knowing no other way to get it, and, as I believe, *encouraged* by our enemies, they demand that Parliament reinstate the Committee of Safety. It's an angry business. The mob has beaten certain men of the Army whom they found there, and led them about by the nose; they have already compelled the Lords to pass an ordinance according to their will, and now they stand on the threshold of the House of Commons shouting, "Vote! Vote!" and permitting no one to go in or out. The House cries, "Alack the day!" and sends messengers to Common Council, asking the City to restore order, but Common Council is in no haste to answer.'

She shivered. 'Jamie Hudson went to look for Captain Wildman at Westminster.'

He was silent for a minute. 'That I did not know. Still, John Wildman's no fool: I have no doubt that he'll put his tongue to good use and 'scape danger.'

'And *Jamie?*'

He gave her a sharp look. 'You're afraid for him?'

She felt her face heat. 'He is my assistant, and ... and a friend.'

'He is a very brave and honest man,' said Sexby, 'and no fool, no more than John Wildman. I have no doubt you'll see them both presently, back at The Whalebone with tankards of Ned's good beer in their hands.'

'God send it!' she whispered again, and Sexby smiled.

She showed him the way to Uncle Thomas's shop and introduced them. Thomas was nervous and grew still more nervous when Sexby began asking about the Southwark militia, but she left them there talking and hurried back to The Whalebone.

When she arrived there she found Jamie and Wildman in the yard with tankards in their hands, exactly as Sexby had predicted.

She stopped short, gazing at Jamie with eyes that stung. He was sitting on the cobblestones, leaning against the wall of the tavern and listening to Wildman, who was on his feet recounting something or other. His face was turned towards his captain, and all she could see was the tip of his nose and the dirty hair hanging below the wide brim of his hat – and yet she had no difficulty in recognizing him. The slouching shape of him was intimately familiar and fitted exactly some empty spot within her heart.

Jamie Hudson! she thought in despair. Of all people to fall in love with! *Why?* An ugly, hulking, slow-speaking, awkward ex-blacksmith ex-soldier from Lincolnshire! What on earth was she thinking of? She'd dodged aside from Ned –

a far better match! – the moment she realized he was interested. Jamie would be a disaster. Their joint earnings wouldn't even be enough to pay the rent.

She would simply keep her feelings to herself until they passed. She took a deep breath, then marched over. Jamie looked up as she approached and smiled his slow, twisted half-smile. 'So there you are!' she said briskly.

'Aye.'

'And Captain Wildman, too!'

The captain stopped speaking and looked at her questioningly.

'I'm pleased to see you well, sir,' she said politely. 'We were worried for you.'

'So Jamie told me,' said Wildman. 'I was in no danger. I managed to slip out before they closed off the House. Jamie met me by Westminster Stairs and vouched for me to the watermen keeping watch there.' He grinned. 'It never occurred to them to ask who had vouched for *him!* It is a sad spectacle, though, to see the Mother of Parliaments besieged.' He began speaking again, telling his audience about a fellow-officer's servant who'd been beaten by the mob.

Jamie was still smiling at her, as though he knew what she was feeling. She reminded herself that he couldn't: he was simply pleased to see her. 'Since you've found Captain Wildman safe and well,' she said sharply, 'we should go back to work. If the Committee of Safety's back in the saddle, there'll be more need of our services than ever.'

'Aye,' he agreed and got up.

Eight

The House of Commons did indeed yield to the mob – though not, as Sexby had contemptuously said, as eagerly as a whore offered gold. The members were outraged by the disorder, and the House held out at Westminster all that long July day, capitulating and reinstating the Committee of Safety only at about eight o'clock that evening, and only after the rioters had actually invaded the House and threatened the members. The Independent members were so shaken that they fled from London before the next session.

The result, though, was to leave the Presbyterian majority in complete control of London. The Committee of Safety resumed its place in the Guildhall and at once re-enlisted the Reformadoes who'd put it there. It sent out a summons to the militia, ordering the men to muster on pain of death.

The day after the order went out, Lucy arrived at the barn to find Ned in the loft beside Jamie.

'A lieutenant of my company sent a warning,' Ned explained grimly. 'He said they were coming to arrest me as a ringleader of a mutiny.'

'Of course they were,' said Jamie placidly. 'How many other sergeants distribute pamphlets urging their men not to fight?'

Ned gave a snort. 'I dare not go home now until this is over with. Can you use another hand with the press, Lucy?'

She left the men printing and went out to buy food: with Ned in hiding there would be no dinner at The Whalebone and they would need supplies.

Half the shops were closed, and there were Reformadoes on every other corner. They were full of swagger and bluster, and Lucy was stopped twice – as far as she could tell, for no other reason than that she was a pretty girl. She gave sharp answers to their questions as to who she was and where she was going, slapped a groping hand and screamed loudly when its owner seemed inclined to slap back: she got away shaken but unscathed. She resolved, though, to return to Southwark early and keep to the main roads. She did not want to meet any Reformadoes after dark or in a deserted alleyway.

Next morning there were soldiers on the Southwark side of London Bridge, watching the crowds come and go. They had a prisoner – a young man in a dark coat, who sat in the mud of the street, his hands tied behind his back, his face bloody. Lucy wondered if he was a deserter from the militia. When the soldiers noticed her looking at him they leered at her, and one advanced; she ducked away and hurried on, head down.

There were more soldiers, and several more prisoners, at the other end of the bridge. Yes, definitely deserters from the militia: they were all young men and, by their dress, likely to be freeholders, neither rich nor poor. It suddenly seemed so *strange* that you could take a man prisoner and beat him, and afterwards expect him to fight *for* you rather than against you – but she supposed that showed her lack of understanding. During the war most of the soldiers, on both sides, had entered their respective armies through the press gang.

She stopped at The Whalebone on her way to work, so that she could give Ned news of how his people were. Rather to her surprise she found the tavern open, but when she came in she saw why: there was a knot of Reformadoes sitting in the common room. Nancy was serving them beer; she came over, looking frightened. 'If you've come to see Ned Trebet,' she said loudly, 'he's not here, and I know not where he is!'

Lucy thanked her humbly and went out again. A block down the road, however, she realized she was being followed.

She turned as though to cross the street: pausing to watch for traffic gave her an excuse to get a good look at the men. Reformadoes, undoubtedly: they were armed with sword and pistol and each had a red ribbon tied about his right arm, the just-adopted token of the Committee of Safety. There were two of them. She recognized one from The Whalebone – that scar across the chin had been unmissable, even in the dimly lit tavern – so that probably meant they'd both been there, waiting for someone to ask for Ned. They were talking to one another, but from the angle of their heads she suspected they were watching her. She crossed the street; when she glanced back a dozen steps later, she saw that they had, too.

Her heart sped up. She stopped, then turned around and started back the way she'd come. The two soldiers hesitated, then stood where they were and waited for her.

She crossed the road again. So did they, and advanced to block her path. 'Where are you bound to, pretty?' asked the older one.

She glanced up at him fiercely. 'Sir, I do not know you.'

He smirked. 'I think I know you, though, puss! Let's see those pretty hands.'

She ignored him and turned to cross the street again. He grabbed her arm, jerking her hand upwards to show the ink stains on her fingers. 'Why, Mistress!' he exclaimed in mock-amazement. 'However did you get such dirty hands?'

She tried to jerk her arm free, couldn't, and screamed. The effect was striking: the Reformadoes recoiled in alarm, and everyone within hearing looked round at them. Her very real fear was joined by hope, and she screamed more loudly: 'Help! Let me go! I am an *honest woman*, an *honest woman*, let me go!'

The man who had hold of her slapped her. 'Quiet!' He glared at the passers-by, who were frowning in shocked concern. 'This woman is being arrested for seditious printing!'

'Lies!' she replied. 'Does he look like a Stationer? I beg you, sirs, help me!'

'We're taking her to the Committee of Safety!' protested the Reformado.

'When was a *committee* a court of law?' cried

185

Lucy. 'You lewd rogue! Please, somebody, help me!'

The Reformado swore, put his hand over her mouth, and he and his friend frog-marched her back along the street. They were followed, though – at first just by a couple of the worried passers-by, but those couple drew in more, and by the time they reached the Guildhall they were trailed by a large and indignant crowd.

One of the soldiers turned on the Guildhall steps. 'See?' he shouted. 'We're *arresting* the wench, as I said!'

Lucy didn't hear the crowd's response because by then she was inside.

There was a disconsolate crowd of militia deserters in the foyer, sitting in leg-irons against the wall. The soldiers hesitated, glanced back, then bundled Lucy through into a small committee room panelled in dark oak. Four or five men were seated around a paper-covered table. They all looked up frowning.

'Excuse us, sir,' panted the lead Reformado, 'but the wench made a disturbance, and—'

'Do you think *I* have time to deal with some shrieking slut?' asked one of the gentlemen with distaste. He was about fifty, richly dressed, with heavy-lidded eyes and a long nose.

'You said you wanted Lilburne's press shut down,' replied the soldier. 'This is the wench that works it.'

'Let me go!' cried Lucy. She finally succeeded in jerking her arms out of the soldiers' grasp. As on the other occasions when she'd been attacked, she was so full of outrage that there was little

186

room for fear. 'You have no right to bring me here! You have no warrant, you have no charge...'

'One of Lilburne's get, all right!' said one of the other gentlemen.

'You found the press?' asked the lead gentleman eagerly.

The Reformado hesitated. 'These two rogues seized me on the *street*,' Lucy cried furiously, '– with many foul lewd words, but not one about printing! God knows what they would have done to me if I *hadn't* "made a disturbance"!'

The gentleman turned an indignant glare on the soldiers. 'Sir!' protested the Reformado. 'We waited at The Whalebone and followed her, but she spied us, so we thought it best to take her up before she alerted her friends. She matches the description, and she has ink on her hands.'

'Well, girl?' asked the gentleman. 'Where is the press?'

'How should I answer such a question? You have no right even to *ask* it! I'm an honest maid, seized in the street by two great rogues, and yet *I* am to be questioned, and not them? You had no cause to take me up: I was doing nothing amiss, *nothing!*'

'Where is the press, girl?' repeated the gentleman impatiently. 'If you will not answer, you must go to Bridewell.'

'I must go to Bridewell for having *ink* on my hands?' she cried incredulously. 'Then your clerk there must needs go to Newgate!'

One of the men smiled at that, but the lead gentleman was annoyed. 'You proud, saucy strumpet! This is easily settled: what's your name, woman?'

'Lucy Wentnor, sir, of *Southwark*, sir – which, sir, is no concern of the Committee of Safety of *London*!'

'Denzil...' began the gentleman who'd smiled. The other waved him aside. Lucy stared hard. The only Denzil she'd ever heard of was Denzil Holles, the leader of the extreme Presbyterians, the chief of the eleven impeached members of Parliament. She'd heard that he'd withdrawn: now, it seemed, he was back again.

'That was the name, I think,' said Holles. 'This *is* the woman said to be working the illegal press.'

'Said by whom?' asked Lucy at once. 'And you *think* that was the name? You would send an honest maid to *Bridewell,* without even checking that you remember rightly?'

'Honest!' spat Holles in contempt. 'No more honest than a maid! This wicked impudent disputation is a harlot's trick!'

'Indeed it is *not*, sir! If a maid won't resist when a man tries to dishonour her, then indeed she *will* be a harlot, very quickly!'

'Dishonour!' exclaimed Holles in disgust. 'You flatter yourself, wench!'

'You would lock me up with whores!' replied Lucy. 'For having *ink* upon my hands! Is that honourable treatment?'

'Denzil...' said the other gentleman again.

'That damned press is behind half our problems in London!' exploded Holles. 'Every other militia deserter we take has one of its impudent sheets in his pocket, and the rest have one at home!'

'But you've no certainty that she's even the right woman!' protested the other man.

Holles grimaced. 'She's one of Lilburne's get! It was plain the moment she opened her mouth! But very well! Weller, check that you have the right wench and *then* send her to Bridewell.'

The older Reformado took Lucy's arm again. '*How* is he to check?' she asked. 'What about a *trial,* Mr Holles; what about *evidence* and the process of *law*? Have you never heard of such things?'

'You, wench, have evidently heard too much of them, from your friend John Lilburne!' snapped Holles. 'This is what comes of it: the lowest of the people prating of law while they strain to get the power in their own hands and lord it over their betters!'

'I have never even met John Lilburne,' said Lucy loudly, 'but I wonder, sir, that you should *boast* of caring less for the law than he!'

Holles got to his feet. 'Take her to Bridewell!' he roared.

The two Reformadoes pulled Lucy out of the committee room.

The deserters in the foyer were all sitting up straight: the door had been left ajar and they had heard everything. When Lucy appeared between her two captors, one of them applauded and cried, 'Brave girl!' The others took it up, and she walked out of the Guildhall to a chorus of cheers, her head held high.

That triumph helped to sustain her during the

189

three days she spent in Bridewell.

It was a foul place: crowded, noisy and reeking of overburdened privy and damp. Most of the female inmates were whores, which added shame to the wretchedness. Lucy spent her first couple of hours there in tears, imagining what her mother would have said.

Work helped, though. Bridewell was officially a 'house of correction' rather than a prison, and the distinction meant that the inmates were required to work, the men shaving wood and the women spinning and sewing. Lucy was assigned to spin thread in a workroom under the watchful eye of a warden. The work was mindless and soothing, and the young women spinning beside her, whores or not, were friendly and helpful. By the time Jamie and Uncle Thomas came to visit her that evening, she was calm and able to put a brave face on it.

It was just as well, because Thomas was distraught: he embraced her, choked an apology, then stood wringing his hands and lamenting that he'd ever permitted her to risk herself. Jamie was much more helpful.

'Take heart,' he told her seriously. 'You'll not be here long.'

'Stark contrary to the law!' choked Thomas. 'Worse even than poor Mrs Overton: they *caught* her with the pamphlets!'

Jamie gave Thomas a pained look: there was a warden supervising the meeting. He said emphatically, 'The Army will soon be in London.'

The warden asked indignantly, 'Here, fellow! What do you know of the Army?'

'Only what any man knows, that has his wits about him,' replied Jamie levelly. 'The Army is on the march, and if you think the militia will fight it, you're blind and deaf, while if you think the Reformadoes can hold the city alone, you're a fool. Soon the Committee of Safety will be gone. What will you say to the new authorities if they ask for the warrant committing this gentlewoman to your charge?'

'How did you know I was here?' Lucy asked him.

He smiled. 'You caused enough stir. Did you really spit in Denzil Holles's face and tell him he cared nothing for the law?'

'Indeed I did not *spit*!' she said indignantly. 'The other, aye, I did.'

The smile broadened. 'And I suppose it never even *occurred* to you to buy your safety by naming friends?'

'Nay!' she said, startled. Give away the press, her livelihood and freedom? Give away Ned, too, come to that: if he was wanted as ringleader of a mutiny, he could be shot. 'Of course not!'

'You're a bright light in this dark world, Lucy Wentnor.'

Jamie's words about the warrant had evidently struck home: after he and Thomas left, the warden was subdued. Lucy had been assigned a foul mattress in the main barracks, but suddenly a chamber was found for her, comparatively clean and shared with only three other women. That might have been the result of a bribe – Thomas must have supplied one to be allowed the visit – but what happened the next morning was not.

191

She was brought before the Governor of the prison, who asked about her meeting with the Committee of Safety. He was unhappy with her replies.

'That I'd been sent to him without warrant or charge would not have troubled him,' she told her friends later, 'except that he feared that those who sent me were not sat firm in the saddle.'

Over the next two days nothing happened to reassure the Governor of Bridewell. The members of Parliament who'd fled *from* London turned out to have fled *to* the Army: since they included the Speakers of both Houses, their presence there seriously undermined the Committee's claim to represent the only legitimate authority. Meanwhile, the Reformadoes were becoming increasingly unruly and increasingly unpopular throughout the city. The borough of Southwark – urged on by Uncle Thomas and his friends – publicly dissented from the City of London. The Committee of Safety remained as belligerent as ever, but London's Common Council, with its support fracturing fast, discovered, as Edward Sexby had predicted, that it had no stomach for fighting against the odds. A delegation was sent to Lord General Fairfax, asking for peace.

The Army was still some two days' march from London, but the gesture was enough to decide the Governor of Bridewell. Lucy was shown the gate and told that, since she had not been lawfully committed, she was free to leave.

It was about noon. Lucy stood outside the gate of Bridewell and tilted her face up towards the hazy sunlight. She was exhausted, filthy and crawling with lice from the prison, but all of that was swallowed up by incredulous triumph. The Committee of Safety, the gentlemen of Parliament – they were going to lose, and *her side* was going to win!

She thought about going straight to her friends, but she was worried that she might be followed, and, anyway, she was desperate to wash and change her shift. She went home.

Uncle Thomas was out, talking to his Southwark friends. Aunt Agnes was sitting outside the shop, darning socks. When Lucy appeared she gave her a look of disgust. 'So,' she said bitterly, 'back you come like a bad penny, with the stink of Bridewell on you!'

Lucy hadn't expected her aunt to be *pleased* to see her, but this was worse than she'd anticipated and it left her speechless.

'Were it mine to say,' Agnes continued, in low-voiced malevolence, 'I'd never let you bring that foul smell into my good house. But you're the apple of Tom's eye, and he'll hear no word against you, so all I ask is that you keep quiet about where you've been. I've told my gentle-woman-lodger and the neighbours that you've been visiting a sick friend, and I trust you'll confirm it!'

Still unable to speak, Lucy ducked her head and went on into the house, walking wide around Agnes as though she were a dangerous dog. Susan was in the kitchen; when she saw Lucy she dropped the dough she was kneading and rushed over. 'Oh, Lucy!' she cried, hugging her. 'We've been so worried for you!'

Lucy burst into tears and hugged her back. She let the maid's affection soothe her and sat in the kitchen drinking a hot posset, waiting while the big kettle heated water for washing. Mrs Penington's maid came in just as the water boiled, and Lucy agreed that, yes, her sick friend was getting better. When Uncle Thomas came in, she welcomed his exclamations of delight and tried to forget about Agnes.

Three days later, Lucy stood watching beside Uncle Thomas as the New Model Army marched through Southwark and across London Bridge.

Southwark had invited them and had opened the city gates. The Committee of Safety had broken in dismay, and its members fled abroad or went into hiding.

Lucy was still nervous of the soldiers, but she had to admit that they appeared well-disciplined. They marched in neat ranks: the horsemen four, the infantry six abreast, each man with a sprig of laurel in his hat. After the vanguard came the Independent members of Parliament, returning in triumph, led by the two Speakers in a grand coach. Behind them came an open carriage, drawn by six matched bays, which was greeted with cheers. A dark-haired man sat there with two women. Several men in the crowd took their hats off. 'That's Black Tom!' one informed Lucy and Thomas.

She stared at the man with interest: so that was the much-discussed Lord General Fairfax? He looked tired and ill, though he smiled and waved at the crowd. 'Who are the gentlewomen?' she asked.

The man hesitated. 'His wife and ... and her maid.'

There couldn't be much question which was which: one of the women was an elegant aristocrat, at ease in her fine gown; the other was stout, red-faced and nervous in a clumsy imitation of it. Lucy later learned, however, that while the elegant woman was indeed Lady Fairfax, the awkward 'maid' was actually Mrs Cromwell.

The carriage rolled by. Another troop of horse followed it; at their head rode a middle-aged man in half armour. The crowd cheered again: 'Cromwell! Cromwell and the Ironsides!'

Cromwell looked disconcertingly *ordinary*: without the armour he might have been any solid, red-faced farmer come to spend a day in London. The iron ranks of his horsemen followed him, though, row after row of buff coats and hats decorated with sprigs of laurel, an endless beating of hooves on cobblestones. They passed under the decaying heads displayed above London Bridge and racketed on, on, into the City. Lucy had expected to feel triumph, despite her fear of the soldiers, but there was something terrifying and relentless about their progress, and she couldn't help remembering that this was a triumph of the sword.

To the citizens' relief, Lord Fairfax did not garrison the City: the Army departed from London again, peacefully and in good order. War had been avoided, and the right side had won. On her way to the next meeting at The Whalebone, two days later, Lucy wondered why she still felt so much disquiet.

She had not crossed the Thames since being freed from Bridewell, and the reformers' council hadn't met for several weeks because of the disturbances. When Lucy and Thomas arrived, Ned hurried over grinning. He flung his arms around Lucy and kissed her.

'God bless you!' he said, while she gasped and gaped at him, torn between pleasure and alarm. 'I've not had a chance to thank you, Luce. You went to Bridewell for me!'

For the press! she thought, but it seemed churlish to say so. She gave Ned a flustered smile and nervously checked that her hair was tucked safely under her coif. Uncle Thomas stared at Ned, equally flustered, evidently wondering if he ought to object to a young man's kissing his niece.

'I wished to visit you there,' Ned went on, 'but Jamie said I would waste your sacrifice if I were taken.'

'Aye,' she agreed. 'It was no great sacrifice, Ned. I was only in the place three days!'

Someone coughed, and she looked round and saw Nicholas Tew. He looked alarmingly healthy, in a new coat with his hair tied back. 'Mistress Wentnor!' he said, extending his hand. 'God keep you well! I've heard of your brave stand and I must thank you for it. Your courage is much above your sex.'

Lucy wasn't sure how to respond to this: she

didn't think she'd been particularly brave and she disliked the assumption that courage was a purely masculine virtue. The last thing she wanted to do, though, was offend Mr Tew, so she shook his hand and smiled.

'I am glad to say you will be spared such dangers in future,' Tew went on. 'Now that I've recovered my health I can take up my trade again. I can even bring my press back to its right home and soon, God willing, print lawfully!'

Lucy felt her smile congeal. Her hands searched nervously for her apron, but, this being an evening meeting, she wasn't wearing it. 'Sir? You'll shift the press back into the City?'

'Aye,' said Tew happily. 'Tomorrow or perhaps the day after.'

'And ... and will you need any help with it?'

He frowned at her. 'You seem troubled, Mistress.'

She muttered something incoherent. Surely she couldn't be dismissed from her job so quickly, with such complacent goodwill?

Tew glanced at Thomas uncertainly. 'I hope the loss of the girl's wages won't cause any hardship to your household, Master Stevens.'

Thomas grimaced uncomfortably. 'Ah, not *as such*. That is ... of course I can provide for my sister's child! It's only that this is sudden – and Lucy's a good, sweet girl who's taken great delight in paying her keep.'

'Well, then, I am sorry to deprive you of that pleasure, Mistress Wentnor,' said Tew earnestly. 'I fear that I need no more help than my own household can supply, but, if you like, I can ask among my acquaintance in the trade to see if any of them need assistance, and recommend you highly to all who do.'

'Oh...' Lucy's heart gave a lurch of hope. 'Aye. Please.'

Someone banged on a table as a signal for the meeting to begin. It occurred to her that this would be the last meeting she attended: in future, it would be Tew in charge of the press. For the past few months she had been part of this company, a comrade-in-arms; now she must go back to being just Thomas Stevens' niece. She took her seat, pressing her hands together to stop them from shaking and struggling not to cry.

Stop it! she told herself. She had known all along that the press belonged to Nicholas Tew. Perhaps he *had* fled London when it was most dangerous and only returned now that it was safe again, but he had spent five months in Newgate. That surely beat anything she'd earned by three days in Bridewell! As for her, she'd done very well out of Tew's press: she'd acquired all the skills needed in a printer. She would only drop back into dependency if she gave up; if Tew kept his promise and recommended her among his printer friends, she need not fear for her future.

She abruptly thought to wonder what *Jamie* would do now. He had no chance of another job printing: no one would take on a maimed printer, a man who could never set type or stitch up a pamphlet. He was unlikely to be offered anything other than menial work. He would probably turn to drink again.

She began to fidget, unable to pay attention to

what what was being said. Thomas gave her a look of surprise, and Ned, still nearby, one of concern. She forced herself to sit still and listen.

It was bad news, confirming her sense of disquiet. According to William Walwyn, the triumph of the Army was not turning out to be the great victory they'd all expected. The eleven impeached members might have disappeared, but the rest of the old Parliament remained, as corrupt and intransigent as ever. The Army's grand officers were pinning their hopes on a settlement with the king, but King Charles had rejected their proposals out of hand, and the Grandees were looking for compromises that would appeal to him. There were rumours that the king had offered to make Fairfax a duke and Cromwell an earl if they sold out.

Edward Sexby, the Army Agitator, stood and spoke vehemently, protesting that *The Heads of the Proposals* had been too generous to the king even in the first draft; to make any more concessions would be a betrayal of everything the Army had fought for. He invited his friends to join the Agitators in drafting an alternative settlement. 'Lord General Fairfax went to the Tower today,' he continued. 'He asked to see the Great Charter, saying that it was what we had fought for, but he never spared a thought for our friend John Lilburne, imprisoned in that very Tower, contrary to that same Great Charter. I take that to be a more honest measure of his commitment to the people's rights than his fine words! My friends, I have no doubt that the Grandees, like Parliament and like the king, would much prefer it if we kept silent and let them dispose matters to their own advantage, but I say, if our voice is not heard now, we will lose it and be dumb ever after!'

The others cheered. Walwyn rose and proposed setting up a committee to work with the Agitators; the motion was seconded and approved immediately, and Walwyn was appointed to it, along with Wildman and a couple of others. Then Tew rose and announced that he was once more in charge of 'the only free press in London', and that he was willing and able to print anything the council wished to publish. There was more applause; the meeting welcomed Tew back and voted him congratulations on his recovery.

William Walwyn looked towards Lucy with a smile. 'We should also take time to thank Mistress Wentnor for her diligence in Mr Tew's absence! It is a hard thing for a young woman to take up a burden that has crushed brave men, but she never failed us. I think we've all heard of her courageous defiance of the Committee of Safety. I move a vote of thanks to Mistress Wentnor!'

'Seconded!' cried Ned, jumping to his feet.

There was applause and cheers. Lucy got to her feet and curtsied, trying to crush the angry thought that she'd much rather have the job than the thanks.

The meeting, as always, closed with a prayer. As soon as it ended, Lucy turned to her uncle. 'Uncle Thomas,' she whispered, 'I should like to speak to Jamie Hudson, to warn him that we are out of work. Could you help me?'

Thomas was already shaking his head. 'It's late now, child. The city gate will be shut. You will have to speak to him in the morning.'

She did not sleep much that night and the next morning she rose before dawn. London Bridge was eerily still in the first grey light as she crossed it, the whole great span empty of movement. Billingsgate fish market was already busy, though, and as she walked north the light grew and more and more people appeared on the streets, so that by the time she reached Bishopsgate, London was itself again. She made her way out of the city among a jostling crowd and picked her way along Moorfields to the barn.

The place was quiet and apparently empty when she unlocked the door. Nothing had been printed since the Army arrived in London, and the drying lines were empty: the press stood alone in the dim light of the interior. 'Jamie?' Lucy called, looking up towards the loft where he normally slept.

There was no reply. She went to the ladder, kilted her skirts, and climbed up. 'Jamie?'

Still no answer, but when she advanced there was a groan from under the straw. She squatted down and brushed some straw away, revealing a coated back. 'Jamie? Are you ill?'

Another groan; Jamie snugged his face against his arm. 'Let me alone, wench!'

'You *are* ill!' She touched his cheek, but it was no hotter than her hand.

'I am most vilely hung-over,' replied Jamie shortly. 'I said, let me be!'

She sat back on her heels and surveyed him: now that he mentioned it, she could smell the brandy. 'You've heard that Tew's back and means to take the press,' she concluded.

He lifted his head and surveyed her with a bloodshot eye. 'Aye. So you've heard, too.'

'He was at the meeting last night. Jamie, drinking won't help...'

'There you're wrong, for it helped a deal!'

'Oh? And it's helping this morning, too, is it? I'll fetch you water, and then we'll talk over what you are to do.'

'God have mercy!'

'Amen!' agreed Lucy tartly, and went back down the ladder.

When she came back with the water, he hadn't moved, but at the sound of her footsteps he squinted up at her resentfully. 'Sit up!' she ordered.

'And if I won't?'

She tipped the flask, dousing him with cold water. He sputtered and flung up a hand to fend it off.

'This is yet half full,' Lucy said sternly, shaking the flask. 'Will you drink it, or will I throw it over you and go fetch more?'

He groaned and sat up. 'You're a hard master, Lucy Wentnor.' He took the flask of water, though, and drank of it. She sat down beside him.

'I was thinking of you all last night,' she told him. 'And it came to me that there's no reason you shouldn't go back to being a blacksmith.'

He made a noise of derision and held up his

maimed right hand. She seized it. His whole body gave a jerk of astonishment and he stared at her, his single eye wide.

'It's not that bad,' she told him, turning the hand over with her own. 'Look, your whole palm is unhurt, and here, you still have the meat of the thumb...' It trembled, and she closed her fingers about it. The scar was rough and warm. 'There are plenty of men in the city with worse, Jamie! Sailors and shopkeepers aplenty do fine with nothing but a hook, and you have *most* of your hand intact!'

'Smithing needs two hands!' he replied. He took his hand away.

'Indeed it does *not!*' she replied. 'Not two *skilled* hands, anygate. Every smith I've ever seen uses one hand to do nothing more than hold the tongs or pump the bellows. Surely with use your left hand could manage a hammer as well as the right ever did!'

'You know nothing of it!'

'I know this much: it's *easier* to wallow in misery and drink than take up your life again!'

'How can I even hold the tongs with *this*?' Again he showed her the hand as though he expected her to recoil from it. 'I've not enough strength in these two fingers to hold anything more than a tankard! The day we met, you called it a claw, and so it is!'

She remembered saying it; remembered how he'd lowered his head after. She'd taken that as a prelude to attack, which now seemed to her wilfully blind: he'd been hurt and shamed. His rudeness had been nothing more than bluster, a defence against a pretty girl's horror. 'The day we met, Jamie Hudson,' she said tartly, 'you called me "puss" and thought to be master at my own press, if you recall! But as to how you might hold the tongs, surely you could fit some sort of brace about your wrist...' – she caught the hand again and circled the wrist with her fingers – '...with a false thumb, here, see?' She lifted her own small thumb where his should have been. 'Curved, perhaps, and padded, so that it won't slip. *You're* the smith! What would *you* make?'

He stared down at her fingers curled about his mutilation. She could feel the pulse in his wrist, beating against her palm. The urge to lean forward and kiss him was suddenly so strong it frightened her. She let go.

'It would take time to master the skill over again,' she admitted. 'You'd need some master smith willing to take you on, but you have *friends* who can help you. I have a little money saved, and I'm sure Captain Wildman would help, too, and Ned...'

Jamie scowled. 'I'll not take your savings! You're losing your place, too!'

'Aye, but I hope I may get another one soon.'

He gave her an angry look. 'Ned's spoken, then?'

She stared. 'What do you mean?'

He was confused. 'What did *you* mean, speaking of "another place"?'

'Only that Mr Tew has offered to recommend me to all his acquaintance. What, do you think I hope to marry Ned?'

'Don't you?'

'Indeed not!' She glared. 'I told him honestly that I'm all but dowerless. I'd not trick any man into marriage!'

He stared at her. 'I think,' he said slowly, 'that Ned may not be so set upon a dowry as you suppose.'

She started to tell him that he was wrong, then remembered how Ned had kissed her the evening before. It should have occurred to her to wonder whether he would kiss her so publicly if he was completely unwilling to be seen as her suitor.

'You do not seem as happy at the thought as I would expect,' remarked Jamie.

'The prospect of explaining to him that I've no maidenhead either doesn't please me, no!'

'*That* he's guessed already.'

'*What*? You told him that? You promi—'

'Nay, nay, nay! I told him nothing. When we were burying Symonds and his friend, though, he asked John and me whether we thought they'd forced you. We both claimed ignorance, but the question knew its answer. He spat on the bodies before we covered them, and wished them all the pains of Hell.'

Lucy was dismayed. She twisted her hands into her apron.

'And still you are not pleased!' said Jamie.

'I've no wish to marry Ned Trebet,' she admitted. 'I like him well, but I've no wish to be mistress of The Whalebone Tavern. I like printing much better.' Her heart added, in bitter secret, *I like you better, too, Jamie. If I'd never met you, perhaps I'd be better pleased with Ned.*

205

There was a silence, and then Jamie said gently, 'You're afraid of men, are you?'

She shrugged: let him think that. 'We were not speaking of me,' she said determinedly. 'We were speaking of you, and I said I see no reason why you should not become a blacksmith again. I'll not let you sink into some swill-pot wallow, Jamie: I'll nag you day and night if you try!'

There was another silence. 'I'd rather sight along a pistol again than suffer that!' said Jamie at last. 'Aye, very well. I'll ask John's help to find a place with a blacksmith.'

Again she almost kissed him; she even leaned forward a little. He had looked away, though, lowering his head so that his hair fell over his blinded eye. He stared down at his bad hand, bringing the good one across to circle the wrist as she had, and folded down his two remaining fingers as though to make a fist.

Nine

Lucy's new employer arrived the very next day.

She'd decided to make the best of unemployment by finishing her gown, which had been half done for a long time now. She'd completed only one sleeve, however, when Uncle Thomas came in from the shop, escorting a stranger.

'This is my niece, sir,' Thomas said seriously.

'Lucy, this is Mr Gilbert Mabbot, a friend of Mr Tew.'

Mr Mabbot was a big, pock-faced man somewhere under thirty; he wore a plain dark coat, none too clean, and had a sword by his side. He smiled broadly at Lucy, displaying crooked teeth. 'Mistress Wentnor! You must be the prettiest typesetter in all London!'

Lucy set aside her lapful of fabric and stood, filled with hope and distrust. 'You're a friend of Mr Tew, sir?'

'More acquaintance than friend,' admitted Mabbot, 'but certainly I esteem the gentleman. I need a typesetter, and my need is like to grow. I hope soon to start a newsbook of my own, though at present I'm but junior partner on *A Perfect Diurnall*. Nick Tew said you'd managed his press by yourself all the while he was in Newgate, that you kept good clear accounts and that you could manage all the business of supply.'

'Aye, sir,' Lucy agreed. 'I'm glad he was pleased with what I did.' *A Perfect Diurnall*! The most popular newsbook in London!

'Nick said that your wages were sixpence a day.'

Lucy almost agreed, but something stopped her. Mabbot had appeared very quickly, and he'd sought her out at home, rather than sending her a message through Tew. She might be eager, but so was he.

'Sixpence *and* my dinner, sir,' she said impulsively. 'If I must buy food at an ordinary, I'll need another threepence.'

207

Mabbot grimaced. 'Ah, I feared it was too good to be true! But how can I pay an unschooled countrygirl ninepence a day, when she must work with printers who served out a full apprenticeship before they earned so much? What would you say, Mistress, to a soldier's wage?'

That, notoriously, was eightpence a day, and Lucy had no intention of paying threepence to eat at an ordinary, not when she could fix herself something at home much more cheaply. She pretended to ponder the offer, already determined to accept it.

'Let it be understood,' Uncle Thomas broke in anxiously, 'that my niece is under no necessity of going out to work for strangers. She first took up printing to help my friend Will Browne after Mr Tew's arrest. It shames me that she ... that she ran into such danger under the Committee of Safety, and that ... that is, I am determined that she will suffer no more insolent abuse!'

Mabbot smirked. 'I can promise you, sir, that your niece will suffer no such difficulties as she did under that ill-famed Committee. Everything I cause to be printed will be properly licensed – for I myself am to become Licensor of the Press!'

'You?' said Uncle Thomas, startled.

Mabbot bowed. 'The Army has been unhappy with the persecution meted out to its supporters in London. Mr Rushworth, the Secretary to the Army, whom I had the honour of assisting, kindly put forward my name to Lord General Fairfax, who has forwarded it to the authorities here in London. So, Mistress Wentnor, if you come work for me, you need not fear the law! How say you?'

'Very well,' said Lucy, her heart singing. 'Eightpence a day. When do you want me to start?'

Mr Mabbot was keen: he wanted her to start on Monday, the very next working day, even though his proposed newsbook was still nothing more than a hope. 'A spell on the *Diurnall* will teach you the ways of newsbooks,' he told her, 'and, God He knows, we need another type-setter. My partner and I have just bought a second press, but it sits idle half the day waiting for a forme to be made ready for it.' He paused, then added, 'Umm ... you should say nothing of the new newsbook to the other printworkers. Keep mum about it to my partner, Sam Pecke, too – to him *especially*. I, uh, have yet to begin this enterprise, so there's no need to spread gossip.'

She wondered uneasily why gossip would be so bad. It seemed likely that Mr Pecke would be unhappy to discover that his junior partner was setting up in competition.

She had dinner at Thomas's house that day, which was rare enough to make her feel that it must be the Sabbath, even though it was only Saturday. Thomas wavered anxiously between congratulating Lucy on her new job and worry-ing about it. Agnes ate in silence, with an occa-sional disgusted glance at her husband. When the meal was finished Lucy collected the dishes and carried them into the kitchen – Susan had

209

finished her own dinner and gone to the market. Agnes followed her.

'You're to get another shilling a week,' said Agnes.

Lucy could guess where this was heading. 'Aye.' She picked up the kettle and started to fill it with water from the jug.

'Look at me when I speak to you, miss!' Agnes ordered.

Lucy set down the kettle and looked at her.

'I remitted you one shilling of the two you owed me every week. Now you can pay it again.'

Lucy raised her eyebrows. 'I was glad to pay two shillings a week into the household account, Aunt, but it was no debt I *owed* to you. You remitted one because you didn't want me at your table at supper-time, and there's no buying supper in the City for less than tuppence.'

'You insolent little slut!' spat Agnes. 'I'll have that shilling!'

Lucy set her teeth. Why should she keep paying the better part of her earnings to Agnes? All the money she'd paid over hitherto hadn't won her any goodwill; in fact, Agnes disliked her more than ever. 'Am I welcome at your table for supper, then?' She asked it to make a point, but even as she did it occurred to her that she *might* be, now that she would be printing a respectable newsbook instead of seditious pamphlets.

Agnes, however, glowered. 'We both know well that you much prefer merry-making with your scandalous friends!'

'They are *not* scandalous! And you know as well as I that I would not have supped in the City if I'd been welcome at home!'

'You proud—'

'I bore it meekly, Aunt! I made no complaint to my uncle – and I might have, you know it! I've wanted only to live peaceably here—'

'Hah! You fell in with that vile seditious rabble of Tom's the very night you first came through my door!'

'*Your husband's friends,* you mean?'

'They were never *my* friends!' Agnes snarled, then stopped, because Thomas, drawn by the rising voices, was standing in the doorway.

Thomas looked from one of them to the other, puzzled and alarmed. Agnes drew a deep breath and pushed past him, leaving the room. Thomas cast a look of appeal at Lucy.

She let out her breath unsteadily and shook her head. 'Money,' she said. 'She wants my extra shilling.'

'Oh,' said Thomas miserably. He hadn't said anything when Lucy was excluded from the supper table. She was certain that he understood what had happened, but he had never asked about it. If he'd asserted his authority as head of the household, Agnes would have made him pay for it.

'I ... I might need it for someone else,' said Lucy – and only then realized that she wanted it for Jamie. He would need help, even if he did manage to get a master blacksmith to take him on. He was unlikely to get any wages while he struggled to relearn his skills. A shilling a week wouldn't be enough for him to live on, but it would be *something*.

'Someone else?' asked Thomas puzzled.

'Jamie Hudson, my assistant,' she admitted. 'He lost his place, too. I think Captain Wildman is finding him another, but I'm troubled for him.'

Thomas looked uncertain. 'I remember the man, of course. When you were taken to Bridewell he comforted me. But, Lucy, he's a poor ugly cripple! He'll not find it easy to get another place, with that face and that hand.'

'I *know*!' she protested. 'I'm not ... not proposing to *love* him! But he was an honest friend to me, and now what will he do? How can I *abandon* him, when I have good fortune and he has nothing?'

There was a silence. 'Well.' Thomas cleared his throat. 'Agnes has no *right* to your money.'

He was willing to quarrel with Agnes for her – but, then, he always had been, if he was pushed by a direct appeal or by public embarrassment. He knew that there would be a cost to pay, though, and so did Lucy. She imagined her aunt's hatred seeping through the house like a poisonous mist. 'I'll try to find out if he needs it,' she said wretchedly. 'If he doesn't, I'll give my aunt ... *some* of it.'

Sunday, though, had to be spent in church and in visiting Hannah, who was now pregnant and more anxious than ever: there was no chance to ask after Jamie. On Monday morning Lucy put on her new, hastily-completed gown and went to work.

She'd visited the *Diurnall*'s printers when she was trying to persuade Samuel Pecke to publish her story about the Reformadoes at The Whalebone, so she had no trouble finding the shop. It was at the corner of Ludgate and Fleet Street, a shorter walk than to Bishopsgate. It felt strange to walk into a printshop that had a sign above the door – 'Jn Bourne & Son, Printers' – and printing presses standing there where anyone could see them. It was both a relief and, oddly, a disappointment.

In the shop two men were working a battered press; they paused when Lucy came in, and the elder of the two came over. 'Mistress?'

'I am Lucy Wentnor,' she told him. 'Mr Mabbot has hired me to set type.'

The man gave her a hard look, then spat. 'Aye, so he told us. Well. Yonder's the new press. The sorts for it are in the case there.' He indicated a second press of fresh unscarred oak, then went back to work.

She hesitated, surprised and hurt, glancing from him to the new press. He ignored her and worked steadily with his partner. She grimaced, went to the press and began setting out the compositor's frame and the type on the table beside it. When she was ready to start setting, she went back to her fellow-workers. The older man gave her another hard look and pointed wordlessly at one of the freshly inked sheets he'd just printed. He ignored her thanks. She stood staring at him a moment, then gave up and took the printed sheet back to her table to set type to match.

Over the course of the day she gathered that the older man was John Bourne; the younger one – also called John – was '& Son'. There was also a Mrs Bourne, the wife of the younger man, a sullen woman with a scowl, who emerged from the house occasionally to ink, then darted back again. All three Bournes made it clear that they were much displeased to have a strange woman intruded upon them. Samuel Pecke, when he turned up mid-morning, was – unfortunately – delighted.

'Why, it's the pretty Leicestershire dairy-maid!' he cried, and tried to kiss her. She jerked away, glaring, and he laughed. 'Nay, come, sweet, give us a kiss! We're to be workmates!'

'When I was a dairymaid I worked with cows,' she told him. 'I never kissed them, and they had sweeter breath!'

Pecke tittered and smote himself above the heart. She saw immediately that 'No' was not an answer he took seriously, and resolved never to be alone with him.

Learning how to print a newsbook was compensation for the company. *A Perfect Diurnall* had been growing for nearly eight years, and its sales now exceeded a thousand copies a week. This was more than could be printed on a single press during one day: hence the second press. Like all newsbooks, it was printed in stages, each day's news being set and printed consecutively. Pecke and Mabbot assembled the news from their various informants, and every morning one or the other or both of them would deliver a handwritten sheet to John Bourne, who was charged with setting and printing it. The front cover and final page were always done last, and if a lot of news came in late, it had to be packed in by using smaller type. The *Diurnall* came out on Monday, but since Sabbath-breaking was unlawful it was finished off on Saturday night, which also gave the sheets time to dry.

The printing itself was little different from what Lucy had been doing before. The pace was a bit faster, and she was no longer free to pause to catch her breath when she wanted to, but, on the other hand, she no longer had to haul loads of paper or ink across London or fear discovery by the Stationers' agents. The thing she most enjoyed about the work, though, was getting the news as soon as it came in – including the items that didn't make it into print. Pecke was full of entertaining anecdotes, good company as long as she kept him at arm's length.

The Bournes were another matter. They didn't speak to her, and at dinner-time they disappeared into their kitchen, pointedly leaving her to eat alone in the shop. (Samuel Pecke invited her to join him, but she declined.) She guessed that Mabbot had hired her without consulting them, and possibly in place of someone they'd chosen. She told herself that it was natural that they should resent this, but their silent hostility was depressing.

The first two days at work she was too busy learning or too tired to do anything about asking after Jamie. The third day, however, she walked out of the shop at dinner-time and went to visit The Whalebone.

She met Ned in the common room. 'Lucy!' he cried, setting down a handful of tankards and catching her in his arms. 'In a fine new gown! Where have you been?'

'I've a new job,' she told him, extricating herself with a smile. 'I'm working on *A Perfect Diurnall*. I can't stay long, but I wanted to see my friends.'

'*A Perfect Diurnall*?' Ned asked in alarm. 'What, with that whoremongering rogue Pecke?'

She was taken aback: previously Ned had been happy to take advantage of Pecke's susceptibility to pretty women. 'Aye,' she said, 'he writes much of it. I was hired by his partner, though, a Mr Mabbot, a friend of Mr Tew – and, anygate, I see far more of the printers than the writers.'

'I'm surprised your uncle permitted this!' said Ned, frowning.

'It's honest work!' she exclaimed, surprised and hurt. 'It's even *lawful!* Mr Mabbot is Licensor of the Press!'

Ned stood silent a moment, still frowning. She suddenly understood that he hadn't expected her to get another job. He'd thought she would go to live quietly with her uncle, and that he could, if he made up his mind to, pluck a grateful bride from her humble dependence. 'Is your uncle so short of money that he must hire you out to strangers?' he asked resentfully.

'Ned,' she said impatiently, '*you* were a stranger when I began printing!'

'Your *uncle* knew me,' Ned replied, 'and you were helping Will Browne, his good friend. I confess I like this not at all!'

'*I* like it well enough! I'm doing honest work for a good wage!'

'Aye, but surely you'd be happier working among friends than—'

'If by that you mean I'd be happier working on Tew's press, aye, I would, and I'd throw this new job over in an instant if I could go back. But I can't, and if you think I'd be happier helping my aunt at home, I'll tell you plainly, you're mistaken! She's an ill-tempered woman and very close with her money.'

Ned scowled and did not reply.

'What ails you?' Lucy asked in exasperation. 'Do you think I'm one to let Mr Pecke or any other man take liberties?'

Ned relaxed a little but he still seemed dissatisfied. 'It's only that it's ... well, I've not thought it through, so I'll say no more. I'm glad to see you, Lucy. Will you have some dinner?'

'I can't, Ned. It wouldn't be honest to dine at your charge when I'm no longer working for our cause and our friends; I'd be ashamed to sponge on you! I've not time to stop long, either. I only came because I ... I missed my friends.'

His expression softened. Nancy Shorby bustled through from the kitchen and looked with dismay at the tankards Ned had set down. 'Oh, Lord-a-mercy!' she cried. 'The party in the panelled room are banging on the table, Ned, wanting those!'

'God damn it!' cried Ned. Nancy and Lucy both stared: it was most unlike him to blaspheme. Ned picked up the tankards so roughly that the contents sloshed on to the floor. 'Come this evening!' he ordered Lucy. 'I need to speak to you!'

Nancy watched him go with surprise, then gave Lucy a doubtful look. 'I thought you'd lost your place to Nicholas Tew?'

'Aye,' agreed Lucy, embarrassed. 'I did. But I found another, printing a newsbook.'

Nancy regarded her a moment warily, then drew her aside into a passageway to talk privately. 'I ought not say this, but ... Ned said you'd warned him plainly you had no dowry. He's a fine young man, and you should know that his friends expect his bride to bring him some money. If he weds a girl with none, there'll be trouble. He has an uncle, in particular, who's promised him a legacy, but might well deny it – and there are other friends he'd be very sorry to disappoint.'

'I've no wish to make Ned quarrel with his friends,' Lucy replied, face hot. 'It's why I warned him.'

'Well, that's fairly spoken!' declared Nancy. She gave Lucy a level look. 'You don't love him, then?'

Lucy set her teeth, feeling her temper rise. 'I like and esteem him,' she said carefully. 'But I would not wed unequally and have all the world cry shame on me. Nor would I have him come to repent his choice and grow to hate me. At present, too, I am my own mistress, and I like that very well indeed.'

Nancy gave a small snort of appreciation. 'Well, I'll tell you, then, that your warning's weighed with him less and less over the summer, and after you went to Bridewell he said outright that he could find no finer girl in all England. We managed to persuade him to consider his friends and think it over for a few more months, but it eased our minds when Mr Tew took back his press: we thought he'd see less of you and there'd be more chance for another maid to catch his eye.'

Lucy noticed that shift from *his friends* to *we*: Nancy had been among the persuaders. She bit back an angry retort, reminding herself that she didn't *want* to marry Ned Trebet. 'He's already seeing less of me,' she pointed out. 'I'll not come again for the council meetings on Thursday, nor yet every day for dinner, but I've no wish to avoid The Whalebone altogether! *All* my friends meet here!'

'Oh, you should never go as far as that!' said Nancy in alarm. 'He'd suspect, then, that we'd warned you off. Just come when you are like to meet other friends here, and we'll try to keep Ned too busy to speak with you. And I'll tell him you're sorry, but tonight your uncle expects you at home, shall I? Thank you, dear, for being so obliging!'

Lucy left feeling shamed, grimly angry and with a strong desire to be *disobliging*. She told herself she was being stupid: if Ned *did* propose, it would be a disaster. If she accepted him, she'd have to give up her work and her independence and ... and any hope of marrying anybody else; she'd have to become Mistress of The Whalebone, a job she didn't fancy, and all of Ned's friends and family would look down on her and disapprove of his choice. If she turned him down, though, he would inevitably be hurt and offended: she would lose his friendship, and *her* family would be angry and disappointed that she'd thrown away such a good match. No, her best course was the one Nancy had suggested: see less of Ned, avoid any private conversation with him and hope that someone more suitable caught his eye.

She was still angry – and bitterly disappointed. Ned would've been certain to know what had happened to Jamie, but she hadn't had the chance to ask. She didn't even know if Jamie had kept his promise to ask his friend Wildman for help.

She was on Coleman Street, only a block from Will Browne's shop, and impulsively hurried to his door.

Liza came into the shop when Lucy knocked: she smiled delightedly when she saw who it was and came over to give Lucy a hug. Lucy realized, with some surprise, that the girl was now taller than she was.

'We've just sat down to dinner,' Liza informed her. 'Come and join us!'

William Browne seemed equally pleased to see Lucy and insisted on giving her dinner. He was deeply interested in her news, particularly the part about Gilbert Mabbot becoming Licensor. 'I've met him,' he said, grinning. 'He may not be a Whaleboneer, but it was *John Wildman* introduced us, and he has great sympathy for our cause. *Excellent* news, sweet, *excellent*! With him as Licensor, those informing rogues will be on short chains!'

Browne had, however, heard nothing of Jamie Hudson during the past week: a second disappointment. It turned out, though, that he was acquainted with the Bournes – hardly surprising, in the small world of City printers and booksellers. 'Honest people,' he said approvingly. 'Godly and hard-working, if a trifle dour.'

'A *trifle*?' asked Lucy unhappily. 'They've scarce spoken a dozen words to me since I came there!'

Browne looked surprised, then thoughtful. 'They wonder at Mabbot's hiring you, perhaps. Or perhaps it's nothing to do with you. Last winter, John Bourne's wife died of the smallpox, along with his daughter and his first grandchild. Such losses would silence any man, and he was a quiet fellow from the start.'

Lucy winced and resolved to give the Bournes another chance.

When she got back to the printshop, the three Bournes were already at work. They paused when she came in. 'Been to see Mr Mabbot?' asked the younger Mr Bourne with a sneer.

'Nay,' she said, surprised. 'I went to visit William Browne, my uncle's good friend. He sends his regards.'

The three looked at her, nonplussed. 'I know Will Browne,' said the elder Bourne. His tone was almost accusing.

'Aye, else he would not have sent regards! Why did you ask about Mr Mabbot?' She suddenly suspected the reason.

The younger Bourne shrugged. 'We thought he was a friend of yours.'

We thought you whored your way in here. 'I never even met the man until he hired me!' she protested angrily.

They looked at one another. Mrs Bourne said cautiously, 'It's strange, then, that he should hire you.'

Lucy considered possible answers and chose the honest one. 'Not so strange. He wanted someone with experience managing a press but didn't want to pay a master printer's wages.'

The elder Bourne looked doubtful. *'You've* managed a press?'

'Aye,' she said coldly. 'Nicholas Tew's press, while he was in Newgate.'

There was a silence. 'Oh!' said the younger Bourne, impressed. 'What, *John Lilburne*'s press, that the Stationers never found?'

'Aye. I started by helping Mr Browne, but then he was sent to Newgate, too.'

There was another silence, this one almost respectful. 'So you're one of *that* crew?' asked the younger Bourne.

She had no trouble understanding what he meant. 'Aye. Though I fell into it through wanting honest work and to help my uncle's friend. I'd never even heard of John Lilburne before I came to London.'

'Is Mr Mabbot of your company?' the elder Bourne asked curiously.

She hesitated. 'I've not heard him spoken of as *one of us*, but certainly he's a friend of those who are.'

222

Mrs Bourne had evidently been thinking along a different track, because she suddenly burst out, 'Why's Mabbot want someone who can *manage* a press?'

'You'll have to ask Mr Mabbot,' Lucy said primly. 'I was simply pleased to find work.' She hesitated, then added, 'I don't think he could be dissatisfied with aught of yours, though.'

'He's young,' said the elder Mr Bourne thoughtfully. 'He thinks Sam Pecke much too cautious. Now he's become Licensor he grows ambitious.' He nodded. 'Well, that's Pecke's concern, not ours. I doubt that aught Gilbert Mabbot comes up with does any harm to the sales of the *Diurnall*.' He gave Lucy the first smile he had ever bestowed on her. It was, to be honest, not much more than a quirk of the lips, but she decided it was *meant* to be a smile and smiled back.

She kept her agreement with Nancy Shorby and did not go to The Whalebone that evening. The following morning, however, she rose early and made her way north to Moorfields. She wasn't sure where Jamie was staying now, but she thought there was a chance he would continue to lie rent-free in the barn, at least until the end of summer.

The barn looked extraordinarily desolate. The press had gone, and all the drying lines; even the loose scraps of paper she'd wedged between the cases of type and the wall had been carefully removed. She couldn't bring herself to disturb the heavy silence by calling Jamie's name. She

223

climbed up to the loft where he slept, but the straw was trampled flat and it was immediately apparent that there was no one there.

She looked around wretchedly, wondering where he was, hoping he was safe and well, fearing that he was drunk in some churchyard or ditch. She should have gone to look for him the day after he agreed to speak to Captain Wildman, just to make sure he'd done it – but she hadn't, and then she'd started her work, and...

She noticed something carved on a beam where Jamie used to sleep. She went over and crouched down to look: it was her name, LUCY, written over and over again, the letters carved deep into the wood.

She stared a moment, then traced the letters with a trembling finger. They were low on the beam; they must have been obscured before by the heaped straw and by Jamie's own recumbent form. She imagined him lying where she now crouched, propped up on his right elbow, etching her name before he slept.

She laid her palm flat against the wood. Her throat ached painfully. She suddenly understood why Nancy had said, 'You don't love him, then?' when Lucy admitted warning Ned about the dowry. If she *had* loved him, the need to have him in her arms would have dragged that warning into silence; it would have emerged late if it emerged at all.

She stood, climbed back down the ladder and trudged back into the City, wondering wretchedly what she was to do. Jamie was God-knew-where doing God-knew-what. Oh, she was sure she could find out what had become of him, but what she could do about it was another matter. He had left her no word to say where he was going. Had he concluded, as she had, that they had no possible future together? As a journeyman blacksmith he would be able to support himself, but supporting a wife was another matter – and four shillings a week might be a grand sum for a single woman living with her uncle but it wasn't enough to set up a household.

To marry in poverty, to bear children in squalor, to struggle to feed and clothe them, to watch them die of cold and disease as you failed – it was a wretched lot. She should put Jamie from her mind ... but, surely, she could do so *after* she'd found out what had become of him?

She arrived at Bourne's printshop to find Gilbert Mabbot there, sitting at her composing table and writing something. When she came in he looked up with a grin. 'Ah, Mistress Wentnor! Well met! I need to discuss some business with you, but I won't keep you from your work. Meet me for dinner at The Cock Tavern in Fleet Street at one o'clock!' He signed his piece of writing with a flourish and bounded out.

The Bournes all looked at Lucy, who shrugged and grimaced, signalling her ignorance.

'Ambitious!' muttered the elder John Bourne, glowering at the door through which Mabbot had just departed.

The Cock was a big tavern: a sprawling place, with common rooms linked by passages and cubby-holes tucked under stairways. Gilbert

Mabbot was in one of these when Lucy arrived. He was talking animatedly with two men, and when they looked up Lucy saw that one of them was John Wildman.

'Captain Wildman!' she exclaimed in delight. 'I was hoping to speak to you!'

'You're known to one another?' Mabbot asked in surprise.

'We've a mutual friend,' replied Wildman, smiling. 'It's *Major* Wildman now, Mistress Wentnor. I've been promoted to ease my departure from the Army. This business of our council and the Army's kept me so busy I neglected my men, and it seemed best to resign my commission and let my lieutenant accept the charge, but my colonel gave me a new rank out of courtesy.'

'It's Jamie Hudson I wished to speak of,' Lucy said breathlessly, sliding on to the bench beside Wildman. 'Did he go to you about the blacksmithing?'

Wildman's smiled broadened. 'Aye, he did. I gather you told him you saw no reason why he should not take it up again. For that, Mistress Wentnor, I am in your debt.'

'You can help?'

Wildman nodded. 'I sent him to an Army blacksmith who owes me a favour. He must relearn his trade, but I've no doubt that if he sets his mind to it, he'll succeed.' He glanced at Mabbot and the other man and explained, 'This is a man who was in my troop, to whose courage I am much indebted. He was maimed at Naseby-fight, and his friends have since been troubled how to help him. He worked for a time on the

226

same press as Mistress Wentnor.'

'So you're a printer, Mistress?' asked the third man. He was about Mabbot's age: stocky, swarthy and hook-nosed, with a gold ring in one ear. 'You're a lucky man, Mabbot: my printers were never so fair!'

Lucy gave him a cold look. Wildman smiled into his beer.

'Come, sweet!' said the stranger. 'How much does our Licensor pay you? I wager it's less than your worth!'

'If you're hiring printers, Nedham, does it mean you're taking up your pen again?' Mabbot asked quickly.

Nedham gave a sly smile. 'I might.'

Mabbot did not seem happy to hear it. Wildman smiled again. 'You are in the presence of the king of newsbooks!' he told Lucy. 'This is Mr Marchamont Nedham – otherwise known as *Mercurius Britanicus*.'

'Oh!' Lucy remembered Uncle Thomas's admiration for that now-defunct newsbook. 'Well, sir, I wish you well.'

'Did you read his "Hue and Cry", after Naseby-fight?' asked Wildman enthusiastically.

'Nay,' admitted Lucy. 'I never saw a newsbook until last spring.'

'"Where is King Charles?"' Wildman quoted with relish. '"What's become of him? They say he ran away out of his own Kingdom very Majestically, and therefore it were best to send Hue and Cry after him: If any man can bring tale or tiding of a wilful King, who has gone astray these four years from his Parliament, with a guilty Conscience, bloody hands, and a heart full of broken vows and protestations, then give notice to Britanicus and you shall be well paid for your pains".' He laughed.

Nedham grimaced and made a dismissive gesture.

'And the king's private letters!' Wildman went on. 'You know they were captured at Naseby, Mistress? *Britanicus* printed them, week after week, with such witty commentary that it made me laugh out loud. My men and I used to read them over again and again in camp, until the paper was quite worn out. It was the best stuff that ever I read in a newsbook!'

Nedham, however, was shaking his head. 'I regret that.'

'Aye, for you and your printer went to prison for it, and you were obliged to grovel for pardon,' said Mabbot acidly. 'Parliament had delusions then that King Charles would agree a settlement.'

'Nay, I regret speaking so ill of His Majesty,' said Nedham seriously.

Wildman gave a snort of contempt. 'You spoke the truth, but at a time when men were not ready to hear it.'

Nedham shook his head again. 'The *truth*, sir, is that it's an evil world, and the king at least fenced us from anarchy. With him down, England is the Devil's plaything.'

There was a silence. Wildman stared in surprise. 'This is a change for the worse!'

'All changes are for the worse,' replied Nedham. 'If you look, sir, at our other choices, mere *pragmatism* dictates a return to monarchy!' He held up a thick-fingered hand. 'There's the Parliamentary majority and their friends the Scots.' He folded down his little finger and ring finger. 'God save England! Better a bishop than a presbyter, and better a devil than a Scots presbyter! Then there's the Independents and their friend Cromwell.' He folded down his middle finger. 'That's to say, the rule of the sword, in the hands of our fiery-nosed St Noll. How can our ancient laws and charters survive under the hooves of the Ironsides? Next, there are these new-fangled Agitators and Levellers, with their prodigious notion of a Commonweath—'

'Sir!' cried Wildman furiously. 'A Commonwealth would indeed be a prodigy, but a glorious one! God has cast down the old order and given into our hands the opportunity to make all things new – to set up justice and freedom such as this land has long desired and never attained.'

Nedham gave him a long hard stare. 'I perceive that *you* are a Leveller.'

(Lucy remembered long afterwards that she first heard that name from Nedham.)

Wildman flushed. 'I reject that title! We have no intention of levelling men's estates. Our desire is for a settlement of government derived from the authority of the people!'

'The *people,* sir, are a mob of cobblers and kettle-menders, screaming for they know not what. A jolly time we should have, should we grant *them* authority!'

'Sir, that is no argument!' Wildman said fiercely. 'That is mere railing! You—'

229

Mabbot reached across the table and caught his arm. 'John, stop! If you start disputing, we'll be here until nightfall and get no business done!'

Nedham got to his feet, sneering a little. 'I will leave you to your business, then, gentlemen! Mr Mabbot, Mr Wildman – *wild man*! a fitting name for a Leveller! – good-day!' He strolled off, untroubled by Wildman's glare.

'It is all *consequences*!' Wildman said bitterly. 'They say we dare not act justly because *they* can imagine ill consequences, even though no man can ever *know* the consequences of a new and untried action! The question ought to be whether or not the action is *just*!'

'Nedham's no lawyer, John,' replied Mabbot. 'Nor, I think, much concerned with justice. But I beg your pardon.' He shrugged. 'I met Mr Nedham in the street and invited him to join us before we discussed our business, because I liked *Britanicus* and I knew you did, too – but it seems he's turned his coat. I am surprised to hear *him* speak for the king!' He frowned. 'And he means to take up his pen again! That's bad news.'

'You think he will write as a Royalist?'

'What? Oh, God have mercy, if I thought that, I would've been bound to arrest him! But I doubt that the king will give him countenance after all he's said of the man. No, I meant that a great many will read his newsbook and it will be harder for mine.'

Wildman put his hand over his eyes.

'Nay, I think I have an opportunity!' cried Mabbot. 'I want your advice on it, as a lawyer.'

A serving-man appeared, carrying a tray. He stared blankly at the place vacated by Nedham.

'The other gentleman left,' said Mabbot, 'but the young gentlewoman is joining us. I pray you, fetch her a pint of small beer!'

The serving-man nodded, set down three dishes of beef and oysters, then fetched the beer. Mabbot waited until he'd gone again, then whipped a newsbook out of his pocket. 'Read this!' he ordered, his eyes gleaming.

Wildman took it; Lucy, sitting next to him, saw that it was *The Moderate Intelligencer,* a well-established newsbook, not as popular as *A Perfect Diurnall* but with a larger circulation than most. 'What am I to look for?' Wildman asked.

Mabbot reached across the table and pointed to a sentence under the heading. It was in French: Lucy didn't know that language, but Wildman's brows rose.

'Well?' asked Mabbot.

Wildman made an uncertain face. 'Well what?'

'What does it say?' asked Lucy.

'"Dieu nous donne les Parliaments briefes, Rois de vie longue",' read Wildman. 'That is, God grant us short Parliaments, and Kings of long life. I don't doubt that most of England would happily say "Amen!", but Parliament won't join them.'

'So I think, too!' said Mabbot happily. 'It gives me grounds to stop his licence to print.'

'And you want to stop his licence?' Wildman asked his friend. 'Why? And who is "he", any-way?'

'John Dillingham,' Mabbot said. 'He who was

231

formerly the *Parliamentary Scout* – and, before that, a tailor in Whitechapel. I've spoken to Robert White, his printer: he's groaning under the burdens laid upon him, and if I provide him with help, he'll happily print for me instead.'

'If White's willing to work for you, why do you need to close down *The Moderate Intelligencer*?' asked Wildman reasonably.

'I don't mean to close it down,' replied Mabbot, grinning.

Wildman's brows rose again. 'You mean to steal the *title*? Publish it as your own?'

'It's a good title! Six or seven hundred people in London pay a penny for it every week!'

Wildman shook his head doubtfully. 'It's a shabby trick, Gilbert. It's an abuse of your new censorship!'

'My fortune won't bear the cost of starting up a newsbook *ex nihilo*!' protested Mabbot. 'And tricks are how business is done among newsmen. Dillingham's played plenty of his own. He's cheated White, for one.'

'Aye, and look at the result!'

'Do you say this would be *unlawful*?'

Wildman thought about it. 'No,' he concluded. 'You can legitimately cancel Dillingham's licence; indeed, I can count off a dozen Parliament-men who would complain if you failed to. Dillingham, however, would keep the right to get a fresh licence, and then he might take you to court to recover his title.'

'Would he win?'

Wildman shrugged. 'It would depend upon the court.'

Mabbot considered that. 'Even if he did, it would take time. I'd have my newsbook running profitably before it was settled.' He turned his smile on Lucy. 'What think you, Mistress Went-nor?'

'I agree with Captain Wildman: it's a shabby trick.'

Mabbot's face fell. Wildman smiled.

'But I don't suppose *printing* your newsbook is any more dishonest than printing the *Diurnall*,' Lucy conceded. 'Am I to speak with Mr White, so that he can see I'm help and no threat to his mastery?'

Mabbot looked surprised. Wildman grinned at him. 'She's quick-witted, our Lucy,' he informed his friend. 'You did well to hire her.'

Mabbot spent the rest of the meal telling Lucy when she should visit Mr White and what she should say to him. When they had eaten, and Mabbot had paid the reckoning, Lucy got up. 'I must go back to my work,' she said. 'Captain Wildman—'

'Major,' he reminded her.

'Forgive me, Major Wildman. Are you like to see Jamie Hudson soon?'

Wildman gave her a warm smile. 'Aye, I'm expected at Croydon for another meeting tomorrow, and his regiment is there. Will I bring him a message from you?'

She'd thought of sending a letter; she'd thought of offering him the shilling a week, at least until he was earning a full wage – but if he was with the Army, he would have his keep, and as for a letter, it presumed too much. He hadn't written to her, not even a word to say where he was going. That stung, though she tried to be reasonable about it. She'd kept her feelings to herself because there was no possible good that could come of speaking out about them, and she now suspected that he had done exactly the same – and they were both right to do so. She should put aside this wistful longing and engage instead with the work Mabbot was offering her, which might be of dubious honesty, but certainly sounded interesting.

A message, though – that much, surely, she could do? 'Aye,' she said. 'Tell him how very glad I am that he's taking up his work again, and...' She stopped, not knowing how to finish.

'I'll tell him,' said Wildman. She saw from his expression that she'd given herself away and that Wildman would tell Jamie more than she'd ever dared to. She regretted that she'd said anything at all.

Ten

Robert White, printer of *The Moderate Intelligencer,* was a slovenly, red-faced lecher. A clay pipe was permanently fixed between his teeth, and his printshop was so full of tobacco smoke that it made Lucy cough. When he set eyes on Lucy he beamed and blessed Gilbert Mabbot, but when he'd been forced to let go of her, he retreated sullenly, rubbing his bruised ribs and shin, and became surly. He had three assistants – two men and a woman – and they all seemed downtrodden drabs. Lucy did not look forward to working with him.

That work turned out not to be imminent. August wore away, and Lucy stayed at John Bourne's printing *A Perfect Diurnall* while Mabbot struggled frantically with his new censorship. She heard nothing from Jamie, though Wildman, whom she saw on a couple of occasions at The Whalebone, reported that he was well. She visited The Whalebone at irregular intervals, always when it was busy. Ned always welcomed her, but his attempts to talk to her were perpetually interrupted.

The name 'Leveller' began to be used throughout London. Wildman told her he'd first heard it from the grand officers at the Army Council at Croydon only days before Marchamont Nedham used it at The Cock: he was impressed that Nedham had picked it up so quickly. At The Cock, Lucy hadn't understood why Wildman had objected to it: she learned his reasons from the reaction of people around her.

'Is it true you would level men's estates?' asked the younger Mr Bourne.

'What do you mean?' Lucy asked in confusion.

'They say that you Levellers wish to do away with property and make men have everything in common.'

'I never heard such an idea in all my life!' she protested. 'We wish no such thing!'

The Bournes, however, were not the only people who drew that conclusion.

It is not known yet whether we shall ever have a *King* again, [said a new newsbook], because the name *Subject* is a *heathenish* invection. We are like to have a brave world, when the Saints *Rampant* have reduced our *wives,* our *daughters,* our *Estates* into a holy *community*: whereby it appears that *Matrimony* must be converted into a kind of religious *Caterwaule,* when the *model* of this new *Common-wealth* has cast all its *Kittens. John Lilburne* and I are all-to-pieces in this businesse, because he has studied the *Laws* so long, that he finds that the only fault in them is, that they allow any *Lords* at all, and says he is resolved to lay the *House of Lords* flat upon their backs. The *Agitators* shall prove good *mid-wives* , and the *Kingdom* shall be brought to bed of that prodigious *Monster* which they call a *full and free Parliament.*

This newsbook called itself *Mercurius Pragmaticus*, and it was widely known that it was written by none other than Marchamont Nedham, the newly converted Royalist.

'Where did he get the money?' fumed Mabbot. 'Starting up a newsbook is a costly business, as I know only too well!'

Where Nedham got the money was quickly established. He had visited Hampton Court, where King Charles now resided; he had begged the king's pardon and been allowed to kiss the royal hand. The guards who'd admitted him hadn't noticed whether the royal hand had held a royal purse, but it was certain that the king and his supporters still had a lot of money. From their point of view, *Pragmaticus* was money well spent: it was popular from the moment it came out, and the king's enemies were outraged by it. It was unlicensed, of course, and Parliament instructed Mabbot to shut it down. His futile attempts to do so were the main reason for the delay in launching his own newsbook.

His job was made more difficult by the fact that the king's popularity was increasing and Parliament was widely detested. All the frustrations and disappointments of the past two years had been crowned by the misery of a poor harvest.

The growing season had been cold and wet; August was just as bad. The harvest was the worst for a generation. Prices had been high ever since the war, but they usually dropped at harvest-time: this year they kept climbing. The beggars on the streets of London, always numerous and wretched, grew in number and in misery. It was obvious to anyone who paused to think about it that many would die during the winter, from cold and illness and starvation. If God really favoured Parliament, people began to whisper, why hadn't He shown that favour to the land? Bring back the king, they murmured; put Charles Stuart on his throne, and then see if the earth yields its bounty!

There was no progress, however, on a settlement of government. Wildman, who was in the thick of things, said that the Grandees were losing patience with Parliament, and the common soldiers were losing patience with the king. Charles Stuart, they said, was the author of the war, and even in defeat he was obstructing peace, refusing to agree to a settlement that set any limits on his power. A belief that the country would be better off as a Republic, though still extreme, was growing as quickly as resurgent Royalism. The middle ground, with its hope for a bounded monarchy, was eroding away under the negotiators' feet.

In this impasse, the Levellers (the name caught on, despite all attempts to reject it) began to have real influence, particularly since their proposals were the only ones that did not rely upon negotiation with Charles Stuart. Richard Overton was finally released from Newgate Prison and allowed to join his long-suffering wife and children in his own house. John Lilburne, however, remained confined in the Tower.

Lucy was surprised to find that she missed her regular attendance at the Leveller council meetings, that when Thomas set off for The Whale-bone in his role as representative of Southwark, she was restless, and when he came back, she was full of questions. She started accompanying him to the Southwark chapter meetings instead. These were held the evening after the general meetings, usually at The Bear Tavern at Bridgefoot. Mabbot and Pecke, who were already in the habit of asking her if she'd heard from Wildman, began asking her about what she heard at the meetings, though the *Diurnall*, ever-cautious of offending authority, rarely repeated it in print.

Sometimes it seemed to her that news was what she breathed, as omnipresent as air, and just as necessary. The question of how England was to be governed, which had seemed almost irrelevant only a year before, was now of so much importance that each twist and turn of events made her heart race: good news elated her and bad news kept her awake at night. When she looked back, she was amazed by the huge gulf between herself and the girl who'd arrived in London less than a year before. She'd begun to write to her brother regularly, but every time she got a letter back it was a shock. Paul wrote to her about the doings of neighbours and relatives – so-and-so married; so-and-so fallen ill – and about the farm, the wretched weather and the price of milk: things which now seemed like the concerns of a foreign country. When he wrote apologetically that he had hard news for her, she was relieved when she discovered that it was only that her one-time betrothed, Ned Bartram, was married. She replied that the news was not hard at all and asked him to give her sincere commiserations to the bride.

Late in August, Cromwell brought a regiment of cavalry to London and stationed it in Hyde Park while he proceeded to the House of Commons with a large force of armed bodyguards; he then entered as Member for Cambridge and called for a vote on an ordinance that the Presbyterians had been blocking. Unsurprisingly, it passed. The more extreme Presbyterians were intimidated into withdrawing from the House

239

altogether: the Independents finally had a majority.

It broke the impasse in the House, but not that with the king. Despite the increasing rumbles of discontent from the Army, Cromwell remained committed to a settlement with King Charles. That, probably, was why, early in September, he went to visit John Lilburne in the Tower: Lilburne could either quiet the Army's discontent or whip it into fury. An indirect result of the meeting was that Lucy met the Leveller leader for the first time.

Lilburne had been imprisoned since June the previous year, ostensibly because he'd slandered a member of the House of Lords. His sentence had no fixed limit: he was held 'at the Lords' pleasure'. He was officially banned from 'contriving or publishing any seditious and scandalous pamphlets'; he was denied access to pen and ink, and his warder was required to watch him whenever he left his cell or had visitors. He'd protested, of course – there wasn't a man in England more willing to protest injustice – and his case had been referred to a Commons' committee; this, however, had been blocked and baffled every time it tried to report. His followers in London had petitioned and demonstrated on his behalf again and again, the Army had called for his release, marched and triumphed – and still he remained in prison.

The ban on publishing had – obviously – never been successfully enforced. Lilburne's numerous visitors smuggled in paper and ink, and smuggled out pamphlet after pamphlet. After

Cromwell's visit, however, the guards were ordered to be stricter and more vigilant, and for a while they obeyed. Some visitors were refused admittance; others were searched and had paper confiscated from them. It was therefore decided that someone who was not one of Lilburne's regular contacts should visit, in the hope that the guards would be less suspicious of someone not actually known to them as a Leveller. Uncle Thomas offered to go, in the role of an old friend of Lilburne's from the days before the war; Lucy came with him because he could properly object if the guards tried to search her. She spent the night before stitching octavo-sized pockets into the inside of a petticoat and hiding paper in them.

Walking to the Tower the following morning, she was jittery. What if the guards searched her? She couldn't be punished for carrying paper, but the thought of a pack of rough louts tearing off her petticoat gave her sick chills. Uncle Thomas patted her arm ineffectually and tried to smile.

When they were admitted to the Tower's outer ward, however, she began to feel steadier. The fortress was huge, and it bustled with activity that had nothing to do with them or their mission. Workers at the Mint jostled soldiers from the Royal Ordnance in the Tower's walks, and there was a noisy queue waiting to enter the menagerie. Even the guards at the entrance to the Inner Ward, where the prisoners were lodged, had very little interest in the comings and goings of the public. Thomas and Lucy were admitted after handing over a mere tuppence tip.

At Coldharbour Gate, where Lilburne was lodged, the warder was more careful. Thomas's name was checked against a register, and he was questioned about why he had come.

'I was a friend of John Lilburne long ago, when he was an apprentice,' said Thomas earnestly, 'and I wish to appeal to him to use his influence to make peace.'

The warder snorted. 'You've come for nothing, then! I once tried to do the same, and he told me that if I were not such an old man, he would fight me!'

'Even so,' said Thomas. He opened his hand, showing a silver shilling. 'I feel called upon to make what appeal to him I can. When he was a wild young man he did listen to me once or twice. Surely no effort towards peace is worthless?'

The warder snorted again, took the money and wrote down Thomas's name as a permitted visitor.

After that they were searched, but not very rigorously. The warder asked Thomas to take off his coat and inspected the basket of food which Lucy had brought as a gift for the prisoner; he asked Lucy to hitch up her skirts and turn about, but he didn't notice the pockets inside the petticoat and demand that she strip it off.

Lilburne had a chamber on the first floor of Coldharbour, above the gate itself; the warder escorted them up to it. On the stairs they heard voices raised in excited discussion, and when they came into the room they found two men sitting at a table looking at a book.

'...wrote it yourself!' the tall fair man was saying.

'Nay!' cried the other, a rangy, dark-haired fellow with spectacles. 'It is by Andrew Horn, a citizen of London in King Edward's day! See here, it says as much by the title!' He had a northern accent.

'Then why do his words sound as though they came from your pen?'

'Because we have both studied under the same masters!' replied the northerner. 'History has taught us to cherish the same freedoms!'

The fair man inspected the title of the book, then grinned. 'I yield: I see that this was translated only last year. No one now can set out to speak of liberty without sounding like John Lilburne.'

'Visitors for you, John!' said the warder.

The bespectacled man turned towards them, an eager smile on his lips. He had only one eye: the socket of the missing one was misshapen, and a scar showed white above and below the black line of his spectacles. 'Why, it's Thomas Stevens!' he cried, and set down the spectacles to come over and clasp Uncle Thomas's hand. 'You that were a master-mercer when I was but an apprentice! And who's this? Your daughter?'

'My niece, Lucy Wentnor,' said Thomas, beaming, snatching his hat off in token of respect.

'I've heard your name before, Mistress Wentnor,' John Lilburne said, taking her hand with a smile. 'Friends have told me of Thomas Stevens' niece, a girl as brave as she is pretty.

You're well met!'

Lucy ducked a curtsey, tongue-tied. This man had changed her life – yet she hadn't even known he had lost an eye or that he was so *young*, surely not much above thirty! She'd assumed that he and Thomas had been apprentices together. Unsure what to do, she presented him with the basket of food.

The other man at once came over to inspect it like a greedy child, and Lucy noticed that he – like Lilburne – was thin and ill-nourished.

'Apples!' he cried eagerly. 'Give us an apple, John!'

Lilburne plucked an apple from the basket and tossed it to him. 'Now get you gone, Lewis!' he ordered. 'We'll feast later; now I'll speak with my old friend.'

Lewis grinned and made for the door; the warder, after a distrustful look at Lilburne, hurried after him.

'Quickly!' Lilburne said, as soon as they were gone. 'Lewis is a Royalist prisoner and must be escorted back to his cell. You brought paper?'

Lucy was already hauling up the side of her gown and turning her petticoat inside-out. Thomas, with a nervous glance at Lilburne, came and held the skirts out of her way. She drew the paper quickly out of the octavo pockets; by the time she'd pulled out the third small sheaf, Lilburne was offering her some folded papers to put in its place. 'Two letters to Henry Marten,' he whispered. 'Copy them over before you deliver them, and print the copies: they tell the truth about the double-dealing of that false hypocrite Oliver Cromwell!'

Lucy shoved the letters into her pocket and pulled out the rest of the writing paper. Lilburne took it and glanced around his room.

'They searched the basket already,' suggested Lucy.

Lilburne shook his head. 'The keeper will help himself from it, the rogue.' He thrust the paper under the open book on his table, just as the keeper returned.

The warder, as predicted, went over to the basket. He removed an apple and a round cheese and sat down at Lilburne's table. He took a bite of apple.

'Thieving scoundrel!' Lilburne said irritably. 'There are no thieves like jailers, Mr Stevens: they pilfer all that comes in, they steal anything lying about, they tax all that goes out, and if a prisoner complains, they clap him in irons. Sir, if you had *asked* me if you might have that apple, I would have given it you!'

The warder glared, swallowed his bite of apple and cut himself a slice of cheese.

'So tell me the news!' Lilburne said, flinging himself into a chair. 'What goes on under the wide sky, while I am buried here?'

'Mr Stevens is come to appeal to you to use your influence for peace,' said the warder maliciously, around the mouthful of cheese.

'Why, so I do already!' replied Lilburne. 'I am as eager for peace as any man in England.' He leaned forward and slapped the table. 'We might *have* peace, swiftly and easily, if our rulers did not set their own greedy interests above the common good!'

The warder rolled his eyes in contempt.

'*Cromwell* spoke of peace!' continued Lilburne, warming to his subject. 'By which he meant, having his own way. He said that I could not be released, for fear of my making new hurly-burlys in the Army, but that if I would be quiet, I might have an honourable employment in that same Army. I told him I will never be quiet until I have justice, and that I would not engage myself for either Parliament or *his* Army for all the gold in the world! And yet, to my shame, I did promise that if I were released, I would go abroad. He professed himself satisfied with this and said he would see to it that I was set free. We drew up a paper together – the warders of the Tower all witnessed it! And now my case has been *referred back to committee*, and God He knows if ever it will be heard at all!'

'If you bore yourself humbly...' began the warder, then stopped as the prisoner straightened and glared at him.

'If Lieutenant Colonel Lilburne had borne himself humbly,' said Thomas with quiet sincerity, 'he would now be a poor mercer, like myself, and we would all be living – most humbly! – under tyranny, for no one would believe it right to resist injustice, however great.'

'I see I have been misled!' declared the warder resentfully. 'You are of his faction. Well, then, your visit is at an end!' He got to his feet. 'Get you gone!'

He chivvied Thomas and Lucy out. Lucy paused on the threshold to glance back at John

Lilburne, sitting alone in his cell. He saw her looking and gave her a tired smile, and she touched her hand to her heart.

When they left the inner ward again, she began to cry. It was a monstrous world: that brave, generous man was locked up in prison, subject to the petty malice and greed of his keepers, while scavengers grew fat and Parliament and the Army Grandees tussled with the king for power. She told herself, sniffing, that it was hardly *news* that the world was evil – yet why should those who were trying to make it better be *punished*?

'Hush, sweet!' exclaimed Thomas. They stopped in the shadow of the Traitors' Gate, and he put his arms round her. 'Don't weep! We *succeeded*.'

'Aye,' agreed Lucy, still sniffing. 'When the Army came to London, I thought it was all over and all would be well, but things are no better than they were!'

Thomas shook his head uncertainly. 'Child, if human efforts come to naught, it is but to be expected: we are sinful and weak. God's ways are as high above ours as the heavens about the earth, and we can but hope that in His great mercy He will strengthen our feeble hands.'

Dissatisfied, she said nothing. If men could only do good through divine help, then why didn't God help them? Did He *want* them to do evil? It was a blasphemous thought, and she tried to put it out of her mind.

'Come!' said Thomas with a desperate effort to

be cheerful. 'We'll visit the menagerie! That will lift our spirits.'

Lucy eyed him doubtfully: she'd seen enough prisoners for one day, she was expected back at work – and Agnes would certainly view the cost of the menagerie, added to what Thomas had already spent on bribes, as insult on top of injury.

Thomas, however, was smiling. 'I took Mark and Hannah when they were babes,' he told her, 'and Bella, and my little Tommikin. Bella cried that she wanted a lion to be her pet, and she and Tommikin fitted out a place for it beside their bed!'

For a moment she was puzzled; then she understood. She'd never before heard Thomas name any of the children he'd lost in their infancy; that 'my little Tommikin' suddenly showed her a grief she'd never guessed at. 'I should like to see the menagerie,' she said, suddenly wanting only to make her uncle happy. He smiled at her, as pleased as though he were a child himself.

The menagerie was in the western part of the Tower's outer ward; the cost of entry was three farthings – or a cat or dog to feed to the lions; Lucy was glad to see no miserable strays in the queue. Thomas paid for them both, and they walked about the tiny enclosures with the rest of the gaping crowd. There were lions, sprawled as though heartbroken on bare earth; there was a tiger, pacing back and forth before the bars of its tiny cage, gazing at the citizens outside with a blind, manic stare. Lucy found the sight painful and disturbing, but Thomas was delighted with the beast and marvelled at its bold stripes and terrible teeth.

They came to some apes. One of the crowd tossed an apple into the cage: an ape caught and ate it avidly, baring its teeth at its companions when they tried to take a share. 'These are more warders of the Tower!' Thomas told Lucy, and she laughed.

Next was a great pale deer-like creature with dark, suffering eyes; Lucy thought at first that it must be a unicorn, but it had two horns, not one. She gazed at the beautiful, exotic animal in wonder and pity. 'That's Lieutenant Colonel Lilburne,' she whispered.

Thomas stared at the creature then shook his head. 'Nay. He's the tiger. He would not be in prison else.' He smiled. 'Why his father ever apprenticed him to be a mercer I know not, for he never had the temper for it. He was ever a bold man, headstrong and ready to quarrel – though withal as generous and warm-hearted as any man that breathes.'

Lucy knew Lilburne's story now: how the young man, charged with illegal printing under the king, had refused to testify under oath before the High Commission; how he'd been whipped at the cart-tail and pilloried and imprisoned for his defiance; how he'd been released from imprisonment when Parliament began its struggle with the king; how he'd fought bravely for Parliament's cause, only to be dismissed from the Army for refusing to take the Covenant. She hadn't, until now, heard Uncle Thomas speak of the John Lilburne he'd known before the story began.

'I'd thought you were apprentices together,' she said hesitantly. 'But you're his elder.'

'Aye,' agreed Thomas. 'He was apprenticed to Thomas Hewson, with whom I did a deal of business before the war. In those days, all Puritans were friends and dealt candidly with one another. Everything was so much simpler then! We could call for liberty of conscience and the true reformed Protestant religion all in one breath, and no one imagined any contradiction between the two. And now many who used to call for liberty call for persecution, and conscience and religion are seen to be quite at odds. It grieves me to the heart when I remember what high hopes we had! Howsomever, John was Tom Hewson's apprentice, and I saw him whenever I came to do business with his master. I thought him a godly young man and a kind one, but something lacking in respect for his elders, and over-ready to take offence.' He shook his head. 'I mistook his honest fervour for bluster. Had I ever been dragged before the High Commission, I would have cowered in terror and done all I could to appease them. John's courage and fidelity shamed me.' He gave her an earnest look. 'As do yours.'

Lucy stared at him a moment in surprise, then caught his arm. 'Never say so! Am I to *shame* you? I am *proud* of my uncle!'

'Oh, dear child!' He patted her hand. 'When Hannah married and left, my house was so empty of joy I could scarce endure it; I am so *glad* you came to stay with us in London! God keep you, sweet!'

It was later in that same week that Gilbert Mabbot took the plunge and launched his newsbook, in the profitable disguise of John Dillingham's *Moderate Intelligencer.* Lucy was at last required to leave the Bournes and assist in the smoke-filled workshop of Robert White.

It wasn't as bad as she'd feared: White wasn't around much, and when he was around, she was able to fend him off simply by taking a hairpin from her coif and pointing it towards him every time he approached. It turned out that he had recently bought a second printworks, and his quarrel with Dillingham had been because Dillingham expected him to oversee printing the *Intelligencer* personally. White would have split with Dillingham over the matter before, except that none of his downtrodden assistants was willing to manage the printshop in his absence. Mabbot had promised to pay for an experienced manager: Lucy was his economical fulfillment of that promise. When Lucy first understood this, she worried about how the assistants would view her; she discovered that the mere fact that she wasn't Robert White told strongly in her favour. The two men considered it beneath their dignity to be subject to a woman, of course, but they were happy to consider themselves subject to White while actually dealing with Lucy. The woman worker was simply pleased to answer to someone who would not molest her. No one, to Lucy's relief, seemed to believe she'd acquired her place by sleeping with Gilbert Mabbot. The Bournes must have scotched that rumour.

Samuel Pecke turned up during Lucy's first day at the printshop, almost spitting with indignation. His complaint wasn't, as Lucy had expected, that his junior partner had set up in competition: it was that his junior partner had cut him out of a profitable new enterprise. Lucy listened to Pecke respectfully, agreed that he'd been ill-used, and told him, quite truthfully, that she didn't know where Mabbot was. Mabbot had, in fact, made very sure that that would be the case: he'd appeared early that morning to give her the sheet of news to print, but told her that he would be 'out' for the rest of the day.

Pecke's visit was on a Friday, the start of a new period of newsgathering. The following Thursday, after their first issue came out, a scrawny man in a good coat turned up, his meagre face blotchy with rage. 'Where's White?' he demanded, glaring around the printworks.

Lucy hurried forward, wiping her hands. 'I manage the works for Mr White,' she admitted nervously.

The stranger looked her up and down with contempt. 'Who are you? Where's White?'

'I'm Lucy Wentnor, sir. I have charge here while Mr White is at his other shop. It's on Thames' Street if—'

'Oh, of course! At the other shop! Did White hire you?'

Lucy winced. 'Mr Mabbot did, sir.'

The other let out a shriek. 'Gilbert Mabbot! God give me patience! Gilbert Mabbot the

Licensor! I have been *abused*!'

'Sir, if you wish to speak to Mr Mabbot, he isn't here, and I know not where he is.'

The stranger whipped a copy of the new *Intelligencer* out of his coat. 'Did you print *this* for Mr Mabbot?'

Lucy swallowed. 'Aye, sir, we did.'

'The whoreson rogue! The lousy cozening rascal! God *damn* him! I'll have the law on him! Where is he?'

'Sir, I know not, but if you would leave a note—'

'He'll take *note* of me, I swear it! You lying whore, where is he?'

'Sir, I know not! He came this morning with the paper of news, and then went!'

'You inky strumpet! This is *my* title! I built it up from nothing to what it is today! You surely knew it was *my* title!'

'Sir, I'm but a hireling! Leave a note or a message for Mr Mabbot, and I'll see that he gets it!'

The stranger glared. 'You tell him this: he's a false knave, and I'll have the law on him!' He stormed out.

'That was Mr Dillingham,' one of the assistants said, awed.

'I guessed as much,' said Lucy sourly.

Dillingham found himself new printers, registered again with the Stationers and resolutely published his newsbook the following Thursday, just as he had before. For the next three weeks two completely different versions of *The Moder-*

253

ate Intelligencer did battle on the streets of London. Mabbot toyed with the notion of cancelling Dillingham's new licence, but he had no excuse to do so, and he was afraid of what the action might cost him if the matter came to court. Both *Intelligencers* carried the imprimatur of Gilbert Mabbot.

Dillingham, however, didn't take the matter to an ordinary court of law: instead, he appealed to the House of Lords, who were officially responsible for overseeing the Licensor. The Lords had resented the Army's interference in appointing Mabbot and were quick to take advantage of the complaint against him. They ordered him at once to yield the title *The Moderate Intelligencer* back to the man who'd founded it.

Lucy was alarmed. Obviously, Dillingham *deserved* to keep the title he'd built up from nothing, but by this time she was thoroughly enjoying the work she was doing for Mabbot. It was both easier and more difficult than managing Tew's clandestine press: easier because everything could be done openly; more difficult because there was more to do. Not only were there three staff instead of one assistant, there were also the 'mercury-women', the hawkers who sold the newsbook on the street. This was a group of poor women who collected copies of the *Intelligencer* when it came out on Thursday morning, and kept everything they earned above the printer's price: keeping track of who had taken how many copies, and how much money was due back, was difficult. On top of this, there was *advertising*. She was already accustomed to setting the little notices in the *Diurnall*: so-and-so would provide lessons in dancing or music; Dr such-and-such announced the availability of his infallible cure for the pox; Mr Blank offered a reward for the return of his stolen horse. Now she also had to check over the text and collect the newsbook's sixpence for the service. All of this involved a lot of accounting and figuring, and she often found herself taking the account books home to pore over them by candlelight. She liked the challenge, though, and loved the sensation of being in the centre of things, with the news flowing out from under her ink-stained fingertips. She did not want to go back to simple typesetting at John Bourne's.

Mabbot arranged another dinner at The Cock to discuss what to do. When Lucy arrived, she found that Wildman had also been invited again. She had just sat down beside him when Robert White came in.

'Ah, Robert!' said Mabbot easily. 'Good day! This is John Wildman, a lawyer friend of mine; John, this is Robert White, my printer.'

White gave Wildman a hard look. 'You're the Leveller law-man?'

Wildman sighed resignedly. 'Aye.'

He was beginning to attain a minor notoriety, if only among those who followed the news closely. He had drafted *The Case of the Army Truly Stated* for a group of radical Agitators: this document strongly protested the failure to act upon all the Declarations and Engagements made the previous summer, and called for the dissolution of Parliament and fresh elections.

'All power is originally and essentially in the whole body of the people of this nation,' it declared, 'and their free choice or consent by their representers is the only original and foundation of just government.' The notion was considered by many to be dangerous and extreme: it not only did away with the need for King and Lords but also ignored all distinction between rich and poor. *The whole body of the people*, it said – not just the few who currently had the vote.

White regarded Wildman uneasily.

'John's a wise man,' Mabbot reassured him. 'And no enemy to property – indeed, he's as quick to acquire it as any man I know!'

Reassured, White sat down beside Mabbot. 'A man's doing well if he can acquire property in these times! What do you deal in, sir?'

Wildman gave a sour smile. 'I've purchased some land that was confiscated from malignants.'

'Ah!' White was now impressed. 'I know half-a-dozen that have *tried* to buy such and failed.'

'It helps to know law,' said Mabbot, 'and to have kinsmen in Parliament. But we're here to speak of my newsbook, not John's business!'

'You mean *Dillingham*'s newsbook,' replied Wildman.

Mabbot made a face. 'I thought the law would grind slow!'

'Justice has been done speedily for once,' said Wildman, amused. 'Gilbert, give it up! You can't have been earning much the last weeks anyway, not splitting the readership with Dillingham.'

Mabbot, dissatisfied, appealed to White. 'Robert, what *were* our sales this past week?'

White jutted his lip, as though he were thinking hard; Lucy was quite certain that he hadn't been following the newsbook closely enough to know. She took out her notebook. 'Three hundred and eighty copies,' she said. 'After costs we had a loss of three shillings and eightpence.'

Mabbot raised his eyebrows appreciatively. 'That's less than I feared.'

'The mercury-women that hawk it say people now ask which *Intelligencer* it is, sir.' She met Mabbot's eyes hopefully. 'I think some prefer the new *Intelligencer* to the old.'

'Still, it is a loss,' said Mabbot unhappily. 'I'd *hoped* to earn money by this venture.' He looked at Wildman. 'Is there no hope of keeping the title?'

Wildman shook his head. 'You must make your choice, my friend. Publish a newsbook that's truly your own or go back to the *Diurnall*.'

Mabbot frowned.

'Sir,' said Lucy hesitantly, 'you wanted your own newsbook in part because you tired of Mr Pecke's caution, did you not? Perhaps you should be bolder in what you write.' She glanced at Wildman and said, 'The Royalist mercuries sell well because many long for the king's return. Perhaps something might be done on *our* side, too. Everywhere we hear Levellers reviled, or else passed over in silence, and yet there are many of us and we are all great readers of the news.'

Wildman gave her a startled look. 'That is a very fair point, Mistress! I, certainly, would be glad to read a newsbook that spoke well of us!'

Mabbot frowned some more. 'Perhaps ... and yet there are a great many people who think ill of you now – aye, I know how falsely you're slandered! But John, if my newsbook closed because readers shun it, how would that help anyone?'

'Mistress Wentnor's point was that it *wouldn't* close,' said Wildman. 'That there are enough of us to make it profitable.'

Mabbot tapped the table. 'I should think on this. Robert – you're happy with Mistress Wentnor's management?'

White had been staring at Lucy with some astonishment; he started. 'What – oh, aye. The wench is hard-working and knows her trade.'

'Then we'll carry on for at least a few more weeks. I can afford patience if the loss is no worse than four shillings a week. Though it seems, alas, that I must find a new title. *The Moderate Intelligencer!*' He sighed. 'I *liked* that. Here, can anyone think of a title that sounds as if it's but a continuation? That way we might keep some of our readers.'

'*The Army's Intelligencer*?' suggested Wildman.

Mabbot made a face and shook his head. '*That* would hardly please the Lords! They are angry enough with the Army as it is.'

'*The City Intelligencer*?' offered White.

'Nay! *That* sounds as though it means to speak of Common Council and its affairs, which is foul ground!'

258

'*The Moderate*?' said Lucy.

'*The Moderate*,' repeated Mabbot, tasting the name. 'Aye. That will do.'

Eleven

The Moderate first came out the following week. It was four pages shorter than *The Moderate Intelligencer* and was published on Tuesday, rather than Thursday; this was to take advantage of the people who liked to send a newsbook to their country cousins on the post-coaches which left London on Tuesday morning. For its first few weeks it continued much like its parent, cautiously neutral. Events, though, made neutrality increasingly difficult to sustain. Mabbot's Leveller sympathies were expressed cautiously, at first; when sales actually *improved* as a result, *The Moderate* became enthusiastically radical.

The king declared his preference for the Army's *Heads of the Proposals* over the strict Presbyterian terms being offered him by Parliament, then refused to negotiate with the Army. He saw the Scots commissioners regularly, however, for long private discussions. The threatening rumbles north of the border which had been sounding all summer were growing much louder. The Scots had made a Covenant with the Parliament of England: would England's Army break it? Charles was Scotland's king as well as

England's: how could the southern kingdom presume to settle with him as though the northern one had no rights in the matter? The summer of struggle had settled nothing, the threat of another war was growing again, and still the country was paralysed.

John Wildman's *The Case of the Army*, with its insistence on the sovereignty of the people, was formally presented to Lord General Fairfax and the Council of the Army. Cromwell, however, was still desperate to come to an agreement with the king. He used all his influence to ensure that *The Case of the Army* was rejected, and made a speech in Parliament dissociating himself from it and praising monarchy.

And thus Cromwell's dear Democraticks being left all in the suds, [*Mercurius Pragmaticus* reported cheerfully] his face is now more toward an Aristocracie than Zion, which has raised a deadly feud betwixt him and the Agitators, who looke upon him as fallen from grace; especially since he has used all his wit and power in the Army to suppresse them, now that he has served his ends upon them.

'What's a Democratick?' Lucy asked Wildman. They were at The Whalebone, where Lucy had gone after work in the hope of meeting friends.

'One that believes in the sovereignty of the people,' Wildman told her. He looked very weary – unshaven, hollow-eyed and dishevelled, not at all his usual immaculate self. 'From the

Greek *demos,* the people, and *kratia,* power.'

'Oh!' said Lucy. 'I thought it meant something bad.'

That drew a tired smile. 'Many think it does. They say that if the common people get power into their hands, they will turn first upon the rich and then upon one another, and all will descend into anarchy and bloody ruin. And yet the Grecians, when they were at their most flourishing, settled upon democracy as the best and noblest form of government.'

Lucy considered that. 'So common people *have* ruled, in the past?'

'Aye, they have!' Wildman roused himself and added fiercely, 'And will again, by God's grace!'

Ned came over with three mugs of beer and, after a glance over his shoulder to check that his staff were coping without him, sat down at the table with them. 'You're speaking of *The Case of the Army*?' he asked them. 'I heard Noll Cromwell's been promised the earldom of Essex for his part in suppressing it!'

Wildman nodded impatiently. 'I heard the rumour. I wouldn't be surprised if it were true. Whenever people are required to make sacrifices for the common good, somehow it always happens that other people make the sacrifices and Noll Cromwell gets the good.' He picked up his beer, had a long drink, then gave Ned a direct look. 'We'll press on, never fear! If they won't accept *The Case of the Army,* we'll try them with *The Agreement of the People.*'

The Agreement of the People was the newly proposed *Leveller* settlement, the result of the

261

committee the Levellers had set up to work with the Agitators back in July. Drafts of it had been circulated around all the Leveller chapters in London, and the initial glut of proposals had been sifted and winnowed out to basics: Parliaments freely elected every two years on a reformed franchise; a set of reserves guaranteeing religious tolerance and equality before the law. The hope was that it could be submitted to the people for ratification, and that the people could be convinced that it really could supply what it offered – 'a firm and present peace upon grounds of common right and freedom' – and abandon their insistence on a king. The latter objective looked more difficult even than the first. There were now more unlicensed Royalist newsbooks in London than legal ones.

'God send you good fortune!' said Ned in a low voice.

'Amen!' Wildman had another drink of beer, then glanced from Ned to Lucy and back again. 'Ned, there's another matter I wished to speak of. Jamie Hudson asked me to ask you about his letters.'

'Oh, Jesu!'exclaimed Ned, with a look of shocked guilt.

'What's this?' asked Lucy.

'Only that Jamie wondered that he'd received no answer to his letters from either of you,' said Wildman. 'He feared they may have gone astray.'

Wildman spoke in a carefully casual tone, but Lucy understood the whole situation instantly. Jamie *had* after all sent her word of how he was, but he had sent the letters to *Ned,* and Ned hadn't passed them on.

'I, uh, I intended to reply,' Ned told Wildman. 'And to show them to Lucy, too. But ... Lucy, I've scarcely *seen* you since Mr Tew took back the press, and when I do see you I'm so cursed busy that it goes from my mind!'

This was true, of course, but Lucy doubted it was the whole truth. She didn't think Ned would deliberately suppress the letters – but ignoring and 'forgetting' them was another matter. He might be in two minds about presenting himself as a suitor, but that didn't mean he wanted to see another man in that position.

'I know I might have written to him myself,' Ned continued, 'but I *thought* I would see you often, as I used to do. I thought we might send our replies together.'

'Where are these letters?' Lucy demanded coldly.

Ned jumped up and hurried out; Nancy Shorby tried to catch his arm as he did, but he brushed her off impatiently.

Wildman gave Lucy a speculative look. His eyes were very bright. 'Tell me quick: how stand things between you and Ned Trebet?'

'That's no affair of yours!' Lucy hissed indignantly. 'But his friends would be offended if he made addresses to a girl without a dowry.'

'And he defers to them?' Wildman replied, grinning. 'I wouldn't have thought him so craven! Were I in his place, I would tell my "friends" to go hang! But I will hold my peace, seeing that it would not serve Jamie's interests to say as much.'

She glared in affront. It occurred to her that any impartial observer would say that marriage to Ned would be very much in *her* interest. Wildman was clearly eager to see his friend win the fair maiden, but he was indifferent to what that might mean for the maiden. She wondered what Jamie had actually said to him about her.

She wondered, in fact, what Jamie *meant* by writing to her jointly with Ned. He had spoken that time as though he expected Ned to propose: was he trying to encourage him? She would, she recognized coldly, do very much better to encourage Ned herself. He was an honest and decent man who could give her a comfortable and prosperous life.

'It's true that Ned's been busy every time he's seen me of late,' Lucy said. 'His people have taken pains to ensure it.'

'Oh!' said Wildman, with an oblivious grin. 'That's how it stands, is it?'

Ned returned with some folded papers. 'Here are the letters!' he panted. 'And I beg your pardon that you did not see them sooner.'

'I know you've been busy,' said Lucy appeasingly, taking the letters. 'Whenever I come here, there are always half dozen matters clamouring for your attention.'

'Aye!' agreed Ned, relieved.

There were only three letters. They were unsealed, brief, proper and addressed to Ned first and Lucy afterwards. The first said merely that Wildman had promised Jamie a place with an army blacksmith; the second, that he was now working with Edmund Davis, attached to Colonel Harrison's regiment of Horse; the third...

To Mr Edward Trebet and Mrs Lucy Wentnor.

John Wildman saies that you aske after my health each time he meets you. Knowe then that I am well, and that I shunn Brandie as it were Poysoun. Mr Davis and I have wrought a brace for my Arme after your urging, and it serves, tho' I think it might be made to serve better. Col Harrison's rgmt is astirr for our Liberties, and I am held in Honour as one that has spent Ink as well as Blood in their defence. There is a press here, it is worked by Mr Jn. Harris, who read all we printed and wonders much to heare that it was managed in such danger by a Lesshire dairymaid. I pray God keep you and all our Friends in health. I wd be glad of News from my Friends in London.

Your Friend, James Hudson

Lucy read it, then read it again, smiling: he might as well not have bothered addressing it to Ned! She looked up, saw Ned watching her closely with a frown, and was instantly certain that he'd noticed that too, and wasn't sure whether or not he should be jealous. She folded it with the others and handed them back. 'Thank you, Ned,' she said. 'I was troubled for Jamie. I knew he would get no more work printing, and I feared he'd end a miserable drunkard, as he was when first he came to us.'

Ned blinked at her uncertainly. Nancy Shorby

265

came over and touched his shoulder. 'Ned, Rafe says—'

Ned groaned angrily. 'Can't you let me be for half an hour?'

'Well, but Rafe says we're out of beef, should he use the bacon?'

'Out of – that's not possible! We've a whole side in the larder!'

'Where?'

'In the ... oh, let me!' He jumped to his feet and strode out of the room.

Wildman shook his head. 'As you said! Why do his people mislike you?'

'Would your friends wish *you* to marry a pauper, Major Wildman?'

He was silent a moment. 'My friends were very pleased with my bride. She is of a wealthy, noble and distinguished family, and the marriage did much to further my career. Her family are all Royalists, she *despises* my politics and we have not spent one happy hour together since I took up the sword against tyranny.'

'Oh,' said Lucy. She hadn't even known that Wildman was married: he'd never mentioned his wife.

'Ned is not your equal,' said Wildman, looking her in the eye, 'either in wit or in spirit. I think you know it: else you would not let his friends cozen him.'

'Jamie,' replied Lucy, 'is as poor as I am myself, *and* he's said nothing to *me* of what I take to be your meaning.'

Wildman blinked. 'Has he not?' He hesitated, frowning. 'I think he must be ashamed to approach you while he can offer you so little. He is a proud man. But I hope you will take no offence if I, as his friend, speak in his place. He has a true and faithful heart, and it is yours entirely.'

Walking back to Southwark she pondered love, marriage and whether to reply to Jamie's letter. She was sure it would be unwise to do so, but she suspected that she'd do it anyway.

She drafted several replies over the next couple of weeks: they ranged from a chilly 'It is not fitt for me to write you further', to a warm 'I thought you had gonne away and left no worde, and when Ned showed me your letters I hadde such joye!' She tore all of them up – except the warm one, which she tore up *and* burned in the kitchen fire. Eventually she sent a brief missive sufficiently impersonal to pass muster.

To Mr James Hudson, Col. Harrison's Rgmt.

I am glad to know that you are well. I am well, & engaged to print Mr Gilbert Mabbot's *Moderate*. He debated much whether to speak out for the Agreement, but now he is resolved, and I thinke will be a strong sheeld against slander, viz this week's copie, which I in close. I pray God we soon obtain what we have so long hoped for, a just Peace! All youre Friends in London send you greetings and pray God's blessing, as do I.

Lucy Wentnor

The copy of *The Moderate* which she enclosed had coverage of the debates at Putney, where the Council of the Army was discussing whether or not to adopt *The Agreement of the People.* Wildman and the Agitators had indeed tried the Army with it, and *The Agreement* had garnered widespread support. Cromwell and his supporters were obliged to bring it to the Council and meet its proponents in debate. Most of the London newsbooks were covering the meeting, but the licensed ones did so with their usual cautious subservience.

The debate discovered so much resolution & integrity in the Generall and officers [wrote Samuel Pecke in the *Diurnall*], that it produced severall votes. This much is certain, that of this party which make such a noise there will not be found above 400 of 21000. The Officers appeared to do like religious and conscientious men, and so did most of the Agitators; there is not that division in the Army our Friends feared and Enemies hoped for.

It was left to the Levellers and *The Moderate* to reveal the strength of support for *The Agreement,* and the bitter clash it had engendered between the Grandees and the Leveller Agitators over whether all free men should be permitted to vote. Cromwell intervened to say that a wide suffrage 'tended very much to anarchy', and that 'they that are most yielding have the greatest wisdom', but it failed to carry the debate. Seeing this, Cromwell tried to refer the whole question to another committee. Colonel Rainsborough, however – the highest-ranking officer to side with the Levellers – called for a general rendezvous of the Army to decide the matter. The Council of the Army agreed to both the committee and – to Cromwell's dismay – to the rendezvous. By this time it was early November, dark, wet and miserably cold. Snow fell early, and the puddles in the streets were skimmed with ice. The price of coal soared and it was impossible to keep warm. In Thomas's house the only fire was in the kitchen: the loft, with its papered window, was freezing. Lucy and Susan slept with the bed pushed up against the chimney-piece, huddled under piles of Uncle Thomas's unsold woollens, and in the morning had to break the ice on their washbasin. The beggars in the streets grew gaunt and few, as all who could scrabbled a place in poorhouse, workhouse or prison, leaving the drunk and the hopeless and the deranged. A beggar woman was found dead in the Southwark stable just up the road, curled protectively around her starved child, both frozen stiff; how many others like her died in the city, no one could tell.

With cold and hunger came disease. Lucy came home from work on the sixth of November to find that Uncle Thomas was in bed with a feverish cold. She brought him a dish of soup from the kitchen.

'Thank you, child,' he said with an apologetic smile, 'but I've an uneasy stomach and I fear even that soup would turn it.' He sat up in bed, however, and asked her the day's news, exclaiming at the Army's plans for a rendezvous. 'If the Army supports *The Agreement,* the Grandees will have no choice but to put it before the

269

people!' he said eagerly. 'God willing, it will be settled before the new year!'

Although he was still unwell the next morning, he got up, saying that he must see to his shop, but when Lucy returned that evening he was in bed again. Agnes was disgusted with him.

'All this to-do about a cold!' she said angrily. 'It's alarming my gentlewoman-lodger.'

When Lucy returned home the following evening, the gentlewoman-lodger had a carriage standing outside the house, and her serving-maid was helping the driver to stow her mistress's gear. Agnes was in the parlour, pleading with Mrs Penington. 'It's but a fever!' she protested. '*And* it's gone down!'

The gentlewoman shook her head. 'That's the smallpox, Mrs Stevens; the rash will come before morning, mark my words. I'll not stay the night!'

Lucy gave her aunt a horrified stare, then ran up the stairs.

The master bedroom was dark and chill; she couldn't make out the bed, let alone her uncle, and had to go back to the kitchen for a candle. When she returned, shielding it with one hand, she found Thomas almost invisible under the quilts. His face turned towards her as she approached, however, and he gave her a tired smile. After what Mrs Penington had said, she'd expected to see him covered with ugly pustules and she sighed in relief at the sight of his unmarked skin. 'How do you do, Uncle?'

He tried to answer, then tapped his throat and framed the word 'Sore!' with his lips.

'Shall I fetch you some broth?'

'Water!' he mouthed.

She fetched him a cup; when she held it to his lips, she saw that they were blistered. He saw her notice, gave another little smile, weary and apologetic, and opened his mouth to show her that the lining was a mass of sores.

Her heart gave another lurch: that was indeed a precursor of smallpox, though she'd heard of it happening with other fevers as well. She went back downstairs, leaving him the candle. Mrs Penington had gone, and Agnes was sitting in the parlour; when Lucy came in, she saw that her aunt was crying.

'Aunt Agnes!' she said, at a loss.

Agnes looked up quickly, with all the old venom. 'It's but a fever!'

'I fear it might not be. His poor mouth is full of sores. Aunt, we should call the apothecary.'

Agnes rose to her feet. 'The *apothecary*, forsooth! It's but a fever! I'll not spend good money to cosset Tom's foolishness! He's just lost us *eight shillings a week*, and how we shall manage without, I know not!'

Lucy glared at her, then went back to check on Thomas. He now lay propped up against the pillows, staring up at the canopy of the bed. She sat down beside him and touched his forehead. It was warm, but not burning hot. 'Tell me truthfully,' she said, 'how do you do? Shall I go to the apothecary?' She was willing to spend her own savings, if she had to.

He shook his head. 'Oh, no, no, no!' he said, in a thin, croaking whisper. 'I'm better than I was.

A good night's sleep will mend me.'

He was mistaken. By morning Thomas had broken out in a rash, and the round red blotches on his forehead were beginning to form blisters.

Agnes had slept in the parlour; when she went upstairs and saw what was happening to her husband she let out a shriek that brought both Lucy and Susan stumbling down from the loft. 'Oh, Jesu!' she cried, pointing accusingly. 'Look!'

Thomas looked back at them in bewilderment, his face damp with sweat and his eyes glazed with fever. Lucy went to him and touched his forehead again: it was like a furnace.

'What is it?' Thomas croaked, then looked down at the rash on his hands, and whispered, 'Oh! Oh, dear Lord, spare us!'

'I'll go to the apothecary,' said Lucy.

The apothecary was the neighbourhood's usual source of medical treatment: doctors were for the rich, and hospitals, like nearby St Thomas's, were for the destitute. The local apothecary had a shop round the corner, in St Thomas's Road; he was a quiet, unassuming man, well-regarded by all his neighbours. He refused, however, to come back to the house with her. 'There's precious little I can do for the smallpox, child,' he said sadly.

'You might purge him, sir,' she urged. 'Or – or bleed him.' That was normally a barber-surgeon's task, but the apothecary had been known to engage in it.

The apothecary shook his head. 'I have not known it serve, once the pustules have appeared;

272

indeed, it does more harm than good. I will give you a tincture which may make him easier, but his best hope is in careful nursing. Take comfort, child! Most men survive this ill if they're cared for tenderly. Make him comfortable, give him to drink, and wash him, from time to time, with warm water and vinegar. I can give you a powder to mix with the water and vinegar.' He looked at her closely. 'But let some other nurse him – unless you were fortunate enough to survive the pox without scarring.'

'I've had the cowpox, sir,' she told him. 'I was formerly a dairymaid.'

He shook his head doubtfully. 'I've heard country people say that confers protection, but it's no more than an old wives' tale. It is a sad, sad thing to see a fair maid disfigured. Let some other nurse him.'

She took the tincture and the powder, promising payment later, and went miserably back to the house, pausing only to buy some vinegar. When she arrived she found Agnes in the bedroom – packing.

'What is *this*?' Lucy demanded in horror.

Her aunt looked up at her, her eyes red and wet. 'I've not had the smallpox.' She shoved her nightgown into a sack improvised from a bolster.

'Agnes!' whispered Thomas weakly. 'Don't leave me now!'

His wife looked at him bitterly. 'Our daughter is an only child now. Do you want her to be an orphan as well?'

Thomas stared at her, his lips trembling, and began to weep silently. 'Forgive me.'

'I'll lodge with Hannah,' Agnes declared savagely, 'until I can safely come back again.'

'But what if you carry the ill to her house?' demanded Lucy, horrified.

'I'm not ill!' said Agnes indignantly, as though Lucy had accused her of a sin.

'Go with God's blessing,' Thomas whispered wretchedly. 'Forgive me!'

Agnes, huffing, dragged her sack of clothing out of the room and down to the parlour. Lucy followed. 'How *can* you?' demanded Lucy, in a low whisper.

Agnes turned on her. *'Easily*! That man has heaped enough misfortune on me, without taking my life as well!' She wiped her face with an angry hand. 'I might have married a gentleman! I was a fool and preferred Tom, because I mistook mere *weakness* for kindness! I've paid and paid again for my error – my poor babies dead, all but two of them, and all our fine goods spent, and then he took my darling boy to that cruel unnatural war and lost him!'

'How can you blame *him* for the war?' Lucy asked in bewilderment.

'He supported that wicked rebellion against the Lord's anointed king! God is punishing us all for what he and his *foul seditious* friends have done! *You* stay and nurse him, if you love him so!'

Susan came in. 'I fetched the carter,' she said nervously.

Agnes gave her a curt nod and returned a baleful gaze to Lucy. 'Susan can nurse Tom: she's pocky-faced already. And you, miss, you may do as you please!' She went out, dragging her sack and wheezing.

Susan turned frightened eyes on Lucy.

'I'll stay,' said Lucy. Despite what the apothecary had said, she *thought* the cowpox would protect her – in Leicestershire they said it did – and how could she leave Uncle Thomas now?

Susan came over and hugged her. 'Thank you,' she whispered. 'Oh, Lucy, my ma *died* of smallpox, and I was sick to the heart at the thought of staying here alone! But you've never had it; should you—'

'I've had the cowpox,' replied Lucy resolutely. 'That's as good. And the apothecary says that most men survive if they have careful nursing, so I think Uncle Thomas will need both of us. One of us can watch while the other rests.'

She wrote notes to White and to Mabbot, telling them why she could not come in to work, found a boy to deliver them, then set herself to looking after Uncle Thomas.

It was weirdly peaceful to stay at home, warm and dry, listening to the wind whistling in the eaves, when she should have been jostling through the dirty streets to work or struggling to set type with cold-numbed fingers. She and Susan made up a bed for Thomas in the kitchen where it was warm, and helped him down the stairs to it. He was an undemanding patient: quiet, obedient to all instructions, deeply apologetic for putting them to any trouble. They gave him the apothecary's tincture, mixed with water, and Lucy read to him from the Bible. When night fell, Lucy and Susan made up another bed for themselves opposite Thomas's: neither of them wanted to go up alone to the cold loft while death stood at the threshold.

Over the next few days the disease followed its usual hideous course: the rash turned into blisters, the blisters into pustules that covered Thomas from the crown of his head to the soles of his feet. He was feverish, sick and in pain, but still apologetic and sweet-natured. The long-winded St Olave's preacher redeemed himself in Lucy's eyes by coming to visit and pray with the sufferer. A worried note from Hannah was delivered: 'My Mother saies I showd not come to see you, for fear the ill showd strike me and the babe unborn, and for the babe's sake I heed her, yet knowe that my thowts are with you, deerest Father, and my prayers each oure of the daie.'

Thomas smiled at the letter and had Lucy pen a reply: 'Indeed you must not come, for the babe's sake and your owne. Your thoughts and prayers are precious to me beyond rubies, deare Child, and I blesse you with a full and lovinge hart.'

On the fifth day after Agnes left, Thomas's fever soared and he fell into a childish daze. He pissed in the bed and cried when they changed the sheets. They boiled the linen and hung it to dry in the master bedroom, though it was sure to take days to dry in the cold wet air. Lucy and Susan took turns sitting by the bedside, wiping Thomas's blistered skin with the vinegar-and-powder solution and dribbling tincture into his disfigured mouth. It didn't seem to help: he moaned when he was touched, and most of the medicine simply ran out from his swollen lips. This misery continued all night and all the next day, and all the day and night after.

The following morning, however, the fever dropped a little. Thomas took some of the tincture and kept it down, and he seemed to be resting more comfortably. Lucy slumped in the chair at the bedside, exhausted by the strain and the broken nights; in the other bed, Susan was asleep.

'Bess!' said a voice, and she looked up to see Thomas smiling at her, his blistered face alight with joy.

'Uncle Thomas!' She bent for the cup of watered tincture.

'I've missed you so,' whispered Thomas. 'Sweet sister!'

She realized that his fevered mind had mistaken her for her mother. She started to correct him, then stopped herself. Why should she break the fantasy if it made him happy? She held the cup to his lips, supporting his head to help him drink. The blisters on his forehead were just starting to sag and dry: the disease had passed its peak.

'Do you remember how we hid the puppy in the hayloft?' asked Thomas. 'Da was so angry! Soft-hearted folly, he called it, and yet he turned out a good dog in the end.'

Lucy smiled helplessly. She picked up the basin with the vinegar and powder.

'I never wanted you to marry Daniel Wentnor,' Thomas whispered. 'He was ever a son of clay, and you were so bright, like the sun upon frost. Ah, but you had the right of it, too, I should never have wed poor Agnes. I thought I might make her happy because I loved her so dearly, and all I've done, it's come to naught but loss. It's an ill world! Pardon my sins, O Lord, and wash away all my iniquities with the most precious blood of your dear son Jesus Christ!'

'Amen,' whispered Lucy, wiping his face gently with the cloth.

Thomas said nothing more, and it wasn't until Lucy had finished washing his face and hands that she realized he'd ceased to breathe.

Twelve

Thomas was buried on a cold day in the middle of November. The gravediggers had to use pick-axes to break the frozen ground, though below the icy crust the earth was heavy with water. Ooze puddled in the hole, and when the shrouded body was lowered into it there was a slopping sound that made Lucy's teeth ache.

Despite the weather the churchyard was crowded. Southwark neighbours stood soberly beside members of the Mercers' Guild, and parishioners of St Olave's touched elbows with Levellers: Thomas had had many friends. Many of them were Levellers – William Browne and his daughter, Katherine Chidley and her son

Samuel, Mr Tew, Mary Overton, William Walwyn. None of the Army men were present, however: Lucy supposed dully that they'd gone to the rendezvous. Ned was absent, too. Agnes had come from Stepney with Hannah and her husband, and she glared at the Levellers across the open grave.

The preacher mumbled a long prayer, then tossed in the first handful of icy earth. The other mourners copied him, and finally the sexton began shovelling the sticky mud into the grave. The crowd watched for a little, then ebbed slowly to the churchyard gate and stood about uncertainly. There was to be no funeral feast – Agnes had declared such celebrations heathenish and unsuited for the sober times – but no one wanted to be the first to walk away.

Will Browne went over to Agnes and offered her his hand. 'I am deeply sorry for your loss.'

She grimaced. 'Indeed.' She turned away deliberately.

Hannah came over to Browne and hugged him. 'Forgive my mother,' she said. 'She is all adrift.'

'Aye, poor woman!' said Browne with pity. 'What will she do now?'

'She will come live with me and Nat,' replied Hannah with an affectionate glance at her husband. 'Help me with the babe, when it comes.'

Lucy felt a touch on her shoulder and turned to find Mary Overton looking at her anxiously.

She liked and respected Mary. Their acquaintance had deepened towards friendship ever since Lucy was released from Bridewell: several other inmates had asked after Mary, and Lucy

279

had passed the messages on. 'He died a most Christian death,' Lucy said now, to forestall the expected condolence. 'I have no doubt that he is rejoicing now in Paradise.'

'Aye, he was a good and godly man,' agreed Mary Overton. She hesitated, then swallowed nervously. 'Lucy, I hope I will not add to your grief, but...' She stopped.

Lucy frowned, wondering what was wrong. Mary was a strong-willed woman, and nervousness wasn't like her.

Mary Overton drew a breath and continued, 'What I must confess is that I have taken your place at work.'

Lucy stared in shocked bewilderment.

Mary winced. 'Forgive me! When your good uncle fell ill and you stayed home to nurse him, Mr Mabbot asked me if I would manage the printing of *The Moderate*.'

'He said nothing of this to *me*!'

'How could he, while you were locked away? I—'

'He might have sent a note! He ... I...' She didn't know how to go on, and at last finished plaintively, 'I'm not to come back to it?'

'Forgive me!' said Mary again. 'I hoped it would not be a heavy blow, but I see it is.' Her pocked cheeks reddened. 'We needed the money.'

Of course she did. Mary had been struggling ever since her husband was arrested. The family's finances had improved only slightly since his release from Newgate: he earned small sums from writing or copying, while Mary set type and stitched pamphlets for one small printer or another. The Overtons had children to support: of *course* Mary had leapt at the offer of well-paid work on *The Moderate*.

'Mr Mabbot said he would have employed me at the first,' Mary continued, shamefacedly, 'only he feared that the children might distract me from the work – but now Richard's taken on some of the writing of the newsbook. That tipped the balance.'

'Your husband is writing for *The Moderate*?' Lucy asked, still bewildered. 'When did that start?' Even as she asked it, she saw that it was a natural development: Richard Overton was one of the Levellers' most gifted writers, and *The Moderate* had become a Leveller newsbook.

She had been numb inside since Thomas died: now she was filled with an agonizing mixture of rage and despair. Even so, she couldn't unleash that rage on Mary – how could she blame her for taking work when it was offered? 'Why did Gilbert Mabbot say nothing of this to *me*?' she demanded instead. 'Why did he leave *you* to tell me – at my uncle's burial?'

'Perhaps he did not wish to intrude upon your grief,' said Mary uncertainly.

'Aye, and perhaps he knew he was playing me a foul trick and feared to do so to my face!'

She'd spoken loudly, and several mourners looked round at her in shocked surprise. Mary made hushing gestures with her hands.

'I have lost everything!' Lucy howled. 'My home, my savings, and now my place as well – and that *cozening hypocrite* Gilbert Mabbot didn't even dare tell me so to my face!'

Agnes, scowling, marched over. 'For shame! Will you shout thus at the *church gate*, and your uncle just in his grave! For shame!'

Lucy wanted to scream and hit her: only the consciousness that she *was* at her uncle's burial held her back. She heaved a deep breath and pressed cold hands against her eyes. The tears flooded hot against her fingers, and she drew another choked breath, then another.

Will Browne hurried over to her in concern. 'What's this about losing your home?' He glanced at Agnes. 'Oh!'

Agnes would stay with her daughter and son-in-law in Stepney: the house in Southwark would be let. The new lessees would never allow the owner's niece rent-free lodging in the loft. Lucy had realized *that* the evening of the day Thomas died, and she hadn't been surprised when Agnes confirmed it in a note she sent round the following morning:

A pore widow must get whatte godes I cann, & you must goe, home to youre rite kin in Lesster-shirr, & why you shud have cum to Lundun & staid soe longe i no nat, but home you must goe, for ther's no plays heer for you, it's a smal hous & scarse monie to keep oure owen.

Browne turned to Agnes. 'You cannot mean to turn our Lucy out into the street!'

Nathaniel Cotman, Thomas's son-in-law, hurried over. 'Of course she will not be turned out

282

into the street!' he said with a stern glance at his mother-in-law. 'We have writ to her father, and I expect he will...'

'I will *never* go back to Hinckley!' Lucy cried vehemently.

'Yes, you will, miss!' hissed Agnes furiously. 'You will go, or I will have you taken up as a common *thief*! There were *sixteen shillings and eightpence* in the shop till when I left the house, and when I looked this morning it was all gone!'

'Aye!' Lucy shot back. 'And every penny of it went on medicine for my uncle! You foul greedy woman, do you grudge *that* cost? Christ Jesu preserve me from malice and slander!'

Agnes lunged forward and slapped her so hard she staggered. Mary Overton caught Lucy's arm to steady her, then hugged her tight. Lucy struggled to get loose again, blind and breathless with fury. 'Peace, peace!' Mary whispered, holding on. 'Don't shame your uncle!'

Lucy stopped struggling, and Mary let her go. Nat Cotman and Hannah, meanwhile, were holding Agnes, who was bright red in the face and crying. The rest of the mourners were staring at her, aghast. 'Forgive my mother!' Hannah begged the company at large. 'She's distraught.'

'You impudent inky strumpet!' shouted Agnes. 'You *provoked* me to it! I am a decent God-fearing woman, but you would provoke an angel!'

Lucy turned around and walked off, blind with tears.

She went back to the house: she presumed that she could stay there until someone was found to rent it, though how she would keep warm and fed she didn't know. She was flat out of money. The medicines for Thomas had in fact cost *eighteen* shillings: she'd had to raid her savings to supply the difference. There'd been bills to pay after Thomas died, too: all the local tradesmen had come round to the house wanting payment for coal and bread and butcher's meat. She'd tried to send them to Nat Cotman in Stepney, who would inherit the estate and all its debts, but they'd been insistent, unwilling to wait until the estate was settled, doubly unwilling to deal with strangers across the river. Lucy had been numb and weary, and nearly out of coal for the fire: she'd given in and paid them until she ran out of savings. She'd been careful to take a note of what she paid and to get receipts, but she was bitterly certain that with Agnes involved it would be a long time before she saw any of that money, if she ever saw it at all.

She let herself into the house and went to sit in the kitchen. Even that room was cold now: the fire had been banked down to almost nothing, leaving only a ghostly residual warmth in the bricks of the chimney. Susan was still at the churchyard, and the house was deserted. Thomas's empty bed stared at her: she and Susan had stripped off the stained sheets and boiled them, but hadn't carried the mattress up the stairs again. Lucy sat down on the floor with her back against the chimneypiece and hugged her knees.

She had come to London to make a new life

for herself. Through hard work, daring and luck she'd succeeded – and now that new life had shattered around her, just like the old one. She remembered Thomas saying that her mother should never have married her father, and she wished with sudden vehemence that she hadn't and that she herself had never been born. She pressed her hands to her mouth to stifle a howl and began to rock back and forth, whimpering.

There was a knock on the door. She ignored it, but it sounded again. She got up angrily and went to open it.

Mary Overton stood there with Will Browne and Liza, all three of them looking worried. 'Might we have a word?' asked Will, taking his hat off.

Lucy made an inarticulate noise, wiped at the tears with her sleeve and gestured them in.

They sat down in the cold parlour. 'I am sorry to have cost you your place,' said Mary cautiously.

Lucy made another noise and wiped her face again. 'No blame to you. You've children to feed.'

'It's true, five shillings a week are a mercy,' agreed Mary, 'but—'

'*Five* shillings?' asked Lucy. 'He only paid me *four*!'

Mary sniffed. 'Small wonder, then, that he went first to you and not me.'

The sly meanness jolted Lucy out of her despair. She snorted, wiped her face again and looked around for a rag on which to blow her nose. Liza got up, handed her a handkerchief, then hugged her. Lucy muttered inarticulate thanks.

'I'd be glad to make what amends I can,' said Mary. 'I can offer you a place to stay, at least until you find other work. In the ordinary way you'd want to stay with your kin, but your aunt seems a most ill-natured woman...'

'She's the most cursed shrew that ever was!' said Will Browne sourly. He seemed to have forgotten his pity for her.

Mary nodded curtly. 'So it would be better if you lodged with friends.'

Friends. Lucy wasn't on her own: her new life might survive this blow. She could go to some other, warmer house and be welcome. The thought set off fresh tears, and she dabbed helplessly at her eyes with Liza's handkerchief. 'Thank you! I should like that very much!'

'We have but the two beds,' Mary admitted. 'I sold the other while Dick was in Newgate. You would have to share with the children.'

'In this house I shared with the maid.' She blew her nose again, glancing round them. 'She's out of a place, too – Susan, I mean: my uncle's maid. She well deserves another one. She's a good, kind, hard-working girl, and faithful. She stayed with me to nurse Uncle Thomas while Aunt Agnes fled across the river.' Her lips curled with anger.

'I will ask among my friends and relations,' promised Mary. 'Indeed, I will mention it at the next council meeting! I am sure we will find another place for your uncle's maid, and for you, too!'

Browne cleared his throat. 'In the meantime, I can find you some piecework with a bookbinder. It won't pay what Mabbot did, but half a loaf's better than none if a man be a-hungry.'

There was the sound of the shop door opening, and they looked round to find Nathaniel Cotman coming in, with Susan on his heels. He stopped short when he saw the gathering in the parlour. Lucy noticed, with a stab of resentment, that he did not take off his hat: he now considered himself master of the house. She remembered with a shock that now that was exactly what he was.

Mary Overton got to her feet. 'Sir,' she said, 'I came to offer Lucy room in my house, since it seems she is not welcome in yours.'

Cotman's face reddened. 'She is welcome in my house until her own kin come to fetch her home!' He frowned at Lucy. 'You *have* kin, Lucy Wentnor; you have a father, and a brother who was anxious to take you home last summer! There was no call for you to shame us in that ungodly fashion, pretending we would turn you out into the street!'

Lucy looked him in the eye. 'I pretended no such thing, sir: it was what others concluded from your half-heartedness. To say you'll keep me until I can be fetched back to Hinckley can scarce be reckoned a *welcome*! And I think even that much would be denied, were it my aunt's to dispose of me.'

'You owe your aunt a duty of respect and obedience,' said Cotman disapprovingly.

'Sir, I have ever tried to pay it! My reward was to be termed a thief before all those people, and then struck when I rejected that foul false name! Shall I show you the receipt, sir, for what I paid the apothecary? And what does it say of *her,* that before her husband was even buried, the first she was back Southwark since his death, she came creeping back without my knowledge to *look in the till* for the money that was left there?'

Cotman blinked. He opened his mouth, then closed it again, realizing that, yes, Agnes *must* have done just that, to know that the money was gone. 'Show me the receipt,' he said at last.

'Sir, that is unjustified!' protested Will Browne, getting to his feet. 'You insult your cousin's honesty, without the least cause!'

Lucy gestured for him to sit down again and went into the kitchen to fetch the receipt. She'd written her expenditure out fair on the last page of her *Moderate* account book, and she'd got the tradesmen to sign or make their marks for what she gave them. Cotman studied the carefully labelled columns, surprised and wary.

'You may *ask* the apothecary and the tradesmen, sir, what I paid them,' Lucy said coldly. 'Their accounts will tally with mine.'

'You've spent twice what was in the till,' said Cotman.

'Aye. The tradesmen came with bills, sir; I tried to send them to you, but they would not go. I was obliged to spend my own savings to satisfy them.'

Cotman closed the account book with a sigh. 'Well. I will repay it.'

'And, I hope, make it public that I am no thief!'

Cotman waved that away irritably. 'I will speak the plain truth: that you spent the money honestly in care for your uncle, but Agnes did not know that and, in her grief and distraction, she jumped to a false conclusion. She mistook you, Lucy, no more than that. Now, will you come back with me to Stepney and live with us peaceably until your family come to take you home?'

'I will not, sir! Mrs Overton has done me the kindness of offering me lodging, and Mr Browne can find me work. You do not wish to be burdened with me, and I have no wish to burden you!'

He gave her a stern glower. 'That is a very saucy answer! I am the head of the household now—'

'Sir, where I am concerned that title belongs to my *father,* not to you! If my father commands me home, I will obey him – but he has no wish to have me in his house again, and that is no fault of mine, as you well know!'

As soon as she said it, she saw that he *didn't* know: he stared at her in confusion. Susan, who'd kept nervously silent until then, touched his arm. 'That's true, sir. Paul Wentnor came without his father's blessing, because a cousin had frighted him with stories of Mr Stevens' wild Leveller friends.'

Cotman looked at the wild Leveller friends but said nothing. He hadn't shared his father-in-law's politics but he hadn't been entirely unsympathetic, either.

'I will tell you the whole tale later, sir,' Susan

assured him, 'but it *is* true that Lucy's da won't want her home again.'

Cotman sagged. 'Very well!' He stared unhappily at Lucy. He was, she knew, torn between a desire to avoid the shame of sending his wife's cousin to live with strangers and his horror at the thought of having Lucy and Agnes under the same roof.

'I will be well, sir,' Lucy told him. 'I will live much more peaceably with Mrs Overton than ever I would with Aunt Agnes.'

'You've a cursed ill-natured mother-in-law there, Cotman,' said Will Browne. 'I'd not take her in for all the gold in England!'

Lucy left Southwark that afternoon, walking over London Bridge between Will Browne and Mary Overton, carrying her small case of luggage. She and Susan had parted with hugs and tears. The maid was going to stay to keep watch over the house until it could be rented. Lucy didn't like to think of her there alone, but Cotman had at least agreed to provide money for coal and food. He'd also given Lucy threepence so she could post a letter to Leicester. She hadn't liked to ask him for money, but she knew Nat Cotman had already written to her father, and, without word from her, Paul would make another descent on London.

The Overtons' house was on Coleman Street, a block to the south of the Brownes'. It was of a good size, but Lucy had gathered that it was underfurnished: Mary had sold most of the furniture while Richard was in Newgate, and the

Stationers' men had stolen everything movable when they arrested Mary. The whole party paused outside it, and Liza hugged Lucy again. 'I'm glad we'll be neighbours!' said the girl happily.

Lucy hugged her back, then followed Mary into her new home.

The first thing she noticed was the smell of tobacco; the second was the sound of men's voices, low and angry. Mary stopped short in surprise, then pressed anxiously on into the house.

The next room was the kitchen. Two men were sitting by the fire smoking pipes. One of them was Richard Overton; the other, to Lucy's astonishment, was John Lilburne.

'Dick!' cried Mary, hurrying to her husband. 'What's amiss? Why are you home so soon?'

Richard Overton groaned and stood to put his arms about his wife and hold her close. Lilburne got to his feet and knocked the ashes from his pipe into the fire. 'I've stayed long enough,' he said. 'I'll hie me home to my own wife and children. Why, Mistress Wentnor! What are you doing here?'

'Oh!' exclaimed Mary breathlessly, disentangling herself from her husband. 'Dick, Thomas Stevens is dead, and poor Lucy is cast upon the world without a penny since we've taken her place at *The Moderate*! I told her she could stay here with us until she finds another place.'

Richard was taken aback and stared at Lucy in obvious misgiving. She clutched her luggage, acutely embarrassed. It had seemed natural to accept Mary Overton's offer, but she should have wondered whether Richard would approve. She barely knew him: by the time he was released from Newgate she'd ceased to attend meetings at The Whalebone.

Then he gave her a tired smile. 'And so she can, of course! I hope you've no objection to sharing with the children?'

'No, sir,' murmured Lucy, relieved.

'Tom Stevens is dead?' asked Lilburne. 'I pray God give him rest! How did that come about?'

'It was the smallpox, sir,' replied Lucy. 'He died most like a Christian, praying that God would forgive his sins.'

'He had but few of those,' said Lilburne. 'I've no doubt, Mistress, that he is entered into the joy which our Lord has prepared for those who love him, while we are left to struggle in the darkness of this benighted earth. I'll home to my wife and children; I bid you all goodnight.'

He left. Mary gave her husband a questioning look.

'We were deceived,' said Richard Overton heavily. 'Defrauded by those we'd set up to govern us. Outflanked, overrid and brought down even unto dust.'

'What!' cried Mary.

'Aye.' Richard sat down again, pulled his wife on to his lap and wrapped her in his arms. 'When we arrived, we found that Cromwell was before us. He had had another proclamation made up in place of the *Agreement,* and he'd had it circulated through the ranks. It claimed to come from the Lord General and the Council of the Army, but the Council never saw it – at least, the full Council never did; it came from Cromwell and his cronies. In it Lord General Fairfax threatened to *step down,* unless *discipline was restored.* Why should it be *restored?* When and where did it *break down*? The rendezvous had been *agreed* by the full Council of the Army, and arranged by the Army's officers and Agitators! But the men are in awe of Fairfax. The threat frightened them, and the rest of the proclamation contained enough of the *Agreement*'s provisions to satisfy them, especially since they believed that it had the blessing of the full Council. When poor Colonel Rainsborough tried to give a copy of the *Agreement* to Fairfax, he was waved aside: the new proclamation supplanted it entirely. Fairfax and Cromwell demanded that all the men sign it, saying that unless they did, they would not receive any of their arrears of pay. Those who tried to stand by the *Agreement* were branded as rebels and disturbers of the peace and were put under arrest.

'Then two more regiments arrived at the field, Colonel Harrison's and the one belonging to John's brother Robert, both zealous for our freedoms. They had copies of the *Agreement* in their hats, with "England's Freedoms, Soldiers' Rights!" in bold type above the heading. Cromwell at once declared that they had *mutinied,* forsooth! – because Harrison's regiment was supposed to have attended a *different* rendezvous, and Robert Lilburne's had been ordered north without being assigned a rendezvous at all! Robert Lilburne wasn't there, nor any of the officers above the rank of captain: the men had been extremely indignant when they were ordered to march north without any opportunity to support the *Agreement*, and when their officers tried to enforce the order they sent them off – but *otherwise* they were orderly enough. They wanted only to claim their right to speak their minds!

'Cromwell and Fairfax ordered the men to take the papers from their hats. When they refused, they rode into the midst of them with swords drawn, snatching the papers and trampling them underfoot. God help us, these men whom they had branded *mutineers* would not lift a hand against their commanders: they yielded, and took the papers from their hats and cast them aside. Then Cromwell was pleased to have those he termed the "ring-leaders" arrested for mutiny – men whom the soldiers themselves had elected to represent them! Three of them were sentenced to death on the spot, but – oh, the Great Man is merciful! – were allowed to cast dice for their lives, and only one of them was shot. They marched him out before the assembled regiments and shot him dead. Arnold, his name was; Private Richard Arnold: may his blood be on Oliver Cromwell's head before the throne of God Almighty!'

Richard delivered all this in a rush, clinging to his thin, pock-faced wife as though she was his only support and he adrift in a raging sea. Lucy struggled to make sense of it: she'd heard no news since Thomas fell ill. She still had no idea why Lilburne wasn't in the Tower, but that had become a secondary matter. Richard Overton was talking about the Army rendezvous which should have determined the fate of *The Agreement of the People*: it had been subverted by Cromwell, branded a mutiny and ruthlessly suppressed. Richard and John Lilburne had gone to – wherever it was – hoping to speak in favour of the *Agreement*, and had instead been forced to watch as all their hopes were crushed.

'Our ancestors' blood was often spent in vain for the recovery of their freedoms,' said the *Agreement* itself, *'suffering themselves through fraudulent accommodations to be still deluded of the fruit of their victories.'* Now more blood had been spent, and still in vain. She remembered Thomas, on the first day of his illness, exclaiming eagerly that they would have a settlement of the government by the new year; at least he'd escaped having his hopes dashed yet again. Now the horrible tussling for power would go on and on, and there would be no settlement at all.

A horrible new possibility chilled her: Richard had said one of the regiments labelled as mutinous was Colonel Harrison's. *'Col Harrison's rgmt is astirr for our Liberties, and I am held in Honour as one that has spent Ink as well as Blood in their defence.'*

'Sir,' she said in an ragged whisper. 'Do you know if Jamie Hudson was arrested?'

Richard looked round at her dazedly. 'Who?'

He didn't know Jamie; of course he didn't. He'd been in Newgate all the time Jamie was working on the press. Lucy would have to discover Jamie's fate from someone else. 'One you never met,' she said numbly. 'Forgive me: I intrude.' She felt ashamed to be standing in the Overtons' kitchen with her little package of luggage, like a poor orphan, especially since she was no relation at all.

Mary Overton kissed her husband. 'I must fetch the children home,' she said. 'We'll talk at supper.'

The Overton children had been left with a neighbour when Mary went to the funeral. She brought them home and introduced them to Lucy: Faith, a girl of eight; six-year-old Dickon; and Judith, who was four. Their mother explained Lucy's presence, and the children asked her how long she would stay with them, and why she'd come to London, and how she meant to find a job printing. Their questions were at least a distraction from Lucy's raw grief and her gnawing anxiety for Jamie.

There was, as Mary had promised, more serious talk at supper. Quite a lot seemed to have happened while Lucy was locked away. Apparently Lilburne had been released from the Tower on bail, ostensibly so that he could prepare his case. Some might say he'd been allowed this because he'd been ill – he had collapsed in front of a Parliamentary hearing – but Richard Overton had dark suspicions that his friend had not been released because of any sudden accession of mercy in his keepers.

'The stratagem at Ware could have failed,' Richard said bitterly – Ware, in Hertfordshire, was where the rendezvous had taken place. 'If it

296

had, why, there was John, conveniently at hand to take the blame!'

'You were there, too,' said Mary and squeezed his hand.

Richard made a face. 'So I was. If he couldn't suppress the *Agreement* in the Army, Cromwell would at least have had the pleasure of discrediting us and discovering another reason to jail us. And there's the business of the letter, too.'

'The letter' was another piece of news Lucy had missed. It had been left anonymously for the king at Hampton Court: it warned him that 'eight or nine Agitators' were planning to murder him. The king had fled the palace precipitously, leaving the letter behind. It was rumoured all over London that Lilburne was the driving force behind a real conspiracy to murder the king, or alternatively, that he'd sent the letter to get the king away from London to forestall a settlement with the Army Grandees. Richard Overton was scathing about both alternatives. 'John wasn't released from the Tower until the day *after* that letter was delivered!' he protested. 'Is he supposed to have conducted his conspiracy under the warden's eyes? And as for wanting the king away from London – Charles Stuart is further from accepting any proposal of Cromwell's than he's been all this year! And John was—' He stopped abruptly, with an uneasy glance at Lucy.

And John was trying to deal with the king himself, Lucy guessed suddenly. She remembered the Royalist prisoner who'd been so friendly with Lilburne in the Tower. She wasn't sure whether she should be indignant or not. Not, she decided. If the king could be brought to accept the *Agreement* as the basis of a settlement, it would solve everything: an alliance between Levellers and Royalists would be invincible.

Of course, a king who wouldn't accept Cromwell's *Heads of the Proposals* would never accept the *Agreement*, which offered him much less in the way of privileges. She couldn't blame John Lilburne for trying, though – nor, with the sentiment among the Agitators running so strongly against the king, could she blame him for wanting to keep his negotiations secret. Richard Overton was right, too: if Cromwell knew that Lilburne was trying to deal with Charles Stuart, then it wasn't *Lilburne* who wanted the king away from London.

'The letter was sent by some other person,' Richard resumed in a low voice, 'and John was released to be a scapegoat. Now, look well at what came of the king's flight! King Charles hied himself to the Isle of Wight because he thought that the governor there, Robert Hammond, would favour him. Why should he think that? Because he'd heard some word, evidently; and yet in the event, of course, Hammond proved himself Cromwell's man. Now the king is locked up in Carisbrooke Castle, a long way from London! Who's benefited from all this hugger-mugger dealing? Oliver Cromwell. The man is as subtle as a serpent, and as cold!'

'What do we do now?' Mary asked, after a silence.

Richard sighed deeply and pushed his dish of

pottage aside. 'We protest. We petition. We print copies of the *Agreement* and circulate it, in the City and in the Army. We must hope and endure all things, dear heart! What else can we do?'

Mary got up, came round the table to him and kissed him.

Lucy found it strangely comforting to squeeze into bed with the children that night. It was like being a child herself again, snuggling up with her little brothers on a cold night, knowing that her mother and father were asleep in the next room and all was safe. Long after the children were asleep, though, she lay awake, thinking of Thomas's body lying in the cold wet earth and imagining Jamie shackled in some rough guard-room, defrauded of liberty by the Army he had trusted.

Thirteen

The following morning Lucy walked the short distance over to The Whalebone. The two people most likely to know what had happened to Jamie were Ned Trebet and John Wildman: Ned was always at his tavern, and Wildman stabled his horse there when he was in London.

The yard of the tavern was quiet for once, and in the main room there were only a handful of customers sleepily drinking their morning draught. Ned was sitting at one of the tables with his own breakfast, with Nancy Shorby and Rafe the cook; he had his feet propped up on the opposite bench but he took them off and sat up when he saw Lucy.

'Lucy!' he exclaimed and came over. 'I – I am most heartily sorry for your loss.'

Her eyes stung at the reminder. 'Thank you.'

He hesitated uncertainly. 'Have you broke your fast yet? Sit down, then, and have a draught and a morsel!'

Lucy sat down and allowed herself to be served with a half pint of small beer and a slice of fresh maslin bread. She was aware, as she nibbled it, that Nancy was frowning: there was no chore at hand to divert Ned's attention.

'Ned,' she began; at the same time Ned asked, 'What will you do?'

'The Overtons have kindly offered me lodging,' Lucy told him. 'And Mr Browne says he can find me piecework bookbinding, which will, I hope, pay my keep until I can find proper work again.'

'What?' asked Ned, startled. 'I thought—' He broke off uncomfortably. Lucy gave him a questioning look, and he went on, 'Well, I thought that perhaps you'd come here to bid me farewell – that you were going back to Leicestershire.'

'That I will never do of my own will,' Lucy said firmly. 'Ned, Mr Overton—'

'Why must you depend on the Overtons?' Ned asked in confusion. 'Has something befallen your aunt and your other kin in London?'

'God forbid! They are well, but they would only keep me until my Leicestershire kin come fetch me – and, as I said, I've no wish to go back. Mary Overton was given my place at *The Moderate* and, conscientious as she is, she had no wish to see me suffer because of her good fortune. I hope I may find another place soon. Last night Mr Overton—'

'What do you want of me?' Ned asked unhappily.

Lucy stopped, surprised. Ned flushed, and she suddenly understood that he thought she'd come to plead for help – for marriage if he'd offer it; for money and protection if he wouldn't.

He hadn't come to Thomas's funeral. She'd scarcely thought about that at the time, but now the omission had a stark significance. He'd been afraid she'd cling – and if she had, he would have pushed her off.

'I thought you might know what has become of Jamie Hudson!' she said bluntly, choking back her anger. 'Last night Mr Overton was telling me of the rendezvous at Ware – have you heard yet what happened there?'

Ned floundered at this unexpected turn of the conversation. Then his face darkened. 'Aye. John Wildman came in late last night and told us of it. As foul a piece of treachery as ever I heard!'

'Is Major Wildman *here*?' Lucy asked hopefully.

'Nay, he's at his cousin's house. But he told the tale when he stabled his horse. He *did* say what had happened to Jamie, too! He's been arrested;

Major Wildman said he *should* have been safe, but when one of his friends was arrested, he protested, and so he was arrested as well.'

'Do you know where he is?'

Ned shook his head. 'That's yet to learn.' He frowned. 'You came to ask about *Jamie*?'

'He's your friend and mine, Ned! Shouldn't I care that he's in prison?'

'I–I...' stammered Ned. 'Aye. It's only – well, Lucy, I thought you might want help. With your uncle dead.'

'Nay,' she said coldly. 'I'd not come here for *that*.'

There was a silence. Ned looked shocked and hurt rather than relieved.

Lucy relented a little. 'I would be grateful, though, if you could spread word that I'm looking for work, printing or setting type.'

It didn't seem to help. Ned might have dreaded the prospect of an old semi-sweetheart clinging to him in tears, but the sight of her determined to fend for herself evidently didn't please him either. 'Aye,' he muttered unhappily, 'I'll do that.'

Nancy Shorby, who'd listened to all this uneasily, suddenly leaned forward. 'I'm at a loss to know why you're so set against your kin in Leicestershire.'

Lucy met her eyes. The question had, she was sure, been asked to embarrass her in front of Ned – and yet there suddenly seemed no reason not to answer it honestly. The shame of what had happened no longer had power to crush her. The rape of a Leicestershire dairymaid couldn't blight the life of a London printworker. 'I'm not set against my kin,' she said firmly. 'My father, though, hates the sight of me because those villains who stole our cows forced me, and it shamed him. I'll thank you to keep that tale out of the tavern gossip.'

Nancy's jaw dropped. Ned opened his mouth and closed it again: if he had guessed this, he clearly hadn't expected Lucy to speak of it. He gave her a look of shock and, strangely, resentment.

'I wouldn't have spoken of it,' she told them defensively, 'only I'd not have people wondering why I'm set against my kin or they against me.' She got to her feet. 'Thank you, Ned, for the bread and ale! If you learn any news or hear of anyone who needs a typesetter, I'll be grateful to know it. I'm at the Overtons' at present, as I said. God give you health!' She walked off and went back to Coleman Street to find William Browne and the bookbinding work he'd promised her.

The piecework consisted of folding and stitching pages for a collection of sermons. Browne gave her a heavy basket of printed sheets; Lucy worked hard all the first day and only earned tuppence. She told herself that it was the same as she'd done when she first came to London, but even that wasn't true: the wages didn't include dinner. She didn't go hungry, but that was only because she lugged the sheets to the Overtons', did her stitching in their kitchen and ate the midday meal along with the family.

She did what she could to make herself useful. She helped Faith, the eldest Overton child, to keep an eye on the younger two, and she prepared the midday meal and cleared up afterwards. She didn't think, though, that it compensated the Overtons for the inconvenience of having an extra person in their crowded house and she was painfully aware that her earnings barely covered the cost of her food. She'd proudly told Nat Cotman that she didn't want to be a burden to him, but she suspected that instead she was burdening the Overtons, who could afford it less and who had no real obligation to her.

However, when she was offered a well-paid printing job after only two days stitching sermons, she didn't see how she could accept it.

Faith Overton answered a knock on the door, then came to the kitchen and handed Lucy a note:

Mistress Wentnor, it has come to my eares that the Licensor has let you go. I am in need of an honest and discreet Printer, as you have shown yourself to be. If you wd learne more, meet me at The Blew Boare in Holborne this evg at 7.
   Yr. srvt Marchamont Nedham

'Who gave you this?' Lucy asked in surprise.

The girl shrugged. 'A man. He didn't tell me his name.'

'What did he look like?'

'He was short and dark and ugly,' said Faith disdainfully. 'But he had a gold earring. In just

304

one ear!'

That sounded like Nedham, all right. If he needed a printer, it was probably because his previous printer had been arrested – that, or decided that the risk of continuing to work on *Mercurius Pragmaticus* was too great. Gilbert Mabbot's men were ransacking the city for *Pragmaticus*. Nedham's newsbook was popular – it sold out more quickly than the *Perfect Diurnall*, despite the fact that, being illegal, it cost twice as much – and its stories embarrassed and offended the government in equal measure. Mabbot's masters were demanding that he shut it down.

Lucy read the note again resentfully. A part of her *wanted* to respond to it: *Pragmaticus* would be much more interesting than sermons and more profitable as well. She had no illusions, though, that it would be safe. Printing Leveller pamphlets had been dangerous too, of course, but she'd *believed* in what she was printing. A Royalist newsbook was another matter entirely. She was not quite sure when she'd started to despise the king, but she did, wholeheartedly. He could have given his poor bleeding country a fair peace at any time over the last summer but he had instead clung to his own privileges. Why should she risk her freedom by printing apologies for him?

There was something very satisfying, though, in the notion of thumbing her nose at Gilbert Mabbot after the shabby way he'd dismissed her.

She struggled with herself, dismayed by how much she was tempted. She told herself firmly that it would be perfectly monstrous to betray the Overtons by taking up Royalism while under their roof and resolved to hand them the note as soon as they returned from work. She expected it would end in the privy.

'There's no harm in meeting him,' said Richard when he returned to the house a couple of hours later. 'If you've no liking for his terms, you can simply walk out.'

Lucy was flabbergasted. 'You – you wouldn't *mind* if I took the place?'

Richard shrugged. 'It's not my affair, Mistress, but it's like to pay well.' He smiled at her. 'I confess, that would weigh with *me.*'

'But he's a *Royalist*!'

'Of late his main target has been Cromwell.' Richard suddenly grinned. '"Crum-Hell", "the Town Bull of Ely", "the Nose Almighty"! Nedham's a very witty fellow and his barbs draw blood. It does my heart good to see Cromwell pricked! If he turns on *us* again, you can always resign. Besides...'

Lucy tensed, suspecting that Richard was about to say he'd like to be able to call his house his own again. If he was, however, he tactfully changed it. 'We say that we're in favour of a free and unlicensed press: if that means a free press for ourselves but none for our adversaries, we're nothing but false hypocrites!'

'Your partner Gilbert Mabbot wouldn't say so,' Lucy pointed out.

'Gilbert *is* a hypocrite!' Richard replied cheerfully. 'He believes in the liberty of the press as I do, but the Licensorship was too fine a gift to refuse.' He sighed and admitted, 'Had I been offered it, I might have accepted it myself. Our Lord threw the money-changers from the Temple, but I've no doubt they crept in again by the backstairs and set up in business once more. I'll never sell our liberties, but still the children must eat. Had Mary been without employment and received that note you hold, I would have advised her to meet with Nedham.'

Lucy looked dubiously at the note. An alternative reason for the invitation had, of course, occurred to her. 'Why appoint a meeting in a tavern? He knew to leave the note here. Why didn't he come in?'

That brought another grin. 'Into *my* house, you mean? The house of the Licensor's partner? Nay. An inn is safer, and The Blue Boar is a fine inn for intrigues. A man has ample opportunity to watch who comes and, if he sees someone he'd prefer to avoid, ample opportunity to slip away.' The grin broadened. 'And any woman pestered by a whoremongering rogue like Nedham would have no difficulty giving him the slip.'

It was a big inn, certainly; a coaching inn, with a large courtyard flanked by galleries. Lucy hesitated in the wicket gate from the street, then told herself it was absurd to think that Nedham would go to so much trouble to seduce a girl he'd met only once months before, and that if that *was* what he had in mind, she would walk out. Her heart was pounding, though, as she walked on: in the back of her mind she could hear her father's outraged voice: 'She agreed to meet a strange man in a tavern after dark? The whore!'

The main room of The Blue Boar was long, low-ceilinged, poorly lit and full of tobacco smoke: you could have hidden a troop of pike-men in it, let alone a fugitive newsbook editor. Lucy stopped inside the door and looked around helplessly. Several of the men sitting nearby took their pipes out of their mouths with appre-ciative stares. A serving-man hurried over.

'I came to meet Mr...' she began; then decided it would be better not to name any names. 'I came to meet a gentleman who offered me work *as a printer*.' She emphasized the final words: she was going to make it absolutely clear that she would have nothing whatever to do with any other suggestions!

'Aye, he's expecting you,' said the serving-man calmly. He glanced behind her, then, con-fident that she wasn't being followed, said, 'This way.'

Nedham was in a cubby-hole of a private room, eating a meat pie and washing it down with a bottle of wine. He beamed when Lucy was shown in. 'Sweet Mistress Lucy! I feared you'd leave me to pine for you! Here, sit down by me! Harry, another glass!'

Lucy took hold of the stool at the end of the table and moved it so that the board separated her from Nedham. 'Nay, I thank you, no wine!' she told the serving-man. She sat primly.

'You're not a Puritan?' asked Nedham in dis-may.

'Indeed I am!' she replied. 'In your note you offered me *work,* Mr Nedham.'

'A Puritan as well as a Leveller!' Nedham shook his head sadly. 'Where's the harm in combining work with pleasure?'

'I see nothing here that would give *me* any pleasure, sir.'

He smote his heart, grinning. She looked him sternly in the eye. 'I am not so desperate for work that I would damn myself, Mr Nedham. If your offer requires me to whore for you, I'll leave now.'

'Oh, oh, oh! The kitten has teeth!' Nedham poured himself more of the wine. 'I *am* offering you work, Mistress Leveller. You managed John Lilburne's press all last summer, did you not?'

'Aye.'

'And then went to work for Mabbot?' He smirked.

'Aye,' she agreed. 'And, indeed, I think that *does* mean that Mabbot would be slow to suspect me. He knows me for a Leveller – and he dismissed me very meanly and will want to avoid me.'

Nedham raised his brows appreciatively. 'Clever puss!'

'If I am a *cat,* Mr Nedham, are you a *cur*? You need someone to print your newsbook and keep your press safe from the Stationers. I know how to do both. I need work and I'm willing, but only if the terms suit. What became of your last printer?'

'He thought he was suspected and told me to take myself elsewhere – which I'm doing now. I can offer you as much as Mabbot did.'

'Sir, what I printed for Mr Mabbot was in keeping with my sympathies; it was also *lawful* and *licensed*. You must offer me *more* than he did!'

Nedham sniggered. 'I'm sure I have it, too.'

'I meant *money*, Mr Nedham.'

'This greed is un-Leveller-like, surely!'

'Consider it my refutation of that foul *lie* that we'd do away with property.'

He laughed. 'Six shillings a week, then! Are all Leveller girls so hard?'

Six shillings a week; a whole shilling every working day! For that sort of money she could rent ... well, no, not a *room,* but certainly a *bed* – and still have enough left to live on. She struggled to keep her pleasure from showing. 'Very well, sir.'

'If you'll whore for me,' Nedham said with a lazy smile, 'I'll double it.'

She jumped to her feet, glaring, and he held up his hands. 'Nay, it was a jest!'

She was quite sure it hadn't been. 'A lewd, sorry one, then,' she said in disgust. 'And they say you're so witty!'

'Jesu have mercy! You know where to strike! I shall try to think of better jests in future. I think we shall agree very well, Mistress Wentnor.'

The serving-man, Harry, came in looking excited. He whispered something in Nedham's ear. 'What!' exclaimed Nedham. 'Are you sure?'

Harry shrugged apologetically. 'Nay. I've not seen them anywhere but a-horse going through London. But I think so.'

Nedham frowned. His eye fell on Lucy. 'Mistress Wentnor. Will you go with Harry here, as though ... as though he were showing you the way to the privy. Cast an eye over a pair of new-come guests, then come back and tell me if you recognize either of them. Don't let them know you've taken note of them!'

Lucy suspected that some of Mabbot's men had just turned up. She bit her lip, wondering if she should walk out before anyone connected her to Nedham. Six shillings a week, though ... She nodded and followed Harry from the cubby-hole.

The main room was just as dark as before and the smoke was even thicker. Harry led the way over to the other side of the room. 'In the corner stall,' he muttered out of the side of his mouth. 'The two Army men with their hats pulled down.' Lucy saw who he meant: they were sitting in a stall in the darkest part of the room and their faces were further shadowed by the wide brims of their hats. Harry, with Lucy trailing him, went up to them. 'One moment, mistress!' he told Lucy loudly. 'More ale, sirs?'

The two men looked up. They both wore the plain buff-coats of ordinary cavalrymen and their swords were leaning against the table. One of them – a fairish man with a pointed beard – was unknown to her; the other – an older man with a ruddy face and red nose – seemed familiar. 'Not yet,' he told Harry.

Harry nodded, then turned back to Lucy. 'Down the passage, and outside on the left!' he told her, waving an arm.

'Thank you,' murmured Lucy, blushing. She went out, then continued on down the passage and outside to the left: she might as well use the privy while she was about it.

She was readjusting her skirts when she remembered where she'd seen that red-nosed farmer's face before: riding through Southwark, with his Ironsides behind him. She staggered from surprise and fought down a mad urge to go to him and demand, *What have you done with Jamie Hudson?* Instead, she went quietly back into the tavern and crossed the main room without even glancing at the stall in the corner.

Nedham was on his feet, pacing, when she returned to the cubby-hole. He gave her a look of sharp question.

'It's *Cromwell*!' she whispered, still aghast.

'Ha!' Nedham stood still, his eyes bright with excitement. 'So Harry thought, too; and if one's Cromwell, then there's no reason to think that he was wrong about the other. Cromwell and Ireton! Now what, I wonder, are those two about?'

'They were dressed like common troopers,' said Lucy, amazed by it.

'Oh, oh!' exclaimed Nedham, grinning. He sat down at the table again, tapping it with his fingers. 'What think you? Are those two holy saints here to meet a pair of whores on the sly?'

'I cannot think any man would take his *son-in-law* whoring with him!' said Lucy, scandalized.

'Ah, you're an innocent maid, after all!' said Nedham. 'I've known it happen. Still, you've the right: old Noll wouldn't want his daughter struck with the clap, blighting the little Nol-livings to come! Perhaps it's not Ireton. You recognized Cromwell; what of the other? You said naught of him.'

'I wouldn't know Ireton from Adam. The man is slight, fairish, with long hair and his beard done in a point.'

'Huh. That should be Ireton. Well, well! I think I will stay here a little longer and see how this comes out!'

Harry came back in. 'They've got a man watching the gate to the street,' he informed Nedham.

'They're expecting someone,' said Nedham. He dug a sixpence out of his purse and tossed it to Harry. 'Here's thank you and well done! I'll wait here, Harry; let me know what they do. And bring me another bottle!'

Lucy hesitated: she knew she ought to conclude her business with Nedham, then go back to the Overtons – but it was possible that Cromwell's business here was something the Levellers would want to know about. She seated herself.

Nedham eyed her. 'You need not stay. I'll meet you tomorrow, at The Fleece in Covent Garden at about ten o'clock.'

'Why there?'

'Because I usually take my morning draught there.'

'At *ten o'clock*?'

'Such as you, Mistress, may rise at the crack of dawn, but I must burn the midnight oil, labouring in taverns such as this to collect the news; I

313

do not rise so early! Meet me tomorrow at The Fleece and I'll lead you from there to the press.'

'I'll wait, sir, until I know why Cromwell came here.'

'What's it to you? Is this woman's curiosity, or are you a Leveller spy?'

'I am a *printer*, sir, as you well know since you hired me! But if I come upon some news that might help my friends, of course I will pass it on to them.'

Nedham stared hard; she stared back. He grinned suddenly. 'Well, then! Come sit by me, sweet Lucy, and have some wine!'

Lucy got up and moved her stool over against the far wall. Nedham glared indignantly, then sighed and poured himself more wine.

They waited for perhaps an hour. Nedham put aside his wine unfinished, took out a notebook and pen, and began scribbling something that involved many crossings out and secretive smirks. At last Harry came back.

'Their man came and spoke to them,' he reported. 'They both rose at once and went out the back way, to the stables.'

Nedham raised his eyebrows, then got to his feet. He seemed to know his way around The Blue Boar because he didn't go through the common room but along a passage, through the kitchen – which was empty, this late at night – and then out into a silent, frosty stableyard. He halted, and in the silence they both heard voices coming from the stable. Nedham walked silently across the yard and along the stable wall.

'—and then you'll let me go?' came a man's

voice, sharp with fear.

'You seem an honest fellow,' was the reply in a deep, steady tone. 'We've no wish to do you any harm. We will dismiss you once we have searched your saddle.'

'My *saddle*?'

'Your *horse*'s saddle, then!' said a third voice impatiently; it was lighter in pitch than the second speaker, a tenor rather than a bass. 'Give it here!'

'But—'

'Give it here, I say!'

There was a silence. Nedham stayed where he was, leaning against the stable wall and listening intently; Lucy stood a yard or so behind him, scarcely daring to breathe. Inside the stable, a horse snorted uneasily; there was a jingle of harness.

'Here!' said the tenor voice. 'Just as he said.'

Another pause, and then: 'I knew nothing of this!' said the first voice, even more frightened. 'I was told to take letters to Dover, b–b–but not *that* one; I knew nothing of *that* one, I—'

'Silence!'

Silence fell, thick and heavy. Lucy tilted her head back and looked up at the November stars, cold and white and beautiful.

'Well?' asked the tenor voice.

'Read it for yourself,' said the deep voice. It now sounded desperately weary. 'He has played us false. God forgive me! I have pawned my reputation for that man; I've offended my friends; I've stood up on my hindlegs in the House and brayed of His Majesty; I have denied

315

my own loyal men and done my utmost to suppress them when they cried out against him – and *he has played us false.* God help us! God forgive us! Deliver me from bloodguiltiness, oh Lord God of my salvation!'

Nedham turned away abruptly. He saw Lucy, stared a moment blankly, then gestured back towards the inn. They hurried wordlessly across the yard and back into the empty kitchen.

'Say nothing of that to anyone,' ordered Nedham.

It was dark in the kitchen; he was only a shape in the dimness. She strained her eyes, trying to make him out. 'It was a letter from the *king,*' she said. 'It was sewn into the saddle. They were waiting to intercept it.'

'I said, say *naught*! If you want to work for me, not a word! Aye, if you keep your lips sealed, you may have a gold angel for it!'

'He might have taken his throne again *last summer*!' she whispered in disgust. 'But the selfish, deceitful rogue wanted *all,* and so the kingdom must bleed again! Why, in the name of God, do you want to protect him?'

He took a sudden step forward, grabbed her shoulders and kissed her.

She jammed a foot down on his toe, got an arm up between them and shoved him off, then slapped him hard across the face.

'God damn!' exclaimed Nedham indignantly, feeling his mouth where she'd hit him.

'Don't you touch me!' she told him in a low voice. 'What, you thought you could silence me by force?'

'By *love,* I thought! Christ, my lip is bleeding!'

'That's your notion of *love,* is it? God have mercy on your wife and children!'

'I've neither.'

'Then God send you never get any! I'll keep quiet about your master's doings, but only because there's no good that would come of speaking out about them. *We* already knew Charles Stuart for a lying knave, and now Cromwell does, too. As for people like you – you don't *care* what he is, do you? If what we heard tonight ended up in *The Moderate,* your Royalist readers would say it was only a Leveller lie or part of some Leveller plot. I'll keep our name clear of it, thank you!'

'If you'll keep quiet, I'll be content.' Nedham sighed. 'Do you still want the work?'

She hesitated, then thought of stitching sermons and of six shillings a week. 'Aye. *If* you'll keep your hands to yourself!'

For a moment Nedham was quiet. Then he laughed. 'Oh, you're a rare one! "'Tis chastity, my brother, chastity: she that has that is clad in complete steel!" Very well: meet me tomorrow morning at The Fleece.'

It was very dark as Lucy made her way back to Coleman Street: the lanterns which lighted the earlier hours of the night were all dark. The streets were foul and icy, and she slipped several times, though she managed not to fall. Her mind churned with questions about what she'd just heard. *He has played us false.* What had been in that letter?

There was an obvious answer: the king had concluded a deal with somebody else, on terms completely unacceptable to Cromwell. There would be another war.

The courier had said he was taking letters to *Dover*, which probably meant across the Channel to France – to the Queen, to the Prince of Wales. They'd been trying to raise a foreign army to invade England in the king's name – but they'd been trying *that* ever since the war started, and if no army had been forthcoming when Charles was free and in power, it didn't seem likely that one would be offered now. Most likely, the letter informed the Queen that Charles had finally made that long-feared agreement with the Scots.

Lucy wondered whether she'd been right to agree to silence. *She* could see no good reason to publicize what she'd heard, but that didn't mean that others couldn't. There was such a fog of suspicion and ugly rumour over everything now, though, that she dreaded the thought of adding to it.

She arrived at the Overtons' house shivering and spattered with mud. She had no key and was forced to knock on the door. It was opened surprisingly quickly by Mary. She was fully dressed and she hugged Lucy and drew her into the house. 'Where've you been so late?' she asked, bolting the door on the cold night. 'We were on the point of setting out to look for you!'

'I'm sorry,' said Lucy, surprised and remorseful. 'It – it took longer than I thought. There

318

was...'

Richard came in, in his coat, with a sword at his side. 'Back safely!' he said in relief. 'Did that rogue Nedham try your virtue?'

'Aye!' she said, surprised that, if he'd suspected trouble, he'd left her to defend herself.

Mary looked dismayed, but Richard raised his eyebrows appreciatively. 'Did you draw blood?'

'When I hit him I did.'

Richard laughed, and Lucy understood, with a surge of pleasure, that he'd *expected* her to defend herself successfully. Mary gave her husband a look of reproach and hugged Lucy again. 'I should have come with you.'

'There was no need.' She wasn't sure whether or not she should tell the Overtons what she'd heard, but she *was* sure, quite suddenly, that she was desperately tired and wanted to go to bed. *In the morning,* she thought, *when my head is clearer.* 'We agreed, in the end,' she told the Overtons. 'Six shillings a week and he's to keep his hands to himself.' She hesitated, then steeled herself. 'I can move out as soon as I've found another place to stay.'

'Oh, as to that, there's no haste!' replied Richard. 'Six shillings a week! That's a handsome wage for any unlicensed printer, let alone a woman! Mary...'

'I've had my fill of unlicensed printing,' said Mary quietly. 'Dick, let's to bed! This is matter for the morning.'

Fourteen

'The Fleece in Covent Garden' was not actually *in* Covent Garden, but on a side street adjacent to the market piazza. Lucy had trouble finding it – she'd rarely been west of the City proper – and arrived slightly late, flustered and out of breath. Nedham wasn't there, and she was miserably afraid that he'd already left. The tavern keeper refused her permission to wait inside unless she bought a drink, so she stood shivering by the door and hoped Nedham would come back.

Just as the clock in the church on the marketplace struck eleven, Nedham turned up, rumpled and unshaven. He stared at Lucy in surprise. 'Why not wait indoors?'

'To spare my purse,' she said sourly.

'Ah, well! Come in while I have my morning draught.'

'You've not had it?'

He belched. 'I had but poor sleep. Come on; I'll no further until I've put something in my belly.'

When they were seated inside the tavern and Nedham had his mug of ale, he gave her a thoughtful look. 'Did you keep quiet, as you promised?'

'I made no promise,' she replied, 'but I kept quiet.'

He gave a snort of appreciation. 'Promise now.' He reached in his purse, took out a coin and held it low beside the table, so that the rich gleam of gold would attract no attention from anyone else.

She hadn't been certain that the offer of a gold angel for her silence was serious. She had never even touched one; the thought of a single coin worth half a pound seemed almost sinful. She licked her lips unhappily. 'Nay.' It was an effort to say it, but she felt better when she'd got it out. She might compromise her principles by printing his newsbook but she wouldn't abandon them completely.

He stared at her incredulously. 'Nay? When you're keeping silent already?'

'I will not promise,' she told him fervently. 'I told you plainly, I will keep silent because I think it best for my friends, but if ever I think it would be better to speak, speak I will!'

'God save me from Puritan Levellers!' groaned Nedham. He stared at her a minute, then grimaced. 'Very well. I doubt it will do much harm even if you do speak out. Be sure, though, that if you do, your days printing for me are done!' He put the coin away and drank his ale. She watched him, struggling not to regret her honesty. She suspected that she'd just thrown a very expensive sop to her conscience.

He finished his bread and ale, and they went back out into the chill damp of the November day. There Nedham halted. 'Will you promise this?' he asked. 'That you'll not betray the location of my press?'

'That I can promise,' Lucy said, relieved. 'I will do all I can to keep it safe.'

Nedham nodded in satisfaction and turned left, towards The Strand.

Covent Garden was a new part of London: the big market piazza had been laid out just before the war, and several of the mansions that had been springing up nearby had been confiscated by Parliament before they were even complete. Nedham led Lucy round the back of one of these – she wasn't even sure which one – and unlocked a door which led into a garden overgrown with winter-shrivelled weeds. He unlocked a second door, into what seemed to be a scullery or laundry – and there was the press.

It was half the size of Nicholas Tew's press; the oak beams that formed its structure were slender but reinforced with iron braces, making it altogether the most elegant machine Lucy had ever seen. It had clearly been designed so that it could be moved from one place to another quickly and easily, but this gave it the additional advantage that it was light enough to be operated by a woman. *Mine!* she thought delightedly.

'There it is,' said Nedham. 'My press – or the king's, which comes to the same thing.' He stroked its side. 'It travelled with the Royalist Army the last year of the war. When the war started, armies would have laughed at the notion that they should carry about a printing press! But now no commander feels complete in his provisioning unless he can bang out tracts and proclamations to keep the soldiers happy. *Aulicus* was sometimes printed on this.'

322

'*Aulicus*?'

'Did you never read it? His Majesty set up *Mercurius Aulicus* to trumpet his cause and vilify Parliament's; John Birkenhead, he wrote it. I owe my career to that witty knave, because Parliament set up *Britanicus* to counter him. We shot poison at one another every week.' He sighed nostalgically at the memory. 'I'll have no such merry sport again. Your friends Mabbot and Overton are honest, righteous fellows, though I'll grant you that Overton writes like a charge of cavalry and has a lively taste for bawdy. Will he trouble you over this?'

'Nay,' said Lucy, blushing a little. 'He urged me to speak to you. He believes in the liberty of the press and, besides, he says it does his heart good to see Cromwell pricked. Yet I do plan to lodge elsewhere, now I can afford it.'

'Excellent!' said Nedham with satisfaction. 'Now, I have leave to be in this house – but only from the rightful owner. Those who've seized it know nothing of our presence here, and it is important that they not learn of it. All the caution you used for John Lilburne, you must employ again. Cold though it is, you can have no fire here – smoke would give the game away – and you must take care coming and going. I have an informant who should give me warning of any unwished-for visitation, but still you should be careful.'

Lucy nodded, and they proceeded to thrash out details: she would be responsible for finding paper and ink but Nedham would pay for it; the text for the newsbook would be supplied the evening before it went to press; he would see that the printed copies were supplied to the mercury-women but she would keep track of the money. He would also supply a 'rascal boy' who would do the inking: he seemed well aware of how much having only one worker slowed things down. He wanted Lucy to start printing the following day, as soon as she could find paper, since there was none in the printwork-scullery.

'Well, then!' said Nedham genially, when all this had been arranged. 'Will you come and have a cup with me, fair sweet printer?'

She gave him a hard look. 'Nay. If I'm to print tomorrow, I must be busy today. Give me the money for the paper, please you.'

He rolled his eyes in disgust, but dug in his purse. He found two shillings and four pence, and frowned at them: it wouldn't be enough. He glanced at Lucy, who was waiting patiently, then handed her the gold angel and a shilling. 'Take your first week's wage from that,' he said, 'and buy paper and ink. Bring me the receipts.'

The weight of the gold in her palm brought another moment of regret, but it vanished quickly. She had her six shillings and tomorrow she would start to earn it.

When she returned to the Overtons' that evening, she was cold but happy, looking forward to the morning. The door opened to a smell of tobacco, and Richard Overton called, 'Mary?'

'Nay,' she replied, coming through into the kitchen. 'Lucy.'

Lilburne was there again, but with a flood or relief she saw that this time John Wildman had joined the pair. All three men were sitting around the kitchen fire, Lilburne and Overton smoking their pipes, Wildman holding a notebook. He stared at Lucy in bewilderment.

'Tom Stevens is dead of the smallpox,' Richard explained, 'and my wife offered Lucy house-room until she could find her feet again.'

Wildman set down his notebook. 'I am sorry for your loss.'

'Thank you, sir.' There was an awkward pause and then she blurted out, 'Sir, do you know if—'

'Jamie Hudson is alive and well, but under arrest,' said Wildman. 'He and the others accused have been sent to Windsor, where the Army is to set up new headquarters.' He glanced at the other two and explained, 'This is a man, formerly of my troop, who assisted Mistress Wentnor on the press last summer.'

'What will be done to him?' Lucy asked unhappily.

Wildman hesitated. 'That I cannot tell. There will be a court-martial set up within the next few days. Technically, Jamie should not be subject to it – he's no longer a soldier but merely a black-smith who chances to be working for the Army. I might apply to have his case transferred to a civil court – only I'm not sure whether it would benefit him.'

Lilburne snorted. 'That's no easy choice! A court-martial would punish him for mutiny; a civil court, for belonging to the Army and being

325

a Leveller and a friend of Agitators.'

'If he's not a soldier, then he can't be guilty of mutiny,' said Lucy hopefully. Despite Leveller denials, it was pretty clear to her that there *had* been a mutiny at Ware. Two regiments had arrived there contrary to orders, and one had driven off all the officers who tried to stand in its way. She had every sympathy for the men's reasons, but they'd given Cromwell a strong case against them.

'An argument which should have protected him,' Wildman acknowledged, 'except that when his friend John Harris was arrested, Jamie struck one of the arresting officers. Under military discipline that's a flogging offence.' He noticed Lucy's expression and added, 'A court-martial might well choose to be lenient! The question is whether Cromwell intends it to crush or to conciliate.' He rubbed his face wearily.

'This business with the Council of the Army...' began Richard.

'We can conclude nothing from that,' said Lilburne. 'It's a thing he's wished to do ever since the Agitators first sat down on it. To him, democracy is but a hair's breadth from anarchy.'

'The Council of the Army no longer includes Agitators elected by the men,' Wildman explained to Lucy. 'Officers only.'

'You say that what happens to Jamie now depends on Cromwell?' asked Lucy.

Wildman nodded. 'And that is one of the weary questions we've been circling about this evening.'

'I still believe he will do his utmost to break

us!' Lilburne declared. 'He knows that he has wronged us and he will not want to leave our supporters in place to work against him.'

'But the men were *deceived*,' argued Wildman. 'That trick he used, of replacing the *Agreement* with his own declaration and acting in the name of the Council of the Army – that gave his actions a veil of legality. If he sets out to crush us, he will strip that veil away and offend many.'

'Then he will strip it away and offend!' said Lilburne. 'I *know* the man, remember: I fought beside him and shared a camp. He's never been one to turn back when once he's set his hand to the plough.'

'But he has others to think of besides us!' protested Richard Overton. 'Enemies in Parliament, and a storm gathering to the north! He can't *afford* to offend the Army!'

Lilburne shook his head gloomily. 'An agreement with the king would give him strength enough to outface them all, and he hopes that now he's put down the faction that were crying out against Charles Stuart, he will get one.'

'Nay,' said Lucy. 'The king has played him false.'

The three men stared in surprise, and she blushed. She hadn't consciously decided to speak out, but the information clearly *would* help them; it might even help Jamie. She was glad, after all, that she hadn't made Nedham any promises.

She told them what she'd seen and heard at The Blue Boar. 'I was in two minds whether to speak to you,' she finished nervously. 'In part

327

only because Mr Nedham said that if I did, I'd lose my place printing for him; but in the main I feared what would come of you knowing. I thought perhaps you might print the tale in *The Moderate*...'

'It would do well in a pamphlet!' said Lilburne, his one eye gleaming. 'The cozener cozened!'

'It would *not*!' she cried desperately. 'Truly, sir, I fear it would do nothing but harm! The Royalists would never take it for true – not from *you*, not from any of us! – but even if they *did*, they wouldn't *care*! They would *praise* the king for tricking his jailers! The only people who'd take real note of it would be Cromwell and his friends – and *they* would wonder how we knew about it. They'd suspect a Leveller plot, and ... and there are so many rumours already! You, sir, are already accused of conspiring to murder the king, or else of conspiring *with* him against Parliament, or I know not what...'

'One would think that even my accusers would see I could not do both,' murmured Lilburne.

'Suspicion is already so thick that reason can't be seen through it!' Lucy replied. 'And I feared that publishing this tale would only thicken it more!'

'And yet you have told us of it,' said Richard.

She nodded miserably. 'You said you were circling about the question. The rest of us rely on you, sirs, to find our way forward. I could not keep back information which might make a difference to your decisions.'

Richard and Wildman both looked at Lilburne.

'She's right, John,' Richard said gently. 'Making this public would harm us.'

Lilburne grimaced. 'You need not coax me, Dick, as though I were a stubborn child! I can see she's right.' He sighed. 'It would have made an *excellent* pamphlet!'

Richard turned a serious gaze on Lucy. 'You say Nedham threatened you if you spoke of this?'

'Not so much *threatened*, sir, as ... well, he offered me a gold angel if I promised to tell no one, and said that if I spoke, I would print for him no more – which I should be sorry for, but I expect I can find another place.'

'Not one that pays six shillings a week,' said Richard, smiling at her. 'There's no need for Nedham to know that you told us.'

She smiled back, deeply relieved and slightly guilty. That morning she'd told Nedham that she'd kept quiet: it had been perfectly true at the time but now it felt like a lie. Still, that discomfort was slight compared to what she would've felt if she'd been obliged to give up her new job.

'Interesting that Nedham feared the effect of this,' said Wildman.

'He was less worried this morning than he was last night,' said Lucy. 'I think at the first he was too shocked to think it through. He had hoped to discover something that would discredit *Cromwell*. Will this help, sir?'

'It will,' replied Wildman and looked at Lilburne.

Lilburne frowned at his pipe, which had gone

329

out, then knocked the ashes into the fire and began to refill it.

'It tells us that Cromwell knows that he will need the Army soon – and need it united,' Wildman urged. 'He cannot afford a contest with us now.'

'*We* cannot afford a contest, either,' Lilburne replied unhappily. 'Not without we risk letting a Scots army into London. Oh, God, that it should come to this! After so much blood spent! But your point holds. Cromwell will try to win us back with promises and soft words. We will have to make certain that we get hard commitments from him.' He gave Lucy a tired smile. 'Your sweetheart should be safe.'

The front door banged; Richard again called out, 'Mary?' and this time his wife's voice answered. A moment later Mary appeared in the door. She surveyed the smoky kitchen equably and asked, 'How many are we to supper?'

Lilburne and Wildman declined to stay for supper and the meeting broke up. As Wildman took his leave, though, he told Lucy, 'I know Jamie would be very glad of a letter. If you leave one at The Whalebone, I will take it with me tomorrow when I ride to Windsor.'

Lucy took the letter round to The Whalebone later that evening. The tavern was as full as she'd ever seen it, every bench taken and more customers standing around the walls: *The Moderate*'s account of events at Ware had hit the street the day before. She would have known the crowd were Levellers even if she hadn't recognized many of the faces: *The Moderate* was being read out in every corner, and everyone who wasn't listening was arguing about it and about how to press forward with *The Agreement of the People.* She struggled sideways to the bar, where Ned was serving ale and arguing that when the Army realized how it had been deceived, it would turn against Cromwell.

'Ned!' she said, and he glanced up with a vague smile of acknowledgement.

'The Army might turn against *Cromwell*,' said the man Ned had been talking to, 'but against *Fairfax*, never!'

'Everyone knows this was Cromwell's doing!' replied Ned. 'Lord Fairfax has been ill all this year with the gout, and never had a stomach for politics even when he was in health, but Cromwell—'

'Ned!' Lucy tried again. She was tired and wanted to go home to bed. 'Can you give Major Wildman this letter when he comes for his horse tomorrow morning?' She took it out of her apron pocket and held it up.

'Aye, I suppose,' said Ned, taking it. He glanced at it, then frowned. 'It's for Jamie?'

'Aye. Major Wildman says he's been taken to Windsor, to be tried by a court-martial.'

'But he's no longer a soldier!'

'He struck an officer, it seems.'

Ned's frown deepened. The man he'd been talking to began to say something more about Lord Fairfax, but Ned waved him to silence. 'And you've writ him a letter?'

'Major Wildman said he would be glad of it.'

Ned looked at the letter in his hand, then looked up again at Lucy. 'A moment,' he told his customer. 'Lucy, a word with you!' He gestured towards the kitchen.

The kitchen was warm, lit by a couple of cressets over the fireplace. The din of voices in the main room just beyond was muffled. Rafe the cook was clearing up.

'Rafe, take charge in the house!' ordered Ned.

'But—' began Rafe, startled.

'Do it!' snapped Ned.

Rafe shrugged, wiped his hands on his apron and went to take Ned's place serving beer, leaving the two of them alone in the kitchen.

'Why are you writing to Jamie Hudson?' demanded Ned bluntly.

His tone stung. 'What is it to you if I do?' she replied coolly.

'Because if he's courting you, he's a false knave!'

'What?' she asked incredulously.

'He knows very well I had my eye on you! He swore he would say nothing!'

'What?' she asked again, now completely bewildered. 'He swore...'

Ned glared. 'He swore he would pay no addresses to you, in deference to me!'

She opened her mouth, then closed it. 'In deference to *you*?' she managed at last. '*You,* who had nothing to say to me once you'd learned I had no dowry?'

Ned had the grace to look embarrassed. 'He knew I needed time to—'

'*He* knew more of your mind than *I* did, then!

But I'll have you know that he kept his oath: he dealt with me as a friend and nothing more. God have mercy! I've heard of a man standing aside to let his friend court a woman, but never in my life have I heard such a thing as this! To make a man swear to stand aside *in case* his friend decides to court a woman! You're like a ... a *Parliamentary clerk*, that will neither do business himself nor permit any other to do it for him!'

'That's a foul likeness!'

'Aye, but a true one!'

'I would have courted you; you surely know I wanted to! But you put me off, first telling me about the dowry and then keeping me at arm's length, and finally telling me plain a thing you knew very well I had no wish to hear! If you'd kept your peace I would have—'

'Oh, so now it's *my* fault, because I wouldn't deceive you?'

'My uncle will settle fifty pounds on me if he approves my bride, but—'

'If you must marry to please your uncle, do it! I never set out to catch your eye, and I've dealt with you truthfully and fairly. Can you say the same?'

Nancy Shorby came in, flustered. 'Ned, the party in the holly room are quarrelling—'

'Will you let me be!' roared Ned. 'Every time I...' He stopped suddenly, staring at Nancy. 'You've done it a-purpose!'

'What?' she asked guiltily.

'Every time I try to talk to Lucy, it's Ned this and Ned that, and please, Ned, you must come and sort this for us – and it's *always* a thing you

333

might've sorted for yourselves!'

'But they *are* quarrelling!' wailed Nancy. 'In another moment there'll be fisticuffs!'

'Let them fight!' Ned shouted. He turned back to Lucy, caught her shoulders and kissed her; she made a muffled noise of protest and tried to push him off. 'Marry me!' he demanded, breaking off.

Nancy groaned.

'I will not!' gasped Lucy. She shoved herself away from Ned and fled out of the kitchen door.

She was in tears by the time she reached the Overtons' and she stood outside the door for several minutes, gasping and wiping her face, until she had regained enough composure to slip up to bed without having to explain why she was crying. She didn't know how to talk about what had just happened, and she didn't want to try.

She spent a largely sleepless night. She was furious with Ned and Jamie both. Something inside her (*good sense,* she thought bitterly) kept trying to tell her that she'd just made a terrible mistake. She ought to go back to Ned; she ought to beg his pardon, explain that she'd been so surprised and so worried about his friends' reaction that she hadn't been thinking clearly; she ought to say plainly that if he still wanted her, she would be very happy to marry him.

The rest of her could not let go of the notion that Jamie might have spoken if Ned hadn't sworn him to silence.

In the morning she rose before it was light, slipped downstairs and by candlelight wrote another letter to Jamie. She doubted that Ned would forward the first one and, any way, she now had more to say.

To Mr James Hudson,
    Ned has told me of that oathe you swore to him. It is the gratest follie and shame that ever I heared in alle my lyfe, that you should deal with me as though I were a parcell of land, and agree to stand aside while your Friend makes up his minde whether or no he will buy. Now he has made his offer, and I have told him plain that I will not marry him, for I like it not at alle, to be reckoned so Doubt-full a Purchase, that he must buye against his better Judgment. As to you, I am verie sorrie you are in Prison, so I will saye no more than that I am ablaze with shame and anger, that you have so slight Opinyon of my Regarde as to barter itt awaye to any man what-soever. And yet I pray God that you come safely out of this Danger, and are soone restored to your Friends and your Freedom.
    Your Friend, Lucy Wentnor

She blew out the candle, wrapped herself in her shawl and silently let herself out of the house. She made her way to The Whalebone in the first grey light of dawn and went straight to the stable without going into the tavern. The ostler who had helped her on the press those first days had just risen and was in the yard fetching water for the horses. He gave her a sleepy smile.
    'I have a letter to go with Major Wildman,' she told him. He took it and promised to hand it on when Wildman came for his horse.

* * *

She went directly from The Whalebone to Covent Garden; it was full day by the time she arrived, and the market was bustling. She slipped quietly into the printworks-scullery, found the text Nedham had left for her the evening before and began setting the type for it.

Nedham turned up before she'd finished, bringing her new assistant, a sullen boy named Wat, the son of Nedham's bootmaker. Lucy showed him how to ink, and together they printed the first segment of *Mercurius Pragmaticus*.

Wat scowled all morning, but Lucy won his heart when she shared her dinner with him. It was only pease and bacon from a Covent Garden cookshop, but apparently in Wat's house dinner in this bitter winter usually consisted of gruel. The bootmaker had a large family and trade was scant: the tuppence a day Nedham was paying the child to do the inking was desperately needed.

When she got back to the Overtons', she found Mary and Richard preparing to set out for The Whalebone: it was Thursday, the evening of the Leveller council meeting. 'Come with us!' Mary offered cheerfully.

'But the meeting's only for the council,' Lucy pointed out.

'Not so,' replied Richard. 'It's for the council *and* the local chapter, and you're now a resident of this ward.'

Lucy had no idea how to answer: The Whalebone was not a place she wanted to visit at present.

'Have you supped?' asked Mary, seeing her hesitation. 'Dick, she needs a bite to eat first! *Next* week she can come with us.'

'I thought...' Lucy began, then stopped. Both Overtons looked at her enquiringly.

'I thought that now I've well-paid work, I should give you your house again and lodge elsewhere,' she said with regret. She would be sorry to leave this secure refuge.

'Ah!' said Richard. He'd been standing in the doorway, but at this he came back and sat down at the kitchen table. 'That. Aye. What would you say to staying on, as paying lodger?'

Lucy was astonished. She looked quickly at Mary.

The older woman smiled. 'If we could have taken a lodger before, we would have, but where could we find one we could set to share a bed with the children?'

'We will buy another bed!' put in Richard hastily. 'We'd soon have need of one anyway, with Faith growing to be such a great big girl. But, aye, it would be hard to find another lodger we could trust to keep any secrets she might chance to overhear, and two or three shillings more each week would be very welcome.'

'I ... I should very much like to stay,' Lucy said. 'But if Mr Mabbot learns what it is I'm printing, surely he will ... will be very angry with you?'

Richard grinned. 'No doubt he would be, but nothing would come of it. I, after all, am prerogative archer to the House of Lords, and he's but

337

the hypocrite Licensor of the Press! I hope he never does learn it, but that's for your sake, not mine. How say you?'

'I should like it very much,' said Lucy, blushing a little.

'Very good!' replied Richard. 'We'll agree the rent later; now Mary and I must away to our meeting.'

The next few days Lucy basked in the sense that she had come home after struggling through a storm. She had work; she had safe lodgings with friends; she had finally made a settlement with her heart. She hadn't realized how much the lack of the last thing had preyed on her: it was as though she'd dropped a heavy burden. The worry about whether Ned would or would not offer marriage; the division in her soul about what she should do if he did; the struggle to suppress her feelings for Jamie – it was all done with and she could let it go. Her settlement might not be wise, but at least her struggle – unlike the kingdom's – was over.

It was true that Jamie was still in prison and that she didn't dare speak to Ned, but she had made her decision, and now all she had to do was wait.

Fifteen

There was a letter waiting for Lucy when she returned from work on Tuesday evening. 'John Wildman left this for you,' Mary told her.

Lucy felt a shock of cold from head to foot: she hadn't seen that rough left-handed writing very often, but it was distinctive, easily recognized. She took Jamie's letter over to the kitchen table, where a candle gave her enough light to read it.

'My verie deere...'

She had to stop there. Mary, who was busy preparing supper, looked at her in concern and asked, 'Bad news?'

'Nay,' said Lucy, smiling and blinking.

'Oh!' said Mary, staring at her. 'Oh, my. Whose is this letter?'

'Jamie Hudson's, whom I ... who was at Ware and arrested for mutiny.'

Mary thought a moment. 'The big man with half a face, a friend of John Wildman?'

'Aye.'

Mary gave her a doubtful look. 'What of Ned Trebet?'

Lucy glared indignantly. Mary put her hands up. 'Well, others than me have noticed!'

'His friends want him to marry a respectable

dowry. They disapproved me and so he havered and wavered. He wouldn't court me, though he tried to put off ... others, until he had made up his mind.'

Mary was silent a moment, studying Lucy with a clear, level gaze. Then she sighed. 'He left it too late, I see.'

'Aye, he did,' agreed Lucy, and went back to her precious letter.

My verie deere,

Do not be angrie with me! If I had knowne that I hadde won your Regarde, I hadde never bartered it for alle the worlde, but I cd. not thinke myself so Fortunate. ~~That I~~ That you shd. refuse Ned Trebet I scars beleeve even now, I am like one that dreames. ~~Deerest Lucy, when once I am Free~~ I hope soone to have my Freedome, and come to Lundon to see you.

John Wildman saies that your Uncle is dead, ~~for which I am~~ which is a grievous loss. I knowe you and he loved one another welle.

I pray God that I shall see you soone, and saye to you alle the things I have at harte, for ink is too weake a messenger.

Yours ever, James Hudson

She read it over and over, smiling over the agitated crossings-out, trying to work out what he'd started to say before he changed it. She spent the rest of the evening in a happy daze.

She ached to see Jamie. When it was Thursday again, she went to the meeting at The Whalebone, along with the Overtons, in the hope that John Wildman would be there and could give her the news.

When she came into the tavern, Ned stared at her hard, his face flushed and his jaw set angrily. She gave him a timid smile. He did not return it but looked pointedly away. After that he ignored her.

It hurt – she had, as she'd feared, lost a friend.

She spotted Wildman shortly before the meeting was called to order. He looked tired, and his boots and coat-hem were splattered with mud. When he noticed her looking at him, though, he smiled.

Lilburne chaired the meeting, as he usually did when he was present, but he called on Wildman to speak first.

'My friends,' Wildman began, 'most of you know that I have been at Windsor, arguing on behalf of our friends who were most unjustly taken up at Ware. First I must report that I have good hope for their release. The Grandees at last begin to despair of a settlement with the tyrant Charles Stuart, and the sinking of that hope compels them to look more favourably upon us. The court-martial which was to have tried our friends has been suspended, and instead their cases have been referred to the Council of the Army. I fear, though, that this is the reformed Council of the Army: the Agitators have been barred from it, and the men have no one to represent them. Like all else in this sad and divided kingdom, the release of our friends has become a subject of contention.'

The contention, however, was not as serious as it might have been: it was over whether the men should be released without charge or whether they should first be required to offer some form of submission to the Army command, rather than over how severely they should be punished. Wildman was optimistic that the matter would be resolved within a couple of weeks; in the meantime, he said, the men were being treated well, and their friends were allowed to visit them and bring comforts. It was a great relief to Lucy.

The rest of the meeting was encouraging, too: it treated the events at Ware as a lost battle rather than a lost war. A new petition had already been drafted and the drive for signatures would be on an unparalleled scale. Meetings would be held throughout London and into the suburbs; the Leveller leaders would visit every part of the city to answer questions about *The Agreement of the People*. The common fund would be expanded; a second treasurer would be appointed to help Mr Chidley to manage it; members would be asked for regular subscriptions. Far from being inclined to surrender, the Levellers were stronger and more determined than ever.

When the meeting ended, Wildman paused and waited when he saw Lucy coming to speak to him.

'He's well!' he told her before she had a chance to ask. 'But I know he would be glad of another letter.'

Richard Overton had followed Lucy; at this he grinned. 'I never thought to see you play Love's sweet messenger, John!'

'Ah, I am a man of infinite resource!' replied Wildman. 'But I fear I have displeased our host.' He glanced at the bar, where Ned stood glowering at them. 'He did not even give me any ale tonight!'

'I had none either,' said Richard, also looking in that direction. 'And yet I can't find it in my heart to blame the man. He has suffered a cruel disappointment.'

Wildman shrugged. 'Let it be a lesson to us all of the dangers of hesitation.'

December started out bleak, dark and bitterly cold. Lucy imagined Jamie shivering in a stone cell. She wanted to send him warm clothing but didn't have enough money saved to buy any. She considered going to visit the Cotmans in Stepney and asking Cousin Nat for the repayment he'd promised, but she feared what might happen if she did. Nat Cotman was already angry with her: he clearly felt she'd shamed the family by going to lodge with strangers. To make her first visit because she wanted money seemed likely to prolong the quarrel.

She hoped that the Cotmans would invite her to visit on a Sunday. Dull as Sabbath afternoons in Stepney had been, she did not want to be at odds with her only kin in London. Cousin Hannah's baby – Thomas's grandchild – was due in a couple of months, and Lucy wanted to be part of its admiring family. No invitation came, however. Near the end of her third week at the Overtons she sent a hesitant note.

I beg leeve to informe my Cozens that I have good worke printing. If any message has come for me from my kin in Hinckley, may I come to collect it? I hope my Cozen Hannah is welle, and the rest of my kin also.

There was no reply.

That Sunday, greatly daring, she accompanied the Overtons to their church. They were what her father would call 'heretics and blasphemers' – specifically, General Baptists. She was mildly disappointed to find nothing in the service to shock her: Baptist preaching wasn't all that different from the Presbyterian variety. There was less about Hell and more about Christ's love, but the flurry of scriptural references and the style of preaching were much the same. If the congregation groaned in penitence less, it shouted more.

The Brownes attended the same church, and after the service Liza hurried over to give Lucy a hug. 'I've not seen you for *weeks*!' the girl cried. 'And I thought I'd see you every day, now you live but down the road!' She turned to her father. 'Da, can Lucy come to dinner?'

'Aye, why not?' said Will Browne, smiling.

It turned out, however, that Liza had an ulterior motive for the invitation.

'Is it true that Ned Trebet asked you to wed and you refused him?' Liza asked breathlessly, when they were seated at table in the room behind Browne's bookshop.

'Liza!' protested Will Browne.

'Aye, but is it true?'

344

Lucy set her teeth: Mary Overton had been right that Ned's interest had been widely noticed. 'It's true.'

'Why did you refuse him?' asked Liza in bewilderment. Her father cast his gaze towards Heaven.

'His friends disapproved me because I have no dowry,' replied Lucy tactfully. 'I had no wish to cause a quarrel between him and his friends.'

'You hear that, Liza?' asked Will Browne approvingly. 'Lucy's a wise woman: she knows that a marriage undertaken against the wishes of friends is a hard road!'

Liza frowned at her father. 'Do you think Ned's friends would disapprove of *me,* too?'

Lucy suddenly grasped the reason for Liza's invitation. For a moment she was tempted to laugh; then she realized that Liza must be almost fourteen. That was more than old enough to marry, according to the law, and Liza thought Ned altogether wonderful; Lucy had been vaguely aware of that for some time without giving the matter any thought. She wasn't sure whether to be worried for Liza, vexed that at least one young woman already had an eye on Ned – or relieved because, if it all worked out, she might recover a friend.

'*You* have a dowry,' Browne said affectionately.

Liza lowered her eyes, satisfied.

December wore on slowly. *Mercurius Pragmaticus* began to mention Christmas – a festival which Parliament had banned as an idolatrous excuse for gluttony and licence. Lucy's family had never celebrated it, but many of the citizens even of godly London strongly resented the ban, especially in this grim year of poverty and hunger. Marchamont Nedham had much to say about Parliament-men who banned innocent merriment while engaging in all sorts of corrupt practices themselves, and his writing fed the restless anger that was everywhere in the city, flaring up suddenly into violence in tavern or marketplace quarrels. Lucy took more care than ever on her way to and from work, dodging through side streets or waiting in doorways if she heard raised voices ahead.

Around the middle of the month, Lucy came home to find Susan sitting in the Overtons' kitchen. She exclaimed delightedly and rushed to hug her.

Susan returned the hug, then let go and looked searchingly at Lucy. Lucy was shocked to see that the maid was worn to the bone, her eyes darkly circled and her pock-marked skin pale and dirty.

'Your aunt's dying,' Susan told Lucy quietly. 'She asked for you.'

She told Lucy more as they walked eastward towards Stepney. Agnes had been suffering the first feverish forepangs of smallpox even at her husband's burial. She had taken to her bed as soon as the family returned home from the church, but everyone had put it down to grief – until the rash appeared three days later. She had survived the disease itself but had now con- tracted pneumonia and was not expected to live through the night.

Lucy remembered her fatuous hopes for an invitation to Sunday dinner and was horrified and ashamed: she had blithely gone about her work, unaware of the disaster unfolding for her kin. 'Is Cousin Hannah...' she began, then stopped, unable to finish.

'Aye, she caught it from her mother,' said Susan. Her voice was strangely hard. 'Mrs Stevens was beginning to recover when her daughter fell ill. She miscarried the baby. It died, poor little thing, before it ever saw the light. But Hannah lives; indeed, she's on her feet again and growing stronger every day.'

'Thank God!' said Lucy fervently. 'You nursed them both?'

Susan nodded wearily. 'I nursed *all three* of them. Mr Cotman caught it, too. He'd sent for me as soon as he saw Mrs Stevens had it.'

'Oh, dear Lord!' Lucy was struck by a sickening thought: what if she'd been *wrong* about the cowpox? She'd gone to the Overtons' in the bland assumption that because she hadn't already succumbed to the disease, she was clean, but in fact it had been too soon to be sure.

Lucy swallowed, thinking of the Overton children. That she'd been *right* about the cowpox was no credit to her. She wanted to call it a mercy from God; only then she was left wondering why God hadn't been merciful to Cousin Hannah.

Susan, who'd trudged in silence for a little while, suddenly said, 'It's an ill wind that blows nobody good. The Cotmans' maid upped and left when she saw that Mrs Stevens had the small-pox, and my place is safe now.'

'I'd meant to speak to you about that,' said Lucy apologetically. 'Mrs Overton put the word about that you were seeking a place, and—'

'That's good of you,' said Susan, without giving her the time to finish, 'but I'm well where I am now.'

The Cotmans' house in Stepney, where Lucy had spent so many boring Sabbath afternoons, was in disarray: unswept and festooned with wet sheets. Nathaniel Cotman was sitting alone in the parlour, huddled in a blanket. When Lucy was shown in, he glanced up with a stunned look. The smallpox scabs had fallen from his face, but the marks they'd left were still an angry red.

Susan went to him. 'I fetched Lucy, sir,' she said, gently adjusting the blanket. 'Do you need aught?'

'Nay,' said Cotman with an effort. 'Let her see her aunt.'

Agnes was upstairs, propped up in a big bed. The bubbling wheeze of her breath was the first thing Lucy noticed on coming into the room. Cousin Hannah was lying in the bed beside her mother, under the covers with her back to the door. There was a candle burning at the bedside and a fire in the grate, but both had burned low. Susan went at once to the grate and began to build up the fire.

'Aunt Agnes?' said Lucy, coming closer. 'Cousin Hannah?'

Hannah lifted her head, then sat up. Her face

was much more pocked than her husband's and the disease had thinned her hair, so that the angry red scars could be seen through it all across her scalp: she looked hideous. She smiled weakly, and Lucy, wrenched by pity, came and hugged her.

'I am so very sorry!' she whispered.

'It is God's will,' said Hannah faintly. 'The Lord chastises whom He loves. My mother was asking for you.'

Agnes made a choking sound and glared at Lucy. The smallpox scars on her face were scant and already beginning to fade but there were sores around her mouth and the whites of her eyes had turned yellow. Her cheeks were covered with a livid network of broken veins. Her expression was baleful and indignant.

On the walk over to Stepney, Lucy had been imagining a tearful reconciliation. That had clearly been a fantasy. 'I'm here, Aunt,' she said.

Agnes made an indistinct noise and turned her face away. She wheezed repeatedly, struggling for breath, then gasped, in a bubbling whisper, 'Take it, then, and go!'

Lucy blinked. 'Aunt?'

Agnes made a horrible sound, part cough and part retch. 'The silk! The damned silk! Take it and go!'

'Aunt, I don't understand!' Lucy protested.

'The silk!' said Agnes angrily and burst into a bout of coughing. Flecks of pus and blood sprayed from her mouth, but when Hannah tried to support her, she shoved the gentle touch away.

Lucy looked at Hannah and Susan in bewilderment and saw that, though they were shocked, they weren't confused at all.

'My father left you a legacy in his will,' whispered Hannah. 'He said you were to have "the bolt of rose tabby" to wear at your wedding. We searched all the house for it and found nothing but woollens and linens. My mother said you must have taken it without leave. Nat was so angry!'

Presumably this had happened before the smallpox made itself known. 'I know nothing about it!' Lucy protested shakily.

Hannah nodded. She again put an arm about her mother's shoulders. Agnes stopped coughing with a groan and leaned against her daughter. 'Mother,' said Hannah softly, 'tell me what you did with the silk. It will ease your passing.'

'Tom *loved* that inky slut!' said Agnes, starting to cry. 'What right had she to come and steal his love away from those who had most right to it?'

'Shh, shhh!' said Hannah, rocking her mother like the baby she'd lost. 'That's all past now, part of this present darkness, and you are facing into the light. Let it go, Mama.'

'It's in the bottom of my linen press,' confessed Agnes. 'I put it there for you. It should have gone to you.'

'Shh, shhh!' said Hannah again, and with a small movement of her head signalled Lucy to go.

Lucy went out and stood dazedly on the landing. After a minute, Susan came out as well, holding a bundle wrapped in canvas. She led Lucy back downstairs. Nat Cotman was still sitting in his parlour.

'Sir,' said Susan, 'Mrs Stevens had hid that bolt of silk in the bottom of the linen press. That's what she wanted Lucy for: to give it her. Here it is.'

'Oh, dear Lord!' exclaimed Cotman. He looked wretchedly at Lucy. 'When she came here that morning, with her things in a sack, I nearly sent her home again. Her husband ill with the smallpox, so she must needs bring it *here*? But Hannah was tender-hearted and said of course we must take her mother in. So she stole the silk?'

'She said it should have gone to Hannah,' said Lucy numbly.

He got up, took the bundle from Susan and opened it. Silk the colour of a summer sunrise, of a dog-rose with the dew on it; a shimmering stream of pale streaked with dark, as beautiful as an April morning. Cotman drew it off the bale in rough arm-lengths. 'Damascus tabby,' he said bitterly. 'Seventeen shillings the yard. Ten yards, more or less.' He stopped, his arms full of the stuff. 'A handsome legacy, certainly, but Hannah had the whole estate else!' Lucy realized that he was starting to cry. 'The foolish, greedy, wicked old woman! To fret about her husband's gifts to his kin and not give a thought to the ill that killed him!'

'Sir!' she said, touching his shoulder.

'Why did she come here?' he demanded, looking at her with wet eyes.

'She – she thought that falling ill was her husband's failing,' said Lucy, giving him the honest

351

answer. 'That she was immune to it. She would not have come here if she'd believed Hannah might catch it: of that much I'm certain.'

He let out his breath slowly. 'She's paid for her folly, and so have we. Take your legacy and go.'

'Sir.' Lucy ducked a curtsey. 'I am very sorry, sir, that you and Cousin Hannah should have suffered thus, while I knew nothing of it. I beg you, don't ... don't shut me out again.'

He regarded her, his expression softening. 'Well, then!' he said at last. 'That is a most honest and cousin-like plea! Cousin Lucy, you'll be welcome here whenever you choose to come.' He glanced at the shuttered window and added, surprised at it, 'It's late! You should not make your way back to the City alone so late. Stay for the night.'

'Thank you, sir. I should be glad of it.'

She ended up cooking soup for the household, since no one had eaten supper. Afterwards she tried to clean the house a little. In a stack of papers she found a letter for herself, from Paul: nobody was sure when it had arrived. She was too tired to face it that night and so put it aside until the morning. She slept that night beside Susan in the maid's room: a comfortingly familiar arrangement.

Hannah stayed beside her mother all night, but Agnes confounded expectation by waking in the morning as baleful as ever.

Lucy walked slowly back to Coleman Street at dawn, Paul's letter in her apron pocket and the package of silk tucked under her arm. Ten yards of rose-coloured Damascus tabby at seventeen

352

shilllings a yard: eight pounds and ten shillings' worth of silk. More than half a year's worth of the good wage she was getting now. When had Thomas bought it? Had it been in the loft all the time she slept there?

Probably it had. Probably he'd bought it before the war when he was rich and put it aside when the struggle ruined the market for such things, then decided at last, in his soft-hearted way, that it would do for his niece's wedding gown.

The thought of how Thomas must have imagined her wearing the silk gave her a twinge of guilt: she already knew that she was never going to make a gown of this beautiful, impractical stuff. No: she was going to *sell* it, though she'd cut off a little first, to remember Uncle Thomas by. Hard cash was a lot more useful than a gown she'd wear only once.

She was so numbed by what had happened that she didn't remember Paul's letter until halfway through the day, when she felt a paper in her pocket and took it out to see what it was. It did not make pleasant reading.

My deare Sister,

Oure cozen Nat and Aunt Agnes have used you ill, sending you to lodge with Strangers, & I blush thatt oure Father wille not stirr himselfe in your defens. I have spoke to him, & tolde him itt is shame to alle oure Familie, & he shd goe himself to Lundun & fetch you home, but he saies it is no Tyme of Yeare to travelle, & you are well wher you are. I will come myself whenne I can, but I think it will not bee this moneth, for no bodie is going to Lundun this moneth. I feare you must bee payshent and I pray you suffer no ill.

The newe Cowes doe very well, for they were so fewe that wee had ample pasture for them dispyte the ill weather alle the Yeare. Cheese is six Pence the Pounde, so we are well, and it is God's mercie, and yet the Haye is mouldie and we must be oute turning it every Daye. I pray God keep you well.

    Yr. loving Brother Paul

Lucy's first thought was that Paul couldn't have received her own letter when he wrote, but then she realized he must have, because Nat Cotman's letter had assumed that Lucy *would* lodge with him until she could be fetched home. She groaned, set the letter down and glared at it. How *could* Paul have managed to read her letter and still come away with the conclusion that she needed to be rescued?

She wrote a reply that evening, though she knew it wouldn't leave London until the following week: that week's post north had already left.

Agnes clung to life for another two days before she finally succumbed to her pneumonia. Arrangements were made for her to be taken back to Southwark so that she could be buried beside her husband. Lucy was invited to the funeral and endured another long-winded mumble from the St Olave's preacher before Agnes's shrouded body was lowered into the earth beside

Thomas's. The thought of those two lying together for all eternity made her queasy. She told herself repeatedly that earthly concerns were left behind by those who'd entered Paradise, but she still had trouble imagining an imperishable Agnes, purged of all greed and selfishness. Perhaps, she thought, Thomas, who'd known the carefree girl, would find it easier.

There was no general funeral feast after Agnes's burial any more than after her husband's, but there was to be a dinner for the family, to which Lucy was invited. The Cotmans had hired a coach to carry the body to Southwark and had ridden in it themselves – neither Nat nor Hannah was recovered enough to walk so far – and Lucy rode back in it with them.

It was the twenty-fourth of December – Christmas Eve, if Christmas had been permitted. The streets were busy. Lucy had taken a day off work, much to Nedham's annoyance, and she enjoyed travelling in the coach, looking out at the bustle of people on foot. When they crossed London Bridge she noticed that the entrance to the church of St Magnus the Martyr had been decorated with rosemary and holly. She pointed it out to Nat, who frowned at it. 'Godless idolatry!' he said severely. 'I wonder it's permitted!'

'I doubt it is,' said Lucy. She felt uneasy: if the authorities tried to clear the Christmas decorations away, there would probably be violence.

As they rode eastward through the City, they passed more churches decorated for Christmas, but when they got to Stepney the greenery vanished: the suburb had long been a stronghold of the godly. The coach stopped by the Cotmans' house, and Nat climbed down stiffly and paid the driver.

Some of Nat Cotman's kin had offered to prepare the dinner while the family attended the burial, so Lucy was not surprised to find the house unlocked and full of people. She was shocked speechless, however, when she walked into the parlour and found Paul sitting there – with her father beside him.

She hadn't seen her father for what felt like a whole lifetime. In her mind he was always a tall, stern, frightening figure, and it was strange and disturbing to see him sitting beside Paul and realize that he was a scrawny man of no more than average height, with greying hair and a lined face. His clothes were plain and travel-worn, and he looked nothing at all to be afraid of.

Daniel and Paul Wentnor both got to their feet when Lucy's party came into the room and stood respectfully holding their hats. Nat Cotman stared at them in bewilderment: he had met Paul only briefly and had never met Daniel at all. Nat's sister Deborah emerged from the kitchen and said, 'Nat, these two arrived but ten minutes ago. They say they're kin to the Stevenses.'

'My father, Daniel Wentnor,' whispered Lucy by way of introduction, 'and my brother Paul.'

'Well,' said Nat, rocking back on his heels and regarding the pair warily. 'You're too late for the funeral.'

Paul cleared his throat nervously. 'We – we

had no notion of it. We came to fetch my sister home.'

Nat shot a quick glance at Lucy; apparently satisfied by what he saw on her face, he declared, 'She told *me* very plain she'd no wish to leave London, and she borrowed threepence of me so that she could write and tell you the same.'

'It is not fit for her to live with strangers in this terrible city!' proclaimed Daniel; the sound of that familiar harsh voice sent a shiver through Lucy.

'You must take that up with *her,* then,' said Nat. 'I writ you, as you know, asking you to fetch her from my house, but she had other ideas.' He glanced round and noticed that Hannah was leaning weakly against the doorpost. He took her arm and steered her over to the bench by the parlour fire, where she sat down heavily.

Nat seated himself beside her and turned back towards Paul and Daniel. 'Sirs, my poor wife miscarried but a fortnight ago, and we are both newly recovered from the smallpox. Our house is in no state to entertain guests. Had you writ to *ask* if you might come, I'd have advised you to wait.'

Paul ducked his head in uncomfortable apology. 'We beg your pardon, sir. We knew nothing of these afflictions.'

'We will take Lucy and go,' said Daniel.

Nat frowned at him a moment. 'You're kin, of a sort,' he conceded, 'and fresh-come from the road, to judge by the state of your clothes. You're welcome to stay for dinner.'

'We will not trespass further on your house,' replied Daniel stiffly: that remark about arriving uninvited had stung him. 'I am heartily sorry for your afflictions, sir. Lucy, come.'

Lucy stood frozen where she was. She had a horrible vision of being bundled straight into a cart and driven directly back to Hinckley. 'Sir,' she said and swallowed. She had no right, in law or custom, to refuse a direct order from her father.

Maybe she had a natural right.

'Sir,' she said again and found her voice small but calm, 'My cousins had kindly invited me to dine with them. For me to walk out when the meat is almost on the board is discourtesy.'

'For us to walk *in* is worse,' replied Daniel. 'And, truth to tell, their hospitality has been somewhat lacking.'

Nat sat up straight in offence.

'Sir!' protested Lucy. 'I know that you and Paul feel that they should have had me to lodge with them, but, as I tried to explain, the blame for that must lie with me, not them.'

'Aye!' agreed Daniel with a hard stare.

A year before a stare like that would have made something inside her curl up in shame; today it just made her angry. 'And I did nothing wrong, neither!' Lucy told him, her voice rising. 'I was offered lodging by friends of my uncle, honest and godly people. I keep myself by honest work!'

'Honest work!' spat Daniel in contempt.

'Aye, honest work! Printing!' She held up her hands, showing him her ink-stained fingers. 'A trade that flourishes here in London! *You* sent me here. What did you think would become of me? Or did you not care, as long as you never had to look at me again? I'll have you know I've done *well* here! I learned a trade; I made friends; I am treated with kindness and honour by all around me! I am *happy* – as I was not, sir, in your house! Why must you come here to put a stop to it and drag me off to a place where I don't wish to be, nor you to have me?'

Daniel stared at her in consternation.

'Peace, Cousin!' said Hannah in distress. She started to get to her feet, and Lucy hurried to her and made her sit down again. 'Peace!' Hannah said again, leaning back against the chimney-piece. 'It's not fitting to speak thus to your father!'

Lucy glanced back at Daniel unrepentantly. She felt light-headed, almost exhilarated: she had finally spoken her mind to him. A reply that it was fit he hear the truth was in her throat, but she checked it. What she'd already said was a monstrous defiance: if she made it any worse, he'd feel he had no choice except to beat her.

'Lucy,' said Paul, 'don't you see it's different now? Da's come all this long way to fetch you home!'

That was, certainly, a new and surprising development, but Lucy did not for a moment believe that her father's presence was occasioned by *love*. Paul had nagged him until he was *ashamed* to leave his daughter dependent on strangers. Neither he nor Paul could credit that she wasn't *dependent* at all. 'I don't want to go!'

Lucy replied. 'God is my witness, I told you as much, last summer and again in my letter!'

'This is a most strange defiance!' said Daniel, recovering his voice. 'Lucy, you are to come away with us. Now.'

Lucy stood facing him a moment, her head high. She would *not* go back to Hinckley: she was determined on that.

Then she glanced at poor, worried Hannah, and at Nat, who was furiously indignant.The Cotmans' parlour, in front of Nat's guests, was not the place to fight it out. She turned to Nat and curtsied. 'I am sorry, sir, that I am obliged by my duty to my father to be so discourteous to you as to leave suddenly. I trust you know I mean no disrespect to you and Hannah, or to my Aunt.'

Daniel flinched, opened his mouth as though to protest, then closed it again.

'Cousin Hannah, I pray you quickly recover your health,' Lucy said. She gave Hannah a quick hug, then wrapped her shawl around herself and made for the door. Her brother and father followed her out.

Sixteen

The day was overcast and icy, with a cold wind blowing from the river. Lucy began walking westward with quick determined steps.

Paul hurried up from behind her. 'Where are you going?' he panted.

She turned to face him. 'To my lodgings, Paul! Surely you don't mean to carry me off without so much as a change of linen?' She fixed her eyes challengingly on her father, who stood at Paul's shoulder. 'Mr and Mrs Overton have been very good to me. Is it your intention to have me leave them without a word, so that they must run hither and yon seeking what's become of me? That would be a cruel trick to play on those who never did you any harm!'

'That was never my intention!' protested Daniel. He was bewildered now. He had come to London expecting to find his daughter shamed and broken and needy. He couldn't understand why things were so different.

'Then, sir, I will go home and explain to them that, *notwithstanding* the agreements we made for bed and board and rent-money, I must return suddenly to Hinckley. If they ask what urgent need brings me there, I will say: none! But my father has a whim, and therefore willy-nilly I must go!'

'I *wrote* to you to say I would take you home!' said Paul, before Daniel could think of a response.

'Aye, and sent the letter to our *cousin*'s house! I never saw your letter before last week! Why didn't you send it to the Overtons'? I'd given you their direction!'

'I'd never met them! How could I know that our cousins were ill with smallpox?'

'And therefore you couldn't wait until you'd received an answer?'

'You are grown very proud,' broke in Daniel forbiddingly.

Lucy met his eyes. 'Not so proud as to hate my bloodkin because they were injured and brought low. Sir, when I was broken and in need of your aid, you sent me away. God gave me a new life here, and why you should come to take it from me and break me again, I cannot understand.'

Daniel stared at her in shocked confusion. She waited for a reply but none came. She turned on her heel and set out again.

She walked quickly, and Paul and Daniel, unfamiliar with the city, struggled to keep up. She thought to wonder how they'd come to Stepney. Presumably they'd travelled to London with a cart or on horseback but stabled their animals before setting out to find the Cotmans' house. Given the time of day, they might well have arrived in the city the previous evening – in which case they had a room at an inn somewhere. They'd want to spend the night there: it was already too late in the day to set out again.

Good. She had at least overnight to work on them.

They re-entered the City of London on Aldgate Street; Lucy led them on past Leadenhall Market, heading back to Coleman Street, all the while desperately pondering how to persuade them to go away and leave her alone. She was not sure whether an introduction to the Overtons would help. On the one hand, they were obviously respectable people – a godly, hard-working married couple with three children; on the other hand, they were heretics. She was so engaged in thinking how she might persuade them to skate over this latter fact that she wasn't watching for trouble as she usually did. The riot was on top of them before she noticed it was there.

As they approached the junction where Leadenhall Street became Cornhill, there was a sudden roar from somewhere in front of them, and then all at once there were people running towards them.

Jolted abruptly alert, Lucy glanced around, then bolted for the nearest doorway. A gang of men in padded jerkins ran past. For a moment there was a snarling tangle in the road before her, and then they were gone, pelting off in the direction of Leadenhall Market. Another group was coming after them – young men with holly in their hats, waving staves and clubs, whooping with excitement. There was an obstacle in the road before them.

Lucy suddenly realized that the obstacle was Paul and her father, crouched in the mud of the road. Most of the holly-decked men ran past them, but a couple hesitated, ready to swoop on the strangers. Lucy pushed herself away from the wall. 'Let them be!'she screamed.

Startled faces looked round at her. The men were even younger than she'd first thought, well under twenty. Apprentices, she realized: the group of Londoners always most inclined to riot. One of them started to jeer.

'They're strangers to London!' she shouted before they could swagger their way to doing harm. 'That's my *father*! The men you were chasing knocked him down!' – because Daniel was indeed on his hands and knees in the filth of Leadenhall Street.

The apprentices had another look at Daniel. Then one of them caught him by the arm and hauled him to his feet. 'Here, Grandad!' he said cheerfully. 'You need to watch where you're going when you're in London!' He led Daniel over to the side of the road, then gave Lucy a broad grin. 'Merry Christmas, sweeting!' He and his friend ran off along Leadenhall Street after the others.

Daniel sagged against the wall; to her horror, she saw that blood was streaming from a cut on his head. Paul stumbled over, holding their father's hat in both hands, and gave Lucy a stunned look.

'Da!' cried Lucy.

Daniel groaned and slid down to sit against the wall. He put both hands to his bleeding head.

Lucy ran to him, then crouched down beside him and tried to examine the cut. There was already so much blood that she couldn't see how bad it was, and Daniel wouldn't move his hands out of the way.

'Oh, oh!' cried Paul. 'He's hurt, he's bleeding!'

'Where is your inn?' demanded Lucy.

Paul stared stupidly.

'We need to get him off the street!' said Lucy impatiently. 'Do you have an inn here in London? Is it close by?'

'The Nag's Head,' said Paul, understanding. 'I–I don't think it's far away.'

There was a Nag's Head in Cheapside; it was four or five streets away, about the same distance as Coleman Street – and both destinations were the other side of Cornhill, the direction the rioters had come from. The street around them was empty now, but the air was full of the sound of shouting, angry and ugly and not very far away. Lucy hurried to the middle of the street and stared towards Cornhill: yes, there was a big crowd there. Whatever was going on, it wasn't over yet. It might well shed more trouble down Leadenhall Street.

'We can't go that way,' she told Paul. She tried to think. They could try to go round Cornhill to the north, but that would take them a long way round – not an easy distance for an injured man. It would be better just to take Daniel to the nearest inn or tavern, where they could see to his injury and wait until the trouble was over. She looked up and down the road and spotted an inn-sign a short distance away, back the way they'd come. She pointed it out to Paul, then went back to her father.

Daniel was now slumped over with his back against the wall, still clutching his head. The blood had covered his hands and dripped through his fingers to make damp patches on his muddy breeches. 'Da?' she said, but he didn't respond. Her heart began to beat very fast: his injury was even worse than she'd first thought. She found a handkerchief and managed to get it under his hands on to the cut, pressed it down to stop the bleeding, then looked around for something to tie it with. Paul was no help: he just stood there gaping, still holding Daniel's hat. Her father had a scarf wrapped round his neck, though. She pulled it off. He made an angry noise and tried to take it back.

'Hush!' she said shakily. 'I only want to bind your poor head!'

He groaned and bent over, resting his head on his muddy knees. The handkerchief, already soaked with blood, promptly fell off into the gutter. Her eyes stung and she wiped them furiously: she could not afford to break down in tears *now*. She left the handkerchief where it was and bound Daniel's head with the scarf. She took hold of his arm and tugged.

'Come on, Da!' she said. 'We'll take you somewhere you can lie down.'

He huddled himself into an obstinate knot. Paul came over and took his other arm. 'Come, Da!'

'God damn you!' Daniel said thickly. 'Let me be!'

Paul and Lucy stared at one another in shock

366

over his bowed head. Then Lucy tried again, 'Sir, there's an inn just down the road...'

'Let me alone!'

'Lucy!' cried a new voice, and she looked up and saw Jamie.

He was on horseback, riding an ugly thin-necked roan which at that moment seemed to her the most beautiful horse in the world. He jumped down from the saddle and hurried over with the reins looped over one arm. 'Lucy!' he said again.

'Jamie!' she replied and jumped up and into his arms. The arms closed round her, and when she tilted her face up, he kissed her. It was nothing at all like being kissed by Ned. It was like nothing else in all the world.

'Oh, Jamie!' she said when she could speak again, and she pressed her cheek against his shoulder. A huge rough ache of wanting seemed to find the shape that filled it, there in the bone and muscle of his arm.

'Are you hurt?' he asked her anxiously.

'Nay,' she said, picking her head up and sniffling a little, 'but my father is. He was knocked down and he's cut his head. Jamie, can we use your horse?'

'Your *father*?' repeated Jamie in surprise, but he was already leading the horse over to Daniel.

'Aye,' she said. 'He came to fetch me back to Hinckley, but I'll never go! You remember my brother Paul?'

'Aye,' agreed Jamie with a nod to Paul, who was gaping. 'Sir, how do you do?' This last was to Daniel, who muttered incoherently, not lifting his head.

'He's dazed?' Jamie asked.

'Aye,' Lucy replied. It was a huge relief to deal with this quick, competent understanding. 'He needs to rest out of the cold. There's an inn just back down the street, but he won't get up.'

Jamie nodded. 'Hold the horse,' he ordered Lucy, handing her the reins. He took hold of Daniel under the arms and hauled him to his feet. For the first time she noticed that he had a brace on his bad hand, a complicated iron thing.

Daniel groaned and tried to push Jamie away. 'Can you ride, sir?' Jamie asked briskly. When there was no reply, he simply hauled Daniel to the horse and hoisted him up over the animal's swayed back. Daniel cried out, tried feebly to get off again, then was horribly sick down the horse's side. The horse put its ears back and stamped. Jamie put an arm over Daniel's back to steady him and nodded to Lucy.

She led the horse carefully down the road to the inn. Daniel had gone limp now, face-down over the horse; Jamie held him steady. Paul followed, still clutching the hat. Behind them the noise of voices rose angrily. Another group of apprentices came past at a run.

When they reached the inn, they found the door was shut and bolted. Lucy beat on it.

'Who's there?' called a cautious voice from inside.

'Travellers, sir, caught on the street!' Lucy called back. 'My father's hurt; for pity's sake, let us in!'

Pity – or perhaps the reassurance of a woman's voice – worked: the bolt was drawn back and a worried innkeeper frowned out at them. Jamie at once pulled Daniel off the horse and carried him bodily to the door. The innkeeper stood aside to let him in, then told Paul, 'You can take the horse round the back.'

The inn was crowded, but the customers made way, and Jamie carried Daniel over to the fireplace and set him down gently on the hearth. Lucy followed and knelt down by her father. It was too dark to see what was wrong with him: the inn's windows were few and the clouded winter light was dim anyway.

'What's happening out there?' asked one of the customers anxiously.

'Some city apprentices decked the pump on Cornhill with holly and ivy,' replied Jamie. 'The ward officers sent the Watch to tear it down, and the 'prentices set on the watchmen and chased them off. When I rode by, the Lord Mayor was hasting there with a troop. Is there a lamp?'

Somebody handed him a candle, which he lit at the fire and held up so that Lucy could see; she was relieved to notice her father's eyes focusing blearily on the light. 'Might I have a basin of water?' she asked. 'My poor da was knocked down and hit his head.'

'Damned rogues!' muttered Daniel thickly. 'Christ!' He closed his eyes.

Jamie secured the candle to the hearth with a dribble of wax and went off. He presently came back carrying a pot of water and some cloths from the kitchen. Lucy untied the bloody scarf and gently began to wash the blood off her father's head. Vomit had mingled with the blood, some of it catching in his hair, and she had to ask for clean water once she'd got the worst of the mess off. Paul came in from stabling the horse just as she started cleaning again. He elbowed his way to the front of the circle of onlookers.

The cut was a jagged tear in the scalp on the right side of Daniel's head. The flesh around it had swollen up like a duck's egg.

'That was done by a cudgel,' said Jamie quietly.

'Aye!' agreed Paul hotly. 'Those whoreson knaves *struck* him because we didn't get out of their way fast enough!'

The inn's customers tut-tutted in shock. 'Damned 'prentices!' said one. 'There's never any trouble in this city but they're in the thick of it!'

It had been the Watch, not the apprentices, but Lucy didn't bother to correct him. A woman had appeared with a pot of balsam; Lucy thanked her and smeared some on to the wound. Daniel opened his eyes again with a yelp.

'I can stitch that for you, if you like,' offered the woman who'd brought the balsam – it turned out later that she was the innkeeper's wife. 'I've stitched broken noggins enough before.'

Lucy thanked her and moved aside to let her stitch up the wound. Daniel whimpered a little but didn't struggle. He was starting to shiver, so Lucy took off her shawl and tucked it round him. Seeing her father like this – hurt and bewildered and weak – turned all her anger into pity.

When the woman had finished stitching, Daniel looked around, moving his eyes without

370

shifting his head. 'What is this place?' he asked faintly.

Lucy was relieved that he seemed aware of his surroundings again. 'It's a tavern on Leadenhall, Da. It was the nearest place we could find to bring you.'

'Oh,' said Daniel. He closed his eyes, then opened them again. 'Someone came with a horse.'

'Aye,' agreed Jamie, kneeling down beside Lucy. 'That would be me.'

Daniel stared at him, his gaze snagging on the missing eye. 'And who are you?'

The good side of Jamie's mouth quirked. 'Your son-in-law, sir, if your daughter will have me.'

Daniel stared at him as if he'd gone mad. Lucy turned and stared, too.

Jamie took her hand with his left hand, then with his right as well. She found herself looking down at the complicated iron brace he'd made for himself. It had a kind of metal thumb, hinged, with a strap that passed across what was left of his real thumb so that he could move it; another piece of metal where his index finger had been was padded with leather.

He followed the direction of her gaze. 'It's not pretty,' he told her quietly, 'but it works well enough. Like myself, Lucy, if you'd have me.'

She felt as though she were suspended in a void of silence, where nothing else existed but his serious scarred face. For better or for worse, her decision had already been made. 'Aye,' she said fiercely. 'You and none other.'

371

'Lucy!' exclaimed Paul in horror.

She glanced up at him impatiently. 'What's it to you, Paul? He's not asking aught from *you*!'

'But we don't know anything about him!' protested Paul.

Jamie was still holding her hand in both of his; he was smiling so hard that the scarred half of his face was in knots. She reached up with her free hand and touched his cheek, wanting to keep that smile for ever. 'Speak for yourself,' she told her brother. '*I* know all I need to.'

'You want to marry Lucy?' asked Daniel in weak bewilderment.

'Aye, sir,' agreed Jamie. 'With your good leave.' He glanced at Paul. 'Sir. By birth I am a gentleman, the third son of George Hudson of Bourne in Lincolnshire. I was apprenticed as a blacksmith and finished my indentures just before the war. I've lately returned to my trade. It's true, sir, that I have no land, but my trade is a good one and I have besides a small allowance from my father.'

Daniel blinked several times: Lucy could see him trying to make sense of this offer for a daughter he'd written off as unmarriageable.

She was trying to make sense of it, too. A *gentleman*! The son of a *landowner*! She hadn't known, and it did make a difference. A third son wouldn't inherit the land, of course, but it could be presumed that his family would help set him up in business: he wouldn't need to eke out years as somebody else's assistant. Marrying Jamie needn't mean abject poverty after all.

She supposed, though, that she *had* known that

his family wasn't poor. Poor men didn't learn blacksmithing. He'd been in a cavalry regiment, too, which meant that his family had money enough to supply him with a horse. Besides, a man wholly reliant on the charity of his friends wouldn't have been able to drink himself stupid with brandy. She should, she thought, have *asked* him, but she had been too afraid of the answer.

'She has little dowry,' Daniel said at last.

'I ask none,' replied Jamie.

Paul had been frowning at a memory and suddenly he exclaimed, *'You're* the one who—' He managed to stop himself before blurting out, *'murdered Lucy's ravishers.'*

Daniel frowned at his son. Then his brow cleared. 'The one who smote the evildoers!' he muttered. 'Aye.'

Both men gazed at Jamie with approval now.

'And you're a *gentleman*?' repeated Paul delightedly. Gentle birth wasn't as good as freehold property, but still acceptable. Lucy was glad that Paul didn't know she'd turned down Ned Trebet.

'A gentleman's son,' agreed Jamie. 'Sirs, may I hope for your approval in my suit?'

'I might find some money for Lucy's portion,' Daniel muttered, embarrassed, 'in time.'

Lucy gripped Jamie's hand hard: that had been consent.

'Sir, it were shame to press you now, while you are still dazed,' Jamie said gently. 'Rest, and we can speak of this again when you feel better.'

* * *

373

The inn's customers were delighted by this drama in their midst, and when Lucy and Jamie looked for a place to sit and talk, they were offered their choice of any seat in the house. They settled in a nook in the corner, and the innkeeper brought them ale. 'On the house!' he said jovially, 'to celebrate your betrothal!'

Lucy looked at her betrothed and grinned. 'I never knew you were a gentleman!'

'Not a rich one, alas,' he told her, smiling back. 'My father has four girls to dower, as well as myself and my brothers to provide for, and his estate's not large. You say your father came to fetch you back to Leicestershire?'

'Aye.' She twined the stained fingers of her left hand with his. 'You came just in time!'

He smiled at her. 'You would never have gone with him even if I hadn't.'

'Not willingly, no! And I hoped I might persuade him to let me stay. But to settle me with a *husband*, oh, that's another matter! That's a fine and estimable estate! And with a *gentleman*, forsooth! For that he'll even condescend to love me again!' She grinned. 'Oh, but he'd think well of *you*, anyway, the way you appeared a-horse to rescue us, when he was struck down and bleeding, and Paul and I sorely at a loss! Indeed you *were* just in time!'

He shook his head. 'I was no more than *convenient*. Had I not come along, you and your brother would have carried him here anyway!'

'Shhh! Let him think you a noble hero! Likely he *can* find a dowry of sorts, if he sets his mind to it. We must get as much as we can. How did

374

you chance to come this way? I thought you were still at Windsor!'

'I came to find you,' he said simply. 'The Overtons said you'd gone to your cousin's in Stepney.'

'The Army discharged you?' she asked eagerly.

At that, though, he looked away. 'Nay. Lucy, I confess that I can stay but briefly. You know that those of us who were taken up for mutiny were required to make formal submission to the discipline of the Army?'

She nodded: it had been reported in the newsbooks and through Leveller word of mouth just two or three days before.

'There was some debate as to what that might mean for me,' Jamie went on, 'since I was not a soldier. I hoped I might just have leave to go, but the Army has need of blacksmiths, and I have been acquiring a reputation as a cunning smith who can be relied upon to contrive things that are out of the ordinary.' He held up his right hand with its iron thumb. 'Once I'd made this many people remarked it. Some have asked that I make like contrivances for friends who've lost limbs; others have wanted fancy hinges to fasten together odd-shaped pieces of baggage and the like.' He sighed. 'To speak plainly, I caught the eye of some who thought that such a man as myself might be useful, and to obtain my liberty I was obliged to swear that I would work for the Army.'

'For how long?' she asked in dismay.

'That's not clear,' he admitted unhappily. 'I'll

apply for a discharge as soon as I can and forgo any pay owed if it helps me get free, but I am at the mercy of my commanders.'

She was silent. She hadn't had time enough to imagine what it would be like to live with him, but she now understood very clearly that she would be obliged to live without him. He would come at irregular intervals – a day here, two days there, and then weeks of absence. If the Army moved further from London, the weeks would be months. If there was another war...

She refused to think about that. 'How long do you have now?'

'I was granted two weeks' leave, to come to London and speak to you. Forgive me, but I had to tell them of you. Else I would have had no leave at all.'

'Well,' she said slowly, 'two weeks is better than nothing. It's a mercy that my father *is* here, to give his consent, or we might have had trouble finding anyone to marry us.'

He was watching her closely. 'I had thought of that. I had thought I might have to content myself with a betrothal – if you were willing to accept such a poor bargain at all, that is.'

She met his gaze. 'I would have accepted it if I had to, Jamie, but I'm glad my father *is* here.'

He relaxed and his smile came back again: she saw that he'd feared that she might refuse altogether. 'Aye.' He was quiet a moment, and then said, 'When I told them that I wished to go to London to speak to my sweetheart, the clerk of the court laughed. He asked what sort of sweetheart such a monster might have.'

She reached out and touched the scarred side of his face; it seemed something she'd wanted to do for a long time. She traced the pattern of the injury, then laid her palm against his cheek. 'One that was hurt, as you were.'

He put his good hand over hers. 'Oh, but you are so bright a light! When you come into a room every man in it looks and smiles!'

'That's false flattery, Jamie! When we first met you thought me a scolding shrew! Confess it!'

He smiled. 'Nay, that was John, not me! Marriage to a scold has made him wary. *I* thought you the prettiest hoyden in London and I hated my wounds all over again. *You* thought *me* a monster, confess it!'

'At first,' she admitted. 'But, Jamie, I stopped minding your scars after the first day!'

He beamed, then leaned across the table to kiss her. 'I must beg your pardon again that I promised Ned not to court you, but it seemed to me that I was forswearing something I could never win anyway. When John came and laughed at me and said, nay, she likes you *well*, I thought it nothing but a friend's raillery. I could not believe that *you* would love *me*! And you truly refused Ned? Was he very angry?'

She hesitated. 'Aye. He's not spoken to me since.'

He seemed pleased at the thought of their friend's disappointment. 'What will you do this next year? I can write to my father and ask him to pay my allowance to you, but it's not much – and, as for my pay, all the world knows the Army provides it but scantily.'

'Keep your allowance!' she told him. 'I have a place with the Overtons and I have work. I'll be well enough till you are free again. But see if you can work on my father to provide a good sum for us. I want to buy a printing press.'

She hadn't meant to say that last but the words came out very naturally, surprising her. She supposed the seed of the idea had been planted with the legacy of silk. With savings of a few shillings, the idea of owning a press was a fantasy; with savings of eight pounds, it seemed possible – even though she'd need as much again to achieve it.

'A printing press!' he exclaimed, smiling again. 'With that and a smithy, we're like to have a noisy house, my love!'

'Amen to that,' she said and kissed him.

Historical Epilogue

I know, I'm out of my period. The English Civil Wars were things I knew nothing about until I started research: I was so ignorant, in fact, that I didn't even know they were plural. Their history turned out to be fascinating but vastly more complicated and challenging than I anticipated, and I know I haven't done it justice. However, for what it's worth, the political events that form the background to this piece of fiction really happened, and many of the characters are based on real people. The greatest liberty I'm aware of taking is making *The Moderate* newsbook start up a few months earlier than it actually did. Be warned, though, that this is one viewpoint and that events would look quite different if seen through another character's eyes.

All but one of the documents quoted are real; the exception is the newsbook article at the beginning of Chapter Six. The personal letters, however, are invented, though I've tried to make them sound like letters of the period. I apologize if readers find the language of the dialogue irritating. I was trying to make it sound sufficiently seventeenth-century that it would fit in with the quotations, while keeping it sufficiently modern that it would be intelligible to twenty-first century readers. Tastes being what they are, I've probably annoyed traditionalists and modernists alike.

For those who'd like to know more, the best history of the Civil Wars is still S.R. Gardiner's four volume *History of the Great Civil War,* first published in 1889; those looking for a shorter and more accessible work might like to try Diane Purkiss's *The English Civil War: A People's History* (2006). The latter contains a bibliography with suggestions for further reading. For my part, I owe a particular debt to Joseph Frank's *The Beginnings of the English Newspaper 1620–1660* (1961): if I hadn't stumbled across it, I wouldn't have embarked on this novel at all. Hmm. Considering how hard I've had to work, maybe I should be blaming not thanking him!

I must also mention a debt to two websites, which I looked at every day I wrote: british-civil-wars.co.uk and pepysdiary.com. The first has timelines, biographies and links to various documents; the second, though slightly out of period, is great fun and provides everything from recipes to the price of a seventeenth-century hackney cab. If any of you on either web community are reading this, keep up the good work!